RUINER

TELLERS, BOOK I

RUINER

by Lara Messersmith-Glavin

Ruiner
Tellers, Book I

ISBN 9781849355940
E-ISBN 9781849355957
LCCN: 2025936924

Please contact us to request the latest AK Press distribution catalog, which features books, pamphlets, zines, and stylish apparel published and/or distributed by AK Press. Alternatively, visit our websites for the complete catalog, latest news, and secure ordering.

AK Press
370 Ryan Ave. #100
Chico, CA 95973
www.akpress.org

AK Press
33 Tower Street
Edinburgh, Scotland EH6 7BN
akuk.com

Cover design by Suzanne Shaffer
Cover art and interior illustrations by Casandra Johns

Printed in the USA on acid-free paper

For Tana

RUINER

See the back of the book for a dramatis personae and map of Soogway

MA'SHIFRA SPEAKS: THE NATURE OF COMBAT

What does it mean to fight?

Think.

Long gone are the days when People drew blades and spilled blood upon the sands, calling it victory—ancestors be thanked. Now your stories are your weapons, your strength.

Pay attention, girl. I know you don't care now, but one day you will.

Combat is a great intimacy. A dance. In battle, you are partnered, you become the reason for the other to be, and they become yours. When you win, you take a piece of your opponent inside of you. Do you hear me? You will never be the same. Victory changes you. When you lose, they take a piece away, and part of you becomes part of them. Either way, you are altered.

Yet you must win. That is your purpose. You must be able to find both harmony and dissonance in the telling. It is a careful balance, offering truth while also holding your defenses, but one you will learn to maintain. After all, to fight is to dance, but to win is to disrupt.

You are not simply telling the better story. You must understand your opponent's rhythms, their intentions. You must match them step-for-step, until you don't. To disrupt, you must listen. You must be fully present to them, more aware of your rival than they are of themself.

Remember, girl. It is an honor to be met in combat. Never will you feel so heard or so well understood as by a worthy enemy.

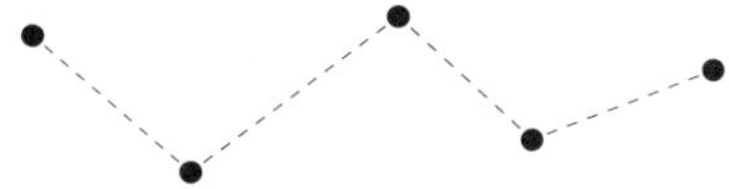

The Serpent: Eastern horizon

1. THE OLD WAY

Sand skittered and hissed across the plain. It spoke with voices of the ancestors, Kell knew, whispering through the endless flats and rolling dunes of Home. She breathed a prayer of gratitude to them as the warm wind tugged at the loose folds of her scarf. With one hand, she drew a length of the thin fabric over her head and around her face to keep the sand from her nose and lips. The device in her other made a sharp buzzing sound, followed by a crackle of static. She cursed as its signal light flickered weakly and went out. Looking up, she found Jor's eyes on her, his lips twisting to contain a laugh.

"You broke *another* one?"

She glared at him, and the laugh escaped.

Kell turned the wayfinder over in her hands and tapped at the control core under the lower carapace. A small puff of dark smoke answered, the scent of hot wires lost quickly to the breeze.

Good riddance, she thought. *I hate these things.*

Given how machines tended to malfunction in her hands, she figured they hated her, too. Kell considered tossing it aside, imagined it scoured by the sun and swallowed by the slow waves of sand that roamed the expanse of the desert, but the thought of the dead tech being left behind, a tick burrowed into the skin of the dunes, made her itch. At least the parts could be traded for something more useful. Like sandbeast dung.

"I don't know why I let you talk me into using it," she snapped, stuffing the broken bug into the shoulder bag beneath her scarf and wiping her hand as if the tech were unclean. "That's the last time." She flashed Jor a daggered look, daring him to argue, but he only grinned. She bit back a smile and settled into an easy stance so she could tune the way.

The *old* way.

Tuning to stones was as easy as walking, really, or listening to the direction of a voice. The trick was not to confuse your own heartbeat for the pulse. She closed her eyes and held her palms up, then waited.

There.

She caught a corner of it, a warm thrum, landing square in the center of her right palm. She cupped her hand as if gathering droplets from a cave spring, turned it slightly, listening with her whole body. A few seconds later, she felt it again. Like catching a sunbeam, a heavy ray of light.

Long moments passed as the sand shushed around her, Jor's feet shifting on the surface of the dune. Behind them, she heard the clank and snort of sandbeasts laden with supplies, the soft murmurs of the scouts waiting for the pathfinders to do their work. The breeze was sharp with sulfur here in the yellow zone. She wrinkled her nose beneath her scarf.

At last, another pulse. This one in her left palm, slow as syrup and much fainter. It drummed against her hand, buzzing her bones all the way to her elbow. It was far, but gods, was it strong. She counted her breaths as her right hand continued to pulse, time slowing to a sleepy drone as the sun poured down upon them. The breeze snapped the ends of her cloth and dried the sweat on her upper lip. At length, the left pulse came again.

"Got it," she whispered. She opened her eyes.

"Well?" Jor held out his own wayfinder bug, showing the coordinates it had located so she could pair it with her own and triangulate their position relative to the stones.

"You know the Way doesn't work like that," she said, squinting at him.

Jor rolled his eyes and deactivated his device. Sighing heavily, he removed his bag to place the wayfinder inside and pushed up his sleeves to settle in for his own tuning.

She watched him, wondering. He was slow at it, this big, strong brother of hers. Fast at flirting, slow at tuning. He was good with night work—his knowledge of the stars was among the best in the camp—and like their mother, he had always been a great hunter, even as a child. What was it about navigating as their ancestors and the ancestors before them had done? The pulsar stones were gifts from the gods, and reading them was in their blood, as natural and easy as a vulture riding an updraft. Jor's preference for city gadgets left her skin cold. *Ancestors be with us.*

Now that she had the pulses in her palms, they were easy to hold. She found herself swaying in time to their staggered rhythms as she regarded her brother, waiting for him to find his own stones. While the endless walking of their caravan had whittled her lean, he was thick through the chest and legs, built more like a city man than a Roamer. The breeze tugged his scarf from his head as he tuned, eyes closed, revealing the tight braids that zagged across his scalp like cracks in parched riverbeds. Another difference between them. Hair was hot, an unnecessary vanity in a desert. She hated having her head touched, and so kept her own scalp closely shorn, which she could do herself. In all things, what Jor was, she was not: tall, fearless, popular, enamored with anything new. He was the sand between her toes, rubbing her raw, making her keep going. Yet she couldn't sing the Way without him, ancestors help her.

She hummed the first lines of the Way at Ease as she waited. The story-song gathered around her neck as a thin snake, green and smooth, and slid along her breastbone, though she felt nothing. It twisted away from her body and curled in midair before slithering downward in a tight spiral until it reached the earth. It glided above the ground, twining around her ankle.

Jor growled with effort. It was hard for him to pay attention, she realized. She thought the wayfinders had made him lazy, that his skills had grown weaker as bugs and electric lanterns and other bits of severed city tech slowly became commonplace in camp.

At last, he opened his eyes. His gaze passed through her as he furrowed his brow.

"What is it?" she asked. He shook his head, letting his left hand drop to his side. So, he'd only found one. Fine.

He began singing his part of the Way at Ease under his breath, and another snake formed, this one a flashy copper with a small red feather sprouting from the end of its length. It slithered around Jor's neck before twisting through the air and into the sand, where it met hers. Kell continued singing, harmonizing with her brother's clear tenor as the two snakes intertwined, swallowing one another's tails, sliding and merging into a tangle of green and bronze. They formed at first a knot, then a ball, and finally an egg. As the siblings' voices rose, the egg shivered and cracked, the shell vanishing into smoke, as a red-feathered serpent the length of Kell's arm beat tiny wings and lifted into the air. She heard the scouts ready the sandbeasts and shoulder their packs. The serpent writhed through the air at shoulder height, carving out the path before them at an easy walking pace. Its tongue flickered in and out, scenting the way. It aimed its arrowlike head across the ridge, pointing through the dunes to the plateau where their caravan would have set up camp. Kell smiled at her brother.

"The feather was a nice touch," she said.

He shrugged. His mood had gone heavy, but she wasn't about to let him drag hers down with it just because she'd broken her wayfinder. Again. If he was the grit in her sandal, then she was what staked his tent against the winds of his temperament. Her job was to stay steady and true while he flapped and sagged around her, chasing whatever caught his eye.

Kell's own heart was light as they turned their footsteps after the serpent, the sand whispering underfoot. It had been a quiet scouting mission, a week of circling through the dunes to intercept any caravans with whom they might trade, though they'd seen no sign of anyone but the raptors wheeling overhead. No tracks but those of snakes and lizards, quickly erased by the breeze. No voices but those of the fiddler bugs and the sun wrens, and the occasional lonely scream of an eagle. *And the ancestors*, she thought, and they began the last stretch of the walk back to where the People were waiting.

"Know when you can bully them and when you need to twist the knife."
—Shade's father

2. THE PIT

The din was incredible. Nobody in the Box cared about hearing the story, Shade knew—they just wanted to watch someone lose the fight. Lamps swung low and spattered the small arena in grimy electric glow, leaving most of the crowd in darkness. Shade could barely make out faces in the crush of bodies that leaned over the stone railings banking the pit, shouting their wagers and bloodlust. Here and there bookmakers pressed through the crowd, tracking the odds and disappearing the desperate fistfuls of money pushed into their hands into the metal purses at their waists.

Shade ignored it all. They spared a glance at their opponent. He looked like he hadn't missed a meal in years, and by the bulk of his arms, Shade figured him for either a butcher or a mason in the daytime, something honest and hard on the body. By night, though, well—we all found ways to make ends meet. The man glared at Shade, pulling himself up in the shoulders and grinding one fist into the other. As if that kind of intimidation might work on someone who'd grown up on the streets. This was all Shade needed to know.

They gave a quick nod to the referee, a sharp-eyed, underfed man whom Shade often saw in the early morning hours in the alcove behind the bakery, curled around an empty bottle. He didn't own the little underground arena and bar known as the Box—in fact it was quite the opposite; whoever *did* own the Box owned the referee, too. But that was not Shade's problem. Getting rid of this meathead then getting out of the arena with their skin and some chips was.

The referee put up his hands, and a hundred pairs of eyes burned down into the pit, the sudden pause in the noise more deafening than the clamor had been. He turned to Shade and held up a palm. Shade slid their own across it in a promise of fair play. The referee took the few steps to the other side of the arena, and Big Arms did the same.

"You all know the rules," the referee droned in a nasal voice. "No crowd assists, no blackmail, no evasive treading for longer than a minute, no heart stories, and no collaboration between the fighters." He recited the words like he'd said them in the exact way a thousand, thousand times. "And no draws," he continued. The crowd cheered at this, hissing and spitting, spraying fine mists of hooch down over the railing as they pulled from flasks hidden in pockets and passed bottles from hand to hand. "Crowd interference results in a forfeit of your bets and an unresolved end to the match," he went on. Boos from the crowd. Shade was itching to get on with it. They gave a quick touch to their amulet beneath their shirt, noting as they raised their arm that a wash wouldn't be a bad idea. "Maximum time, ten minutes. Loser cedes the tale. May the best story win."

The referee retreated into the dim at the edges of the pit. Shade settled into their heels and locked eyes with Big Arms. With their slight build and diminutive stature, Shade was too small for strict dominance plays. Though they had a few big wins adding to their repertoire of tales, they still needed to rely on what their father had called "twisting the knife." Fully legal, if not entirely ethical, manipulations of pathos. Shade had stopped growing when they were still young and never started again, giving them the look of someone several years their junior—not that they knew exactly how old they were. Everyone underestimated them because of it, which was fine by them. This meatbrain was a perfect mark. They held out their casting hand.

"Stop me if you've heard this one," they began. A smile tugged at the corner of their mouth.

Big Arms led with a crash, as they'd expected. One of the conqueror tales. Within moments, the wriggle squirming in the man's platter of a palm poured onto the concrete floor of the arena, congealing into something that looked part steer, part squid with mallets at the ends of its tentacles. The teller's voice boomed in a cadence that set the creature's feet stomping.

A chanter, Shade thought with a grain of surprise. *Give the big guy five points for style. OK, then. My turn.*

"Picture your home," they said in a voice so soft it slipped beneath the chanter's bellows. They could barely hear their own words through the howling of the crowd. "Not the meager stone walls that you slog back to every evening, the ones your wife dresses with dried flowers, hangs tapestries from to keep out the damp, scrubs to remove the stains but they always look dirty. And you—you're too tired to notice. Not the place where you shovel stew into your mouth and roll into bed at night with aches no balm can soothe."

That last was a line they'd gained from a match that had won them two loaves of excellent bread in the market some weeks back, and they had been eager to try it out. A small bird leaped from Shade's hand, glowing a yellow so like the lamplight it appeared translucent as it flitted easily between the slamming tentacles of Big Arms' beast. It darted and wove, its head turning this way and that to shine a bright eye onto the massive creature that swung at it, earthbound.

"Not that home—think back. Picture the place your roots live. Imagine those roots still dive deep into soft, dark earth alive with tiny micro-organisms and rich with nutrients and water. Imagine the network around you, the constant flow of exchange and care, death and life as your body soars upward into the warm light. Every branch and twig of your body reaching and gathering energy from the sun."

The bird gave a silent chirp and spiraled upward, tracing figure eights around the lanterns. Then it swooped around the arena, racing past the fists and faces of the bettors. The scant few who'd taken the long odds whistled in support.

Big Arms was just coming to the part where Caldo the Great passes the test of the Enchantress and receives the Golden Scythe in reward.

Smart, Shade thought, *a public classic*. The steer-squid backed toward its master, slamming the ground in time with his voice. The illusion was so effective, Shade thought they could feel the floor tremble with the rhythm. They pushed aside their admiration to prepare for what would no doubt be a charge.

"Above his head he swung it now
The sun upon its blade
The battlefield would groan beneath
The weight of all he slayed—"

Big Arms' voice boomed like a battle drum, and he raised his arms as if he himself held the Golden Scythe. The crowd roared, only their lust for winnings keeping them from adding their voices to the familiar chorus. Instead, they kept time, stomping and screaming, spit flying. The room smelled of sweat and rotten hooch.

Shade braced themself. This was going to hurt.

Sure enough, the creature charged, growing as it did, lengthening so its tentacles easily reached the bird dancing among the lights. The mallets flared into barbed hooks and lashed at Shade's story, lunging for it. The bird dodged and wheeled.

Shade wanted to close their eyes to concentrate but didn't dare lose sight of the beast and its movements. Their casting palm shone with sweat. They hated these old stories from the ancient, barbaric past where people fought with blades instead of words. It made their stomach queasy to hear crowds cheer for crude, physical violence. Their plan was starting to feel like a gamble. Maybe they'd misread the audience.

The forest, they reminded themself. *Take him to the forest.*

Shade began to speak more quickly now, piling description on description. They told of clear rivers full of fish, of ferns the size of carriages, and dappled sunlight warming patches of moss. Big Arms was looking straight at them, not at the creatures they'd each summoned, but at *them*. A vicious smile crept across his face as he stomped his own foot in time with the old chant's rhythm.

Caldo the Great was devastating his enemies, and the steer-squid began to do the same. One tentacle wrapped itself around the bird's wings, and though the bird flapped desperately, the creature dragged it downward, its head turned leonine with sharp teeth glinting beneath the lights. The bird struggled in the creature's grasp, and Shade's heart hammered, birdlike, in their chest.

"It was all like this once," Shade whispered. "It could be that way again."

The bird melted.

There was a gasp from the crowd, and the referee took a step out from the shadows, looking for evidence of a cheat. But there—they could all see it now: an asp, twining around the lion-steer-squid's tentacles, squeezing. A spiral, growing tighter as it slithered downward toward the creature's torso. Tighter.

The chanter stuttered an impromptu line, but the old classics were set—one trick only, and it had to work. Coming up with new endings to old rhymes on the fly was not part of Big Arms' skill set, it seemed.

Shade murmured the snake slowly down the length of the creature, describing sadness in its curves, loss and longing in its deadly pace. The beast thrashed and twisted its head this way and that but could reach the serpent with neither tentacles nor teeth. The snake hissed silently as Shade spoke of alienation, of homesickness, and the creature shuddered. The crowd was quieter now, rapt by the movements of the asp, straining as if to hear, finally, what Shade was telling.

The smile had faded from Big Arms' face. In its place was a knot of fury, choked by something more that dragged the corners of his mouth downward. His chanting had ceased. Shade almost felt sorry for what was going to come next.

"I see you," they said to the chanter, looking into his eyes. "Your hands are gifts. In another life, you wanted to be a woodworker."

The crowd was silent as the asp sank its teeth into the beast's neck. The creature swooned, collapsed, and dissolved back into a puddle of light. The snake bunched and gulped, the defeated story disappearing inch by inch down its throat.

There was a pause. And then the crowd erupted. The referee was shaking his head as if to clear it from drink, staggering into the arena. He gripped Shade by the wrist and thrust their arm into the air, declaring them the victor. Across the pit, the chanter slumped. Shade knew he'd no doubt needed that money for food.

The referee handed them a light pouch. Shade heard the thin clatter of chips inside and tucked it into their shirt for safekeeping, eyeing the stands and looking for the nearest exit. It would be time to bolt, soon. They closed the story and pulled the snake back into themself with its new acquisition. A conqueror tale would definitely come in handy.

The crowd around the railing was booing, an angry mob, with the few who'd backed the underdog crowing and clapping one another on the backs. The bookmakers were swiftly trading chips and cubes among the winners and losers, their eyes alight with profit.

And then it came.

"Cheater!" screamed a voice from the crowd. "Forfeit! Cheater!" The voice was shrill and panicked. They'd no doubt lost a tidy bundle of chips. "That was a heart story!" The crowd picked up the call.

Yep, Shade thought. *It's time.*

They bolted.

MA'SHIFRA SPEAKS: THE STONES

Long our ancestors wandered in this place without truly knowing it, without means to find their way. They traced the vanishing marks left by jackal and snake through the sand. They followed the arrows of birds in the sky, seeking springs. They waited for darkness and read the circling map of the stars. These things they knew and knew them well, but under cover of clouds or in the absence of animal guides, they were lost. The place was hostile to them, scoured clean of landmarks and deep knowing. They each carried a hole in their hearts where the winds blew. They had an emptiness in their veins, their hands, their tongues. Their stories were toys, pleasing and thrilling, or records, memories, and lessons. But not guides. Their stories were only reflections of what they and their ancestors knew. They could not use them to find their way. Our People prayed to the gods for an end to the restlessness in their hearts, and the gods provided.

You were not there when the stones first arrived, yet you feel it still, do you not? You feel in your blood the shudder, the impact. Imagine—a torrential rain, not of water or ice but of flaming rock, shards and jags, dust and shrapnel, massive, molten boulders hurtling into the ground. The gods answered our prayers with a storm that scorched the sky and sent the very air burning.

There were many who gave themselves as offering to the gods. They stepped into the torrent with arms raised, as if greeting the first rains that fill the springs at sunretreat. All who were struck perished instantly, some run through, pierced like a fish on a spear, others flattened and buried beneath the crushing weight. When the sands settled and the air was again breathable, our ancestors found that those lost lived on, their heartbeats perceptible through the stones themselves.

The gifts of the gods were terrible things, frightening things. They were too hot to approach, too powerful to behold directly. And yet the People could feel them, feel their pulse and life force, even at great distances. The hollow place within our ancestors was filled with this rich power, the emptiness now an echo of return, a dense web of landmarks, each with a personality and pitch all its own, as knowable as kin. They are our family, our blood. No other folk in this world belong to the stones as we do, and no other folk can find their way as we can. The gods gave us the gift of knowing, and it is through the stones we understand not only where but who *we are.*

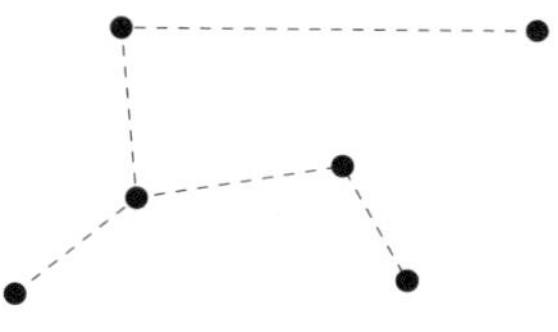

The Hunter: South; bird migration

3. THE HUNTER

The scouts spread out around them, braiding their tracks, communicating in whistles that traveled farther than voices as they ranged wide. Jor was uncharacteristically quiet, his conversation whittled to grunts. Kell tried to draw him out, asking about his latest kill, his newest device, details of recent lovers, but it was like dragging a sandbeast away from water. Even though most of their news had been spent in the week since they had left camp, she and her brother seldom lacked thoughts to share. Kell fidgeted with the edge of her scarf as they continued in silence.

The sun slid westward, and they walked into their own lengthening shadows. The serpent that guided them picked up its pace and straightened, like an arrow flying true, which meant they were drawing near to camp. Kell felt a grain of unease settle into her chest.

Out of the corner of her eye, she watched Jor clench and unclench his jaw, making the tiny white constellations tattooed into his cheeks and neck dance. They stood out against his skin like stars in the night sky, an effect that she thought was both beautiful and excessive, a mating display. Given his allure for many from their caravan and at bazaars, she assumed that was rather the point.

She timed her footfalls to match his, hoping to create a feeling of connection, but either he ignored the gesture or was too wrapped up in his thoughts to notice. She knew what would capture his attention—and she resented him for it—but she needed to crack this dark facade before they made it back to camp.

"Do you remember the story of the Hunter and the Ibex?" she began. He turned toward her, his eyes glittering, seeing her for the first time in hours. She took a deep breath and made a sweeping motion with her hand, as if binding him inside a loop. His face softened. He always looked like a little boy when she told him stories. She held up her casting palm, and a glimmer twitched and jerked there, like a tiny fish gasping for breath.

"The Hunter was a great one," she intoned. She could feel all the voices that had told it blending with her own. She loved this feeling of communion with the past, of being part of something greater than herself, even if she hated the attention it drew, the eyes upon her. Even now, she saw one of the scouts pause and glance in her direction, feeling the pull of the words, and she turned her back toward them, focusing on her brother.

"Mmmm—a great one," Jor nodded, adding his energy to the telling.

The light in her palm grew.

"She was not afraid of man nor beast."

"No, not afraid."

Their footsteps were in unison now. She knew her ancestors would guide her path as she told, so she did not watch the ground or the way.

"Fast of foot was she, and long of limb. Some even said she could disguise her shape, so she would become a stone by a watering hole or a sister beast, running alongside the herd in their skin."

The glimmer stretched and expanded, taking shape. It swelled into the form of a glowing hare, its feet furred and its ears long and listening. Then its legs continued to lengthen, changing, leaping from her palm and across the dune on sharp little hooves.

"Yet there was one beast who had always eluded her, the sleekest and fleetest of them all."

A pair of ragged wings sprouted from the creature's shoulders, and long fangs shot from its whiskered snout as it danced and crouched. So many tellers had left their marks on this story—the result was a chimera of traditions, a wondrous mix that climbed the air like a goat and raced circles around them as she spoke.

Kell told of how the Hunter saw the Ibex drinking by a pool, how she crept toward it, but its keen ears and nose picked up her intent. When she told of the chase, Kell's voice leaped with the fear of prey and the lust of the predator. Her hands molded and moved the air before her, as if her words were formed of clay and not of breath. The creature that was the story raced and turned and cowered and played, turning from gold to rose to flame as the sun set behind them. Kell had given herself over to the story, could no more direct it than she could change its ending from the one that had been spoken by countless tellers before her. The force of it, the tradition of it, pulled her from her body so she scarcely felt the ground beneath her sandals.

"At last, the Ibex could run no more," she said, tilting her head back, her eyes tracing a path upward. "It climbed to the top of the sunset mountains, and there it put one hoof upon the evening star. Finding it sturdy, it took another step, balancing carefully. Once it was again sure-footed, the Ibex leaped into the sky, tiptoeing from star to star, seeking shelter in the far horizon."

The creature vaulted higher and higher until it paused, becoming hazy around the edges. Then it shivered once and appeared to shatter. Golden dust rained slowly down like pollen caught in a breeze.

"The Hunter climbed the stars like scaling a wall, one hand over another, until she, too, balanced in the firmament. She stepped on the stars as if jumping from rock to rock across a river, fording the darkness with fire underfoot. There she walks, to this day, still seeking the Ibex in the sky."

Glittering specks drifted down onto Jor's upturned face, animating the constellations in his skin. When he looked back at her, she could see a tear streaking the dust on his cheek. She twirled her fingers together, closing the story, and the specks vanished.

"Jor—" she took a step toward him. "What is it?"

"It's nothing." He smiled weakly and wiped his face. "That's one of my favorites." He avoided her eyes and looked out past the serpent, which was fading into shadow. Fear clutched her.

They had crested a small rise and could look down into a valley below. The fires of the camp were visible, the tents arrayed in concentric circles, the livestock and supply structures set up near the outer rims. The sweet warmth of homesickness she felt at seeing the caravan so close was chilled with worry.

"Kell," he said, his deep voice barely more than a whisper. "I couldn't find the other stone." Relief turned her knees to sand.

"You scared me, you severed fool. Gods be thanked, despite your terrible wayfinding, we have still somehow arrived."

"No," he waved away her jest. "That's not what I mean. It wasn't that I couldn't pick up the pulse."

She shivered, though the air was still very warm. "What are you saying?"

He looked into her eyes as if trying to press his memory into her mind. "I mean, it felt like a hole. Like it wasn't there."

Ancestors help us. Her brother, flapping away again like a loose tent in a storm. If there was one thing they could count on, it was the ancient stones. She clicked her tongue and looked at him sideways. "You just spend too much time with that bug in your hand and not enough time listening," she teased.

He forced a smile. "I hope you're right."

"Good pacing doesn't always mean fast. Keep them hungry."
—Shade's father

4. THE WINNINGS

It wasn't a heart story. Not technically, Shade thought as they ducked under a metal stool that just missed their shoulder before clattering to the ground. Shade had never been to the forest, so they had no genuine memories to share—just scraps they'd gleaned from their parents' stories. They darted around one swinging fist and dodged another, pivoting just in time to shove the fist's owner as more angry bettors swarmed the pit. Though punching had long fallen out of favor, patrons of the Box weren't above throwing a knuckle or two when the mood struck, and Shade preferred not to be on the catching end. They stumbled backward and fell, scooting briefly on their butt before getting their feet back under them and pushing toward the exit, as the crowd of losers demanded their money. The yelling was higher pitched than it had been before the fight, now with cries for Shade's hide, as infectious panic crushed body against body.

The referee knew the difference. Even Big Arms knew the difference. They fought their way toward the rear of the Box. *Woodworker had been a lucky guess. But I can see how it might have looked like a low blow.*

The concrete floor of the arena was covered in spray and spit, clumped with spatters of overripe fruit. This had always occurred to Shade as an odd waste. With the Fresh Tax, who carried fruit just to throw it?

Amid the uproar, they could just make out the doorway leading to the outside passage and aimed for it. A bottle of hooch sailed through the air in front of them and shattered against the stone wall. They braked on their heels and jumped over the broken glass. Shade gagged at the reek of home-brew rotgut as they turned the corner into the narrow hallway, banging their shoulder hard as they did so. The passage was completely dark, but Shade lunged forward, leaning into their run, their hat in one fist and long braids trailing behind them. They made it four steps before a hand snaked out of the shadows and grabbed for their hair, yanking hard and bringing them to the floor. Their scalp blazed in pain, and they kicked out, hoping to hit shins.

"Thief!" a voice hissed from somewhere above them. "You little shit, you'll pay for this!" The hand that wasn't buried in their hair clutched at Shade's shirt and arms, but they could hear the drink in the voice, and the grip was clumsy. Shade kicked again and this time connected, hard. The voice yelped and cursed, hands releasing, and Shade scrambled to their feet, running as fast as they could until the sound of their footsteps and gasps no longer echoed back at them. When their outstretched hands met the door, they pushed through and into the alley behind the Box, cramming their hat back on their head and shoving the door shut behind them.

They panted in the night air, taking in the heaps of baskets and metal garbage cans and the dumpster that cluttered the alley. They scrambled to push the dumpster to block the door, but it was too heavy, so they dragged a few metal cans in front instead, and then another in front of those. The glittering eyes of trashcats watched them, unafraid, as they picked through mounds of refuse with their little hands. One even hissed at Shade, and they hissed back. Shade jogged light-footed down the alley, out toward the maze of streets that made up the neighborhood.

Clattering cans behind them announced pursuit, and Shade took off again at a dead run. Two streets later, they zagged right, then left again at the next turn, hoping to lose their tail in the familiar labyrinth that made up the Arbor.

The night was damp, and Shade's shoes slapped against the stone of the streets. The irony of calling this filthy concrete warren an "Arbor" was lost on no one, especially since no trees had grown outside the private gardens of the Capitol Temple itself in the Imperial City of Soogway for nearly a hundred years. When the last dynasty had established the neighborhoods, they had bestowed them all such names. Perhaps they thought it would offer the lower classes a touch of bucolic fantasy to cling to, but those who now lived within the walls of places like Arbor, Glen, Orchardtown, Greenwood, or Sylvania curled their lips at the cruelty of it. Shade slowed their pace, letting their heart rate come down in case any of the safes had eyes out. It was no good sweettalking a safety enforcer while panting like you'd been on the run.

The next street yielded the smells of fried dumplings, and electric light splashed across the cobbles. Shade ducked into a doorway and curled up in the small drift of plastic garbage that had settled there, wincing at the clatter they made. Under the guise of sleep, they slipped the pouch from beneath their shirt and peeked inside. It was more than they'd thought. Shade drew out four chips with practiced fingers, tucking one into each sock and pants pocket, then replaced the pouch inside their shirt. Under the loose cloth, they felt the reassuring edges of the ironwood cubes. Those were worth a hundred dumplings each.

They yawned, stretched, and stood up slowly, as if working out stiff muscles, in case anyone was looking for a short storyfighter on the move. They kicked off a plastic sack that stuck to one heel. Dinnertime.

Shade bought three dumplings straight from the fryer, handing over the chip from their left pocket. They wrapped two in a handkerchief they stuffed inside their jacket, and the third they ate quickly, taking quick gasps of air around each hot mouthful. The filling was spicy and warming. They felt considerably better as they wiped the grease onto their pants and got their bearings. Just a few quick stops and then home.

Their footfalls pinged through the narrow concrete canyons of the Arbor but were soon lost on Commercial Street, swallowed by the rumble of carriages rolling, even at this hour, the repetitive jingle of happy boxes singing their vapid distractions, and the buzz of electric signs offering late-night snacks, hooch, plastic toys, produce. Shade danced around a trashcat who refused to yield the right of way and bared their teeth at it. It hissed and waddled on.

Shade passed an alley where a small pack of street kids were staging combat. They paused to watch two glowing rats wrestle as their young tellers made up rapid-fire nonsense on the fly. The rest of the pack was squealing and cheering favorites in whisper-shouts. Shade had gotten their start brawling in alleys just like this one, and they felt a swell of protectiveness, though they knew better than to interfere with the serious games of children. Shade nodded to the urchin posted as a lookout. They couldn't have been more than six, Shade figured. The lookout gave a solemn nod in return.

The next set of stalls flooded the street with the smells of baked goods, and Shade's stomach growled, despite its dumpling. They poked their head behind a curtain that glowed blue around the edges with electric light. An old man turned away from a small happy box balanced on a metal stool, his lined face branching into a wide smile as he recognized Shade.

"Kiddo! How'd it go?"

Shade pulled the chip from their right sock and held it up. The disk was real ironwood, laser-cut with an image of a tree. They handed it over to the old man, who palmed it and hid it with a fluid sleight of hand that belied his age.

"You always pay up eventually," he said, offering a coarse laugh as thanks. "Wanna sit for a bit?" He gestured to the crate beside him.

"No thanks, Cheap." Shade gave the old man's shoulder a squeeze. "I'm wiped. I'm gonna head home."

"OK, then," Cheap patted at Shade, already turning back to his box. "You be good," he added as the curtain fell.

Shade's next stop was a shadowed doorway with no door. They stepped inside and found it almost completely dark. They gave a low whistle. After a few moments, another whistle answered from above.

"I need a light!" Shade hissed.

There was a click, then a flood of pale yellow from a lantern overhead dimly revealed the foyer of a concrete building that looked as if it had been abandoned for ages. A spiral staircase curved above them, but its bottom story lay in a heap, blocking the way. To the right, a pipe ran up the wall and over a banister, and it was this Shade climbed, gripping with both hands and inching their feet from junction to junction to worm their way to the second level. Once they reached the top, the light was extinguished.

They walked down a corridor, running their hand along the wall to count the doorways by feel. At the third, they knocked softly. It opened, and Shade entered a small room lit by a happy box with the volume low.

Two children sat before it, their faces slack, their eyes reflecting the light from the device. A third peered behind the open door.

Shade hesitated, their stomach growling, then pulled the two dumplings from inside their jacket. At the smell, the two seated children seemed to wake up. They turned toward Shade, expectantly.

"Look what I brought," they said. The third at the door, who was a little taller than the other two, received the dumplings reverently and carefully tore each in half. One part for each, plus one for the lookout downstairs. The two crammed their portions into their mouths, chewing quickly and licking the hot oil off their palms when they'd finished. The child at the door smiled at Shade.

"Did you win?" Her voice was small.

"Of course I won," Shade said, ruffling her dark hair. "Here," they said, bending down to retrieve the chip from their other sock while also digging out the one in their pocket. They held their hands out to the girl as if she should choose a fist. She tapped their left.

"Wrong," they smiled. "You get both." They opened their hands to reveal two whole ironwood chips. The girl's eyes grew wide, and she snatched them as if Shade might change their mind, then wrapped her arms around their waist in a tight hug. Shade stiffened and patted her head awkwardly. They didn't like being touched.

"You smell," she said, wrinkling her nose.

"Thank you," they said. "Now go get some food." The girl nodded, beaming. The other children's attention was already back on the box as they absently sucked their fingers. Shade backed out of the room as the girl closed the door after them.

Shade couldn't have explained why exactly they bothered looking after the D Street kids, bringing them the odd snack and making sure they knew someone noticed them, checked in on them. It wasn't like they were the only orphans around. The city was crawling with feral children no one gave two shits about. Shade had been one once. Their family wasn't even from the city originally, but far to the west, where Shade would return as soon as they had the money. They just needed to make sure the little ones stayed alive in the meantime.

MA'SHIFRA SPEAKS: THE PEACEMAKER

What makes a Person a Person?

Is it that we walk upright, balancing on our two feet as we pace across the earth?

No, my People. See the stork and the tallhare. They are upright, too, and though we call them cousins, we do not call them People. That is not what makes us who we are.

Is it that we create things, things of use and things of beauty?

No, my People. See the spider spinning her web. See the magpie solving puzzles at play. Many are the creatures who make things, and we thank the gods for such wonders. But that is not what makes a Person.

Is it that we speak and sing?

Hear the sunwren with his lilting call. Hear the vulture hiss and the desert fox yap and lament. Hear, too, the stitch and hum of insects. Do we doubt the sense and meaning of these sounds, deny that all creatures are linked in voices, communicating like with like?

No, my People. Our language is not what makes People—yet there is something different in the way we use our words, is there not? It is not the sounds we make, my People, but what those sounds can do.

Long, long ago, there were humans who walked upright, who created beautiful things and useful ones, who talked and sang to one another as they worked and lived as we do. Yet they also ran, they hid, they made dangerous things, sharp things and hot things, things of death. They used their words to lie and to trick. And their contests were not ones of telling but of blood.

Yes, these beings had language and perhaps even knew the gods, but they had not yet learned to use their words as story, had not learned to summon and shape the light. They were dark creatures, sad ones, frustrated like tired children, and they solved their quarrels with fists and teeth and blades. Often these conflicts grew to engulf whole families, entire camps—groups fought groups and left their bodies to rot where they lay, spilling blood instead of light, using their force instead of their wits, their historics, their truths and wonders.

The gods at last took pity upon them and sent a dream to teach one the art of story. The Peacemaker learned quickly in her sleep and then carried that knowledge to the rest like a gift, a jewel, an offering. At first, they thought her mad, but it was she, the first teller, a visionary, who lifted those beasts from human to People. She saved us from our own violence and gave us a better way, a way we must continue to follow.

It is our stories and our capacity to hear and learn from them that make a Person a Person. Nothing less, nothing more.

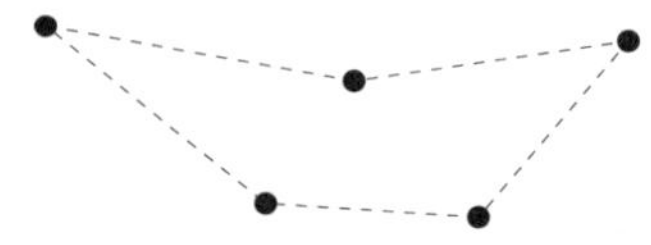

The Hearth: Overhead, windy season

5. THE SCOUTS RETURN

A rainbow of small children ran to meet Kell and Jor as they approached the perimeter of the camp, some trailing tiny glittering creatures of their own storymaking. "Ma'ani," she greeted them, smiling and bending to stroke the tops of small shorn heads and others tight with braids. "Ma'ani, it is good to be home. Yes, you too," she said and pushed away the paws of a large, exuberant desert cat. The sandbeasts snorted and groaned as they scented the rest of the herd. They began to trot, and the scouts holding the animals' leads jogged to keep up and remove their packs. Kell glanced to her brother, who looked happier now they were back. He needed to be reminded of what mattered sometimes. *Has his connection to the stones really grown so weak?* she wondered. *If he one day has children, ancestors save us, will they learn the old ways at all?*

These thoughts were quickly driven from her mind as the smells of the cook fires promised dinner and a welcome change from the trail meals they'd eaten for a week. She searched the array of tents, looking for Ama's mark on the side, not an easy task in the deepening twilight. The People set up camp differently at each stop, giving everyone the opportunity to be near the center or at the perimeter. The shift followed star transits and something to do with circumference, though Kell had seldom paid much attention to its precise calculation. The People's strength was their fluidity, like the sands taught them, but, gods, was she hungry and in no mood to learn the new layout.

"Do you see it?" she asked Jor, who had a better memory for the rotation pattern.

He pointed somewhere between sunrise and the Finder's Eye, the star that led north. "I think she's on the outer rim this time," he said. They pushed their way past dozens of small fires where evening stews were bubbling, exchanging wishes of peace with everyone whose path they crossed. The firelight threw shadows wild and leaping against the sand-colored tent walls, and faces shone, the murmur of voices split here and there with sharp laughter. Some tents glowed blue where the families inside chose the cool, interior lights run on city tech over the collective warmth of the fires.

At last, they came to the perimeter, where the air grew chill and the fires more widely spaced. Kell could hear the munching and grunts of the sandbeast herd, smell their comforting, oily funk. Despite being faded by the sun, Ama's mark stood out on the tent wall like a beacon, filling her with relief.

Now we are home, she thought. Their grandmother was not outside, but one of the cousins was tending the meal. A rich mix of spices wafted from the pot, and her mouth flooded in anticipation. Jor hailed the cook, who embraced him and offered Jor a taste. Kell was about to ask for a spoonful herself when another scent made her pause—something under the mix of sandbeasts and stews and warmth leaving the weave of the tents for the day. It was a golden-green smell, unfamiliar to camp. She heard a shuffle and huff. Walking into the shadows behind Ama's tent, she saw them, their legs hobbled, their soft noses in bags of feed on the ground.

Horses.

Their own caravan did not use horses. The areas of Home they frequented in the red and yellow zones were not ideal for horse travel, though she had seen them ridden on many occasions, and once even seen a story-joust on horseback, which had been thrilling but difficult to hear. Many of the People from other regions of the desert liked horses for their speed and sheer beauty, and she could see why, but those People generally lived in the hard-earth parts of Home, like the clay zone or the Riverlands, where scrub grass was more plentiful and the horses' legs less prone to snap in the shifting sands. The presence of horses in camp could only mean one thing: visitors. A thrill danced up her chest.

Kell walked back to the front of the tent and offered to help her cousin cook, but he waved her away and sent her in to Ama. He politely avoided mentioning how her tendency to break things often extended to recipes.

The front flaps of the tent were closed, which was odd at mealtime. She pushed aside the heavy drapes that kept out both sand and storm winds and found herself in a scene much different from the joyful homecoming she had anticipated.

Ama sat in her customary place at the rear of the tent, legs crossed beneath her on the worn pillows. Though her eyes lit up at the entrance of her granddaughter, she did not rise to welcome her. She lifted her hands toward Kell as if asking to be helped up, and Kell went to her and clasped them in her own, kissing the tops of each.

"Ma'ani, Ama," she said softly. "It is good to be home."

"May you find home wherever you are, child," Ama responded solemnly and gestured for Kell to take her seat next to her brother, another cousin, and Si'Denna, another head of family. Across from them sat four strangers. Even in the smoky, flickering light, Kell could see from their clothing and the tattoos one bore along their neck and wrists they were Roamers as well, though the cut of their tunics was different. They had the same dusty look that she and Jor shared after a week out of camp. Two even looked vaguely familiar to Kell—scouts, probably, with whom she might have exchanged water and news on a lookout run in the past. Her eyes traveled to the fourth and stopped. A woman her own age, long and rangy. She sat folded on her cushion like a gazelle, all angles and lines, her attitude a dare. Her hair was twisted into neat locks, and her face wore a look of such ferocity that Kell wondered whether she should prepare a story for combat. A jackrabbit leaped in her chest.

Gods, she was beautiful.

She dragged her attention back to her grandmother. The oil lamps on the ceiling swung gently from her entrance, and shadows danced back and forth across Ama's stern face.

"Your return is well timed. Riders from the clay zone have come to share news," Ama said, indicating the scouts. "The City of Soogway has overstepped our trade agreements and extended their reach farther into our territories than we had imagined, it seems." She looked to the riders, inviting them to speak.

"We made a full sweep of the area we were tasked and saw no one," Kell blurted out. "—Ma'Shifra," she finished awkwardly, remembering her formality at Jor's nudge. Ama hushed her with a hand, glaring at the interruption.

The older Roamer spoke. "What Ma'Shifra says is true," he began. "The city has changed their focus from the Broken Forests of the west and south and turned their attention northward, to our Home."

"It seems," Ma'Shifra continued, "That they have their eyes on the pulsar stones."

Kell's stomach dropped. Beside her, Jor coughed. The room weighed thick, the air sweetened with burning resins now dark and unbreathable. Kell looked from one face to another, waiting for someone to take the words away, but none did.

"That doesn't make any sense," she said at last, filling the heavy quiet. "Ancestors protect us, the stones aren't pebbles for the city to collect in their pockets. They aren't even sources of ore. What on dry earth could Soogway possibly want with them?"

The older scout shook his head. "We don't know, but we have come with dark news. Gods be with us, I—I am afraid that one is already gone. We knew that you, too, would feel it missing, but we witnessed its taking. It was...awful. A horror." His voice clotted with grief. "This could not wait for market season to be shared. We decided it is our duty to inform other camps in the region so we can prepare to protect the other stones."

One is already gone.

Kell gripped Jor's knee. He covered her hand with his own and squeezed, too tightly, until she met his eyes. There was something there she could not quite name—fear, certainly, but something else, too. Could that be satisfaction she saw? Could her brother really be so petty?

"How did this happen?" Jor's voice cracked as he spoke. He cleared his throat and sat a little straighter, releasing her hand.

This time the woman answered. Her voice was low and rusty, and Kell warmed at the sound of it, even as anxiety gnawed at her belly.

"Our camp has a long history of ignoring the city's overtures," she said. "The only transactions we allow include small amounts of ore for the metalworking that goes into our riding tack. Nothing else." Her eyes flicked around the room as if daring judgment. “Soogway sent a formal dispatch when we were at the south end of the yellow zone. They arrived with a full unit of security forces with them. The city came in with a negotiator and offered several trade deals, but when our People refused, they demanded formal combat.”

A murmur went around the room. Kell had to close her jaw.

“Turned out, they had come with a combat teller ready—one of their generals,” she continued. “The trade offers were a farce. They had no intention of leaving without the stone, one way or another.”

“But how can they do that?” Kell heard the shrill edge to her own voice and felt the room tilt. None of this could be happening. “They can’t just *take* it—that’s ridiculous . . . that’s not—your teller must have fought for it. Even against a general, the ancestors would protect you.”

The woman turned her eyes on her. It was like being sighted by a snake before a strike.

“My sister fought,” she said. “And she lost.”

"They have to believe you, or you've already lost."
—Shade's father

6. STOCKING UP

Shade's steps were lighter as they exited the building, even as they noticed for the first time how tired they really were. Their stomach protested the loss of the other two dumplings it had been promised, but Shade reminded it of the remaining cubes around their neck, and it agreed, reluctantly, to be patient. They paused in the doorway and glanced down the street. The ragged nighttime trade bustled on—sanitation workers pushed worn bamboo brooms across the pavement, chasing feral plastic bags; porters lugged baskets and crates in two-wheeled carts; hawkers shouted their gadgets from rickety bamboo stands. No sign of the safes.

Electric lights punched holes in the darkness, and the glow of oil lanterns spilled onto the cobblestones in narrow pools. Shade reached into their shirt for the pouch. Not wanting to risk showing the contents in this part of town, they dug around inside, counting their winnings by feel. No more chips, it seemed. Only a small handful of ironwood cubes, which made Shade's chest warm—*Not bad for a weeknight*, they thought—and posed an unusual problem. Not a lot of food stalls around here were keen to break a cube for a snack. Shade pulled out a cube, running their fingertips over the intricate carvings on its faces, before disappearing it into a pocket and returning the pouch to its hiding place. It was the end of the day. Maybe they'd get lucky.

Shade passed two more dumpling stands and a bakery. Their mouth watered, but a cube would be no good there. They were going to have to do something outrageous: go shopping. On the far corner sat a grocery that sold through a window at night to prevent theft. It yawned a weak yellow electric light onto the street, and the tinny sound of a happy box crackled from within.

The shopkeeper raised an eyebrow when Shade put their forearms up on the counter. It was at an awkward height, and they had to reach up, like a child. Shade pretended not to notice the indignity and pointed to a loaf of bread. The shopkeeper stared at them with a tired look Shade knew meant, "Money first." They feigned nonchalance as they drew the cube from their pocket and placed it on the counter. This raised both eyebrows, but the shopkeeper said nothing and turned to pull the loaf from the shelf. He set it on the counter and waited. Shade directed him to a hard sausage, two imported apples that shone with some edible coating, and in a fit of extravagance, a small cheese wrapped in thick red wax. The shopkeeper silently delivered these things into a small pile on the counter.

Shade swallowed hard as they scanned the shelves, crammed high with colorful goods. Preserved fruit, cigars, baked sweets, soda in glass bottles. The plastic beads some wore around their necks to trade with others. Bits of distraction tech. Things they never let themself see, let alone consider, were suddenly in reach, glowing with temptation. Shade licked their lips and blinked. *No*, they scolded themself. *Just the basics.* The shopkeeper's mustache twitched as he held up a bar of soap, his eyebrows a question. Shade glared, then nodded. *And a sense of humor to go with that mustache*, they thought. The shopkeeper produced a thin plastic bag with a flourish, snapping it so that it ballooned, and began placing Shade's items inside. Shade watched him, eyes narrowed. This was taking too long.

"Oi! You!" a deep voice barked. The shopkeeper froze mid-motion, looking past their shoulder into the street. He flicked his eyes to Shade, who mouthed a silent curse. This shopping spree was going to cost them more than a cube if the man didn't hurry.

Heavy boots scuffed the pavement, and the safety enforcer cleared his throat. Shade lifted their empty hands and began to turn around as slowly as they dared. Inside, their heart was pounding, ready to flee. The safe stood with his arms crossed, blocking their exit. "Where does someone like you get chips for all that?" he growled, smiling. Night safes were the worst: that terrible mix of bored and spineless that enjoys hassling street folk. Shade glanced down at the enforcer's side.

This safe's unit was, predictably, in the shape of an enormous dog.

"You're nothing but a worthless leech," the safe intoned, his voice taking on the edge of a formal accusation—Shade's least favorite kind of story. The dog bared its teeth in a silent snarl, swelling larger. Its shoulder came up to Shade's waist now. "I'll bet you're a thief, and you stole that money." Shade flinched as the enforcer's breath reached them. They kept their hands up above their ears and dropped their eyes to the ground. The safe's uniform was rumpled and soiled around the cuffs, and he swayed unsteadily.

Great, they thought. *Bored* and *hooched.*

"I didn't steal it," they muttered. Their mind raced as they tried to think of a way out that allowed them to keep the sack of groceries on the counter behind them. Their truth story glimmered from their upright casting palm. An egg. It shivered and fell onto the cobblestones, cracking open and spilling glow in a smear at Shade's feet.

The safe laughed, a short bark that reminded Shade of the Greenwood bullies who lit trashcats' tails on fire and crowed as the animals tried to put themselves out. "See?" he sneered. "Thief. Nobody like you carries money like that."

The dog sniffed at the broken egg. It opened its mouth to lap up the story when the glow shivered and popped up into the shape of a frog.

"I said, I didn't steal it," Shade repeated, louder. The frog hopped toward the dog. The unit raised its ears and showed its teeth again. Small spikes prickled along its spine.

"How'd you get it, then?" The safe leaned into Shade's face, and their stomach turned at his sour hooch and sweat stink. Shade was sweating, too: pit fighting was a worse offense than pickpocketing. They leaned away from the enforcer as far as they dared, their shoulders resting against the counter behind them.

"I . . . I worked for it." For who? For Cheap? Shade wouldn't drag him into this. For the Box? Chances are the owner would never vouch for them, especially not since they had cost the house a fair amount in tonight's fight—though Shade figured the house had hedged plenty. The frog hopped anxiously on the wet cobbles, resting then leaping erratically as the dog edged closer. It snapped at the frog just as the frog lurched between its legs, and the dog's teeth clamped only air. It peered under its own belly and then from side to side, trying to track Shade's story.

"Oh yeah?" The safe's finger pressed into Shade's chest, his breath in their face. "What work do you do, thief? You a baker, maybe?" The enforcer squeezed Shade's bicep as if testing their muscles. "You a teacher?" He prodded their breastbone again, close to both the pouch and Shade's amulet. Too close. Shade gritted their teeth and looked him in the eyes. Their look blazed with hate, they knew, and they didn't care. The safe grinned. "You a stoneworker, *thief?*"

"That one works for me," said a voice.

The safe turned his head, and when he saw who had spoken, he stood straight and backed away. Shade let their breath out in a rush.

"No kidding," the safety enforcer looked back at Shade in appraisal. The man who'd spoken was well dressed and clean. He stood casually, hands in his pockets, but his smile said he was accustomed to being obeyed. The two shook hands, and Shade saw the safe pocket whatever chips the man had palmed him. "Well, how about that," the enforcer said. Shade shivered. "You two have a good night, now." The safe gave a last malicious grin and turned to go, his unit padding quietly after him.

"You can collect your story." The man nodded toward the frog, which had found a puddle to sit in and was flexing its throat in a silent croak. Shade twirled their hand and pulled the story closed. "And your things."

They did as the man suggested. The shopkeeper handed the bag over the counter, along with a great number of chips in change. Shade figured the shopkeeper saw plenty from his corner shop, so one more little run-in with the safes wasn't worth comment. They hurriedly stuffed the chips into their pouch and returned it beneath their shirt.

The man made a gesture of invitation, and Shade followed, though a little voice in their head was telling them to run.

"Nice evening for groceries," the man said. They strolled down the damp, filthy street as if they were a couple of bosses visiting the Temple gardens on a sunny day. Shade never walked like this, especially at night. Their teeth chattered with nerves, so they pulled off a corner of the loaf in their bag and chewed it. The man had an easy, avuncular demeanor that they found both calming and distressing. He put an arm around their shoulder, and Shade stiffened.

"You can call me Mr. Go," he said, as if Shade had asked.

Shade felt they were supposed to offer their own name in return but chewed harder instead. The two walked to the end of the street, and Mr. Go paused at the alley where Shade would normally turn toward home. They wondered vaguely if that was coincidence. Mr. Go smiled, not releasing their shoulder.

Shade was tired. They wanted to go home, stash their winnings, and eat in peace. Maybe even sleep for a day. Whatever this mister wanted, it was unlikely to include any of those things. If there was one thing they hated, it was owing people. Men like this, in particular.

"You can cut the shit," they said around a mouthful of bread. "Why bother scramming that safe? I don't work for you."

Mr. Go's eyes were black in the lamplight. His fingers tightened on Shade's shoulder, and they felt themself fall limp like a stray caught by the scruff.

"That was true." His voice was soft, almost sleepy. "But you do now."

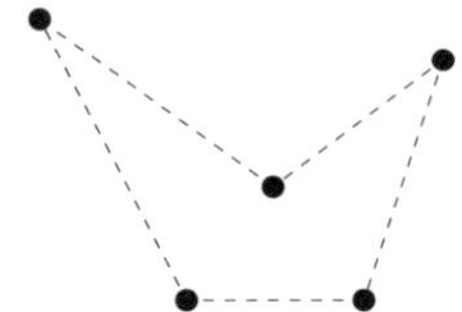

The Falcon: Western quarter, market season

7. FIRESIDE

Kell's heart was a sandstorm. *A pulsar stone missing? Soogway combat generals, here, overpowering the protection of the ancestors?* The city sometimes sent small research teams to test for minerals or stage temporary mining works in exchange for pieces of tech, but this . . .

Home felt suddenly unfamiliar and corrupted. The desert was endless, perfect, and yet this one violation poisoned her entire understanding of what was possible and true. The stones were massive, ancient, sent from the gods. How could the city could just march in and take the heartbeat of the land itself?

Ama listened to the group as they came to their fears aloud. Voices leaped and tangled in anxious murmurs and bold shouts as people talked over one another. Everyone needed to say it with their own mouths to understand.

"They just *took* it."

"How could they even approach?"

"—must be returned!"

Kell watched Ama draw closed in the way she always did when she was planning. The lines on her face betrayed years of worry and the creases of many smiles. In those lines, Kell saw a map of their traditions formed over countless generations, solid and sure as bedrock. But there was something else on Ama's face, something tired and full of doubt. Kell realized with a jolt that her grandmother was *old*. She knew this, obviously, but the word felt different in her mind now, offering not only wisdom and perspective but frailty, too. It occurred to her that Ama would be an ancestor one day, that her warm grip and rough voice would no longer be there to bark at her weakness or reassure her through her endless mistakes. Kell shivered and tried to put a lid over the hole that yawned open in her chest, lest she fall in and disappear.

"My People," Ama said at last, bringing her hands together before her. The room quieted. She was again Ma'Shifra, the eldest of the council in this camp, beaming confidence to the group. The formality of her tone was a comfort, and Kell seized on it like a fledgling to a branch. "We are grateful to our family who have ridden far to share this important news with us. We must think on what we have learned and ask the ancestors for their guidance. In the meantime, let us share a fire and a meal and stories from better times," her grandmother concluded.

Kell's comfort was short-lived as a new worry took hold. A story would be a perfect distraction, provided she didn't have to tell it. The thought of doing so in front of strangers right now made her sink into her cushion. She stole a glance across the room, searching out the fierce scout with the locks, and was startled to find her looking back. The visitor's face didn't soften, exactly, but there was something to it that suggested a smile. Kell reddened and examined her fingernails, still dark with travel. Ama rose from her pillow with the aid of her walking staff, and the occupants of the tent filed out from back to front, in order of seniority, as the ancestors had taught them.

Once they were all seated around various fires with bowls of stew in their hands, it was easier to pretend that everything was back to normal. Across the circle, Jor was surrounded by a handful of suitors of all genders who laughed and leaned into his words. Ama and the elder of the visiting scouts sat knee to knee, Ama's eyes lost in a wrinkled smile as she listened. Sparks danced around the elder scout's hands as he spoke, though no real stories materialized. Anyone could be a teller, Kell reminded herself, but not everyone learned to shape storylight.

The fire cast a coppery glow on the multicolored faces and tents as voices mixed with the crackle of the wood settling. Kell settled, too, basking in the familiarity of being back at camp, and attacked a large piece of dried fruit that had gone plump and soft in the stew.

"May I join you?" a voice rasped above her. Kell looked up to find the fierce woman towering above her. Her heart lurched as the visitor folded herself into a seated position beside her in a single, fluid move, her eyes fixed on Kell as if she were still awaiting permission. The fruit in Kell's mouth became huge and unmanageable, growing juicier but no smaller as she chewed. She covered her face with her hand as she strained with her mouthful and ducked to avoid the woman's gaze. Kell could feel her companion staring and stole an apologetic glance, nodding in awkward welcome. She chewed faster, but the fruit remained too large to swallow.

The black eyes burned into her.

Look away, please just look away. She considered spitting her bite out into the sand beside her, but as dribbles of juice ran from the corners of her mouth, she prayed silently to the ancestors that she would simply choke and die.

Mercifully, the woman gave up on receiving a more graceful invitation and said, bluntly, "I'm Silaya," before turning her attention to her bowl. Kell forced the stubborn fruit down, leaning into the shadows as her eyes watered.

"I'm so sorry," she coughed, clearing her throat. The fire was far too warm. "I'm Kell. Red sandbeast," she added, offering her camp's primary zone and mount in what she hoped wasn't an excess of etiquette.

Silaya laughed, a low chuckle that made Kell's insides feel like butter. "Clay horse."

Kell's mind raced, searching for something engaging to say. "So," she began weakly. "Horses." Her face flamed.

Silaya continued to eat as if Kell had said nothing.

"I mean," she tried again. "What's it like?"

"What's *what* like?" Silaya asked. Her voice was sharp, and Kell flinched.

"What's it like to ride a horse?"

At last, the right question. Silaya's face changed, the hard angles of her eyes and mouth turning to long lines of pleasure. She looked at Kell when she spoke. "You've never ridden a horse?"

Kell shook her head.

"It's like flying," she said. "It's like riding the wind in all its strength." She took a bite of stew and chewed.

Kell studied her as the orange light danced over the dark planes of her cheekbones. The shape of her eyes reminded Kell of the slender obsidian chips they sometimes used as hand knives. It was easy to imagine this face mastering the winds.

"It is like dancing with a partner," she went on. "My horse is my best friend, and we respect each other. I am not her master," she finished as if hearing Kell's thoughts.

"Our sandbeasts travel slowly, and we're almost always on foot. It's hard for me to imagine moving so quickly."

Silaya gave her a look, and there was something wicked in it that made Kell's skin tingle. "You would get used to it."

Kell poked at the food in her bowl. Silaya, on the other hand, seemed to find the act of eating a waste of time and was rushing to have it done. The sound of her spoon scraping the bottom of her bowl filled the awkward pause between them.

"You and your sister—you're both tellers?"

"I'm no teller," Silaya said gruffly. She drained the last from her bowl and set it in the sand beside her.

"Really? I took you for combat."

Silaya looked at her evenly, her dark eyes unreadable.

"I am no teller," Silaya repeated. "Just a pathfinder. I'm only on the scouting missions to tune the stones. My cousin and I triangulate." Like Kell and Jor. Some stones only spoke to certain people, so good pathfinders traveled in complementary pairs. "Back at camp, I'm a weaver," she said.

Kell considered this. Silaya had fight written all over her—it was hard to imagine those powerful-looking hands devoted to the repetition of a loom. Kell wondered whether there was a piece missing from the story but didn't ask.

"And you? You're a pathfinder too, yes?"

Kell nodded around a mouthful and swallowed.

"And at camp?"

Kell sighed. "I'm a teller—not a good one," she added quickly. It was a habit she'd learned to deter people from asking her to demonstrate. "I'm not much of a performer. Too many eyes on you when you tell, too much responsibility for the outcome. I don't really have the instincts for it."

Disappointment—or was that boredom?—shadowed Silaya's eyes.

"I love the telling, the stories themselves," Kell clarified. "Just . . . not the rest of it." She glanced at Silaya to see if she understood. "Ama—I mean, Ma'Shifra wants me to be a combat teller in her place, but . . . " She trailed off.

"You don't like to fight?" Silaya asked.

"No. Not really. All that strategy—" she made a face. "I'd rather do lore, honestly. Ritual work. History, memory—anything. But telling in defense or negotiating trade exchanges just so we can adapt city tech?" Her eyes flicked briefly to Jor and saw the wayfinder still sticking out of his shoulder bag beside him. "I trust the old ways."

"Ancestors be praised," Silaya said. "More People need to stick to the old ways. Like I said, we don't waste time trading with Soogway except when we absolutely have to. We don't need their severed gadgets to find the Way." She spat in the sand.

Kell nodded, emphatic. "My brother, his skills have gotten weak because he relies too much on the bugs. And so many—" She gestured around the camp at the tents lit blue with tech, flaps closed to the communal fires. "They forget what makes us People."

Silaya smiled at her, a real smile. "Yes," she said. "Exactly."

Kell's chest heated with pleasure. She chased another lump of fruit around her bowl but didn't dare eat it. The stew was delicious, rich with sandbeast milk and pungent spice bark, but she felt full already, her insides too alight with questions and the spark of attention from this visitor. Food was never wasted—especially stews with their precious liquid—so she offered the remainder of the bowl to Silaya, who took it without comment. It vanished in seconds, and Kell found herself wishing she'd kept it to have something to do with her hands.

"Can I ask you something?" Kell began, absently tracing a circle in the sand. Silaya's eyes reflected the firelight as she looked at her. "What happened? With—with your sister. How did she lose?"

Silaya was quiet a long moment.

"Upepo used a heart story," she said. She sat cross-legged, and her hands twined and twisted together as if she would wring the tale from the air. Or the city general's neck. "Something tender and real . . . It's always a sure win, right?" The husky voice cracked.

Heart stories were the deepest currency they had. Some were passed down among generations and used to teach and shape, the purest form of cultural transmission. Others were private and holy, moments of epiphany or joy that were shared only as an act of great intimacy or vulnerability. They were the essence of a Person and of the People. And like all stories, if the teller lost in combat, the heart story was consumed by the opponent. It would be taken from the teller—and the culture—forever. Kell had seen Ma'Shifra lose a heart story in combat once, several years ago. It was the only time she'd seen her grandmother cry.

Kell's hand moved to Silaya's knee in awkward comfort, and she clicked her tongue in sympathy. She knew the loss was deep, one felt by an entire community. Silaya only carried a piece of it. Then Kell's mind returned to the stolen stone, and the sudden fresh grief of it snatched her breath away.

Please, ancestors, Kell thought, staring into the fire. *Guide my words.*

"We will get it back," she said with a certainty she did not feel. "The stone, I mean."

Silaya looked at her and nodded, her fierce mask back in place. "I want that general to feel it when we do."

Kell smiled. "Don't worry. If they show their face around here, we'll chase them off with a story of mudworms in their food."

Silaya blinked. "A cloud of grasshoppers to chew through their ugly city clothes," Silaya said, a smile forming at the edges of her mouth.

"A wind made of cactus thorns to blind them," Kell countered.

"Of flying, hungry jackals. Teeth snapping at their asses."

"Of sand lice on their balls!"

"A flash flood of flaming shit!"

As they laughed, Kell felt herself ease into the sand a little. She was grateful the color of the flames hid the blush she felt rising into her cheeks.

A long rattle interrupted them. Near the fire, a woman from another tent stood, holding a staff bristling with wire and pebbles made from bits of glass and shards of tech. Her long hair streamed darkly behind her, and firelight limned her in gold. She stamped the end of the staff into the ground, and it rattled again. Conversations broke off as people scooted closer. Kell melted with relief at not being called upon to tell. She leaned toward Silaya.

"A'Lan is one of my favorite lorists," she whispered, grinning. "She's who I've done most of my studies with, besides Ama." Silaya nodded and leaned in, as well, until their shoulders touched. Kell's skin felt like it often did right before she broke a gadget, charged and alive with static.

A'Lan shook her staff, and the rattle became the low warning of a snake. She stabbed it upward, and it was a crack of thunder. She swept it in a wide circle, casting the listeners in with the sound of rain on tents, sweet and rare. The audience was bound to her.

"You remember how we came to know our Home."

A'Lan's voice was gentle, but it carried well. Turning as she began her telling, she made eye contact with everyone around her as if welcoming each to the circle, adding their strength to the story. Kell felt herself tugged gently forward as A'Lan's eyes met her own, her energy claimed.

The lorist upheld her casting palm and took them all back in time, to the Lost Period, when People did not think to wander and had no sense of Home. A large golden lizard shimmered in the air before her, sunning itself. A'Lan told of the rootlessness of the People, the loneliness they felt having no connection to the earth. How travel was a hazard, how the winds would erase their paths in the sand, and the few People who dared to wander never returned. The glowing lizard rolled off an invisible rock. The crowd gasped as it fell against the sand and shattered into a cloud of termites.

"Our ancestors knew this had to be fixed," she continued. "And so, they called upon the sky and gave themselves to the earth." Kell murmured along under her breath, as did many around the fires. The combined strength of their telling caused the termites to swell, rising until a whirlwind of luminous insects boiled the air above them. The audience leaned back as one to watch. Stories were climbing and twisting above other fires in camp, as well. The night sky was golden with their telling.

"The ancestors sang and danced until they wore paths in the rock. The earth vibrated with their music, their memories turned to pattern and rhythm. The quaking of the ground shook the sky, and the gods themselves trembled. And they were moved by the dancing of the ancestors. A rain came then, not of water, but of fire and stone."

The termites spiraled together in a helix, twisting ever tighter until they coalesced into a dragon. Kell felt her heart clutch as it always did at this part, her lips moving to the words.

"The stones tore their own paths through the sky, and many ancestors offered themselves up to their fire. The ground shook with the impact of the sky-stones, and many People fell beneath them. As the stones settled into their places, each had a living heartbeat drawn from the heart of an ancestor, each as different as the People themselves. Those who remained gathered close to listen."

The dragon unhinged its great jaw in a silent roar, swooping above their heads. As A'Lan spoke of the First Pathfinder's hands catching fire, the voices of the listeners grew. She told of how the People learned to cooperate to read the stones, to feel the pulses, to sing the Way at Ease, the Way in Haste, and the Way to Water. How their stories would always show them the truth of Home. Kell's heart burst with gratitude for the ancestors and their sacrifices. Silaya's shoulder pressed against hers, solid and warm.

The dragon climbed the air, higher and higher, until A'Lan reached the tale's final line, and the audience was silent, leaving it to her to end the telling.

"And that is how we found our Way."

The dragon disappeared, replaced with a constellation against the black of the sky, then reappeared only to dive headfirst toward the listeners. Kell heard Silaya's quick intake of breath as the dragon hurtled toward them. The beast rushed downward and plunged itself into the fire, vanishing in a puff of sparks.

Around them, listeners clapped and offered sounds of appreciation. A'Lan took her seat again, and Silaya turned to Kell, her eyes bright and face flushed.

"We tell it almost the same, but with a falcon. The dragon is . . . " She searched for words. "Wonderful."

Kell's smile faded as she again remembered why these horse riders had come. A pulsar stone had been defiled. *Taken*. Is that why A'Lan had chosen this story to tell?

Silaya nudged her. "Come on," she said, as if sensing the shift in Kell's mood. "Let me show you something." She stood and took Kell's hand, pulling her upright with a grip that did not invite refusal. Sunwren wings flapped in Kell's chest.

The two rinsed their bowls with sand and returned them to the stacks outside Ama's tent. The night was cool shadowside, and they rubbed their arms, pulling their loose scarves around their shoulders. Silaya led her into the darkness behind the tent, where the air was rich with the smell of horses. Kell followed, nervous and excited at once. Unlike sandbeasts, who knelt in the cool night sand to rest, the horses remained quietly upright like sentries. They seemed far larger than they had in the fading daylight, their backs nearly up to Kell's shoulders, and she worried she might be crushed as Silaya led her between them. The horses just stood, however, stamping an occasional foot into the sand. One nickered as if enjoying a private joke. They were like sandbeasts in some ways, she thought, but also so incredibly different.

Silaya had disappeared into the shadows.

"Here," came her voice. Kell followed.

She was stroking the neck of a brown horse. It was no larger than the others, and yet the way the light caught the muscles that bunched its withers, the restless energy coiled inside it, Kell felt certain this horse was special. It was like Silaya, she realized.

"Do you want to touch her?"

Kell nodded. She reached out a shy hand for the horse's nose, and it quickly pulled away. She jerked her hand back, and Silaya laughed.

"Gently," she said. "Like this."

Kell allowed her hand to be placed on the wide flat of the horse's neck. She moved it slowly down the length of it, marveling both at its softness and the raw feeling of strength inside it. Silaya was standing close enough that she had the electrical feeling in her skin again. Trapped between the fierce woman and the giant animal, she swallowed a delicious sense of panic.

"What's her name?" she whispered. She cleared her throat. "What's her name?" she repeated, louder. She stroked the horse as it flicked its ears, their thousands of tiny hairs backlit by the faint light from camp.

"I don't know yet."

Kell turned to face her. Gods, she was standing so close. "What do you mean?"

Silaya reached up to touch the horse's neck as well, leaning into Kell to do so, her arm over Kell's shoulder. "I don't speak her language," she explained. "So, she hasn't told me. We don't name our horses unless we know what they call themselves. But she and I have our own way of communicating."

Silaya's eyes were black and bright, her face nearly lost in shadow. Kell felt her press into her, felt the warm bulk of the horse behind her. The ache over the stones felt far away, like the taste of a bad dream left from the night before. Silaya smelled like leather and red sand and dried roses, and Kell could not remember why she had been afraid. Her heart pounded as if she had been running the dunes. Silaya paused, her face now so close Kell couldn't see her, only feel her breath against her lips.

Silaya's mouth was hot as it met her own, and surprisingly gentle. The kiss was a question.

This?

Kell put her hands on Silaya's waist and pulled her closer.

This.

"A seed of an idea is alive. Let it grow."
—Shade's father

8. A BAD JOB

Shade felt like they'd slipped from the safe's dog only to find themself between the paws of a very large cat. *Be quick, street rat*, they thought. With a limp bob-and-weave, they shifted their bag to their other shoulder, easing out from under the man's well-groomed grip. Familiar tension returned to their body the moment they stepped out of reach.

"I'm not for sale," they said, gesturing down at themself as if their slight build was obviously unsuited for whatever this man had in mind. "Besides," they added around a chew of bread. "I already have a job."

Mr. Go nodded, still with the same confident slouch to his tidy, well-fed frame.

"Of course you do," he said mildly. The streetlights painted his features in exaggerated shadow, and Shade could not tell if his expression was a smile or a scowl. Either way, he emanated a quiet menace that turned the food in their mouth to paste. They were ready for this day to be over. Let this cat find something else to play with.

"Thanks, then," they said as they backed away, plotting a route back to their nook that wouldn't show Go where they lived, though they had the uneasy feeling he already knew.

Mr. Go picked at his teeth with something that flashed in the dark. "It'd be a shame," he began in a soft voice that made Shade feel like their fur was being stroked the wrong way. "A sad ending, for you to get picked up one of these days, lose all those chips you've been working so hard to amass."

Shade froze, their heart hammering in their chest.

"You haven't even heard what kind of job I have in mind," he continued calmly. The blade in his hand glinted. "I assure you, it falls neatly into your set of—," he paused, waving at Shade's entirety with the knife, "specialized skills."

They swallowed.

"It's simple, really. You need money, a fair bundle of it. And papers. I know where you can get it all. In exchange, you do for me what you do best."

"What's that?" Their voice was a squeak.

"Same as always: you fight."

"I don't fight for owners," Shade growled. The Box and places like it had plenty of ways of making money for people who weren't doing the actual fighting. Good tellers getting into debt, working off accounts that never quite balanced. Shade had had plenty of offers but avoided them like poison.

"I know, I know," Go said, neatly folding the knife and replacing it in his pocket. He gave off a faint scent of flowers, and Shade wondered what kind of man wore cologne to prowl the Arbor. Imported oils cost a fortune.

"The thing is, I only really need you to fight once," he said. "One time should be enough."

Shade's eyes searched for the man's face. It was so hard to see clearly in the scant light.

"One time," they parroted. Their mind poked at the corners of it, looking for the trap.

"It'll take some training, of course," Go sighed heavily. "You're not ready yet. Not for a fight like this."

It was an obvious taunt, but Shade bristled, despite themself. "Doubt it," they said. "I can beat anyone in the Box." Go smiled, and Shade wanted to spit at his feet.

"I'd like to sponsor you for the Cycle."

Shade gaped. The man chuckled and put both his hands in his pockets, as at ease standing on filthy street corners and promising the impossible as he would have been lounging in pajamas. Shade knew there was a catch, knew the wire hovered just above their neck, but the bait, for once, was worth it.

"I take it you know about the Cycle?" Go asked.

Shade nodded. Every teller knew about the Cycle. It was an annual tournament hosted by the Temple Council, full of spectacle and explosions. Shade had sneaked into the cheap ticket area to watch a handful of times, and though they had only been able to steal glimpses through the standing crowd, it had been the grandest, wildest display of talent they had ever imagined. All the greatest fighters took a swing at it sooner or later, pitting their storytelling skills against one another in the arena for a shot at a treasure in prize money. More than Shade needed to save up in a single shot. Word was that was also how many combat generals got their jobs. But competing was little more than a fantasy for folks like Shade—the entry fee was months' worth of chips. Almost nobody who fought in places like the Box ever set foot in the arena.

"I'd like for you to win," he said. That soft voice prompted an uncomfortable shiver. "And I think I can help you do it."

Shade didn't know what to say. The Cycle was a fantasy, something kids daydreamed about but left behind as they grew older and reality soured, when such dreams felt more like weights than wings. They had never allowed themself to think seriously about entering—the entry cost alone had cut short any thoughts their father may have had about it, and that was doubly true for them. And begrudgingly, they knew Go was right. They weren't ready.

"So, you're a teller, too?" The man likely expected a "sir"—the power of his station fit on him like a comfortable suit—but Shade was damned if they were going to give him the satisfaction.

Go's face changed, though Shade struggled to follow the shapes it made in the shadow. Eventually the man shrugged in a gesture of false humility.

"Of a sort." His voice was nearly a whisper.

Go began to murmur under his breath, and a glimmer appeared

in his hand. Shade leaned in to hear his words—they didn't like stories they couldn't hear—and the glimmer quickly grew, spiraling up from his palm. The light of the telling revealed Go's face, the shape of his narrow eyes, the disappointed sag of his cheeks.

A curious sensation spread through Shade's chest, a tingling and a tugging. The spiral sprouted extensions—tentacles again, Shade thought, but no—the edges were sharper and more vein-like. They ranged upward, and Shade saw that they were branches, a gnarled trunk reaching up into the sky, roots seeking downward to invisible earth. Not an animal at all, but an ancient tree with golden twigs that burst forth into golden buds and unfurled into golden leaves. The leaves shuddered in a noiseless breeze and then fell. The tugging feeling inside Shade turned to grief.

Go muttered on, too quietly for Shade to make out the words, yet it had a pulse and rhythm to it, almost like a chant but soft, so soft. The tree stood naked for a moment, its leaves carpeting its base, and then it twisted again like a rag being wrung. A form appeared, human and delicate, the features slowly molding into recognizable shape. The form took a step toward Shade and reached two hands to their face. They looked into the figure's eyes, and for a moment, one moment only, Shade saw the face of their mother, as clearly as if she lived. She smiled at Shade sadly, her glowing hand just brushing their cheek, then vanished in a swirl of leaves that settled onto the concrete and winked out. The vision was gone as quickly as it had appeared. Go collected the story back into his palm, and the street again was dark.

Shade stared into the space where their mother had been. They wanted to scream.

How had he done that? A real tree, a real memory—

It was like a heart story in reverse, one the stranger had pulled out of them as they watched, which was, well, impossible. Cunning tellers guessed at things all the time—like the woodworker tonight—but . . . that was far from conjuring the face of someone they'd loved. They swallowed the bile that leaped up the back of their throat. Their pulse surged through them, singing, *Run, run, run.*

Their mind, though, yearned. *Teach me. Tell me everything.* They looked at Mr. Go, but his face was lost in the trick of the streetlights.

Shade's voice was hoarse. "I'll do it."

The man was silent for a moment, then produced something small and pale from his pocket. He handed it to Shade, who stuffed it into their own without looking at it. They hated this man.

"I'm glad we understand each other," Go purred. He extended his hand, which was damp and folded around Shade's own like dough. "I'll be in touch," he said. Shade snatched their hand away and darted down the street, away from their homeward alley, away from the man who was going to give them everything they'd ever wanted.

They ran blindly for blocks, their rat-heart thumping in their chest. Their bag slapped against their leg as they went, their footsteps too loud and easy to follow. They felt naked and watched, the dark windows and blooms of box light like eyes following their path. When they finally slowed, a voice in their head said, *Up*, and they began to climb, grabbing one railing then another without thinking, jumping from concrete ledge to ledge, not looking down, not caring whether they slipped. They found a pipe leading upward and yanked, testing it against their weight. Shade climbed hand over fist.

Once they made it to the rooftops, they paused, panting. Here they felt safe, or at least without pursuit. Away from the eyes of fat-cat tellers. They slinked past the dark shapes of stairwells and thickets of clotheslines, picking their way by instinct. They jumped a few gaps that were wider than they'd usually risk and had to climb down into an alley, over a dumpster, and back up the other side again to reach the building they called home. This time, they took the outside route, traversing the concrete wall until they came to a glassless barred window. They reached through the bars to work the pins that kept it locked, then swung it open, tumbling into the small nook that was their room. It was dark and damp, a concrete box. It was secure.

Shade collapsed in the corner where their mattress lay, lit only by streetlights in the alley outside. They curled onto it, shivering, and pulled their jacket around them. Both their amulet and the pouch of winnings pressed into their sternum, and they leaned into the sharp edges, seeking the bright points of hurt. The glowing image of their long-dead mother reaching for them burned on the insides of their eyes. They closed them tightly and shoved her image down deep, clamping a lid over her memory. They forced themself to count their breaths. Eventually, their hands stopped shaking. Shade tried to push their meeting with Mr. Go into a hole in a corner of their mind as well, tried to stuff the entire evening down into the dark. *But the Cycle.*

Their stomach growled, and they sat up and dug into the sack of food, tearing off another hunk of bread. Cheese and sausage could be saved, but bread didn't keep long in the damp, which was a good excuse to eat most of it, and quickly. As they chewed, Shade removed the pouch of winnings from around their neck, spilling the contents onto the bed. Five cubes remained, an incredible haul for one night, enough to keep them in dumplings and fruit for months and still have some left to share with Cheap and the D Street kids. Maybe get a sweet bun for their friend at the shipping docks, too, and a new pair of scissors for Ma Bud, ones that didn't hurt her hands. There would still be enough to save.

Shade reached under their mattress and felt around for a familiar tear in the fabric. They dug further, their fingers doing the seeing, until they reached the rough edges of another pouch. They gripped it and pulled, bringing bits of mattress stuffing with it. It had been a while since they had counted it all, and emptying the pouch now made their heart first rise then sink in their chest. Four years they'd been saving, and yet the mound of chips—and now several cubes to boot—wasn't nearly enough to escape the grip of the city, to purchase the requisite travel papers and passage to the Broken Forest. To set up a new life far away. Shade's hand strayed to the amulet on a cord at their neck, their fingers tracing the tiny edges and sharps of its curve. A very small acorn.

When Soogway had taken the trees, many forest folk had moved into the city looking for work and a new way of life, Shade's parents among them. The couple had always hoped to return, but Shade's father, a gifted teller, had been taken into the guard and lost too many battles, spent too many heart stories trying to survive. As his memories of the forest faded, so did he. Shade's mother soon followed.

Shade had still been a child then, and the neighbors had told them it was cancer that had taken her, a product of the chemicals she had worked with dyeing capitol cloth. But Shade knew, even then, it was a broken heart. Theirs had broken, too, and something else inside of them. Ever since, Shade had been trapped in a strange and desperate present, scrabbling to survive but never truly feeling the satisfaction of change, never seeing evidence of real progress outside the pouch that grew with agonizing slowness. The same fights. The same roasted beans, the same dumplings. Even their body had stayed small and slender.

Their childhood had been filled with stories of the Broken Forest, the green of it, the leaves and needles and ferns, the mosses and bugs. They had grown up hearing about symbiosis, root networks, words that meant sharing and safety. Shade didn't know exactly what a fern was but knew the forest was full of them. Their parents remembered ferns. And Shade remembered their parents.

Their mother had removed the acorn from around her own neck. A relic of an old life she no longer needed, she'd said, but one that she hoped would live again. With shaky hands, she had tied the amulet around Shade's nape and let it slip beneath their shirt. *It's from our home*, she'd explained, her voice rattly and sweet. *Someday you will go back there and see it, Shade. You will plant it, and it will grow.*

The glowing hands, reaching for their face.

A'LAN SPEAKS: SANDSTORM SPIRIT

Breathe with me.

In, then out.

Again.

Feel now the clarity as it enters your lungs, that precious air, so clean and cool here in this place. Feel how it fills you, allows you to grow. Feel its safety and abundance.

You know what it is like when this is not the case. You remember the storms when they come, the air that turns to pain, no longer round and cool but sharp, hot, heavy with grit, scouring the skin from any place you have left exposed. You remember what it is to fight for breath. You know how to cover your eyes, to balm your nose, to sink until the spirits pass.

Yes, you do. You remember the spirits.

How can something so cold bring so much heat? How can something so lost find us in this place?

My People. You remember Si'Pala. Pala is but one of many, for storms are great and thirsty, but it is of Pala I will tell.

Pala the third child, Pala the Weak. Si'Pala whose two older brothers, Ma'Donok and A'Mene were strong and well-liked, who lived in the community with grace. How many acts does it take to sour a heart? Count them upon our fingers. One? Two? Ten acts, enough to form fists? Was it the first time Donok teased him that Pala withdrew his love for others, that he forsook his place at the fire? Was it the hundredth time he watched a girl admire Mene's long legs and easy smile that Pala came to want those looks for his own?

When a man cannot easily gain what another has, he will misunderstand the path by which it has come to the other. He will simplify it in ways that are brittle and false, seek a shorter route to the place he wants to be, but the Way in Haste will not lead you if you do not have the song, my People.

Pala craved attention and adoration, two things that he mistook for power. He imagined that Mene held sway over people like a rope around a sandbeast's jaw, not that people would come to him of their own accord, drawn to him like moths to the lanterns of a tent. Though he did not have the pull of his older brother, nor the laughter and wit of the other, Pala vowed to wield power too. The only means he could find was by hoarding what should have been shared.

What must be shared? You remember.

Water, yes. Food. Healing. Shelter. Voice. Memory. Space. Stories.

Yes, my People.

But Si'Pala did not do this. When he crossed the yellow and red zones, he carried water in plenty. But when he met travelers in need, he denied them, sent them scratching at their throats and raving into the wastes. When his father, a great teller, passed, Pala allowed the stories to slip away, to climb the night like sparks from a fire, lost to the People forever. These acts did not bring him pleasure but something akin to satisfaction. In the suffering of others, he saw his own hungers reflected and pulled tight at the rope he thought he held.

Years passed, and Pala grew ever colder, distant from the fires of the group. He became insatiable. His blood went sour from eating alone. When his body was ready to return to the sands and his spirit to dance with the ancestors, the ancient ones turned from him. He had not spoken their names nor had the communal fires lit his face. They did not know him.

Frantic, Pala raced across the desert, seeking any spirit who would see his face, behold him, keep him and share his name. But all he came upon were memories of those he had wronged, reminders of his bitterness and the suffering he had created.

At last, he found a knot of spirits who recognized him. Their eyes were twists of shadow, and they moaned instead of sang. Perhaps once they had been People, but they were now wraiths, horrors made of pain. Thirst drove them, shredded them, and they whipped and screeched and clawed at him. Their forms were made of grit and tumult, their voices the groan and rumble of discontent, the shriek of want. Souls that had seen great torment, they were—or had inflicted it upon others. Only here would Pala find his place, and only here would he find others drawn to him in the way he once had longed. But instead of peace, Si'Pala was condemned to roam, desperately seeking the water he once had denied others.

This is the sandstorm, you remember. The thirst and the fury. The wandering and the rage. When the storm comes, these unseen spirits seek your moisture, your rest. That is why we must sink and hold one another close, lest we be torn apart and lost.

Breathe with me.

This is one of the many gifts we share.

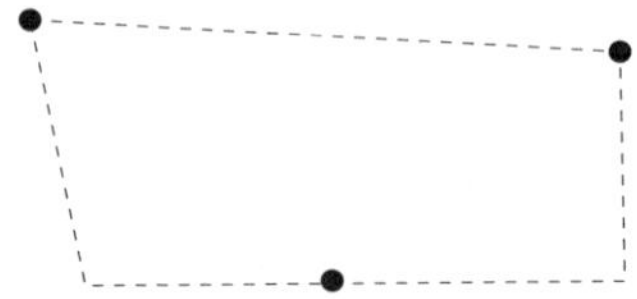

The Cauldron: North, flood season

9. PRAYER AND PREPARATION

The next morning began with sounds—the chatter of voices around the small breakfast fires, the shriek of early-rising children chasing desert cats between the tents, the clack of spoons against pots as tea brewed and flat breads baked on hot stones. The inside of the tent was dim and smelled of resin and warm bodies. Kell rolled onto her side and looked at the sleeping figures. The visitors had placed their bedrolls along the opposite wall for the night and now were stirring. Silaya had slept near her people, and Kell felt a tug of longing, wishing they could have curled up together. Ama's spot was already empty. She often woke early and went walking around the perimeter of camp to think and greet the sunrise.

Jor snored quietly beside Kell, a friend from another tent sprawled against his other side. Kell couldn't remember his name—Mina, maybe?—but he'd been around before. He and her brother sometimes slept together, especially when nights were cold. Privacy could be hard to come by in camp, but such casual relationships, both brief and enduring, were common and welcomed. The People valued family over romantic connection, so long-term couples living together were rare, though there were, of course, exceptions. Kell's mother was one, wherever she was. Mina's eyes were open, and he was watching Jor sleep, one finger lazily stroking her brother's arm. He looked at Kell as she sat up, and they both smiled.

Kell felt giddy and light. It was good to be home, which felt renewed with the addition of visitors. She regretted that Silaya would have to leave, and likely soon, but the sweetness of the night before had left her belly full of fluttering wings. She rubbed her shorn head, feeling bits of sand in the fuzz that had grown out, and looked across the tent to see Silaya sitting up and unwrapping her hair. Their eyes caught, and they both grinned. In the morning light, Kell felt strangely shy.

She busied herself with her morning routine, rolling up her bedroll and tucking it off to the side where it could serve multiple purposes, as did most things in their camp—as a cushion for tea or unfurled as an extra windbreak in a sandstorm. Still bleary-eyed, she clicked on an electric lamp that hung on the wall within reach. It crackled and sputtered briefly to life before going dark again, a stain against its side showing where it had burned out at her touch. She sighed, then stepped softly over sleepers and wakers. At the rear of the tent, she knelt at the small, two-tiered altar set behind Ama's seat and bedroll.

While most of the tent floor was layered in thick woven blankets to protect from cold desert nights, the altar rested on a corner of bare earth. She spat into the sand before it, offering her water to the gods and the ancestors. The altar was little more than a low table covered in fabric, but it had the magnetic power of a holy thing. She held her hand above the small oil lamp that burned on its bottom tier, letting the heat awaken her senses, and then opened the wooden box containing sweet, gold resin. She held a tiny bit of it to the flame and set it in the offering dish, letting the rich smoke curl upward. The lower level was for the ancestors. The upper was for the gods. Right now, she needed the intervention of both.

This daily practice of gratitude and request for guidance was a welcome bit of discipline that made space between her mind and her thoughts. Beneath the thrill she felt at meeting Silaya lay the seed of why the other Roamers had come in the first place, and Kell felt a cool dread growing roots in her heart. Something would have to be done to retrieve the stone and protect the rest from the city's generals. Storytelling—and especially combat—followed clear rules of engagement, predictable arcs, and known patterns of conflict and resolution. The city's deviation from this was a violation of more than an individual stone. It was a perversion of respect she found difficult to grasp, and this morning she struggled to take comfort in the ritual.

She closed her eyes, tried to let her worries settle like sediment in a jar and focus on breathing. She heard the soft sounds of people moving about the tent and felt an electrical heat against her shoulder as someone knelt in prayer beside her. She smelled leather and roses. Silaya waved her hand over the flame, selected her own piece of resin, and spat. Taking a deep breath, Kell centered herself, feeling a great sense of rightness. Jor still made offerings from time to time, but it had been years since he'd been consistent. Even if Silaya's camp apparently spat in the wrong order, Kell found that she'd missed the feeling of praying alongside someone, and her heart opened in gratitude.

Some people saw visions when they prayed, Kell had heard. The ancestors spoke to them directly, offered glimpses of the past to be used in the present. Kell envied these people. What she felt, instead, was physical—as if her veins flowed toward her heart but originated outside of her skin. The strength of the ancestors animated her body with every pulse. She felt *connected.*

The gods were silent, majestic, distant, offering creative force and wonder but having little interest in the everyday dramas of people. The ancestors, on the other hand, remembered life and how to live it. When they spoke, they did so through stories. The words that came to Kell were theirs—with lore, the teller was merely the conduit. Even the telling she did of her own imagination was animated with the ancestors' shadows, their thoughts and habits making the images dance. Their guidance was rich with symbol. And yet sometimes . . . sometimes she wished they'd simply tell her what to do.

Shouts from outside broke her reverie, announcing the approach of more riders. Whispering quick thanks, Kell took two more breaths and got to her feet. Silaya, too, unfolded beside her, her long body tense and poised to spring. *A weaver, indeed.* Kell met her eyes, and both headed outside.

Scouts returning from the red zone were dismounting their sandbeasts. A pair of pathfinders did the same, and tenders rushed to remove the beasts' saddles and packs. One of the council elders from another fire strode forward to embrace the returning party, which the scouts returned hurriedly. They spoke with sharp gestures, pointing in the direction from which they'd come. Kell could not quite make out their words, but the message was clear enough. The council elder looked grim.

A small crowd began to gather, Ama included. Kell reached a hand toward her, and the old woman made her way over, leaning heavily on her staff. Silaya stepped aside to make room for Ama, and Kell took her grandmother's hand. The grip that squeezed hers back was strong and reassuring.

"Ma'ani," Kell said softly.

"It looks like we'll have even more guests," Ama said wryly and winked at the two young women. Kell leaned and kissed her grandmother on the cheek, and the old woman took her leave to join the other members of the council now gathering at the edge of the camp's perimeter. The eight of them conferred as more onlookers continued to congregate.

Jor appeared at Kell's elbow, groggy and rumpled. His friend was nowhere to be seen, but Jor had snagged a bowl of tea and two flatbreads on his way past the cookfire and offered her one, lounging against Kell's shoulder as if she were a convenient stone. She rolled her eyes at him but took it, tearing it in half and offering a piece in turn to Silaya, who attacked it as if it hadn't just come from the flame.

Maybe she's not fierce, Kell thought. *Maybe she's just hungry.*

At last, the council turned to face those who crowded in the space between the last row of tents and the open expanse of the desert. The sun was just peeling off its morning cap and now burned the lip of the horizon. The light changed from pale to golden in an instant, and Kell felt a flush of heat against her left side. The council members chose this moment to speak, awash in the amber sunrise. Ama always did remind her to use atmosphere for effect.

"An envoy from Soogway is on their way to our camp," one of the council members announced. "Scouts have spotted them less than a day's ride by sandbeast, but they are traveling by sled, so will be here in a matter of hours."

She felt Jor stand up straight. Kell looked at her brother and then at Silaya as the sweet warmth of the morning drained away. What if the envoy was bringing a general? Was a combat teller—was Ama—going to have to fight? Was *Kell*? She clenched her non-casting hand, and Silaya took it in her own.

"The representatives from the city will not be taking us by surprise," Ama spoke now, looking as solid and immovable as a stone. "Let us prepare to greet them with full hospitality." A murmur went through the listeners, but heads nodded in agreement. Ama bowed to everyone present, and the People bowed their heads in return. "May they find Home wherever they are," she said, her voice clear and final. Kell saw a falcon in her grandmother's fearless yellow look. The crowd dissipated to prepare for a formal welcome.

The three turned to go back to the tent to change, but Kell stopped at Ama's summons. Nodding for the others to go on without her, Kell faced her grandmother, steeling herself. Ama grunted as she approached, her staff holding her up, and Kell again was reminded of her age. With her free hand, Ama reached toward Kell, and Kell took it in both of her own.

"A'Kell," she began, pinning her with her raptor gaze. Ama almost never used her formal name, and hearing it called forth a sense of duty Kell hadn't realized she possessed. "You will be my second."

Any relief she might have felt learning she wouldn't be the primary combat teller was quickly replaced by anxiety. The old woman did expect a story battle—a formal fight with legally binding results. She thought of Silaya's sister and swallowed the panic yanking at her stomach. She could only guess how fierce any relative of Silaya's must be, but Silaya's sister would have lacked the advantage of age. No amount of fire could beat Ama's experience, not with the ancestors on their side. Kell bowed deeply, still holding her grandmother's hand between her own.

"Yes, Ma'Shifra."

Her grandmother held Kell's gaze for a long moment. Kell felt as if she were being sorted into piles, the fear and broken bits being swept aside to clear a space for the storyteller she needed to be. She clenched her fist again and caught herself, forcing a deep breath as she imagined her hand over the altar flame, the sweet smoke offering its focus. She returned her grandmother's gaze and tried with everything she had to feel courage instead of terror.

"Kell." Her grandmother's voice was hoarse and gentle. "We will not lose." When Ama smiled, Kell mirrored her, then turned and headed back to the tent to prepare for battle, stopping only once to vomit tea into the sand.

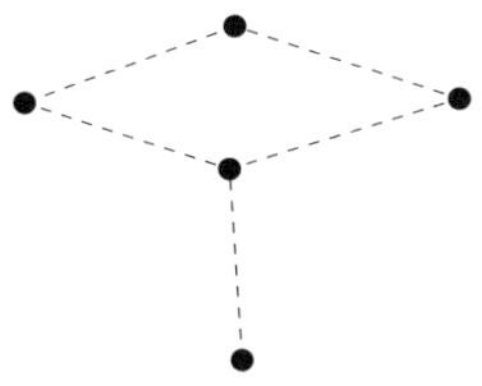

The Two-Headed Sentry: Western horizon, early springs

10. A FALSE GOD

When Kell reentered the tent, having drunk from a waterskin to clear her mouth, Jor and her cousins were already inside, changing into formal wear. Silaya looked uncomfortable.

"I didn't bring anything with me," she said.

"You can borrow something of mine." Kell shrugged. "We're practically the same size." Silaya was, in fact, inches taller, but Kell doubted it would matter much. She liked the idea of seeing Silaya in her clothes and having a task would distract her from the anxiety buzzing in her blood.

Kell guided her past her family in various states of undress. Nakedness was seen as a natural state among the People, and the communal spaces of the tents made modesty impractical, anyway. Though sand ablutions were often done in private to allow the bather to thank the gods without distraction, all genders dressed together, particularly for events that required finery, when extra hands were often helpful for fastening clasps or tying things behind one's back. Kell tried to think of an outfit that would require Silaya's assistance and touch, her body flashing between chill at the fight to come and heat at the preparation.

A row of colorful cloth bundles lined a corner of the tent, and Kell dragged one of these out, inviting Silaya to sit. When she undid the knot holding it together, it fell open into a giant scarf wrapped around a jumble of clothes. She dug a second, smaller satchel from within, which jingled as she untied it to reveal a tangled collection of bracelets and thin chains. She rooted through the pile of fabric, mostly the sun-faded things she wore every day, looking for bright spots of color. One by one, she held up an array of options as Silaya frowned and shook her head. At last, Kell offered a simple black wrap with flared sleeves that was sufficiently formal and earned less scorn from the horse rider, who pulled off her own scarf and tunic and stripped down to the loose travel pants she'd been wearing for days.

"Will these work with it?"

Kell eyed the dusty maroon fabric, trying to ignore the curving expanse of mahogany skin that stretched upward from Silaya's waist.

"I think they're fine. They'll barely be visible. But try this." She pulled a long chain from the pile of jewelry and held it up. It was studded with pale blue stones at the junction of each wide link. The belt had been a gift from her mother, so Kell never wore it. She thought it would look perfect on Silaya, however. Silaya pulled the black cloth over her head and arranged its layers around her shoulders, then took the chain and wrapped it around her waist, fastening it along her side. It held the wrap in place at an angle that accentuated her long lines, which Kell appreciated.

"Here," she added, drawing a dark purple scarf from the pile. Silaya draped it around her shoulders and gave it a loop to put around her face and head in case of sand. She posed and allowed herself to be admired. Kell obliged.

"Now what do I wear?" she wondered aloud, frowning at the mound of clothes. *What will make me feel both invisible and strong?*

The two dug through the pile and settled on variations in green—loose bottoms the color of young cactus and a flowing tunic in rich emerald, shot through with threads of gold. It tied together at the base of the spine, where Kell could reach, but the brush of Silaya's fingers in the small of her back was worth feigning helplessness. Kell added a thin gold scarf that was so sheer it was almost invisible, little more than sunlight settling across her shoulders. Silaya nodded approvingly and selected several large gold hoops, fastening them around Kell's neck, wrists, and into the holes healed into the tops of her ears. There was muffled laughter across the tent as Jor and a cousin wrestled while helping one another lace something up. Kell rolled her eyes and pulled a narrow diadem from the pile. She stepped forward and reached up to place it on Silaya's head, nestling it into her locks to make it stay.

They regarded each other.

"Are you ready?" Silaya's face was somber, anger at the city lighting her skin from within.

Kell offered a weak smile. "I'll have to be," she said.

Silaya put both hands on her shoulders and looked her in the eyes. "Kell—the story that the general used, it wasn't like a real story. It wasn't anything I'd seen before."

"What do you mean?" The look on Silaya's face was unnerving. Underneath the wrath, her eyes held the shadows of real fear.

"I mean, don't let Ma'Shifra use a heart story. She will lose. The story the general fought with was pure spectacle, like it had nothing living to it at all. And yet it was so powerful, so *aggressive*, no emotion could touch it. It didn't even hear what Upepo had to say—didn't listen, didn't care. It had no honor."

Imaginary insects crawled up Kell's spine. A story like that was hardly a story at all, she thought. The idea was repellent to her, like something diseased, something she did not want her People's stories to touch. Even in combat, there was a sense of mutual respect that came from pitting oneself against another. Why bother if there was no dance, no honor? What would a fight like that prove?

"We have to tell Ama," she said. The two quickly gathered her things back into the scarf and shoved the bundle into place.

Ama was sitting quietly on a cushion as one of Kell's older cousins wrapped her cloud of silver hair into a tall, multicolored turban. The turban was snug, and the weight of it pulled at the edges of her face, elongating her falcon eyes and accentuating the already sharp lines of her cheekbones. She was every inch Ma'Shifra.

She listened impassively as Kell stammered out a warning, anxiety pushing her voice too high. Kell's cousin finished tucking in the wrap and stepped away to allow the tellers to talk. Ma'Shifra asked Silaya to repeat what she had told Kell, and she did, adding further details about the unnatural way the general had beaten her sister's story. Ma'Shifra's face betrayed no emotions other than calculation and focus. Kell twisted the edge of her scarf, then stopped herself when she saw it was wrinkling.

Ma'Shifra was quiet for a long time before she spoke.

"Severed fools," she said softly.

Kell opened her mouth and was silenced with a sharp glance.

"I believed we still had time to play to their sincerity," Ma'Shifra continued, her tone full of steel. "I assumed we could lean on the agreements Soogway had made and hope that the ancestors would lend their strength, but that was foolish. We've been behaving like children. Clearly, we need a different approach."

To Kell, this bordered on blasphemy, and she disliked hearing it from Ama. Stooping to the level of the city in order to win felt like no win at all. What could they rely on if not the ancestors?

"We need a god, instead," Ma'Shifra said.

A tinder lit in Kell's belly, and as she breathed in, it gusted into flame.

A god story. Ama's tactical boldness never failed to awe and alarm her. The gods were scarcely concerned with humanity, but they held massive power at their disposal. A god story would be indifferent to the city's creature but contain the potential for incredible destruction. The idea was a wild one, excessive and grandiose, like using a rockslide to remove a fly, and yet the thought made her hands pulse with energy.

She frowned. "But Ma'Shifra—" she said, uncomfortable even shaping the question aloud. "What happens if we lose? What happens to the god?"

Ma'Shifra gave her a smile Kell had not seen before, a smile of cunning and tricks. "My child, we would not give up one of our gods to these city folk. They have no hearts to begin with, no way of understanding even what they had gained."

"I don't understand."

"A'Kell." Her name sounded like a command in Ma'Shifra's mouth. "We are going to create a new one."

Kell shuddered. *A false god?*

Silaya, too, was smiling her wicked smile. She nodded, folding her arms across her chest.

"This is a good idea," she said.

Kell swallowed. Ma'Shifra held her gaze for a long moment as if willing Kell into alignment. It *was* a good idea, just—a frightening one. Could she imagine a false god? Would the ancestors help? She looked at her casting hand, flexing her fingers. Kell wasn't sure she could do it. She prayed that Ma'Shifra would need no second.

"Be brave, now." Ma'Shifra took her casting hand in her own. "This is how it will happen. Listen to me."

"There is always an opening. You gotta stay sharp to see it."
—Shade's father

11. SOME GOOD ADVICE

Shade hated the smell of the gator hole, the swampy rotten-fish funk of it, but nothing beat a tourist trap for picking a few pockets. The story they'd heard as a kid was that some rich guy long ago had wanted a gator for a pet, and because he had one, then all the rich folks had to have one. But as the gators got bigger, keeping them in their homes went from status symbol to disaster, until finally the fad ended, and everyone released their gators into the sewers. There they ate rats and mucked about for a time, but when they got hungry, they'd creep out of pipes and snag small children—or so little Shade had been told—until the safes had rounded them all up into this concrete pond, where they lived on trash and clumsy birds and the occasional fish that didn't get sold in time. Some fishmongers set up their stalls close to the hole, and wealthy visitors would buy a fish or two to throw in and watch the creatures snap at each other. It reminded Shade of the Box.

There was a good-sized crowd leaning over the railing, pointing down into the pond and cheering on their favorites as young men jostled and pretended to push each other in. From below came the sounds of scuffle from the muck. Children asked to be held for a better view, while some of the more sensitive among the crowd covered their noses with scarves or kerchiefs. Shade couldn't blame them. Pulling their hat down low and tugging their braids flat in front of them, they skirted around the onlookers. They peeked between shoulders, as if to see the action, and leaned in close, creating just enough pressure that their marks didn't feel it when they dipped a quick hand into a pouch or a purse. Never the whole thing—that was too hard to deny if you got caught. Just a chip here and there. They'd learned that taking a little from a lot of folks was a better bet than taking a lot from just a few.

That was one of their first rules—don't be greedy. Keep it so nobody notices what's missing until it's too late.

Their second rule was never to steal from poor folks. It was easy to tell who was who. In Soogway, the rich liked to flaunt what they had: their clothes were tidy and spotless, their bodies soft with plenty. Alongside the sharp, hungry angles of the poor, the rich looked like plump dolls to Shade, blank and superior, spending time on the streets as a thrill. Shade's mother had always encouraged them to share, and they saw it as their duty to help redistribute wealth a little more fairly.

Their third rule was that combat wasn't like stealing; if they were fighting, the first two rules were off.

Two of the D Street kids were shouting at each other on the far side of the hole. They were dirty and one was barefoot. One shoved the other and then fell upon them, raining down fists with their mud-smeared face screwed up in anger. Careful eyes would note, however, the punches didn't land. Shade thought the display was overdone, personally, but several adults stooped to intervene and correct this taboo behavior, oblivious to the third child who'd slipped between them, relieving them of the contents of their pockets. The little ones often worked in teams like that—distraction was most effective at that age, when they were too small to stall-and-bump or be threatening in a straight-up mugging. Though Shade had once seen a crew of tinies who all carried chains that they swung around their heads, and the effect had indeed been intimidating, since small children couldn't be relied upon to honor social norms.

Shade spat. That side of the hole would be picked clean, then. Good for them. Shade contented themself with just a few more dips and came up with five chips, three falsies, and a piece of candy covered in lint, which they cleaned off as best they could before they popped it in their mouth. Falsies were the homespun coins fashioned by poor folks when they couldn't score real laser-cut, ironwood chips. They were made out of whatever might be on hand—ceramic, bamboo, pounded bits of soft metal. They served more like IOUs for the black market, but they still spent if you knew where to use them, and Shade never turned them down, even if they didn't count toward their travel savings. With a little sleight of hand to distribute their findings among their various pockets, Shade left the gator hole to spread some chips around.

Cheap's snack stand was little more than a bamboo rack slung with plastic tarps and stacked with bins full of roasted beans. He didn't exactly do a brisk business, but kids could afford handfuls there now and then, and the salty crunch appealed to folks well into their hooch. The stand's resident happy box spat out its incessant rattle of tunes and stories designed for short attention spans. The old man sat stooped on his stool in front of it like one of the vultures who lurked the killing yards, eyeing the cattle before they became meat. But unlike the vultures, Cheap didn't have a baleful bone in his body, and he lit up when Shade poked their head under the plastic to check on him—once he was able to tear his attention away from the happy box.

"Kiddo!" His voice was small and tired, but glad to see them. Shade let him ruffle the hat on their head as if they were a child, trying not to flinch away from his touch, and then promptly pulled their braids straight. Shade flicked Cheap a chip, who held up a scoop of beans from a bin at his feet. They took off their hat, flipped it over and held it out to Cheap, who dumped the beans into it, turning the floppy back of the peak-brimmed hat into a snack bowl. Shade switched off the happy box and set it on the ground so they could lounge on the stool and eat. They didn't like how much time Cheap spent with that thing.

The old man sniffed. "You take a bath or something?"

"Thought I'd try it, see what the fuss was about."

"You want a riddle or a joke?" the old man asked.

"You pick." Shade smiled as they crunched.

"What do you call a safe with no story unit?"

Shade thought for a moment, unsure whether it was a joke or a riddle. Cheap's eyes twinkled.

"A drunk?" they guessed. They both chuckled.

"All bark and no bite," said Cheap. He wheezed, his shoulders shaking. Shade still wasn't sure if it was a joke but kept smiling, just in case.

"Speaking of, I ran into a safe last night. After the fight," Shade said.

"After you came here?" Shade nodded. "Those good-for-nothin' . . . " Cheap mumbled under his breath, shaking his head. "You get picked up?"

"Nah," Shade shrugged, as if it weren't a big deal, suddenly uncertain whether they should tell Cheap the truth of what happened. They felt as if they had brushed up against something dangerous, an infection, and wanted to make sure it didn't spread. "I got out of it."

Cheap looked at them, his eyes bright and calculating. Shade knew they were the riddle, now. It was hard to keep things from the old man, even with his poor eyesight and hearing. Shade took comfort in having someone who always knew when something was wrong.

"Somebody kind of stepped in," they offered carefully. "Some rich guy. He was just out walking, and he called the safe off. Gave him some chips to scram."

Cheap whistled and raised his ample eyebrows at this. "And he did?"

Shade nodded, tossing another fistful of beans into their mouth. They made a satisfying crack between their teeth.

"What sort of rich guy we talking about, here?" Cheap looked wary.

Shade relayed the encounter with Mr. Go, his perfume and finely-tailored clothes. They told him about the strange story, the great tree that had drawn out one of Shade's own memories and made it real. The snack vendor's face grew dark at this, but he nodded for Shade to continue. For a moment Shade hesitated, then the words tumbled out of them in a rush. They explained Go's offer to sponsor them for the Cycle, to train them in exchange for—whatever it was he wanted. It felt good to say it out loud. It sounded ridiculous, more like an absurd dream and less like swimming in dark water where they couldn't see the bottom.

"What did you tell this guy?" Cheap asked. His eyes searched Shade's face. They examined the beans in their lap, suddenly afraid they'd made the wrong choice.

"I—I told him I'd do it," they stammered.

Cheap nodded slowly, not taking his eyes off Shade. There was a fierceness to it they didn't like. Cheap was supposed to be soft and worn out, like a pair of triple hand-me-downs. This sharpness in him only added to Shade's sense of unreality. Was this a riddle or a joke?

"Attaway," Cheap whispered. He sat up a little straighter, as if a heavy thought had passed, and then thumped Shade on the shoulder, harder than Shade had expected. It nearly knocked them off the stool, and they clutched at the hat to keep from spilling their beans. "You go get it, kiddo." Cheap laughed then, a sound like a rusty saw, and Shade couldn't help but smile.

"Get what?"

"Whatever the hell you need," Cheap replied, still laughing. "This Mr. Go, he's your ticket, kid. You got a shot now—you can get back home and everything. You just gotta watch your toes now, you know what I mean? I figure that fella has eyes on all the elbows."

Shade wrinkled their nose at the image. "Do—do you think he saw me at the Box?"

"*Of course* he saw you at the Box!" Cheap laughed again. He lowered his voice and said, "A talent like yours, kiddo. You weren't gonna go unnoticed for long."

Cheap patted Shade's knee, and Shade saw his eyes flick toward the happy box. It was like watching a hoocher eye a bottle, and their heart sank a little. They were reaching the limit of the old man's attention.

"He gave me this," they said, and produced the small, flat object from their pocket. It was a white card printed with letters in dark green ink. Cheap's mouth made an O of wonder, and he reached for it with gnarled hands that betrayed not the slightest tremor of age.

Cheap turned it over in his fingers, rubbing the surface the way a tailor might feel fine cloth.

"Say," he said in genuine appreciation. "This is real paper, kiddo."

They nodded. They'd thought so. The paper was thick and heavy, the surface rough with bumps like wool. Shade had stared at it for a long time that morning, marveling at the material.

"What's it say?" They leaned close and pushed the last fistful of beans into their mouth.

Cheap gave them a look.

"When ya gonna learn to read?"

They shrugged, crunching. "I can read my name. That's enough."

Cheap clucked his tongue and turned to the card, holding it far away from himself and squinting at the fine lettering.

"It's an address," he announced. "Looks like it's over in Greenwood. Doesn't say what place it is."

"Do you think it's where he lives?" Shade asked.

"Doubt it," said Cheap. "This looks more like a business, if you're asking me." He gave Shade a devilish grin and elbowed them in the knee. "Which y'are."

"So, do I just go there, or . . . ?"

Cheap's face turned serious once more.

"You listen to me now, Shade." They swallowed. He almost never used their name, and it reminded them that there was more to Cheap's story, that he hadn't always been a sweet old snack man hunched over a happy box. "This Mr. Go is a big fish. He's not like the owners who troll the pits. Sounds to me like he can *do* things, you know what I'm saying? Whatever you do, don't let him get close to you. That one memory isn't all he'll be able to use."

Shade shivered, recalling the sense of odd violation. Seeing their mother in Go's storylight hadn't taken that memory from them, but then it wasn't combat. What if Go had done that in a fight and Shade had lost? A slip of panic hit their gut.

"And you," Cheap continued. "Think what you could do with that trick."

Shade looked Cheap in the eyes and nodded.

"Take him, kiddo." Cheap's voice was low and fierce, his eyes bolted to Shade's. "Take him for everything he's got."

"Rhymes don't have to be perfect. They'll only hear what you want them to hear."
—Shade's father

12. GREEN RESISTANCE

It felt strange to spend more than a chip at a time, but it was the kind of strange Shade hoped to get used to. One of the cubes from the fight had yielded more than just extra food. They had bought supplies for all the D Street kids and their friend at the docks, the one who let them know when produce was brought up the river, and they bought a new pair of scissors for Ma Bud, who sometimes made them new clothes in exchange for small things she needed. Shade was lucky that they had stopped growing early. A lot of their pants got worn through at the knees, but at least they didn't hike up around their ankles in that awkward way they saw on some of the lankier street kids who outgrew their surroundings like pet gators. Ma Bud tsked at their lack of height, muttering things about meals, but never complained about fixing up a tear or two. The jacket they wore had come from her hands, and every stitch felt sturdy.

The Arbor was too hot to be wearing it today, but Shade needed the pockets. Sun slanted into the narrow stone canyons between the tenements, and curls of steam rose from the cobbles and pavement. The ground was an uneven patchwork of rough slabs and concrete, bouncing the sun back like an echo. They looked up, pulling their hat to their brow to avoid squinting. Drying laundry dripped from lines slung across the alleys, window boxes offered weak spots of color with their ragged blooms tilted toward the light. Stone filigree curved from the edges of even the humblest buildings, evidence of a determined aestheticism on the part of the craftspeople who built them—even these grim structures had some beauty for its own sake.

The statuary so prevalent in the wealthier neighborhoods was scant in the Arbor, but here and there stone shapes sprouted from the sidewalk, geometric arches and twisting organic abstractions, all reminiscent of, but perversely different from, the absent trees. Shade ran a hand along the curve of one as they passed. It was smooth and worn, oiled from the repetition of this gesture by countless passersby. It wasn't good luck to touch the statues, exactly. It was more like a wish: I wish you were a tree.

Shade's parents had come from a part of the Broken Forest where many of the trees did not have leaves that dropped in the autumn. Instead, the trees bristled like hedgehogs, their mother had said, and remained stubbornly green year-round. Shade had grown up thinking this must be a wonderful thing, to be surrounded by green all the time. The relentless grays and brick reds of the city felt wearing, interrupted only by jolts of blue plastic and electric pinks and yellows. For as long as they could remember, Shade had enjoyed picturing the forest in their mind's eye and painting the landscape in as many greens as they could imagine, inventing new hues for each evergreen.

Their mother's favorite trees, though, had been oaks. She had always pronounced the word as if she were ringing a bell made of wood. She'd clicked the back of her tongue when she said it, and the sound had made Shade's scalp tingle in a way that left them shivery and calm. Sometimes now Shade practiced saying it as they walked, but the effect was never the same.

"Oak," they tried. Nothing.

Ma Bud's shop was not at street level, so you had to know where you were going and why, like she was making you earn it. If you could navigate the streets and the stairwell and the maze of doors on the third floor, you would be rewarded with her company and expertise.

Shade knocked tentatively at the door, and it swung in.

"Took ye long enough."

She marched from the door without a glance, and Shade followed her inside.

Ma Bud's home and sewing shop was a study in precision. Bolts of material lined the shelves in careful rolls organized by color, which gave the sensation of stepping into a boxed rainbow, a slice of wild nature held carefully and unequivocally in check. Not a stray thread or snippet of cloth dared clutter the floor. Even her pin cushions were orderly. Shade stood up a little straighter.

"It's too hot for that hat," she announced. Shade removed it politely. Ma Bud stared, waiting for whatever they had brought. She might as well have put out her palm.

"I brought you something," they said.

She put out her palm.

Shade drew the scissors from their pocket and presented them with two hands, like a proper gift. Ma Bud tilted her chin up to look down her nose at them, but they saw her pupils widen and knew she was impressed. She sniffed.

"Didja swipe 'em?" She glared through narrowed eyes, suddenly suspicious. Shade knew she couldn't care less if the scissors had been stolen—she even sewed hidden pockets into Shade's clothes for just this purpose.

"I paid for those," they said. She grunted.

Ma Bud slipped the handles over her misshapen fingers and snipped the air. The scissors made a satisfyingly sharp sound. She nodded and then turned to her cutting table, crisscrossed with a grid for measuring and flanked by a basket holding chalks and pins and other essentials. She inserted the scissors into the slot where scissors went and removed the old pair, which then vanished in a trick of organization. Shade hoped the new ones would feel better for her hands. Ma Bud complained often of arthritis in her joints, but it didn't seem to affect the precision of her stitches.

"You aren't eating right."

Shade twisted their hat.

"Here," she commanded and stumped over to the curtain that separated the main room from the small window balcony that hung off the side of the building like a tiny pocket. It was barely anything, the balcony—not large enough for the two of them to stand on, but wide enough for a window box cramped with motley flowers, the only messy thing in Ma Bud's domain. She pawed through the plants as if searching for a dropped pin, pushing aside thin sprays of green dotted with small yellow flowers. Something with dark red blooms bobbed alongside. Shade had seen those blossoms dried and hung from the wall as decoration before. Window boxes were one of the only sources of nature in neighborhoods like these, and nearly everyone who had one used it, trading seeds and starts as gifts.

There was a snapping noise from under the yellow, and Ma Bud produced something large and green, which she put in her apron pocket before shuffling to a thin metal trellis along the far wall. A vine covered much of it that appeared to have withered some seasons before, but when she pushed aside its large brown leaves, Shade saw that there was another, fresher vine clinging to the metal behind it, one with tiny white flowers and hanging dangles of bright green. She popped several of these off and tossed one in her mouth, crunching loudly. She returned to the room, drawing the curtain shut again behind her.

Half of the room was a living area, and she made her way to the small kitchen, with its gas-bottle stove and basin for a sink. She poured water from a pitcher into the basin and rinsed whatever she had pulled from the window box, blotted it all with a hand towel, and carried it back to Shade as if they were jewels. Which, Shade realized as they saw what rested there, they were.

Ma Bud had harvested several fistfuls of plump pea pods and one very green vegetable the size of Shade's two fists put together. Their first impression was of a cloud, all bumpy and round, but then she turned it sideways, and Shade realized it looked like nothing so much as a diminutive tree, its branches terminating in dense clumps of minute green buds.

"Take it," she ordered, pushing the towel toward them.

"What is it?" they asked, stuffing peas into their mouth and pocket, relishing the burst of sweetness between their teeth.

"It's called 'broccoli,' you ignorant little so-and-so. It's too hot for it these days, but the flowers make good cover."

"Cover for what?"

She tsked, but then her attention snagged on a small tear at the elbow of Shade's jacket.

"You think I'm paying city prices for peas?" She snorted, sitting heavily and producing a needle and thread from thin air. "These days, I barely make enough to fill the rice bin every month. Ha." She gestured for Shade to hand over the offending garment and attacked it with the needle, her hands moving more quickly and subtly than Shade could follow. "Folks trade plenty," she muttered. "But nobody's got chips."

Vegetable gardens were expressly forbidden in the city. It was one of the many ways the government sucked funds out of the empire—they imported produce from the outlying farm regions on the Nong Plateau and shipped it in on the river, charging exorbitant prices for it in the city markets. The Fresh Tax, it was called. Swiping greens was one of Shade's occasional side gigs.

"So, you hide vegetables under the flowers?"

Ma Bud scoffed. "Who doesn't?" She tugged at the thread in her hands and cut it neatly between her teeth. Shade thought of all the miserable flower boxes they could see from the street, the drooping plants hanging over the edges of the stone like they were trying to escape. They'd assumed they were just meager decorations, never having considered the subversive potential of vegetables. The mess of their arrangements made a new kind of sense.

"The window boxes seem . . . small," Shade said carefully. She tossed their mended jacket back to them after giving it an evaluative sniff.

"You seem small," she retorted. "And a launder wouldn't kill you."

Shade shrugged the jacket back on.

"I've got tomatoes on the roof under some plastic," she continued. "And a bunch of onions around the fire exits. Keep 'em little enough, they look like weeds."

Shade thought of all the rooftops they scrambled across and wondered how many secret gardens they'd passed, not knowing what to look for. Their skin prickled in the uncomfortable way it did when they missed an important detail in a storyfight. They had to be sharper.

"Keep an eye out for a line on silk thread," she said. "I'm out, and there's none in the market." She began arranging and rearranging some small projects in progress on a workbench by the cutting table. Shade realized they had been dismissed and moved to leave.

"Oh, and Shade—"

They stopped at the door and turned.

"Mr. Go says to tell you it's time you came by. He says you know where to find him."

She continued her puttering without a glance in their direction, as if it were the most normal thing in the world.

A'LAN SPEAKS: THE WEEPING SPIRIT

The gods delight in creation and destruction. They know that another name for life is change. Before the time of People was the time of beasts. And before the time of beasts was the time of the elements. The rains were patient sculptors, dripping and pounding the earth into its future shapes. Restless tremors unsettled entire regions, lifting some plates and sinking others, the earth jostling and rearranging until the very stone coughed and jittered in motion. Winds danced across the wastes, twisting and swirling, toying with bits of sand and small leaves, anything they could pick up. When small, winds are playful beings, given to mischief. When they grow to gales, they can be pompous, overpowering, pushing things from their path. Mountains of fire forged new, rich earth in their bellies and spewed it forth in molten offering, bold and proud.

In this time of making and unmaking, the gods looked on, curious at the creations of their offspring yet disinclined to interrupt the processes their power had set in motion. Strange spirits were birthed from the land, urges brought into form—spirits of wildness, spirits of autonomy, spirits of quiet and of celebration. As many feelings as the world could feel, so did a spirit arise to embody it. Anxiety, awe, patience, carnality, union, pride—each grew and danced and wandered, shaping the elements and being shaped in return.

In this heady time of creation, one spirit caught the attention of the gods. It was not a feeling, nor an element, but rather an impulse: the spirit of static state, the resistance to change. It moved slowly, like a cloud upon the ground, a dead space that held everything in its range in suspended animation. Within its grasp, nothing grew. Nothing aged or died. Nothing happened at all.

The gods watched as the static state drifted. The more it stilled, the larger it became. A miasma of nothingness, a thick, stubborn weight against the flux of energy. It was the antithesis of change, and the gods knew it could not be allowed to continue or it would eventually consume all they had set in motion and bring a cool, inert death to the world.

They took the spirit and sealed it under a rock, crushing it. The spirit struggled, for it only knew its own nature and meant no evil in particular. Yet the gods held it fast underground, trapping it for all eternity where it could not interrupt the flow of change. The spirit wept then, its pain condensing into tears that bubbled up from under the stone as a spring. From the spring, new things emerged: plants and greenery, algae and mist, rainbow light from the sun, and after eons had passed, a place for animals to drink. The spirit had become its opposite, a source of life, and this made it cry all the harder. For change is a painful thing, even when it offers the world exactly what it needs. The gods know and protect us from our own resistance.

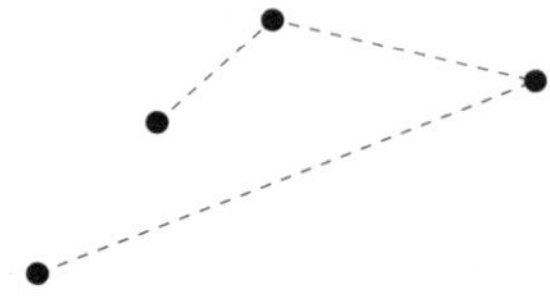

The Antelope: Southern horizon, dry season

13. THE AMBASSADOR

By the time they ducked under the open flaps of the tent and out to the bustle of camp, the sun was already blazing, and the smell of roasting meat filled the air. Despite the grave occasion, the mood was festive, and Kell felt like a simmering pot. Something new stirred in her, a feeling of heat and force that sought an outlet. When she thought of the fight to come, she discovered her anxiety had been replaced with something lunging and hungry. They would protect the stones at all costs, a false god at their fingertips.

Am I . . . looking forward to this? A rush of power answered, and for a moment, she felt she could throw a boulder if she tried. She thought of the story of the sandbeast who startled at the scent of a lion, who fled wildly until it collapsed with exhaustion, unable to fight back when the patient predator caught up. She hoped this surge would last long enough to be able to use it.

She didn't have to wait long. Scouts announced the approach of the emissaries even sooner than expected—*gods, those sleds must be fast*—even though they had been seen taking several wrong turns along the route. Kell felt a pleasant stab of superiority as she realized how poorly their wayfinder bugs must have worked.

Runners were sent among the tents to muster everyone for a formal welcome, and the People had just enough time to gather with the council of elders at the front before the sleds came into view. Appearing first as shimmers in the heat and then as shadows, the fast-approaching shapes took on detail and color until they pulled to a stop in formation less than a stone's throw away, dust swirling in their wake.

Each sled was long and ornate, like all things from the capitol Kell had seen. The runners and curlicues that served as sides, tie-downs, and grips were all made of shining metal, and Kell wondered whether they grew hot to the touch in the sun. She was fascinated and felt guilty for it. Each sled was harnessed to a small team of antelope, leggy, nervous creatures who stamped and flicked long ears as they fussed against the reins. Antelope were common enough in the desert, elegant and wild, but Kell had never been this close to one that hadn't already been killed and cleaned for food. She wondered how they were tamed, and hated that the city had managed it.

Each musher was wrapped toe to head in black gauze to keep out the sand, and they gripped the reins like statues, their goggles flashing in the sun. Most of the sleds were mounded with crates and bundles, though the sled at the front of the formation bore the lightest load, which moved and revealed itself to be a person. They had been seated backward to avoid what was no doubt a relentless and painful spray of sand at the speed the sleds traveled.

The emissary dusted himself off, standing slowly as if his joints had gone stiff from the ride. He made a great show of unwrapping his own scarf and shaking it out, dumping a small cloud of sand all around him. One of the council members opened her arms wide in a gesture of welcome, but the emissary appeared not to notice the entire camp of People waiting to offer their warmest hospitality. Clenching her teeth, Kell fought the urge to bury him in a swarm of story ants.

The ambassador from Soogway, if that's what he was, at last acknowledged the patient crowd. He cleared his throat and offered a feeble hand gesture that Kell assumed was meant as a greeting.

"Manny," came a nasal voice. He cleared his throat again, then muttered something to his musher, who tied off the reins and turned to dig a canteen out of a cargo pouch, hustling to hand it to the man. The ambassador took a long drink and returned it to the musher without looking. He repeated himself. "Manny!" he demanded.

Kell looked at Jor and her cousins, noticing how nice they all looked. Jor's friend had attached wren feathers to the ends of some of Jor's braids, and the effect was beautiful. She felt plain in comparison.

A council member stepped forward. "Ma'ani," she said, enunciating slowly and clearly. An almost imperceptible titter rippled through the crowd.

Don't you dare, she warned herself, biting her lips to keep from laughing.

Her eyes scanned the four other sleds, some of which carried passengers, who were now also dusting themselves off after their long ride. *Which one is the combat teller*? she thought, her eyes straining to pick out details in the bright sun. *Where are you, General?*

Ma'Shifra spoke. "Greetings to our friends from the south," she said. "May you find home wherever you are. You have traveled far and must be tired and thirsty. We have prepared food and shade for you and would share with you our tea and our stories. In the eyes of the gods and the ancestors, please allow us to extend to you our hospitality." She made the gesture of welcome again, which was repeated by the rest of the council and echoed by many in the crowd.

A child was nudged forward and scampered to the man, bearing a bowl of cool tea flavored with ease-herb, the traditional offering to travelers. They held it up with both hands, their gaze toward the sand. *Very polite*, Kell thought. The child's braids had been redone for the occasion and made a pattern like meandering rivers across their scalp. The man looked at the gift, sniffed, and gestured again to the musher, who stepped off the sled, took the bowl from the child, and set it aside. Another ripple went through the crowd. The child returned red-faced and was comforted by all who stood nearby. Such callous refusal of water was beyond rude.

"Er, thank you," said the man. Kell hated the whine of his voice. "We won't be staying long."

This time, the collective gasp was audible. Kell shuffled her feet nervously. She felt as if she were in one of the dreams where she was telling a story and suddenly forgot all the words. What came next, if not combat?

At a sign from the ambassador, the newcomers all went into motion at once, animated shadows in their black wraps. They went to work unlashing and unstacking the crates and bundles from the sleds, carrying them forward, and setting them down in the sand in a line, creating a curious barrier between the ambassador and the People. Lids and sand wraps were opened, revealing a dozen containers of various tech: one crate was full of new wayfinder bugs; two were stacked with happy boxes of varying sizes; another was filled with large beads. Kell realized these were in fact small disposable power packs used to run the devices—utterly impractical in the desert where everything needed to be reused and repurposed for as many cycles as possible.

Kell's stomach turned. What was this, a bribe? Were they afraid to fight? Her skin tingled as if she might discharge lightning. She wished she could race forward, grab every piece of city tech and break them herself. There was an uncomfortable pause as the People and the city folk regarded each other.

"We are grateful for your gifts," said another of the council elders at last, "but we have little use for such things here."

"Speak for yourself, old man," came a mutter from somewhere in the crowd. This was met with both shock and some murmurs of agreement. Kell scanned the People to see who had spoken. This was what the city people wanted, she realized, this lack of unity. This was what happened when People strayed too far from the old ways. Her mouth soured as she realized that many of the families gathered there might genuinely welcome Soogway and all it stood for.

"We would invite you to the shade to talk about the trade relations between our Home and yours," the elder continued.

"Yes," said the ambassador. "That is rather why we're here."

The man drew a plastic parchment from within his clothes and unscrolled it. He cleared his throat, and with a last, awkward look at the crowd, began to read aloud, lazily proclaiming every word in his awful, nasal drone.

"Whereas the Imperial City of Soogway, in full right and capacity thereto, did, by its assembly and through decree of both its magistrate and royal governing council, in this cycle of seven thousand and twelve, marker one-three, season two, three days past the dark moon, give peace to the lesser tribes who know themselves as People, and receive unto the burden of the Greater Empire the protection and care of a number of geologic resources as best serves and benefits the greater common good . . . "

Kell's head swam. *Geologic resources? Gods—he's talking about the pulsar stones.*

The voice intoned on, " . . . the People do hereby acknowledge, do hereby renew and confirm the collectivity of this resource in the lines beforementioned, to the end that it may be and remain an agreement between the People and the City of Soogway in perpetuity."

He eyed at the crowd as if to reassure himself they understood before continuing.

"The People and their respective tribes, and their heirs and descendants, for the consideration beforementioned, do release, quit claim, and cede to the City of Soogway all such geologic resources, in true and absolute propriety, forever."

An awful silence followed. Kell felt frozen in place, locked in as she did in the nightmares where her mind was awake but her body still slept. The ambassador rolled up the scroll and crossed the gap between the sleds and the council, looking uncertain as to whom he should hand the document. He gravitated away from Ma'Shifra and shoved it in the hands of the tallest man. He gave a brief bow.

"The city thanks you for your contribution," he said. "Extraction teams are already in place."

The ambassador turned and made a brief hand gesture, and the mushers and riders all resumed their positions on the sleds. He quickly wrapped his scarf back around his head and took his seat at the rear. With a crack of reins, the antelopes leaped forward and carried the emissaries away, the sled runners hissing on the hot sands.

Kell stared after them. Around her, the crowd murmured and shifted, uncertain, but then people began to push their way to the front to peer into the crates of tech. Some pawed through the piles, others picked up their finds delicately, like shoppers examining spiny fruit at a bazaar. She felt strangely heavy and immobile. A hand touched her back, and Kell gasped, realizing she had been holding her breath. She took a gulp of air, and it came back out as a whimper, a keening, desperate sound that she hated. Shaking, she clapped her hands over her mouth to stop it.

"Kell—" Jor was there, his beautiful feathers fluttering at the end of his braids. Ridiculous. As if he were attending a dance at The Wheel gathering rather than witnessing an uncontested pillaging of all they held most sacred.

Severed fools.

His hand was warm on her shoulder. He turned her toward him, his eyes searching for hers. Her own were wild and staring, rolling left and right, unsure where to look. She let his eyes hold her, and she stared into him, like she would never blink again.

"I didn't say anything," she whispered through her fingers. Her heart was racing now, her blood pounding like—like an antelope. "I didn't say anything to stop it."

Jor stooped toward her, shook his head, assured her it wasn't her fault, but she shrugged off his grasp. She stared out at the horizon where the sleds were dissolving into the morning heat. Her breathing was too fast.

Where was Ama? People were busy unloading the crates, passing out wayfinders and happy boxes, small earpieces and flashlights, handfuls of batteries. They all moved as though everyone had just awoken from a troubling dream they were eager to forget. She searched for her grandmother and the other council members, but the milling crowd had swallowed them up.

She turned and saw Silaya, her eyes trained on the receding sleds like spears.

The god story. I was ready, Kell thought.

The adrenaline she'd felt earlier had gone bitter, and her stomach cramped. She dropped her hands away from her face and hugged herself. Tears burned her widened eyes.

I was ready to fight, and I didn't do anything at all.

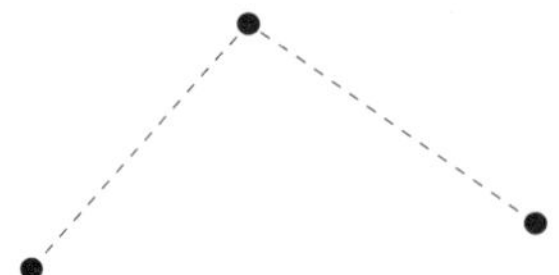

The Fallen (or, The Slain): Northeastern quarter, bird migration

14. THE MISSION

That evening, there were fewer faces bathed in the ruddy wash of the fires; more tents glowed blue from within, their flaps closed to the collective warmth. Kell thought they looked like bruises, like wounds to the camp. She glared at the spaces where People should have been.

"Do you want to tell a story?" Silaya nudged her, gnawing on a piece of roasted meat.

Kell shook her head and took a bite of her own. She had no appetite, but she imagined it was antelope and that helped her get it down. She picked at the flatbread that served as her dish and rested her meal in her lap. She was still wearing the formal greens. The gold scarf glinted at her shoulder, and she pulled it over her head miserably, wishing it were black and she could disappear.

A large desert cat sniffed at her elbow and nuzzled her neck. She pushed its head away, but it flopped against her and stretched out, nearly as long as she was, rolling onto its back in the cool evening sand. It blinked at her upside down, and she relented, handing it her piece of meat. It quickly flipped right-side up, spraying sand across her lap as it did so, and took the meat gingerly between its enormous teeth. She gave it a scratch behind the ears, but it growled and padded off into the shadow with its treat. Kell looked down at the sandy flatbread.

"I'll eat it," said Silaya.

Kell handed it over.

Silaya seemed unaffected by the day's events, which bothered Kell in a way she didn't know how to reconcile. She knew Silaya was angry, that she cared about the stones as much as Kell did. But the arrival of the emissaries and the announcement that the stones were now property of Soogway hadn't surprised her, while Kell felt completely uprooted by what she'd seen. What did it mean that a city official could just come in and make a declaration, and what power did it have? Since when was Home a part of the empire? Why hadn't they taken the opportunity to fight?

And if she were honest with herself—why wasn't Silaya more disappointed in Kell's failure to intercede? Had she expected Kell to fail? She ground her teeth in shame.

While the rest of the camp ate, the council members were deep in discussion in the Great Tent. She knew she should leave it to them to figure out what the next steps should be—but waiting was hard, and Kell couldn't shake the feeling that she had let everyone down. Even though she had only been Ama's second, she had known the plan for combat. She could have wiped that proclamation off the face of the desert. He hadn't even been a teller—there wasn't a glimmer of story in what the city had done. She tried to imagine what Ama's god tale would have done to that bureaucratic heap of dung.

Jor offered Kell his bowl of tea, and she sipped it without meeting his eyes. He had stayed close ever since the sleds had left. He might not understand her, but he knew when Kell was hurting. When they were little, he had always tried to protect her when she fell or got tired on long travels, as if she were his responsibility and not their mother's. Not that their mother had ever offered much in the way of care. Ma'Deena hadn't been neglectful, exactly. But Kell had never been able to keep her mother's attention for long. If Kell had been a better hunter, like her mother, instead of a storyteller, perhaps.

When Kell had been maybe five years old, she had strayed off from their mother at a bazaar, fascinated by some toy or caged bird or bit of ribbon. When she'd turned again, she had seen only the rows upon rows of spread blankets mounded with goods and the milling legs of a hundred strangers. She'd wandered for what felt like an eternity, crying. It had been Jor who found her, brave Jor who tracked her like a fox and held her hand, singing to her under his breath as he guided her back to their mother. Though he was only a few years older, he had seemed so big to her then, so wise and safe. Kell would have followed him anywhere.

Jor was turning an object over in his hands beside her now, the feathers still fluttering in his hair, moved by the occasional gusts of heat from the fire, his white tattoos in sharp relief against his skin. He pressed a button on the top of the device, and a thin strand of music curled up from it like smoke, tinny and strange. The chords that formed were unnatural and incomplete, the melody too simple.

"You have to admit, this is pretty amazing," he said. The sound muffled as he turned the object in his lap to examine its workings.

"No, I don't," she snapped. "That's not even music."

Jor shrugged. "Sure, but the tech itself—what if it were playing *our* music?"

Kell shuddered. Music was music because it was *alive*, because you sang or played it with others. Sealing it into a device then coughing it out with a button was abhorrent to her. This wasn't music—it was the ghost of music, captured in a box and forced to perform on command. It reminded her of the spring where a spirit had been trapped to protect the world from its influence. Its tears flowed through the rocks and kept the spring alive. That's what that sound was—a cramped, weeping spirit.

Silaya had finished her second flatbread and was licking her fingers. She eyed the tech in Jor's lap suspiciously.

"I don't like the way it feels," was all she said.

Kell stared into the coals at the base of the fire. The red chased the black around the burning wood, the glow and shadow trading places as the heat devoured the fuel. There was a coal in Kell's chest as well, flashing black then red, anxiety and anger taking turns. She felt that as long as she kept her eyes on the fire, she could pretend it was all happening outside of her and not behind her breastbone, that she could walk away from the sting and panic and cool herself shadowside when she chose. She wanted that very badly—to walk away and find everything as it was only days before.

A polite cough interrupted her thoughts. She looked up to find one of her older cousins standing behind her, his face serious and blank.

"The council wants to speak with the three of you," he said, and offered a hand to help Kell up. She ignored it and stood on her own, brushing the sand from her pants. Silaya reached for her, and Kell took her hand, following her cousin and Jor into the Great Tent.

The Great Tent was much emptier than the other tents because it belonged to everyone and no one at once. It was nobody's home, so it lacked the clutter and personality of family dwellings. Instead, it was simply a shelter, a great open space to keep out sand and heat and large enough to accommodate big gatherings and assemblies that could not take place outside. Children often played there during the heat of day while the adults were napping in their tents. There was room to run and tumble, and the blankets that lined the floor were less worn than in the family tents, their colors more vivid. There was no altar, no residue of incense here. Instead, it smelled like nervous bodies and stale air.

More than a dozen people were gathered in a horseshoe shape in the meeting space, seated or kneeling on the floor—the council members and a few heads of families. Ama was there, and Si'Denna, and the visiting scouts from Silaya's camp. Their faces all looked weary but resolute.

The three new arrivals greeted those assembled and took their own seats at the ends of the horseshoe. The crackle of the fires and soft sounds of conversation drifted in through the open tent flaps. There was a moment of quiet in the Great Tent as everyone waited for the newcomers' attention to catch up with their bodies. Then it was Ama who spoke.

"We have decided to make a formal petition on behalf of the People," she said. "We will send representatives to the city to seek an audience at the temple and demand the return of the stones. They likely underestimate us and our capacity to navigate their system, which is to our advantage. If the battle is one of bureaucracy, then we will answer in kind."

It sounded simple said like that. And it would require no combat. In hindsight, the god story *did* seem excessive, a plan born of emotion more than reason.

"The stones belong here," Ama continued. "It should be a straightforward task for our emissary to demonstrate their rightful cultural and natural home, given their unique properties. Those that have been taken must be restored, and those intact must be left alone. In *perpetuity*." She drew out the ambassador's word with a cold smile.

Thank the gods, Kell thought. Perhaps the Soogway government didn't understand the proper use of the stones. They did build wayfinder bugs, so they must have some sense of their utility in navigation, but did they realize how unnecessary that technology was? Sending representatives to explain how essential the stones are to the People, to our travel and finding water in a landscape that was constantly remade by the winds—representatives who could speak the convoluted language of the emissary and be both persuasive and firm—it was a good idea, a reasonable one, but Kell did not envy those chosen to do it. The weight of that burden would be immense.

And the ancestors will help them carry it, she reminded herself.

"In the event that the petition results in a challenge, we will be sending a solo combat teller as well as a diplomat. For simplicity's sake, we will not be sending along a second." *Ama.*

Kell supposed formal petitions were just as dull and procedural as they sounded, but of course there was the potential for a challenge—as Upepo had learned. Perhaps Ama would get to use her false god story after all. She felt a twinge of jealousy that she wouldn't get to witness it firsthand, the spectacle of Ama unleashing the power of creation on city functionaries.

Kell looked at her grandmother, her cheekbones elongated by the weight of the head wrap she wore, her quiet magnificence that made Kell feel safe. At the same time, Ama's copper skin looked gray in the light of the tents, the circles below her eyes dark and sagging. Ama was beautiful, a force, but very tired. *Old.* Kell tried to imagine her making the long trek to the city, lurching along on the back of a sandbeast or walking alongside with the aid of her staff. Though the People were nomadic, they moved at the pace of the slowest among them and never too far in one trip. The thought of her grandmother enduring such a long and hasty journey reignited the coals of rage in her chest. She thought again of the sandbeast pursued by the lion.

Would Ama even have the strength left to fight when she arrived?

"Ma'Jor," Ama used his formal name, identifying his seniority in birth order. "You will be our diplomat."

Kell's eyes met her brother's from opposite ends of the horseshoe. He sat up straighter, swallowing his nerves. Jor was a good choice. He was personable, charming, sympathetic to city tech. Gods help her, everyone liked him. He would be a good balance to Ama's wise strength.

Picturing him leaving brought Kell a new slip of panic. They were seldom apart, hadn't been since they were children, she realized. This would mean she couldn't go scouting until the party returned, since her brother was her triangulation partner. She tried to picture wayfinding with someone else and felt a creepy tingle in her spine.

"A'Kell." Kell's look snapped to Ama's face. "You will be our teller in the event of combat."

The room darkened to a single point as if the entire tent had collapsed, and Kell felt the weight of its walls and poles heap on top of her chest. She failed to inhale, and when her breath finally returned to her, it did so in a great audible gulp, as if she'd just clawed her way from under a sandfall. Silaya stiffened beside her, and Kell tried to speak, to recapture a single scrap of dignity, but she panted instead as her heart raced in her chest. Someone handed her a skin of water, and she gulped at it, eyes closed.

When she was again able to master her breathing, she opened her eyes. Her vision cleared, and she could see that the entire room had leveled their gazes at her. Silaya seemed irritated; Jor, concerned. The council looked as if they were having second thoughts.

Yes! she screamed in her mind. *Choose someone else!*

Ama narrowed her eyes at her but said nothing. Then the leader of the Roamers from the clay zone spoke.

"As a gesture of solidarity among the People of all camps, we offer two of our riders and their horses for swift passage to the city. Rather than camp on the outskirts and wait for a resolution, they will leave the two of you at the city gates and return when you have completed your audience with the temple."

"Wait—" Kell blurted out. A faraway part of herself heard the shaking in her voice. "How long will an audience take? We show up, we explain, we demand the stones back, maybe we fight. And then we leave, right?"

"The wheels of bureaucracy are said to turn slowly," he replied.

"Unless they're taking something of ours," Silaya spat.

"It could be days, or it could be a matter of weeks," he said gravely.

Weeks! She looked from Ama to Jor and back, but their faces were impassive. Was she the only one to whom this sounded crazy? Gods help her. She was going to ruin everything.

"Silaya, you will ride for Kell. Kiche—," Silaya's cousin, the one she triangulated with for wayfinding, raised his head. "You will ride for Jor." He nodded. "Expect the trip to the city to take a few days longer than the return because you will have the weight of extra riders. Plan for five days there and three days back. We will await you here, rest for a day, and then depart for our own camp." A sense of finality filled the room.

One of the council members stood and swept their gaze over those assembled. They opened their arms wide in the ceremonial gesture of both welcome and leave-taking and said, "We are grateful to our friends in this moment, for it is their feet that guide us swiftly across the sands. May your way be solid and far from storms." Everyone in the room nodded—except Kell, who sat as still as a jackrabbit in the eyes of a hawk. "We are grateful to our ambassadors, who will do what is right and what is needed to restore things to their proper order."

Kell was glad she had eaten little of the meat, as the entire contents of her stomach threatened the rug beneath her knees.

"And we are grateful to our ancestors, who witness our struggles and offer wisdom in the most trying of times."

A murmur of prayer rippled across the room like distant thunder.

Ancestors help us.

"They're just stories, Shade. They can't hurt you."
—Shade's mother

15. PAPER

Shade squinted at the shapes on the paper and then again at the ones above the door. They seemed to match, but Shade wasn't sure. The shapes above were carved into a metal plate bolted to the stone archway over the entrance. *Fancy*.

They didn't bother with things like that in Shade's neighborhood. They just painted marks on the walls or gave directions by landmark—the door across from the second-best dumpling stand, that sort of thing. This door was red, patterned to look like wood, they guessed. Maybe it *was* wood, though that seemed an extravagance too great even for this place. It had a little window in the middle set with amber glass, and small bars spanned the opening. The effect was oppressive—too much like a gaol cell for Shade's taste.

Shade wiped their hand on their pants and was about to knock, but the door swung open as they reached for it. A tall man stood before them, his look suggesting that Shade was unwelcome but also late.

"I—"

"Come in," the man interrupted, and Shade was relieved they didn't have to give the speech they had prepared. They held up Mr. Go's business card as if it were a ticket, but the man only turned and strode down a dim hallway. Shade followed, hearing the door close behind them with a resounding click.

It took a moment for Shade's eyes to adjust after the harsh sunlight of the street, and they had the impression of being swallowed, the walls gulping them into the wealthy underworld. Shade made it a habit never to go into a building where they didn't know a back way out, and this rare exception made their heart hammer in their chest so loudly, they were sure it echoed in the confines of the hallway. If the tall man could hear it, he made no sign. Shade gritted their teeth, willing their nerves into silence as they tried to memorize the route as they went.

A few more turns led them to an unmarked door—this one was wood, for sure—where the man gave a soft knock, turning to glower at Shade as he waited for a response. A tiny bell rang, and the man opened the door, gesturing for Shade to pass through.

Sun streamed through broad windows, rendering every color pale. It looked as though they were on at least the second story, though Shade didn't recall having climbed any stairs. Across the room was an enormous desk—also wood, they realized with a thrill—covered in sheets of . . . could all of that be *paper*? The wealth it represented made their head spin. Behind the desk sat a plain man with narrow eyes. He looked up from the papers he was studying and offered Shade a small smile that invited them to approach.

In the daylight, Mr. Go was much less intimidating than Shade remembered. He looked soft, contented—pretty much like any rich man in Soogway. Though after asking around a bit, Shade had learned that Go lined his pockets through betting and the black market rather than the usual usury and price gouging of more sanctioned trade. Shade tried to stay sharp, to remember what Go had done with their memory of their mother, what he was capable of. But now that they were here, seeing Go at his desk, the anxiety Shade had felt at the door faded into curiosity. What could a man like this really want from them?

"Hello Shade," Go purred.

Shade paused, unable to recall having given the man their name. They stood a little taller. "I heard you wanted to see me," they said, as if Go had pulled them away from important business.

"Indeed," Go agreed, with a touch of amusement. "Thank you for coming." He leaned back in his chair and took Shade's measure. As if finding Shade scrawnier than was satisfactory, he asked, "Can I offer you some refreshment?"

Shade shook their head, but the gesture knocked loose a hungry gurgle from their stomach, and they winced. Go reached across his desk to a tray of small bells and gave one a brief ring. The sound was different than the one that had allowed Shade entry, and Shade wrestled the impulse to run to the tray and ring all the bells, just to see what they would make the tall man do.

"Have a seat." Go gestured with his eyes to a large, overstuffed chair opposite the desk, and Shade sank into it. The arm rests were uncomfortably high, and they struggled to sit upright, endeavoring not to look as if they were being eaten by the upholstery.

Go began shuffling the papers on his desk, straightening them into tidy stacks, and for a strange moment, it was as if he had forgotten Shade was there. To pass the time, they ran their fingers over the carved wood of the armrests. It was satisfying—slippery and smooth in whorled shapes that their fingers could trace like a maze. They craned their neck to survey the room. Paintings crowded the walls, and a bookcase overflowed with books. This is what owning folks gets you, Shade thought bitterly. Being surrounded by paper and fine furniture and everything interesting to the touch. Having someone jump when you ring a bell.

When their attention returned to Go, they found him finished with his task. He sat with hands folded, regarding Shade blandly under heavy-lidded eyes. Despite its mildness, Shade could feel every inch of themself being weighed by that gaze. They tried to give the impression they were measuring Go back.

"I've seen you fight," he said finally, breaking the silence. "You're very clever."

Shade's chest heated with pleasure, but they knew better than to trust a compliment. Rich people were like that, always pretending to give you something so they could get more of whatever they already had. They shifted in the softness of the chair.

"Who taught you?" Go's voice was so gentle, Shade responded without thinking.

"My father, mostly."

The combination of the warm light and the deep cushions made them feel a little sleepy. They sat up, trying to stay alert, but an unexpected drowsiness tugged at them, loosing something inside. "He was a guard for a long time, got commissioned to work off some debts, and then gave his life to it," they found themself saying, though they didn't know why. They reminded themself to stay guarded against Go, but the thought was distant and growing fainter.

Images of their father flickered up inside them like light bouncing off water. Shade pictured his hands, the way they cupped the storylight and shaped it. The way those hands felt on Shade's shoulder, heavy and warm. The way they had formed story creatures that had lived in the Broken Forest and how they had brought his home there—their mother's home too, the one Shade's parents had left behind—so clearly to life. They recalled the hollow look that grew on their father's face after he lost fight after fight, spending his heart stories until there was little left of him but a ragged, bitter shell of the man Shade had loved. Toward the end, he didn't even remember Shade's name most days. Suddenly Shade blinked against the memories, unbidden and unwanted, and returned to themself. Was this another of Go's weird tricks?

Mr. Go was watching quietly, and Shade's stomach began to squirm. They had the uncomfortable feeling he could see every thought in their head. Cheap's warning echoed in their ears. *Think what you could do with that.*

There was a knock at the door, and Shade started. Go rang the bell for entry, and the tall man carried in a great tray laden with food and drinks. Go gestured for him to leave it on the desk, and the tall man retreated without a word, closing the door soundlessly behind him. Go indicated the food with his chin, and Shade eyed it for a moment. *Traitor*, they thought at the saliva flooding their mouth.

"Gimme a break, kid," Go said, helping himself to a fat sandwich. "Just eat. Like I'm going to go to this much trouble just to poison you." A sound escaped Shade that wanted to be a laugh. Go took an enormous bite, his jaw popping to accommodate the thickness of it. A bit of lettuce dangled from Go's mouth as he chewed, and he chased it with fleshy lips. Shade examined the tray, selected a sandwich of their own and a full mug of something that smelled sharp. Shade took a sip. It was cool and tangy, sour and sweet at once, like lemons and sunshine.

"He teach you the trick you used on that chanter the other night?"

"You were there?"

"Of course. You made me a nice stack of chips." Go chewed noisily. Shade swallowed carefully before answering.

"That was something I figured out on my own. My dad was more traditional in a lot of ways. He knew all the classics." The sandwich was stuffed with meat and some kind of creamy cheese Shade had never had before. They had to force themself not to wolf it down. "He was creative too, though. A dreamer. He had a real vision for how he wanted our lives to be."

"And what happened to him?" Go asked around a mouthful.

"He died," Shade said. The words came out flat. It had been a long time since that sentence had brought out the old howling pain in their chest, they realized. Now there was only a hollow ache, a feeling that something essential was just . . . missing. "He burned up all his heart stories." Shade was grateful for the mug of citrus so they could clear the lump in their throat.

"Ah," said Go, not unkindly. "That happens with visionaries, doesn't it? They care too much and are willing to give it all, to use up that core if it can save the dream."

Shade nodded. It felt good to talk about their father—nobody ever asked. Cheap knew it was a sore spot and avoided it. The D Street kids weren't exactly conversationalists, plus they had all lost their parents, too, so it wasn't anything worth bringing up. Shade found themself wanting to say more, as if thoughts of their father were something fizzy in a bottle, and Go had just given it a good shake.

"He was a good fighter," Shade said finally, as they finished the rest of the sandwich in three rapid bites. Shade felt bolder now on a full stomach, more in control. "It wasn't his fault that he lost. The city made him fight a certain way, only let him use certain kinds of stories in the guard. But he really knew how to win. He taught me all about stances and how to read people's bodies, how to know when you'd hit a nerve. That sort of thing."

"Fundamentals are important," Go agreed. His eyes were difficult to see. It occurred to Shade that Go was reading them just like that now, sizing up what would hurt and where he could press for more.

Shade decided they didn't care. There wasn't anything about them that they needed to keep secret. Even as they thought it, though, a slender ribbon of alarm snaked up their spine, Cheap's voice reminding them to be careful. Secret or no, information was powerful when you fought an opponent.

"Why don't you just fight in the Cycle yourself?" Shade asked. It had sounded less rude in their head. Go's face changed, that smug comfort hardening briefly into something hungry and sharp before fading again.

"I have been . . . " Go lingered over the words, selecting them with dry irony. "Disinvited," he said. "Prohibited." Shade snorted.

"You? Banned from competing? Why?" They gestured at the room as if to say Go could easily buy his way onto the brackets, if that's what he wanted.

Mr. Go finished his sandwich and carefully wiped his hands and face with a handkerchief he produced from an inside pocket. "The Temple Council find some of my methods unconventional," he said. "They do love their traditions in this city, and it sounds like your father paid the price. If you ask me, they have a very limited understanding of what story combat is, of what it can be. The rules are simple and fixed; the only one who gets to break them is the city itself, and then only in the most boring ways."

His eyes crept up to Shade's, then, pinning Shade to their chair. "They have an impoverished notion of what is possible, Shade." They shivered at the sound of their name in the man's mouth. "They don't know what a story can really *do*."

Shade felt cold all over. The light in the room was too bright, the food in their stomach too heavy. What had seemed like comfort only moments before took on the soft, imprisoning quality of a dream.

"What *can* it do?" Shade's voice came out quieter than they liked.

Mr. Go withdrew a knife from his pocket, unfolded it, and began cleaning his nails. Shade recognized it as the knife from the other night, but any sense of threat was lost now to sheer distaste. How rich did you have to be to groom yourself in front of others? Go turned the tip of the blade to his teeth. He removed a bit of green from his gumline and slipped the knife back into his pocket.

"What *is* a story, Shade?" Go's voice was patient, but his tone indicated clearly this was a test.

"It depends," they shrugged. "A story can be a fantasy, a distraction, a little bit of culture, or a lesson dressed in costume." Their father used to say that a story was a secret that everybody knew, but they didn't feel like sharing that. "Sometimes it's just a trick. Sometimes it's more than that, like a wish—" *Or a memory*, they thought, Go's story image of their mother's face still glowing behind Shade's eyes.

"Sure," he said, waving away Shade's words like a small, pestering insect. "But what is it you're really *doing*?" He leaned across the desk as if pushing his meaning into them. Shade thought that if he had some smart answer he wanted them to say, he could go ahead and say it. They waited, arms crossed.

"Stories make the truth, Shade." Spittle flew as the words came out, and Go wiped his desk with a fingertip. Shade was seeing entirely too much of Go's mouth.

"I mean, yeah, you can create things, but they aren't *real*," they said, cringing as the man licked the crumbs off his finger. "As soon as the story is over, it's gone. It's not like you can conjure a meal that will feed someone. Storylight doesn't last."

"Doesn't it?" Go asked. "Doesn't it leave a mark in all who heard it? Doesn't it alter the world, even just a little bit?" Shade shrugged. Other tellers might argue over whether the audience was changed by the stories or the outcomes, but Shade didn't really care—they just needed to win fights. And they said so.

Mr. Go shook his head. "That's not what winning means. It's not just entertainment, Shade. It's not mere tradition, habits reproducing themselves over and over so that people can take comfort in the familiar. Telling is not simply distraction." Shade eyed him, sensing some kind of move they couldn't foresee. Go raised his eyebrows, inviting them to disagree.

"The strongest tellers remake reality," he went on. "They change what is."

What do you know about what is? Anger spread through Shade like an itch. Rich folks always thought they knew what the world was all about. But what they didn't get is that there are two worlds, and the one Shade lived in was not filled with paper and bells.

"Stories don't feed my friends," Shade growled, running out of patience. *And they don't bring back the dead. They don't get me to the Broken Forest.*

"But they do," Go hissed. "They *do*. Stories bought your friends those dumplings. They can make you money. They can buy you freedom to get where you want to go. That's real change."

Shade bolted out of the chair. "You don't have anything better to do than watch me all the time?" Enough. This creep could keep his offers and fancy food. Go gestured as if to settle a spooked animal.

"Easy," he said. "A lucky guess." But his eyes flashed with satisfaction under their soft lids.

Shade was done with this conversation, but they weren't sure they could find their way out of the building, and they didn't think they could break past the tall man who was no doubt still standing outside the door.

"You're just talking about tricks," they said, starting to pace. "All that is in people's heads. I already know how to do that."

"There's so much more, Shade. I want to show you how to win. Really win. I can teach you how to remake it all in the ways you want. You can walk in and take the Cycle—you can even keep the money. It's not about that to me."

"And why would you do that?"

"Because I want the council to lose." A shadow passed over Go's features, but his eyes still glittered. "They might keep me out, but my ideas can still tear them apart. I want them. To pay. For their lack. Of vision." He emphasized his words as if spearing each one with a knife. The careful control was gone, the smug softness Go wore as his veil of power. Beneath lay nothing but raw blades and sharp teeth and something else, something vicious and calculating and not entirely well.

Shade stopped pacing.

"That's it?" They fought to keep their face bland despite the tension climbing inside them. This man would not see them afraid. "That's all? You want to make the council look bad for hurting your feelings?"

Mr. Go stood, and Shade could have sworn that the light in the room dimmed. Go began murmuring something they couldn't quite hear. Storylight peeled from his palm, first like leaves, like pages of a book being turned, then like wisps of smoke, tendrils drifting and creeping from his hand as he rounded the desk, his eyes drilling into Shade's. The storylight congealed into a spider the size of a fist. It gripped the desk, its furred legs silently tapping a route between the stacks of papers and other items cluttering its surface. Instinctively, Shade dropped into a defensive crouch, the first words of a counterstory coming to their lips. Shade's eyes danced back and forth between the creature and Go.

The spider crawled down one of the desk's legs and skittered toward Shade. The story driving it was little more than a growl from Go, unintelligible yet clearly effective. Shade's mind raced as they sifted through counters, settling quickly on a rhyming ditty that produced a leggy waterbird. The bird settled onto the floor, stabbing its beak in the direction of the spider.

The spider was much faster. It raced up Shade's pant leg and vanished into their pocket before Shade could switch tactics. They yelped and reflexively smacked at their hip, feeling nothing. But then there was a sensation of heat there, and a tugging. Shade gasped, looking at Go and then down at their pocket as the spider tugged the business card in it free and then melted back into formlessness as the card dropped to the floor.

"How—" Shade began and then stopped. They swallowed, their mouth suddenly very dry.

Go twirled the story back into his palm and leaned to rest his weight, placing both hands on his desk behind him, lounging. The hunter again replaced with the lazy gambler accustomed to getting his way. He jerked his chin as if to tell Shade to read the card.

Shade stooped to pick it up and saw that the symbols had shifted, unwound and rearranged themselves into the only shape they could recognize: SHADE.

They lifted their eyes to Go's.

"Remake reality," he said softly. "Change what is."

"Just listen, *dammit!"*
—Shade's father

16. HOW TO THROW A FIGHT

Shade didn't like being wrong, but they needed chips more than they needed to be right. The man could for sure do things they didn't know how to—yet. The business card thing was a magician's trick, they were sure of it. But after Shade had settled down, Go had shown them a couple small tips that, they had to admit, would be pretty useful in a fight. The one where you got the other teller to look at you instead of the story, how you faked your body language so they reacted to your gestures and not your words? Shade wished they'd thought of that. They'd definitely trot that out in the Box. Once they were allowed back, that is.

Go had wanted to show Shade something in action. They would make a lot of money in the process, he'd assured them. So Shade waited as yet another of Go's bodyguards ushered them through a series of unmarked doors, each requiring a password and a visual identification of Go himself. At each, a small window slid open, eyes peered out, codes were muttered, locks disengaged. Shade thought it was all a bit much, really.

They were in the basement of a building somewhere in Glendale, Shade guessed, though they'd walked so far out of Shade's usual terrain that they weren't entirely sure where. Not their favorite feeling. After three secret entrances and some chips exchanging hands, concrete underfoot gave way to thick red carpet, and Shade found themself being steered down an increasingly well-appointed hallway flanked with curtains and decorative panels. They tried to shrug Go's hand from their shoulder, but the man gripped their collarbone as if he would snap it.

"Remember," Go said flatly. "You do *exactly* as I say." Shade nodded. "Or?" asked Go.

"Or no deal," they echoed, chafing at the words.

Go released his grip as the bodyguard opened a final set of doors, and they entered what appeared to be a small, underground auditorium. Shade's first impression was of the Box—if the Box were made of velvet. A swank version of the pit.

Very swank.

Instead of rickety metal chairs and benches were soft, cushioned seats. The tiny arena was recessed—not so deeply as the Box but enough to give the mezzanine a clear view of the tellers—and a dozen or so people sat, their eyes returning expectantly toward the space that would become the field of combat. Silk orb lanterns hung like glowing fruit, bathing the space in a warm light that draped shadows across their faces. They could use that to their advantage, Shade thought, to hide or exaggerate their own expressions.

If the Box was a hooched-up dog kennel, full of howling, sodden lowlifes, this place was a solemn temple of power, a theater of secrets for the wealthy. Shade tried not to gawk as they looked around, taking in the clothing, the muted reds, the ornate gold filigree in the form of leaves and vines. The acoustics were such that the smallest sounds leaped across the space, so voices were kept to low whispers. A man in a fine suit approached and greeted Go, who murmured something in the man's ear then nodded briefly toward Shade. The man didn't bother to glance at Shade but offered Go a slight bow and indicated empty seats along the railing above the arena. The bodyguard went first, then Go, and Shade followed, as they took their places. Shade ran a hand on the railing. It was smooth, polished wood.

Of course it was.

A woman appeared at Shade's shoulder, and they flinched as she placed a hand on their arm. They looked up in alarm to find she was offering them something with tongs from a woven basket.

"Take it," Go growled in their ear.

Shade took it, and found it was a warm, moist cloth that smelled faintly of the sweet resins that scented the public baths. Go took one as well, and Shade mimicked his actions, unfolding the cloth, using it to wipe their face and neck first, then their hands. The woman took the dirtied cloths from them with the tongs, returning them to the basket, then smiled expectantly. Her bald head gleamed as she bent obligingly toward Go.

"Tea?" Her voice was high and flute-like. Go nodded, and the woman vanished, reappearing moments later with three steaming cups on a tray. She handed each to them before withdrawing again behind what Shade now noticed were enormous, embroidered curtains at the back of the amphitheater. Shade sipped their tea, which was too hot, and studied the other patrons in the audience. All elegant, puffy rich folks that sat with the same lazy ease that Go had.

Go indicated the arena with his chin. "Keep your eyes on the stage."

They did.

The first few bouts were pretty standard fare, Shade thought. A handful of interesting tricks by a folklorist gave them a couple new ideas, and a surprise win by a teller using flexible satire provoked sounds of outrage from the audience that cracked the pretense of relaxed calm they all cultivated. It wasn't about losing money, Shade knew; it was just pride.

Go kept quiet for most of the matches, so Shade was left to discern the system on their own. Some of the tellers looked to be sponsored by those in the audience—owners were typical at the Box, too—while some were unaccompanied, free agents, as Shade had always been. *Dogs and birds*, that's what their father had said. Dogs fought for others. Birds flew on their own wings.

Does this mean I'm a dog now? The thought was uncomfortable. Shade looked at Go, who had finished his tea and was nursing a glass of expensive hooch, swirling it as they regarded the arena through heavily lidded eyes.

More like a rat. They frowned.

The next match was about to start. One teller stood from beside their sponsor at the railing and made their way down the short staircase that led to the arena. Another teller stepped from behind the embroidered curtain at the back. *One dog, one bird.* The bald woman made her way again around the mezzanine seats, quietly taking bets.

Go extended a finger from his glass, indicating the free teller. “Watch her.”

Shade gauged the two combatants. The one with the sponsor was twitchy, angular. He jumped up and down in place as if jostling his nerves loose, rolling his shoulders and twisting his neck back and forth. The other, however, swaggered to the center where she made a show of wiping her nose on her hand and then stuffing her palms into her back pockets.

Cocky. Shade had to admit, they liked her style. What exactly her style was, however, was difficult to say. Nothing on her body looked like it had come from Soogway. She wore dusty brown pants and a matching shirt, both of which were absolutely covered in straps, clasps, and pockets. It was as if she might need to carry thimblefuls of everything all at once—or as if she might fall to pieces if she weren’t securely buckled together.

The referee stepped between the combatants and looked to both their faces to verify they were ready and knew the rules. The twitchy teller sank into a defensive crouch and made a flourish with one hand. The woman laughed a huge, braying laugh that echoed in the chamber’s acoustics. She shook her head like a dog just come from a swim, her hair springing about her head in wild curls, and took her hands out of her pockets. Shade raised an eyebrow. This was going to be good.

Storylight pooled in the man’s hand as he launched into his tale, a carefully plotted crime puzzle that was sharp and convoluted right out of the gate. He used a series of hooks that drew Shade in immediately, and their eyes grew wide as the light formed into an elongated fish with a snout like a saw, jagged teeth razoring out from either side. The fish sprouted wings and radiated an uncanny number of fins around its body, steering itself into quick turns as it darted around the stage. Meanwhile, the strange woman in brown was still clearing her throat.

Why doesn’t she say anything? Shade wanted to shout at her to do something, anything. Stalling was against the rules—and anyway, it was a very boring way to lose a match.

The fish cut circles in the air as the man charged through his plot. It had nothing to fight, so paraded around the arena in a victory lap.

Shade liked the story, though they were pretty sure they could guess how it would end, which ruined some of the effect. He was telegraphing the twist, they thought. They had expected better from such an opening.

Then the woman opened her mouth, and a song poured forth just as storylight poured from her hand. *Hands—both of them!* Shade hadn't even known that was possible. They glanced at Go, but his face was a mask of placid observation.

She sang. Terribly.

Her voice cracked and quavered. Paying as much attention to pitch as she had to etiquette, she veered close to notes then slid off them again, powering through a rhythmic beat. It was a work song, Shade realized, the kind of thing crews would sing to offload a riverboat or to build a warehouse out of mortar and stone. Yet something about it was haunting, lovely. Strangely . . . *disruptive*.

Her storylight broke into pieces then, scattering around the stage, and each formed its own creature. There were small, furred things with bushy tails and tiny creeping things that inched along the floor. Long, leggy animals, all joints and digits, clambered up invisible tree trunks, while beasts composed entirely of wings flapped and soared in a flock that engulfed the saw-toothed fish. Each creature moved independently of the rest, as if carried by one mote of the wild, fractured chord of her voice. The fish snapped at them, whirling as it attacked, spiraling on its strange, fletched fins. It was outnumbered, though, and the sharpness of its approach was no match for the sheer complexity of the woman's song. Soon the many small creatures descended upon it, pinning it in place, and taking many small bites until the long fish was entirely consumed.

The woman cleared her throat as she gathered the light back into her palms. She offered a small wave to the other teller, who stood slack-jawed in defeat. She winked at him, and then turned to survey the audience, which murmured and shifted at the victory.

"I don't get it," Shade said. They turned to Go. "That shouldn't have worked. There was no urgency, no tension." It bothered them. Something wasn't right about it.

"You're next," was all Go said.

A thrill shot up Shade's stomach. *Finally*. They knew exactly what they'd do to take her on. First, they'd—

"Lose."

Shade froze. "What?"

"I want you to lose," he repeated.

Shade blinked. "But you said—"

"You agreed: You do as I say."

"You said I'd make money!"

"And you will, Street Rat." Mr. Go's level voice was oily, a sound that could slip under doors. Shade narrowed their eyes at the nickname.

"I don't throw fights!" They hissed, keeping their voice low but wanting to scream. They could feel the other patrons' attention turning their way.

Go finished his glass in a single swallow, and the bald woman appeared at his side to take it as if summoned. Go didn't even bother to look as he said, "It's your choice. Do it and learn. Or leave and don't come back."

Heat squeezed out of Shade's eyes as they blinked, clenched. Something large and burning rose in their chest, and they took a few panting breaths to push it back down. The referee had returned to the arena and was looking in their direction.

"Tick-tock, Shade." Go's voice was calm, almost bored.

They pushed their way out of their chair and stood, fists clenched at their side. So stupid. They didn't throw fights. They *won* fights. If they lost, they lost to tellers who could beat them, not to nonsense stupid work songs that didn't even have a plot. Shade stomped to the stairs and entered the arena, aware they were making entirely too much noise.

The woman in brown flashed them an enormous grin that showed her teeth, and Shade ducked their chin, hoping the shadowed lights would hide their red-rimmed eyes. The referee gave the signal. Shade glanced at Go, who watched them mildly from the mezzanine, though somehow they could still see his eyes glittering, set in their soft folds.

Do it and learn.

Shade let out a long breath and opened their hand, sinking into their familiar stance. They mentally rifled through some options and settled on a recent acquisition they wouldn't mind letting go of—the chanter's classic they'd just won at the Box. They began tapping their foot in time and wondered briefly whether this woman was dumb enough to use the same trick twice. She winked at them and began a folktale about a butterfly and a ghost, one Shade didn't recognize.

Shade filled their lungs with air and summoned the deepest voice they could muster:

"Caldo once was a man like you
You wouldn't have known his name
But when he found his calling true
He also found his fame."

The squid-steer from the chanter's telling was sleeker in Shade's, lither and less poundy, but the idea was the same. Its tentacles unfurled into mallets and began to wave around. They saw a flash of delight in the woman's eyes as she realized Shade was using a public classic.

Just kill me now, they thought miserably, but the chant was catchy, and it got into their blood even as they spat the words from memory. They threw themself into it, their eyes flicking to Go at the railing and then back to the folktale, which had taken the form of a saber-toothed badger with enormous, diaphanous wings.

The badger hovered in the air as the woman spooled out her fable. It was clear she was taking liberties, as the badger's face distended and shrank, growing small antlers that stretched into antenna and then melted back into whiskers. The badger rolled on its back, batting at the squid creature, flitting out of reach of the mallets, then licking its front paws like a cat.

The audacity was too much. Shade sharpened their chant, layering snaps and claps to their stomping beat, a polyrhythmic intervention that sped the story along, carrying Caldo quickly through his meeting with the Enchantress. They even riffed briefly about the jewels that adorned the hilt of the Golden Scythe. It was a gamble, as rhyme flow wasn't Shade's strong suit, but they'd be damned if they let this woman mock them. The tentacles flattened into blades, and one whipped up and struck the folktale, shearing a wing from the badger's shoulder.

Shade saw the surprise register on the woman's face at the precise instant they sensed Go sit up straighter in the balcony. Maybe they would just win this thing. Maybe they weren't going to be a dog after all. Shade's voice rang through the auditorium as they went for the badger. Go's eyes burned into them from above, but Shade ignored him, feeling the rhythm of the chant as it shook the small arena like a pulse.

The woman's brow furrowed, and her telling took on a surreal quality, the badger careening now on its single wing, its tail growing and thickening into something wide and flat. It spun toward the squid and slapped it soundly with its tail before hurtling away again, not entirely under its own control.

The squid pursued, Caldo reaching the battlefield with his army and laying waste to his enemies and allies alike. It was a disgusting story, really, but crowds loved it. A quick glance at the soft faces surrounding the arena, however, suggested otherwise—maybe Shade had misjudged these rich folks' taste for ancient blood battles after all. They cursed to themself as they saw the flat reactions of the onlookers, saw the folktale growing longer claws as it hunched on the floor, preparing to strike.

The woman was good. In her tale, the ghost had coalesced as a transparent prison of hope, a walking miasma of butterfly wings. That image alone stilled Shade and left them wanting more. Now the badger was creeping toward the squid, folding its remaining wing across the squid's eyes as it latched on with claw and teeth.

Caldo whirled the Scythe overhead and stood on the battlefield, panting, but the crowd did not rise, roaring in triumph. The final phrases of the folktale rang eerily in the room, and Shade watched as their squid-thing folded beneath the badger's talons, crumpling in on itself as if it were made of paper. The badger lapped up the squid, taking small bites of it until there was nothing left, then it began grooming itself once more in a feline manner as if it had found the whole business mildly distasteful. The creature melted back into storylight mid-lick, disappearing into the woman's palm and taking Shade's story with it.

They glared at her. Somehow it was even worse, knowing they had tried to win. Sort of.

A glance at the balcony showed the bald woman presenting Mr. Go with a large bag of what Shade presumed were chips. How the hell had he worked that? Had people actually bet on them?

Go met their eyes and gave a satisfied smile. He nodded at Shade. Shade bowed their head in response.

Take him, kiddo. Take him for whatever he's got.

They just hoped it would be worth it.

A'LAN SPEAKS: AMULET DEVELOPMENT

Stories belong to no one and to everyone, girl. They are like water, commonly held, moving through the land and the sky and through our bodies, changed and returned but always in motion. To tell is to open oneself to this flow and receive that which travels, that which remembers. If we had only one life through which to learn, one story to weave and to know, we would be as infants until we died of old age, helpless and simple. We would eat the poison plant, fall into the hidden quicksand; we would weep for lack of meaning. The ancestors watch and speak. They lend us their lives, their lessons.

Thanks be to them.

How do we call the ancestors, my child? How do they know when to come? How do we open ourselves to their wisdom, loose our tongues that they may use them to speak the truths they carry on our behalf, fill our lungs that they may breathe again?

Listen well. There are three means the teller has to create a point of entry, an amulet. One is Object as Amulet. The second is Movement as Amulet. And the third is Body as Amulet. All three forms can draw your own attention and that of the audience, can act as invitation and gate through which the ancestors may arrive. Each has its strengths and each its dangers.

Object Amulets are simple. See my staff, the way it shakes and casts. Hear its rhythms as I stamp and sweep. These pieces here, the wires and stones, the glass and tech, the feathers—these remind us of the world and its many faces. My staff is the gate, but only because it is mine. Endless are the forms an amulet may take: ring or cloth, cup or stone, burning brand lifted from the fire. These amulets are temporary, and unique to the teller.

No, child. This is no magic. It is just how things are.

Movement Amulets are rituals, reminders that trace one's steps back to the story. Through movement you rise to meet the ancestors at the gate rather than summon them forth. You dance with them, pluck them from the air, creep to them with fingertips and eyelashes, call them to you with your look. These amulets are body but not body. Memory of shapes and motion. These are shadows we inhabit that overlay the past and now.

Yes. Body Amulets burn hottest, child.

You may be tempted to use this too much, as your heart, my child, is close to the gate already. You will want to swallow them, to call them with your voice and your skin. Once summoned, you will want them to live within you—to carry them that you may feel them with you always, to fill in the dark gaps you are afraid to touch yourself. The body is already a living temple to the ancestors. Your blood and shape their blood and shape, your colors and fears their own. But you are also now, *and they are only now through* you.

Take care you live your new life that they may continue to learn.

•

The Finder's Eye: North

17. RIDING THE WIND

Silaya had been right—it *was* like flying. The first day whipped past in a blur, the hard desert earth melting away beneath the horses' hooves in a steady cadence of speed. Kell wondered at the shapes of it, the way the familiar roundness of the dunes became a rolling pattern of waves as they rode, like fabric billowing in a hot breeze. She leaned her chest into Silaya's back, her arms wrapped tightly around Silaya's waist, her body alight with the warmth of her.

This. I just want this. No battles, no ambassadors. Just keep going, horse, whoever you are. The constant nearness created a sense of connection that felt deeper to Kell than conversation could forge. She breathed in Silaya's rose and leather scent, realizing the latter came from the saddle and riding gear, which were as much a part of Silaya as her own body. Silaya was completely at ease on a horse, her edgy manner melted into a will to motion, and Kell allowed herself to submit to this, to feel safe and utterly out of her own control.

The second day was harder.

Kell was sore in places she had never considered, and the initial thrill of the ride gave way to monotony. Though they moved through the landscape at a new rate, these were still the familiar dunes and plateaus of Home, territory she had scouted with her brother countless times, and it lacked a sense of discovery to distract her from their purpose. Every hoofbeat brought them closer to Soogway and her mission, every step toward her potential failure. Kell felt this like a sickening drop in barometric pressure, as if they were riding headlong into a storm.

At the end of the day, they stopped to make camp near a rock outcropping that boasted some rare greenery and a small copse of short, scrubby trees.

A spring, thank the gods. Kell's eyes were stinging and dry, and she nearly fell climbing off the horse. She wanted to race toward the water source, but on her numb feet, she could barely manage a bent hobble. Her legs ached, and her groin felt as if she'd been bruised with a hot poker. She stumbled her way toward the green and the sound of dripping.

Silaya chuckled as she walked the horse to water. "I thought you said you rode sandbeasts," she said, her eyebrow raised.

"They're different," Kell sniffed. "And I usually walk," she added, though her attention was captured by a small animal that darted out then disappeared under one of the trees. The trees here were little more than woody bushes, bent by years in the sun and the wind. Kell wished they were larger so she could hide as well. She could live here, a tiny rodent eating hardy plants and sleeping with the sound of water bubbling up through the rock. She wouldn't need to confront any bureaucrats or fail her people or spend three more days on a horse.

I could just die here and become a spirit of the spring, she mused, *let my tears water the trees and provide oasis for countless desert creatures*—though on brief reflection, crying for all eternity quickly lost its appeal.

She looked to Jor and Kiche approaching on the other horse. Silaya always rode a little faster than her cousin, whether through the strength of her mount or her competitive nature, Kell couldn't be sure. Singing the Way in Haste together required them to stay in visual range—but only just. The hot blur of their travel companions solidified into shadow and then shape as they drew near, and Silaya murmured to her horse, stroking its neck as it drank. Kell knelt and drank from the spring, as well. When the others got close enough to make out their faces, she could see that Jor looked as tired as she felt, but he sprang from the saddle easily and walked with no apparent discomfort, which only irritated her further.

Kell soaked a part of her scarf in the trickle of water carving its patient path through the stones and wrapped it around the back of her neck. As often happened on scouting missions, they had spent the entire day in the sun, and her head felt as if someone had placed it in a bind and was spinning it around. The water was surprisingly cool, likely from a deep source, and she sucked a corner of the scarf, enjoying the rivulet that ran between her shoulder blades. For a moment, she felt almost peaceful.

"Too sore to help us make camp?" Jor grinned as he helped Kiche unload his horse, and her calm evaporated.

"I didn't realize you were in such a hurry to get to sleep," she snapped, but it was a weak barb, and she turned away from the spring feeling both foolish and resentful. Silaya smirked as she unbuckled the straps holding their packs to the saddle, and Kell said nothing as she retrieved her things.

The evening was clear, and as the light fled to the west, the sky extended overhead like a vast pool of water. Wordlessly, the four agreed to sleep without a tent for the night. There was no sign of bad weather, and the air felt clean and good on their skin. Countless stars danced above them as they unpacked their bedrolls and coaxed a small fire from the dried sandbeast dung they carried and the scant tinder they could gather from the scrub. Kell had tried to light it using only dry twigs and friction, as the old scouts once did, but after several failed attempts and broken twigs, Jor pulled out a small lighter from his pocket—only minor tech, his shrug said—and a small fire bloomed.

They chatted quietly as they ate.

"You watch your hands, there," Kiche teased. "You get too close to that last piece of fruit, Silaya maybe eat your hand, too!" He pointed at the dried juba fruit they were sharing as Jor reached for it. Everyone laughed. Silaya's cousin was as different from Silaya as he could be—gentle, rounded, easygoing. He had grown up among Roamers who mostly ranged in the far north of the clay zone, he explained, which was why his accent sounded different from hers, though they still looked a good deal alike. Kell was grateful for his banter as it crowded out her growing anxiety.

"You know about the lights they got in the city?" he asked. "They don't need to burn nothing—they just go *light*, like that!" He made a flaring gesture with his hands. "They use the juice, like with happy boxes and bugs and all, but they get the power from the wall." He shook his head.

Jor looked at him, fascinated. "Where does the juice come from?"

Kiche shrugged. "They make it go in the walls, in the floor. I dunno how they work."

"You've been to the city before?" Kell asked, leaning in. "What was it like?"

Kiche shook his head again. "Yeah, I've been there. It's like . . . " He paused, thinking. "It's like those folks don't know how to be together, so they make themselves as apart as they can. But they're all smushed up." He pushed his hands close as if squeezing an invisible body. "They're all so close, so many people in one spot, but they got all walls and that. They don't tell stories together or think about others. They just buy buy buy this and sell sell sell that. They got story, but they'll also still hit you, still cut you if they need." He shrugged again, his eyes far away in some memory of Soogway where the others couldn't follow. He looked up then and laughed. "They're missing out! But they do have some stuff."

Kell found herself staring. What else was he thinking? She had a sudden, desperate urge to hear everything he could tell about the city, as if he held a key to their mission.

"Did you go to the temple?" she asked, hopeful.

"Nah," he said. "Too fancy for me. I just helped my family trade a bunch of blankets in the market one time. Nice work. We sold a lot." He nudged Silaya with a foot. "Weavers," he said. "She's, like, real good."

Silaya reddened in the firelight, looking equally embarrassed and pleased. Kell sought her eyes over the fire and found them. They shone in the warm flicker, and Kell felt a flush rise in her chest. The heat in her skin mixed with her nerves until she couldn't tell what was fear and what was desire.

I want to be worth this, she thought. Silaya gave her a look somewhere between a smile and a threat, like a hungry desert cat, and she went dizzy with the thrill of it. Anxiety crackled in Kell's nerves, a wild energy that urged recklessness. Everything felt dangerous and alive.

Jor's voice interrupted. "What other kinds of tech do they have?"

"They got all the tech," Kiche answered slowly. He rubbed his nose as if to remove the day's sand. "Lights, sounds. They got boxes that flicker, make you feel good. Things that build, things that move, carry." He shook his head as if the technology of the city was beyond belief.

"Things that build? What do they build?"

"Other machines, I think. Things that build the happy boxes, things that make the money."

"The machines earn for them?"

"No, no—I mean they *make* the money. Machines, like, make the chips. The money is special, can't be copied. They make other stuff, too. Make machines that cut down forests and, like, dig out rocks."

Kell went cold. She glanced at Silaya and saw her grief mirrored.

"That's incredible," said Jor with awe.

"What are you talking about?" Kell snapped. "Dig out *rocks*, Jor. As in stones. As in *pulsar stones*. This is why we're going to the severed city in the first place. Don't tell me you're impressed."

"I just think it's amazing what they can do," he said, taken aback by Kell's sudden ferocity. "I'm not saying I like what they're doing with it."

"Well, it's not. It's *not* amazing. It's horrible. All of it. Did you even hear what he said?"

"Just because they're not like us doesn't make them horrible, Kell."

"Not necessarily, no—but in this case, they are."

"You haven't even been there."

"They're destroying our Home!" Kell shouted, keenly aware of three sets of eyes on her in the firelight. "Why doesn't that bother you?" The strain of the past few days grew even heavier as she stared at her brother. Inside her, some thin cord snapped. For a brief, irrational moment, Kell was afraid that last thread had tethered her to the sandy earth, and now nothing would keep her from floating away into the night.

"You think it doesn't?" Jor's face grew dark. His anger was rare but forceful, like a desert flood. "You think I like the fact that I couldn't find the stone the other day?"

Kell swallowed. She had forgotten.

"No, but—"

"You think you're the only one who cares?"

"Of course n—"

"Not all of us want to live in the ancient past, Kell. We could be a lot more, you know. Do more than just drag around the desert and trade the same shit with people who look exactly like us, act exactly like us. We could actually *share* things, *learn* things. What if other people could hear our stories too, huh? Did you ever think about that? Or are our stories too precious for that, other people not good enough?"

"Why would we want others to hear our stories?"

"Because then we'd matter, Kell!" Jor stood up, his body full of frustration and pent energy. "Then places like Soogway would *know* we were People and not just, just—minor inconveniences in the way of their mining operations!"

"You think they care about that?" Kell stood now, too, so she wouldn't feel so small looking up at her brother. With her sore muscles, she stumbled getting up, which only enraged her further.

"They might!" he shouted.

"What gives you any idea they might treat us like People?"

"They're not monsters, Kell. They already give us tech in exchange for—"

"Yes! Exactly! They buy us off with their cheap junk that we don't need and think we'll be distracted by all the pretty lights like the stupid brutes they think we are!" She gestured at Kiche as she said this and immediately regretted it.

"Now wait," said Kiche, holding up his hands as if to ward off Kell's words. "I never said anything about pretty—you asked me, I told you what they—"

"She's right, though," Silaya broke in. "They *are* trying to buy us off."

"And what's wrong with a little trade?" Jor asked, pacing at the edge of the firelight. "Maybe we could use these things in a way that helps us. *Maybe* we could make something even better than they have, and then we'd be the ones to take what *we* want."

"And what do they have that we want?" Kell demanded. She felt horribly exposed and raw, arguing this way in front of two people she barely knew.

"I don't know, Kell. I've never been there before." Jor's voice was low and cold, unfamiliar, and struck Kell with a stab of fear. "But that's what I'm going to find out." He glared at her across the fire, their bodies tensed as if ready to cast. His tattoos flickered in the firelight, a continuation of the night sky.

The fire popped. The scuffles and chitters of small desert creatures made themselves known beyond the perimeter of light. Kell's chest heaved as she willed her breath to remain silent, her eyes locked on her brother. Kiche cleared his throat and rummaged in a pack, drawing out a small bundle wrapped in cloth.

"Tell you one thing they got. They made this." He gestured for Kell to take it, and she did. She sat back down, cross-legged, to unwrap it, and Jor sat as well, though he bounced his foot as the anger left his body. The cloth unfolded to reveal a piece of tech that Kell had never seen before. It was in two parts: one a rectangular brick with a screen, not unlike a happy box. Separate was a small token attached to a thin chain of tiny metal beads. Kell picked this up and poured it from palm to palm. It felt like water and moved like a snake.

"What is it?" she asked, examining the box again. It felt strange to the touch, alive but also dead, like something that had been forced into the world against its will. Her hands grew hot as she touched it, and she worried she might break this, too.

"It's a beacon," Silaya said. "The council said it could take days or even weeks for you to get an audience. Kiche and I can't wait outside the city gates. We will leave you there and come home, and when you are ready for us to come and get you, you turn this on, and we'll come back."

"So, it's like a wayfinder bug but for a person?" Kell shivered. The thought made her faintly ill, as if she'd been touched without consent.

"Basically," Silaya agreed. "But remember that it'll take us a week or more to reach you after you signal us, depending on where our camp heads." Kell nodded. Something about this was making it all feel more real. As bad as the tech felt under her fingers, she was grateful to have a plan for getting home.

Kiche reached for the box in Kell's lap. "That thing, we keep," he said. She handed it over gratefully and held up the token on the chain as if it were a dead scorpion she'd crushed under her bedroll.

"How do you turn it on?"

"Flip it open and push the button," he explained. "Easy." Kiche smiled, and Kell felt a little of the tension in the air melt away. Maybe he'd forgiven her the comment about brutes. She tried a small smile in return.

The token dangling from the chain was round and flat, like a locket. She pressed a thumbnail into the seam around its edge and found that it did flip open, revealing a small red button inside. *Take me home*, she thought. The irony of a piece of tech being her lifeline to the People was not lost on her, and she almost laughed.

"Don't give it to her," Jor said. She looked at him and her smile fled. "She'll just break it. It's what she does."

Kiche raised his eyebrows and let out a low whistle. Silaya just stretched out her long legs, readying for bed. "You two gotta work that shit out," she muttered, wrapping her hair and pulling the edge of her scarf across her eyes.

Kell clicked the locket shut and stared at it for a moment longer before passing it around the fire to Jor. Her eyes met his as she handed it over. Jor put the chain around his neck and slipped the beacon under his shirt.

"He's right," she said.

They let the fire die on its own and all of them readied for bed without saying another word. Kell stared upward at the sky and begged it to take her. Home was no longer safe, so she would rather wander up there, like the Hunter, than remain here and do what was being asked of her. At last, she let go of the earth and the buzzing weight of her body, and drifted through the star-studded dark into sleep.

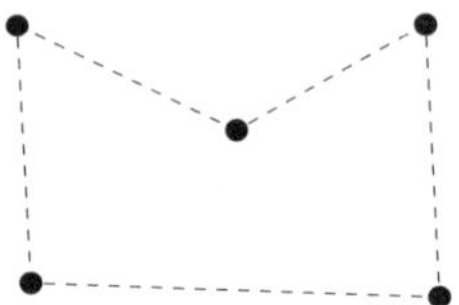

The Suneater: Southwestern quarter, windy season

18. THE CHOKING WAVE

A sound awoke Kell at daybreak, and she sat up stiffly, her hips aflame from their days on horseback. She unwound her scarf from her head and rubbed at her scalp, removing the sand from her hair. Her heart felt tender and hot from the night before, her brother's words no longer stinging but still sore. Kell disliked arguing almost as much as she disliked combat, but arguing in front of others was the worst. She had the sick feeling that something between the four of them may have broken, some fragile sense of purpose and unity. She glanced at Silaya's sleeping face, angular and fierce even in rest. Had Kell lost her chance to be close to her? She rushed to bury the ragged edge of self-pity that surfaced and sought refuge in routine. She would wash and then pray, and everything would feel better.

Kell stumbled to the spring, where she knelt and scooped fresh water onto her face and neck. She drank eagerly from both palms, letting the cool water rinse the sleep from her mind and clear her eyes. The sky to the east was pale pink, like a polished stone, though the rest of the horizon remained shadowed. The others stirred but didn't awaken.

One of the horses—Silaya's, she thought, though both were brown, and she found them difficult to tell apart—let out a series of soft snorts, its ears flicking back and forth. The other was farther from camp, investigating a thicket of desiccated thorns at the base of a small cliff. The horses' front legs had been lightly bound the night before so they couldn't wander too far, but Silaya's mount still paced nervously. Kell was momentarily amazed they hadn't accidentally been trampled while they slept.

A gust of wind brought a brief chill to her neck and sucked all the moisture from her skin, leaving a thin coating of dust behind. She shivered and looked again at the horizon. The dawn was slow in coming. Silaya's horse made another sound, one that raised the hair on Kell's arms. She turned, looking to the west where the night was fleeing.

There were no stars.

"Wake up!"

Kell's shout startled both horses, and they danced nervously, ears back. Kiche was the first to sit up, seeming to rouse instantly. He slipped on his shoes and was on his feet before the other two had fully opened their eyes.

"What—" Jor yawned.

"Sandstorm. From the west. Look."

Kell pointed, but Kiche was already in motion, going after his mount. Silaya began breaking camp as quickly as she could while Jor staggered, looking for his shoes.

"Where should we sink?" Kell asked. They had to choose carefully, or they risked being buried in sand or drowned in a flash flood.

"Can we get to the top of that cliff in time?" Silaya indicated the crag with her chin as she finished buckling her bedroll into the packs.

Jor shook his head. "I don't think so. But we may be able to shelter at its base."

"We don't know how stable that wall is," Kell said as she strapped her own things into a saddlebag.

Kiche approached with the horses. "Sink in place, then?"

They were on the westward side of the rocky spring, so they would be safe from flying branches and other debris. They were close enough to the small cliff at least that it might offer some buffer but far enough that they wouldn't be in danger of rockfall should it collapse.

"What do you do with the horses?" Kell asked. Sandbeasts were native to the desert and its conditions. Surviving sandstorms was in their blood, but Kell had no idea how the horses might fare. Though she knew that horses had been used by the People nearly as long, their sleek legs and restless power seemed suddenly fragile to her. How could such creatures of motion sink in place?

"Is there time?" Kiche asked Silaya. She glanced toward the west where darkness was gathering rather than dispelling and gave a grim nod. The two began setting up low, sturdy variations of the tents. Their movements were quick and sure, anticipating one another like any triangulating pair. Kell blinked and realized she was staring rather than helping.

"Kell!" Jor hissed. He was wrestling alone with another tent, sinking the deep anchors that might prevent it from flying away, burying its stormside edge. She dropped to her knees across from her brother and began anchoring her side of the structure in a mirror of his motions. Its purpose was twofold: to keep sand from their lungs for as long as possible and to preserve a pocket of air in the event that they became buried. Kell had had to dig herself out many times, but it was never an experience she wanted to repeat.

Around them, the wind gathered. Grit was already scouring her exposed skin, though the storm remained miles off. Kell tightened her scarf around her head, covering her ears, nose, and mouth and leaving only a slit for her eyes—though once the winds really hit, she would cover those, as well. The others were doing the same.

She fumbled with the upper support of the low structure then found the correct tension and was gratified when it held. She tested it with the weight of her hand and pushed hard, making sure it could withstand what was coming. Kell caught Jor's eye, and he nodded. Storms were common enough so she wasn't afraid, exactly. But the haste sinking required always brought a flutter of adrenaline to her chest, even as it sharpened her focus. She was relieved to find that the horse People had an identical process for sinking, so little talk was needed once they were all in motion. *The same ancestors guide our hands*, she thought.

The darkness to the west grew, a mimic of nightfall as if the planet had altered its spin, and day was being swallowed in reverse. The storm traveled swiftly, the wall of debris lifted by the winds a visible swirl. The sound of it made the hair on Kell's neck stand on end. As she and Jor sank the stormside edge of a second tent, she thought of the story A'Lan told when they were small. Sandstorms held the spirits of restless ancestors, she'd lamented, those who had been painfully wronged or had made unforgivable choices and were doomed to seek water and rest in the parching wind. Kell herself had never told that story, but the shriek and moan of the storm in the distance sounded just like lost souls to her now.

Gods forgive them and bring them peace, she prayed as she drove the anchors of their tent as deep as she could.

Kiche had led his horse to one of the tents and was tying a soft cloth around its head to protect it from flying sand. Sandbeasts had long lashes that shielded their eyes, and they were able to open and close their nostrils at will. Again, Kell thought the horses were unsuited for the conditions, but she said nothing and marveled when both riders were able to coax the animals into kneeling positions and cover them with the tent flaps.

The wind ripped at them now, causing any unsecured edge to snap and leap wildly. Kiche was shouting something that Kell could not make out through the roar of the approaching storm. She ran through her list in her mind—breath, shelter, water, vision. Kell squinted as she retrieved her pack and shoulder bag and surveyed their sunken camp. Four low tents were now hunched against from the coming darkness like squat beetles. There was nothing left to do but wait.

She knelt and crawled into the nearest tent, shoving her pack into a corner as a pillow. The sound diminished immediately from deafening to merely loud. The scream was gone, replaced by the shushing patter of sand and grit striking the stormside wall. Kell let out a sigh of relief, rolling onto her back and scooting to make room for her brother, who was still retrieving his things outside. The flap opened, and Kell saw with a jolt that it was not Jor who crawled in beside her but Silaya. The fierce woman grinned and cocked an eyebrow.

"Let's let the boys have some quality time, hmm?"

Something in Kell's chest leaped. Incredibly, this beautiful creature still wanted to spend time with her. She exhaled a wordless prayer of gratitude to the ancestors just as Silaya rolled into her, and her breath came out as a snort. Kell was mortified, but Silaya only giggled and shoved her with her elbow.

"You better not snore, though," she teased.

"Gods, you smell better than Jor."

"My horse smells better than Jor."

Their laughter temporarily drowned out the wind.

Kell reached into the side of her pack and drew out a small jar of salve, which she scooped with her finger and rubbed around the edge of her nostrils. She handed it to Silaya, who did the same. They both drank deeply from their canteens and rewrapped their scarves so only their eyes were visible. Side by side in the dim, they lay with the length of their bodies pressed together. The tent walls quaked and groaned as the wind arrived in full force, lashing at them like a desert cat trying to open a tortoise. Kell took measured breaths to slow the pounding of her heart.

"Can I tell you a secret?" Silaya's voice was soft, and Kell strained to hear it beneath the din.

"Of course."

"I hate sinking," she said. "I—I always feel like I'm going to suffocate. When I was little, my mother told me I'd grow out of it, but—" she grew quiet.

To Kell, it was impossible Silaya could be afraid of anything, let alone something as common as a sandstorm. It made her even more beautiful somehow, more real. The chance to comfort her felt rare, and she took it.

"Do you know of the time before the storms?" she asked. Her voice was low, almost a purr. The ancestors who came to her now were very, very old, and she scarcely recognized the sound of them, but she welcomed the story they would help her tell. Silaya shook her head and turned on her side to look at her. Kell raised a palm toward the ceiling of the tent. A warm light glimmered there, casting soft shadows on their faces.

"Our Home is old," she said, feeling the truth of the words in her chest.

"So old," Silaya murmured, adding her strength to the story.

"Our ancestors have found their way through storms and stillness for countless generations, thanks to the gifts of the Pathfinder and the stones. They learned to wander, to know the sands and the space, the springs and the birds."

A tiny, glowing lizard unfurled from her palm and climbed into the air, marching in patient circles above their heads.

"But just as the sands slide to reveal the bones of beasts whose shadows have long lain still, so too do they offer up secrets of the land itself—ancient riverbeds where waters freely ran and sang, stones that were once the trunks of great trees."

The lizard scurried, first tumbled by a flood, then climbing something tall and stately. Silaya's eyes glimmered from between the folds of her scarf, and Kell felt her press her legs more tightly against her own. A thrill raced the length of her, though she felt it at a distance, for the story was taking her. Her body was little more than a future memory as the ancestors filled her with their knowledge.

"See it now, the forgotten face of Home—a rich, dark place cluttered with foliage and branch. Long, long before the stones came, this land was in its infancy, a forest ripe with trees and plants, with the footfalls of pacing creatures and flapping birds. Insects whirred in great clouds, and the ground was a dense, matted thing, thick with roots and vines and difficult to cross. Loud and unruly was this green world. Where we now have the gift of sight, the ability to see for miles in any direction and know the weather and the winds, they had only a few yards before or behind. Their sense of place was thick and busy, and they found their way from trunk to trunk rather than stone to stone."

The lizard's tail stretched long, and its snout grew to accommodate a row of dagger-like teeth. Its tail dragged behind it in a slow swish, leaving a trace of light to fade behind it.

"Here, in this very spot, may once have been a grove, a dim place with thick sentries gathered round, their roots gripping deeply into the dark earth where now pale sands shift and fly. Trees were dense and many then. No sandstorm would budge them. Any storm would have broken against their first line of defense, at the far forest edge. The thickets would rip the wind to tatters there until all that reached this place was a soft breeze, caressing the waterfall that tumbled then from what is now a sere cliff."

The creature elongated further into a serpent, sprouted wings, then spun in carefree, lazy arcs. Kell watched it turn above them, feeling the truth of the story so concretely that she was almost sure the wind outside had stopped, that they would step outside their tents to find not the familiar vastness of the desert but impenetrable woods stretching in every direction. The serpent alit on the ceiling of the shelter and curled into itself, the coil of its body forming a lantern above them.

"Where did the forests go?" Silaya asked. Her voice was rough.

Kell searched her memory for that piece of the story. The ancient lore sometimes came in small packets, rich details easily summoned followed by wide gaps lost to time.

"Drought," she whispered. She reached a hand up and placed it on the tight weave of the tent. It shuddered beneath her palm like an animal. "Fire, cutting." She traced a fingertip above their heads, her skin glowing with storylight. "Time," she said. And then she saw it in her mind: "The rivers went away, hid underground." Another story lurked beneath this one, one she did not remember learning from Ama or A'Lan.

Silaya's hand reached up and covered her own. Her wrist was broader than Kell's, and she slid her hand to fit inside.

"What were they hiding from?" Silaya asked. Kell turned her head to look at her, shifting against her pack. Silaya's eyes burned her, made her feel at once utterly bare and completely secret, as if she had been stripped before the sun but the sole human alive.

"People," Kell murmured, leaning forward into her. The story snake melted and dripped from the ceiling of the tent into her palm. She gathered it in with a twist of her fingers, and darkness came over them. The maelstrom of sand and air outside blotted out the morning light. A relief came over her. The darkness was an invitation, a liberation. She felt Silaya's fingertips drag the length of her arm, then trace upward to her shoulder. She blinked against the grit in the air and knew she should not remove the cloth from her nose and mouth, though she craved this woman's lips more than water, more than air.

She tilted her head until their scarves met and then pressed her forehead into hers. She could hear Silaya's breath quickening, deep and conscious behind the thin material. Kell dropped her hand and wrapped it tightly around the other woman's waist, pulling her close until they were brow to brow, chest to chest. She tilted her pelvis to press into Silaya's and heard her exhale slowly, as if trying to be patient. She felt a hand work under the layers of her tunic, seeking her skin. It found it. Kell gasped. Silaya's fingertips were cold, and she remembered that she had been afraid of the storm. But as Silaya slid her hand up Kell's ribcage, her palm grew warm and then hot, describing her own shape to her in hungry lines.

Kell wrapped one ankle around, dragging Silaya's leg between her own, settling against her thigh and rocking gently as the warm hand found its way to her chest and slipped beneath her bindings. Silaya's thumb dragged across her nipple and a sound escaped Kell that was snatched away by the wind. She circled Silaya's waist with her free leg and cinched their bodies together like a knot, their legs woven and bound. Their hands roved, fumbling in a directionless terrain of frustrating cloth and delicious skin. Kell had to clench her teeth together against the desire to drink Silaya whole, to tear off their protective layers and expose them both, but the need for restraint was a dark thrill of its own, the friction between the rules of the desert and the wants of her body sparking a flame.

Silaya growled in an echo of her own impatience, and Kell felt herself being trapped and spun. The confines of the tent were strict, but Silaya managed to roll atop her with their legs still intertwined, their hips locked together. Then Silaya's hands were suddenly everywhere, her nails raking into the skin of Kell's ribs, her fingertips twisting at her breasts and tugging at the notch at her throat. Her own hands had slid past the other woman's belt and were cupping her ass, pulling her tight as Silaya drove their bodies together, the muscles of her haunches tense and hard beneath her fingers. The pressure made Kell want to scream with joy, and she did. She laughed and sighed and moaned as they weathered the storms inside the tent and out.

"Whenever you get nervous, just remember to breathe."
—Shade's father

19. PRACTICE MAKES PERVERSE

"You're too loud, Rat. How do you expect to hear her if you're the one making all the noise?"

"I know," Shade snapped. They gritted their teeth. Go had plucked "street rat" from their mind and now used it consistently as a term of dubious endearment. Cheap had warned them not to let him in, and now after weeks of training, Shade was only starting to realize how difficult that might be.

Part of Shade ached with relief to be studying under someone again, being the object of attention if not care. It was a warped replica of the days when they had practiced under the guidance of their father, a shadow of the relationship that had once shaped their sense of the fight. As long as Shade could hang on to themself, could protect their core from this man, the shot at the Cycle and its prize money would make it all worthwhile. It had to.

Shade danced in place to loosen the tension in their shoulders and then resumed the position, one foot ahead of the other in a slight crouch, casting hand back and palm open. The girl across from them smirked and mirrored their stance.

"Go ahead," she sneered. "Try again." She was about their age, they guessed, and she wasn't great at combat, but Shade needed someone to practice on, and she was content with the pocket change Go had offered in return. Shade hadn't bothered to learn her name. Instead of sparring with Shade himself, Go hired an endless parade of street urchins for Shade to battle, though they never fought any of them more than once.

Shade narrowed their eyes. Their pride urged them to lash at her like a snake. Left to their own techniques, they knew they could swallow this girl whole, unhinge their jaw and devour her as easily as an egg. It was all this other business they were struggling with, the weird backdoors Go was bent on teaching them. Shade did not like the way these things felt, nor did they enjoy not being good at things. In fact, this entire apprenticeship was distasteful—if "apprentice" was what they were and not a dog, a weapon for Go to wield against the council.

Go glared at them over the head of their opponent, his eyes a warning. Shade took a breath. *No snakes. Time to be a weed.*

The girl had begun her story, the glimmer of it already pooling and spilling between her fingers. Her style irked them—she ended every sentence as if it were a question, which triggered in Shade the urge to answer. Anything that distracted was an annoyance.

Get still. Go down.

Shade's lips moved through the motions of their story—a basic folktale about a traveling musician, something simple they could do in their sleep—but they let their consciousness sink down their body into the soles of their feet. It was a strange feeling, leaving behind their mind in the middle of telling, though it proved easier than they'd first thought. A geometric glow sprouted from their casting palm.

Down, they forced themself.

When their awareness arrived at the floor, they pooled together as much strength as they could and began to push forward, through the concrete of the warehouse, just as Go had shown them. The floors were damp, and a disagreeable smell of mildew and copper hung in the air. Shade pushed again, trying to aim for the girl's feet and keep from scattering through the ground. It felt like blowing into thick liquid with a small straw, only with their whole body. Very unpleasant.

Above, their folktale had emerged as a small monkey with butterfly wings and several fluffy tails. It sprang from their hand and leaped around the room, toying with the fish-cat the girl had sent swimming through the air. The fish-cat sprouted long, needle-sharp fangs beneath its whiskers, and the monkey swung casually away on an invisible vine, its glowing wings fanning the air.

Shade's consciousness sat like a willful puddle below, waiting, pressing forward. It was disorienting, thinking through the ground. They had the vague impression of being crushed, yet they were the one doing all the pushing. At last, they felt something new, a very faint pulse above them through the floor.

It's working! they thought.

The excitement of it almost shot them back into their own head, but they hung on stubbornly to the spot where they could sense the girl above them. It was frightening and gross, somehow, being in both places at once. A part of Shade could feel their mouth working, feel the story tumbling out as easily as spitting melon seeds. But another part was here, in the cold concrete, listening to their opponent's heartbeat. Shade was quite sure she had no idea what was happening—or what would come next. They weren't either, when it came down to it.

Nausea hit them, hard and sudden—the part of themself that was in their body fought back the urge to retch. Go had warned them about this, had told them it would go away with practice, but Shade was finding it difficult to focus because of it. They had the sensation they were suffocating, though they knew their body was unscathed and breathing normally—only their awareness was trapped in the floor. A fist of panic gripped them.

Keep moving, Shade steadied themself. *What had Go said? Plant your root, and grow like a weed.*

They felt their awareness slipping away at the edges, running this way and that. It was like trying to gather spilled milk on a tabletop. Shade pulled the puddle of themself together into the densest pool they could, focusing on the pulse of the girl's heartbeat. It was faint, but audible—or maybe *sensible*. They could hear it, though not exactly with their ears. And then they pushed upward, straining against the immense weight above. Nothing happened.

Shade bore down as forcefully as they could to create tension. This brought on the embarrassing impression that they were trying very hard to move their bowels with the effort of their entire body. Compression strained their thoughts. While the concrete was porous and pregnable, whatever was above them—*It's her feet. You know what it is. You're pushing against her feet*—was not.

Shade pushed again. Nothing. It was like trying to lift a building. The pressure was overwhelming now, and the nausea intensified. Sweat traced down their skin, and their knees and teeth trembled. As if from a distance, they heard Go's voice, angry and sharp.

"Not like that, Rat! You'll blow your brains out. A weed, dammit. A weed!"

A weed.

Shade stopped pushing. Their monkey moved lazily through the air as the fish-cat snapped and lashed, swimming in angry circles though the monkey scarcely paid it attention. The girl looked furious, but Shade only faintly registered this, their eyes offering their mind little more than flickers between stretches of black. Shade wondered vaguely if they were going to pass out.

I'm not a puddle, they told themself. *I'm a seed. A tiny, stubborn seed.*

The spilling, spreading sensation abated. They felt themself condense further, and the feeling of pressure increased. Somehow, it also felt less like they might suffocate, as if they had made room for themself by drawing in.

A seed. Shade pictured themself smaller than a nut, just a speck, a germ of potential. Their stomach recoiled, flooding their throat with bitter acid. From a great distance, a part of their mind noticed that they were approaching the climax of their folktale, where the wealthy merchant would be tricked by the sounds of the musician's instruments. A hot slice of pain crowned their head and abated just as suddenly.

There was a soft popping sensation. Something like cobwebs, a tearing of rotted cloth or gristled joints coming apart. A delicious stretch, a wiggle upward. The concrete had disappeared. The girl's heartbeat was much, much louder now, as if the walls of the warehouse struck with every pulse. Shade felt themself shoot up, unfurling and growing like—*like a weed.*

They were in.

Belatedly, Shade realized they'd never paid quite enough attention to what was to happen next, but they knew it would be quick. Their mind buzzed with a thousand strange sensations—their body murmuring their story, their knees watery, the monkey dropping invisible fruit onto the irate fish-cat and flinging imaginary poo. Shade's own heart felt impossibly distant, while that of a stranger, its rhythm foreign and accelerating, thundered around them.

Something about the breath, they remembered. Another wave of nausea wrenched their body double. They could see the floor, see the girl's feet, see themself inside—*what*? They retched.

The girl was saying something now but it wasn't her story. Her voice sounded strange, and the ends of her sentences went down, not up. The fish-cat wavered. It flopped on its side in the air.

Shade drove further upward. Behind the girl's heartbeat, they could feel something bigger, like tides pulling the river high and low. There was a rush, a great bellows. The girl's breath.

Catch it, they thought.

It was unclear how a weed might steal another's breath, Shade's mind said. But Shade no longer felt they had much say in what was happening—whatever story they were involved with, they weren't the one telling it. They felt themself expanding as the girl breathed in, elongating as the girl breathed out. A weed that thrived on breath. Shade stretched into her, tendrils creeping along what must have been veins—*Don't think about it*—until they could feel all the way to her skin, sense what she was sensing from the inside out. Breathe what she was breathing. Was she still breathing? Shade was breathing. Shade was breathing her. They could hear something. Was that screaming? She couldn't get the words out—the breath was all theirs, now. Shade felt a terrible surge of panic, fear coursing past them, and realized it was not their own. The thought came then that they wanted to stop being a weed and weren't sure how to get out. Like an unchecked vine, the girl's frantic breath was making them grow and grow and grow.

The girl's heartbeat sounded like drums now, many drums, rumbling and syncopated and much too fast. Shade felt her terror as if it were their own. Flashes from their eyes registered the whites of hers, the fish-cat flailing and gasping for air. The monkey, too, was . . . wrong. It was larger now, swelling. Each of its arms was the size of Shade's body, its wings now less like a butterfly's and more like the broad fins of a sailfish, sharp spines jutting through stretches of leathery flesh. Shade felt themself bursting at the tips, a rootbound plant cracking through a pot. There was a rushing sound as they gathered an enormous breath and held it, lest they split through the skin of the urchin girl.

Shade felt their chest might pop, but they held their breath as tightly as they could, sending it into their roots. They could feel themself tapping back into the floor, branching downward now. Their blood fizzed as if the air had turned to bubbles in their veins. Tiny lights flickered in their vision, and they gagged again. Which body was theirs? The warehouse around them was swimming. The fish-cat was not. It drifted in the air belly up, turning slowly as if caught in a current. Shade closed their eyes. Something black was seeping up from the floor, a thick tar sucked up by their roots. They were no longer a weed.

A tree, they thought. Then, *I'm going to drown.* And the black sludge covered their eyes.

When Shade came to, they were lying on the ground. Back in their own body, they were soaking wet and chilled, the floor beneath them impossibly hard. They blinked. A massive glowing gorilla with aquatic fins and several lashing lion's tails sat cross-legged on the concrete, messily devouring a fish. A girl Shade didn't know was screaming, red-faced, her breath coming in ragged, panicked gasps.

"What was that!" she sobbed. "What *was* that! What are you people *doing!*" Nothing she said now sounded like a question. She was shaking, digging in her pockets.

"Take it back!" she shrieked, throwing whatever she had retrieved onto the floor. A handful of ironwood chips clattered to the ground. Shade closed their eyes again and heard her frantic footsteps ringing through the empty warehouse as she ran, still sobbing and struggling for breath. "*There's something really, really wrong with you!*" she howled and slammed the door behind her.

Softer footsteps approached. Shade opened their eyes. Go stood above them, his face dark. He sucked his front teeth as he looked down at them, considering.

"That was pretty stupid, Rat." His voice was soft, like a knife wrapped in felt.

Shade threw up.

"It's not always about the outcome, you know. How you win matters, too."
—Shade's father

20. FRINGE BENEFITS

The river that tumbled down the distant Kushan Mountains, full of angry, icy force, cut its way through the Broken Forest, stalled by log jams, dropping over cliffs, and pooling into backwaters, before arriving at the agricultural reaches of the Nong Plateau, where it was diverted and flooded through countless fields. Shade's father had loved the river back home but mourned what it became once it entered the city. By the time it reached Soogway, it had warmed and fouled to a sluggish green, a dragon reduced to a filthy worm. It crawled past the docks and warehouses of the city's Shipping District, emitting rank smells of algae and dung.

Rickety stone piers sprouted from the edge of the water like the ribs of an abandoned carcass left in the sun. Small boats poled along its surface, moving baskets of fish to market or to popular spots like the gator hole. Flat barges ferried produce, often wilted upon arrival by ox cart to the taxable confines of the city. The docks were busy most times of day, a bustling mix of merchants and longshorefolk, porters and fishers and stevedores.

Shade liked the sounds of the place, the shouts and hails from water to shore and back again, the clank of blocks and pulleys and the creaking of lines. It was different from the noise of the city proper, of haggling at markets, crowds, and buzzing signs. Shade had taken to strolling along the docks, liberating small amounts of produce to redistribute among the street kids they looked after. It helped them think, and lately, they had a lot to think about.

They hadn't been back to see Go since. Part of them wanted to crow with triumph that they had managed to root into the girl's feet, but where glory should have been in their chest, they felt only a queasy sense of having done something unforgivable. *There's something really, really wrong with you.*

They shivered. The smell of fish in the warm day drifted around them and added to the unpleasantness of their stomach. So far, Go had taught them more than Shade had bargained for. They could match a chanter's rhythm and disrupt it. They could shift their telling from narrative to rhetoric midstream and dissect an opponent's story with analytical blades. And they could travel short distances through the floor and eavesdrop on an opponent's heartbeat. Shade hadn't determined how this might be useful to them beyond the breath trick, but they felt there had to be a way to turn it to their advantage on the streets as well as the arena. Stealing the breath like that was only supposed to stall their rival's story—to make them lose their place or rob them of a key line. It wasn't supposed to—

It wasn't supposed to kill them, they thought. *I could have killed her. I could have split that girl in two or choked her from the inside.* That wasn't what storytelling was about, was it?

It's combat. But the whole point of story combat is that nobody is actually harmed, right?

Shade stopped on the edge of a pier, looking out over the water as it moved in slow whorls. Water green was nothing like tree green. They fished a pebble out of their shoe and tossed it into the river, watching it sink too slowly in water thick as goo. They pictured themself in the arena, knew that they were adding to their skill set in frightening and likely unstoppable ways. They were already good—Shade knew that. But Go's tricks would make them damn near unbeatable, they thought. That was what they'd wanted, wasn't it?

To compete in the Cycle. To win enough money to leave this place.

They imagined Cheap in the audience. What would he think of a win like that? The old man was often a puzzle to them, more riddle than joke. Shade commanding the arena, slicing through the stories of the other combatants, stalling their rhythms and snatching unuttered words from their chests. Their parents in the crowd watching—would their father be proud of what Shade could do, things he'd never dreamed of teaching them, things he no doubt never even thought possible?

Their father had always been one for rules, and for keeping things simple and up front. Using heart stories was as low as he would go. Even as a combat teller, Shade's father had felt that honor mattered more than winning—and look where that got him. Shade took a deep breath, clarity entering their thoughts for the first time in a long while, and felt a stab of shame. Even a shot at the Cycle wasn't worth this confusion. They would go back to fighting the ways they knew best, on their own and far from the arena. They would earn their money for the trip back to the Broken Forest the old-fashioned way—by stealing it.

Absentmindedly, Shade fingered the acorn through their shirt and felt a little lighter. They weren't sure yet how to handle Mr. Go, but they figured they'd give it a few more days and a plan would come. Go was a busy man. And after that last mess, he was probably just as eager to be rid of Shade as they were of him.

What Shade needed right now was something familiar, a little boost of energy. The blocks near the pier held a few clusters of commerce—the Fresh Quarter, which was nothing but city-run produce stalls, and a handful of wholesale outlets for goods. They decided to see what was new in the greens department, in case their friend down here could skim some for Shade to resell elsewhere at more reasonable prices than the government stalls offered.

Shade strode down the concrete alleys that lanced away from the river like capillaries, trying to look like someone who might make purchases. It didn't take long for the dock sounds to give way to the roll of cartwheels, for the calls of porters to become the shouts of hawkers announcing the arrival of onions, greens, fruit. The Fresh Quarter was an open plaza bordered by warehouses that stocked all the goods that came in off the docks. Each was guarded by a number of safes and their units, and the structures themselves buzzed with electricity, housing the produce to be sold in the Quarter.

They knew a few folks who had tried to nab some apples directly from a warehouse once; it had gone poorly. Instead, Shade's friend at the docks often let them know what was on the barges and sometimes grabbed a handful of the bruised and wilted stuff that fell off the pallets. Shade ran errands for him in exchange for these castoffs, which they sold outside of Cheap's stand or used for trade instead of homespun falsies. People would pay a lot for a nice bunch of turnips or a bruised peach.

The tables in the plaza were piled high with roots and tubers—carrots, parsnips, taro, potatoes, beets of every color, ginseng, and dark, twisted clumps that Shade could not identify. One corner of the market was dedicated to fresh herbs and sold small, discolored bundles of every imaginable variety. Shade's eyes slid across the expanse of them. Though the tables were shaded with protective canopies of cloth and plastic, these herbs had long since left the ground and had given up their crispness for exhaustion. Shade recognized a few of the leaves as plants they'd seen growing in gutters and on rooftops and thought of Ma Bud. How many illicit herb gardens around the city had Shade mistaken for weeds?

There was a commotion in one corner of the market, and Shade turned to see a handful of dignitaries from the city government, recognizable by their long red robes and wide straw hats. They reminded Shade of ducks on a concrete pond, gliding between the tables with their hands clasped behind their backs as the small entourage behind them quacked and jumbled busily. As the vendors crowded toward them, Shade took advantage of the moment to edge closer.

As always, the servants formed a protective flank around the dignitaries to prevent unwanted interactions. Officials rarely carried their own money, anyway. It was the lackeys and handmaidens in plain white garb that they focused on. Shade lingered over a pile of radishes while studying the group out of the corner of their eye. One of the robed figures made a purchase, a cluster of carrots that looked to still have a crunch to them, and a small page in a white tunic and pants scurried forward to offer payment to the vendor, a chip purse bouncing at their waist. It was a satchel, embroidered with beads of glass and real wood. Its top flap was fixed in place with a wooden toggle. It was almost too easy.

The money bearer returned to the rear of the entourage as the dignitary munched his carrot with a flourish, affirming loudly how fresh and delightful city produce was. Shade worked their way closer, keeping their gaze on the tables and murmuring small pleasantries to the vendors, who were unconvinced by Shade's pretense. They lingered over a mound of small blue potatoes, forcing the dignitaries and their ducklings to jostle by.

The red robes smelled of burned resins and flower oils as they brushed against the back of Shade's rough-woven jacket. They were tall, all of them, and for a moment, Shade had the impression of being stuffed in a wardrobe, buffeted by shoulders and cloth as they passed. The red gave way to white, and Shade cast a deft hand toward the satchel as it went by. They had only a second to work the toggle and reach in—and the toggle wouldn't give. Something held it in place, a hidden second loop or catch that Shade's eye had missed. The catch snagged Shade's finger mid-grasp, and as the page strode past, it yanked the satchel with it. The page yelped as the bag's strap jerked them backward. Shade tried to slip their hand free but found their finger was trapped. The entire company had halted at the page's shout and turned to see Shade with their outstretched arm tangled in the coin purse hanging at an incriminating angle away from the page's neck.

Shade was paralyzed in a blur of panic. *Think, Rat, think!*

Some part of their mind flinched at Go's voice in their head, but it was quickly drowned out by the bellow of a lackey in white.

"THIEF!"

Merciless columns of ivory cloth pressed them into a table of cassava, surrounding them like thick gaol bars. Shade's rat heart thudded so fast it became a vibration in their chest, threatening to explode. Their hands suddenly slick with sweat, they realized they were free of the satchel, but the damage was already done. Faces atop the crush of white scowled and hands reached for them as Shade's eyes darted, searching for a means of escape.

The plaza had stilled, the vendors and buyers all watching Shade and their captors. Murmurs passed through the crowd like one giant animal, shifting in its sleep. Shade heard hard footsteps against the cobbles from several directions, and the white wall parted.

Shade could see a flash of red as the ducklings reassembled around the dignitaries, who had scarcely noticed the goings on. Before the ring sealed once more around them, Shade saw one red-gloved hand exhibiting a yam to another, whose broad straw brim bowed in appreciation. The safety officer who reached Shade first had a large black cat as its unit, just smaller than a panther, though Shade had no doubt it could grow. It bared its teeth in a snarl that matched exactly the look on the safe's face. A second safe flanked the first, a dog at his heels, and then a third arrived with an enormous falcon on her outstretched wrist. All the units fixed Shade with glowing eyes.

Shade wondered briefly how they could snatch the breath of more than one opponent at a time, but they were far too terrified to focus in this moment, something they'd have to work on if they were going to compete in the Cycle. Any tricks they pulled now, they would still be cornered here with a hundred witnesses. This rat was fully caught in a trap.

The three safety officers towered above them, faces hard as clubs. These were no drunken street pacers—these were a special operations unit tasked with guarding imperial property. Shade contemplated playing blind and deaf. They blinked hugely and began concocting a preposterous story about having merely stumbled into the page. It was stupid but as good a plan as any.

The safe at the front took a step toward Shade and readied his unit, his casting palm tensed at his waist. The panther crouched, its haunches settling as if it would very much enjoy pouncing on its prey. The dog paced, flanking Shade. The officer holding the falcon watched them with slitted eyes before giving a low whistle, and the other two looked to her for a moment. She nodded. Dog snapped his fingers and fed something to his unit from a pouch at his waist. Panther began to murmur an accusation story—"You're a thief, having committed crimes against the City of Soogway, your protector and provider. You have violated the community trust . . . " His voice had the mechanical boredom of one who has repeated a tale so many times their words had lost all meaning.

Shade dropped their blind act and considered whether they might be able to disrupt the safe's litany—after all, the rhythm had much in common with a chant—and noted how much Go's teachings had already altered their thinking. There were so many possibilities for intervention, they admitted bitterly. *Too bad I'll never get a chance to use them.* Shade didn't bother offering a counternarrative of innocence. What would be the point? The entourage had moved away from the scene, their indifference to the outcome a testimony to how little Shade mattered in the world.

The safe completed his story and cuffed Shade on the shoulder, knocking them to the ground. The force of it winded them, and as their cheek met the flagstones, Shade realized how rare it was they experienced aggression outside the arena. Their panic chilled into real fear. Shade pulled themself onto their hands and knees, but the dog slinked up beside them, its shoulders a foot higher than their own. Its tremendous jaws lunged at Shade's hands where they were planted on the ground. Shade felt an electrical shock and discovered their wrists had been bound with thick manacles of glowing light, something they had witnessed but never experienced firsthand. As their brain struggled to understand what, exactly, held them, Panther kicked them in the stomach, and without the use of their hands, Shade hit the ground hard. They closed their eyes against the rough cobbles.

"Get up," said the falconer. They opened their eyes and saw her staring, her gaze a perfect replica of her bird's, as if both would as soon eat them as take them into custody. Shade feared they would be sick, but they pulled themself up onto their knees and came awkwardly to their feet. The dog jerked its head, and Shade realized their manacles were attached to a glowing leash, the end of which the dog held in its mouth.

The falconer cut a path through the plaza, under the tarps and awnings that snapped in the breeze off the river. Panther shoved Shade from behind, and they followed after the falconer, the four-legged units on either side, one holding Shade on a leash, and their safes at the rear. It was a dark parody of the city entourage, and they could feel the eyes of the vendors on their back as they passed, feel the heat of their scorn and their collective relief at having the safes leave.

The company turned a corner into an alley beside a warehouse, and the falconer pushed open an unassuming door that slid on a track. Shade followed her inside, their eyes adjusting to the dim. They were surrounded by countless bamboo pallets of greens, including a wall of crates that contained small crimson globes packed in leaves. Shade blinked. Radishes.

The falconer's bird leaped from her arm and wound slow circles in the stale air of the warehouse, the glow of its wings revealing a network of pipes on the distant ceiling. Here it was much cooler than outside, mechanically chilled to protect the produce. Shade wondered vaguely how that worked and what powered it. Their face and shoulder ached where they had hit the ground, and their panic had drained away, leaving them sapped and shaky in the knees. Panther slid the door shut behind them.

The falconer nodded to Dog, who muttered something to the unit holding Shade's leash. The dog coughed, and the leash evaporated. Shade felt a new chill at their wrists, and the manacles disappeared as well. The falconer crossed her arms and eyed Shade, her mouth twisted as if they smelled particularly bad today, though they had washed their jacket the day before.

They rubbed their wrists where the manacles had been, glancing uneasily between the falconer and Panther, whose unit continued to stare at Shade like a snack. No one said anything for several minutes, and Shade's fear turned to tedium. They counted the crates out of habit. They scanned idly for another exit and found none. Dog and his unit were behind them, but Shade didn't dare turn to look.

At last, Dog spoke. "That long enough?" His voice was gruff and slow.

The falconer pursed her lips. "It'll have to be," she sighed.

Shade heard the door roll open again. The falcon landed silently on the safe's arm. It folded its wings and glared at Shade. Again, their expressions matched uncannily.

Panther grimaced. "Let's at least mark 'em," he growled. The big cat elongated in an unhurried stretch, extending giant, luminous paws. It began to clean itself.

"Go said not a scratch," said the falconer.

Shade snapped to attention, their heart hammering again.

Panther made a rough noise of impatience, and his unit paused, tongue extended. Then a thrill of disbelief began to course up Shade's belly.

"Leave," said the falconer, her voice an ice pick.

Shade stared.

"Before she changes her mind," Panther said, his lip curling.

"Make sure you're not seen," she added.

Shade straightened their braids with a pat and strolled toward Dog, and the door, their head held high. They passed a stack of radish crates on a pallet and reached in, tearing off a cool red orb. They paused, looking at the safe and his unit.

"Don't push it, you little shit."

Shade shrugged and popped the whole radish into their mouth, then walked freely into the sunshine.

MA'SHIFRA SPEAKS: MUD GOLEMS

How lucky am I, to live in a camp with so many well-behaved children. None of you would ever wander off, out of sight of the elders. None of you would ever sneak into the dark to test your Way at Ease without your teacher, to play at finding the path home to where the fires burn and the songs are sung and the stories told. No, I am lucky. I live in a camp where children know about mud golems.

What's that? You don't remember? You want me to tell you again?

Such forgetful children . . . over and over, "Ama, tell us about the mud golems."

Well. If you insist. Just because you are so well behaved and would never run away. Because you listen to your families and are helpful and strong.

How lucky are we, to live lives filled with meaning. We remember what our ancestors have told us. We find our way when the stars are hidden, when the Falcon cannot guide us or the Pathfinder is lost to the clouds. We share stories so that our hearts are big and full and hold the many worlds within us all.

Not everyone is so lucky, you know. Jackal sings and yips, but she cannot tell her pups about the making of the moon. Snake hisses and writhes but can only warn—he does not know how to explain why *the mouse should run. We are lucky to be People, to carry light that we shape with the help of the gods and our ancestors.*

There are other beings that walk upright who are not so lucky. When the gods made our People, they scooped us from the lake beds, shaped us from rich mud squirming and teeming with life. They formed us and whispered the stories into us, baked us in the sun so that our skins dried in every color of the earth—brown and ocher, red and rose, tan and black and pale as dust. We are the bodies of change and of growth. We carry experience and song.

But some beings were afraid of the stories and the sun. They did not want to be filled with light or baked under the heat of day. They climbed out from the lakebed and shambled off while the gods were busy giving life to the rest. They hid from their gifts, they slipped away from the gods, and still they roam.

Golems, these creatures are. Not People, not beasts. Made of mud but unfinished, they shuffle and groan, moved only by fear and ill will. They are damp, hollow, incomplete. They are hungry, lacking meaning to feed them, having no stories to show them the way. They wander only in darkness, hiding deep in caves in the daytime and emerging at night to seek out those children from unlucky camps, the ones who disobey and venture far from the fires where they are safe. The golems detest the fire, fearing becoming baked as People are, lurking instead in the shadows where their skins remain damp and sticky, raw mud wet with stink and solitude.

What do they do with the children?

Well, lucky are we that we never have to find out. None of you would ever be so foolish as to let yourself be taken by a mud golem, now, would you? No, thank the ancestors. How lucky I am to live in a camp with such wise little children.

• •

The Dark Star: Northeast, late springs

21. THE WRONG FOREST

Kell's feet were sore. They had left behind the flat reaches of the desert, and the terrain they now crossed was dust and gravel, rough and unpredictable under her soles. Not to mention that they had been walking for well over a week now, doubling the time the trip was supposed to have taken. That week was one in which more pulsar stones may have been ripped out of the earth by the city's machines, a week in which their shared frustrations had brought the four of them closer together and also farther apart. The determined chatter of the first days following the sandstorm had given way to a long, commiserative silence, in which each plodded along to the beat of their own thoughts.

It was Kiche's horse who hadn't made it. It had been horrible to watch the swiftness with which it had been put down, the smell of its hair burning on the pyre they'd constructed. The memory of it made her skin crawl.

The storm had passed in a matter of hours, but they had needed to dig themselves out, a task that only worsened Silaya's panic. When they had finally emerged from the dune that had gathered around them, they found the horse with breath ragged and eyes wild, struggling and still half buried. It had broken both its forelegs in the attempt to free itself. Kiche, who had known his horse's name, felt the animal's anguish as his own. He had ended its misery with a blade to its neck, cradling its head in his lap as he wept. The blood had poured forth and spread into the sand around him like a shadow.

Kiche and Silaya spent the rest of that morning conducting their ritual of passing as Kell and Jor gathered firewood at Kiche's request. When a sandbeast died away from camp, its meat was taken, as was its blood. Its long guard hairs were cut and bundled for weaving, and if there was time, even the hide would be salted and saved. It seemed the People who rode horses did not have the same sense of frugality, and Kell had wrinkled her nose at the waste of these resources. Some of their cooking oil was sacrificed as the horse was put to flame. Perhaps when your mounts were faster, you didn't need to conserve such things, as you would quickly reach another oasis or caravan for trade. Kell watched the carcass smolder and catch and frowned at the wasted flesh. The ancestors' teachings were clear: sufficiency and security are created, not promised.

It took a long time for the horse to burn. The urgency to continue on toward the city had dragged on Kell, making her clench her teeth, though she understood the importance of honoring a lost mount. She and Jor had wordlessly busied themselves with small tasks of cleaning and repair while the black smoke billowed into the sky, the stench of it stinging her eyes. Kiche changed his clothes and sandbathed before he and Silaya sang their song of leave-taking. It was similar to the one Kell's camp sang, she noted, though she and Jor were not invited to sing along. As she waited, Kell had scrubbed the blood from Kiche's clothes with sand and prayed.

May the ancestors find this beast's spirit running freely. May it ever outrun the storm.

Now their pace had slowed by more than half. Silaya's horse carried the bulk of the packs while the People made their way on foot. Kell and Jor took their turn as wayfinders, and though they sang the Way in Haste, their haste was imperceptible to Kell. She longed for the sensation of speed they'd had on horseback. The threat of time lost, of further stones lost, felt like it might choke her as the wayfinding serpent the Way had created led them past the edges of the desert. The ground grew harder and more solid until it was replaced entirely by rock. Gradually, the colors deepened from ambers and golds into reds and browns, from barren soil to lichen and finally to vegetation and scrub. Each step they took was now the farthest Kell had ever been from the desert.

Kell felt as if she had left herself behind in the dunes and was now someone new and strange in the unfamiliar terrain. Her hands seemed different with grasses beneath them, her gait altered without the sand beneath her feet. Under clouded skies, her dark skin looked duller without the glow of the desert sun. There was a growing distance she did not know how to bridge between herself and her sense of the world, a hollow space where she felt her heart should be, and she moved as if without will over her own body. Kell felt drawn forward as inexorably as if she were a character in someone else's telling.

Kiche's warm banter had been chilled by grief, and Jor walked beside him in companionable silence most of the time. Jor seemed to know when to make quiet conversation and when to remain still, sometimes with a hand on the other man's shoulder or elbow. Kiche's smile returned slowly, warming to the attentive care.

In contrast, Silaya now ran unpredictably hot and cool. Her vulnerability that night in the tent had been replaced with a stoicism that Kell found difficult to penetrate as they picked their way across the terrain hand in hand.

"What will you do while we're petitioning in the city?" Kell asked. Her palm was damp, and she tried in vain not to feel self-conscious.

"Return to our own camp," Silaya said simply, as if it were obvious. "Seek out other camps along the way to let them know about the stones. The Soogway ambassador may not have reached them all."

"What if you stayed in the city?" Kell asked, squeezing Silaya's fingers in a sudden rush of hope. "Came with us? Sent Kiche back with your horse?"

Silaya looked at her blankly. "Why would I do that?"

"I—I don't. . .I guess I thought—"

"We need to be ready," Silaya said.

"Ready for what, exactly?" Kell released her hand and wiped her palm on her pants.

"What if the Temple refuses Jor's request?" Silaya's horse stumbled on a loose rock, and she nearly dropped the reins. An image of frail legs fracturing, of carrying their own packs the rest of the way struck Kell, and she sucked in a breath. Silaya murmured encouragement to the animal and continued, "What then?"

Kell thought for a long moment before answering, "Then I guess I fight." In truth, she was afraid.

How many hours had she spent practicing with Ma'Shifra, copying the words and the gestures until they were right, learning all the ways to let the ancestors enter her body and use her voice? How many of their tales did she know by now? Yet somehow, her entire life of dedication and study felt inadequate to the task at hand. The stories that filled her were those of history and memory, of ritual and lore. Not of combat.

Ancestors, guide my thoughts.

Kell startled when Jor shouted, "Look!"

They had rounded a small hill, and beyond it lay a valley swathed in green. They all stopped. From the where they stood, they saw only treetops below. A forest filled the valley, a vast emerald beast sleeping in its basin. A nudge of a breeze raced down the hillside, ruffling the beast's fur like a hand stroking a pelt. For Kell, descending into the valley would mean entering another land altogether, one that was sighing and alive with vegetation.

She had never seen a true forest before. She had been to the Riverlands, of course, where bushes clustered around the waters. And her camp had visited plenty of oases in their travels, seen thickets of thorn trees in the yellow zone and small clusters of palms in the red, not to mention the broad canopies and trunks of the great Walking Trees that roamed the stonier parts of the desert, but this before her was something different. It was so dense she was sure she could walk across the top of it like a carpet in a bazaar.

"We're going through the woods?" Kell asked no one in particular. The idea both thrilled her and prompted a small spike of anxiety. What would it be like not to see the sky under so many leaves?

"That's the road," Kiche said. "It starts here and goes through quick. We come out the other side of the valley."

The road. Another new thing for Kell. There were some well-traveled routes in the stonier parts of Home but none like this pathway carved into the bedrock itself. It was surfaced in cobble and crusted the land like a scab. She couldn't say why a road felt less reliable than the guidance of the Way at Ease or the Way in Haste, but it did. She supposed it was that the Way was mutable, adaptive. It changed depending upon conditions. A road felt strangely constrained. She and Jor let the guiding serpent dissipate and gathered what storylight was left into their palms. Silaya led the horse down into the valley, its hooves clopping loudly on the cobbles. Kell and the others followed.

As they drew closer, what had seemed to be a lush, wild place organized itself into orderly rows. Where Kell had envisioned a rich tangle of species, she saw only straight, wavering trunks that shot upward to towering heights, splitting toward their tops into great plumes of thin, shuddering leaves. As they walked, the rows repeated with unnerving regularity, as if they were moving through a counting table. The branches whispered overhead, but there was no birdsong, no rustle or call of animals. It filled Kell with unease.

"Why is it like this?" she asked. If Kiche had intended to answer, his response was interrupted by a metallic shriek that sliced through the air. The horse balked, and Silaya soothed it, though she, too, was visibly shaken.

"What *was* that?" Jor asked. The sound came again, followed by a series of heavy crashes. There was shouting ahead. Kell's heart raced, and she whirled around, glaring at Kiche as if he were responsible for the road, and therefore, any dangers to which it led.

"We have to turn around!" she hissed. She didn't know what sort of monsters lurked here, but beasts lacked story and so attacked with tooth and claw. Her combat tales would do nothing.

"Relax," Kiche said, offering her a smile. "That's what they do in these places."

"What *who* do?"

"People," he said mildly. "These folks, this is what they do. You'll see." He continued onward, and the rest had no choice but to follow. The hideous shriek continued intermittently, punctuated with further crashes and shouts.

They rounded a bend in the road and saw a great metal cart piled high with the trunks of trees and another with foliage. A team in matching blue clothes worked busily: two on a side, they gripped a massive machine and guided it down a row of trees. At its center was a slicing wire, a blur of knives, that cut neatly through the trunks as if they were made of fat. The trees toppled in sequence, one after the next, before another team in blue fell upon them wielding smaller mechanical saws, stripping branches from the trunks and loading them these onto the carts. Sunshine poured into the newly made clearing, aggressive and pale after the filtered light of the canopy.

"So, they just . . . *take it*?" Kell asked. "Does it grow back?"

"Sometimes," Kiche said. "It's not really a forest, you know. More like a farm. Bamboo grows real fast, so they plant it and cut it as quick as they can."

A farm. Hence its uniform strangeness, the lack of any creatures or other species. Although green was not common in the reaches of Home, she found she craved the feeling of nature taking the lead. Things growing under such tight control, cultivated for the ease of machines, felt distasteful to Kell.

Also, she was disappointed not to see a wild forest, she realized, and the thought surprised her. Home had always been plenty, with its endless varieties of stone and sand, yellows, ochers, reds, browns, and the powdery whites of the salt flats in the pale zone of the far north, where the desert was cold and featureless and had few stones to lead the way. She had never wanted more than what she had.

Gods be thanked.

The road through the trees was nearly too narrow for the horse and the carts both, the bamboo too densely packed in its rows to penetrate, so they awkwardly negotiated passing the work crew. It was not long before they came to a completely logged stretch of the forest—*the farm*, Kell corrected herself—and the sounds of the cutting machine faded to a distant whine.

On the other side of the valley, they climbed through a narrow pass in the hills and found themselves in a broad grassland, the road visible as far as the eye could see. A scar leading through a dun-colored prairie.

"Not too far now," Kiche said. Kell whispered a prayer of gratitude to the ancestors even as she swallowed a lump of dread.

That evening, they sat around their final fire together as a group.

"Tell a story," Silaya said. The rasp of her voice made Kell feel as if she were made of wax too close to the flames. She remembered Silaya's touch beneath her clothes and some part of her turned liquid. "Tell us a story where we win."

Kell looked at her. Silaya's face was a challenge, every angle of her body tensed for a fight and yet relaxed in itself. Kell's own body was all nerves and joints, and no part of her rested easily against any other part. Even sitting felt like an uncomfortable effort, and she envied the other woman's strength.

"I can't think of one," Kell said, tossing a twig into the fire, and it was true. Perhaps she was distracted, or maybe they were too far from home for the ancestors to help. Either way, her mind had gone blank.

Jor did not meet her eyes.

The next morning, Kell arose before the others and went to pray. Their packs had had no room for an altar, but she had brought the items she would have placed on it, bundled into a small scarf. She walked away from camp and settled onto her knees in the grasses, facing the way they had come. With a flint, she lit a tiny oil lamp and sprinkled resin from a small pouch. The scent of it made her ache. *Ancestors. Can you find me in this place? Can you follow?*

Kell's thoughts were answered by the plaintive call of a bird she did not recognize. A breeze rustled the grasses all around her, and she closed her eyes to the whispering of it, a thousand unfamiliar voices. The breeze carried the smoke away from her, and she pictured it traveling all the way to the desert, Home, where it would be received and understood.

It's a long way, she thought. The realization struck her as clearly as if someone had splashed her with cool water, and she opened her eyes. Ama was not here. The ancestors were not here. It was just her—her and Jor. She would have to find a way.

The thought filled her with a stony resolve. She would not let her People down.

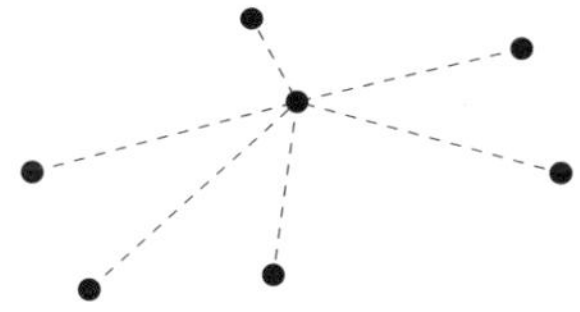

The Hornets: Southeastern quarter, windy season

22. THE CITY

They broke camp in silence. Jor was driven and at ease as he gathered his pack and readied for the last day of travel, but Kell felt like the ground beneath her were falling away, piece by piece. Now she floated, uncertain how she continued to move through space. Silaya was absorbed in tending her horse, and Kiche was lost to his thoughts. They would be returning Home soon, and Kell somehow felt as if they had already left, while she and Jor stood in the terrain of the unknown. They were less than a stone's throw away but already worlds apart.

Kell scarcely noticed the land through which they passed as they made the final approach to Soogway, though there was something strange about the grasslands here that Kell struggled to place. They looked naked and bruised to her, the bushes and scrub battered by the pale light that fell from the overcast sky. Everywhere, as far as she could see, were cylindrical protrusions that, at first glance, she took to be rock formations, but which she quickly realized were not.

"Look at that," she said to Silaya, who was lost in her own thoughts as they walked.

"Look at what?"

She pointed. "Those were all trees."

Silaya made a sound with her tongue.

"They cut *all* of them?"

"Yeah," Kiche broke in. "These city folk, they don't know when to stop, right?"

"Was it another farm?" Kell asked.

"Nah," he shook his head. "See how they're spaced? That was natural."

"What do you think they did with them?" asked Jor, but no one answered. Kell thought of the pulsar stones and wondered how long they had until the city tried to take them all.

The road widened, and other roads from other directions flowed to meet it, like a river running in reverse toward its source. The sky was overcast, and it was difficult to tell the time, but the heat and clouded glare made Kell guess that midday was pressing down on them as they began encountering other travelers. Cart wheels, animal hooves, footsteps broke the silence among them, and she couldn't help but stare at the range of vehicles and people all making their way to Soogway.

A tall, rattling platform balanced on enormous wheels rolled past their left. It was piled high with small cages woven from grass, and from inside each came peeps and songs and twitters. A thin person dressed in bright colors sat at the fore of the platform, holding the reins and clucking encouragingly at the oxen drawing them forward. They nodded to Silaya and Kell as they passed, doffing the floppy thing that served as a hat and whistling in cheerful company to their cargo.

A troupe jogged past in matching orange garb, all small and compact, chanting in time under their breath. They reminded Kell of the tumblers she'd seen perform at the vast annual market festival known as The Wheel. Crackling music spilled forth from some kind of tech strapped across the shoulders of the one in the rear of the group. Occasionally, one tumbler or another would interrupt their progress to roll or hop onto a nearby stump in time with the rhythm. The music faded away as they trotted over the crest of a hill out of sight.

"They're quick," Silaya said.

Kell made a noncommittal sound. "Imagine listening to that all day long," she groused. Silaya did not reply.

A row of sullen old women cloaked in brown cloth far too heavy for the climate trudged in the ditch that traced along the road. They bore giant bundles of cloth on their backs, which Kell assumed was laundry or clothing for sale, but as she passed them, she could have sworn one of the bundles squirmed.

Kell looked to the others and saw Kiche was nonplussed, his eyes fixed on the road ahead. Jor, though—she couldn't help but laugh at his expression. He turned and smiled sheepishly at Kell, the tension between them thawing. For a moment, she enjoyed the relief. She was going to need him in this severed place.

They crested a hill, and Kell's stomach dropped.

Soogway.

From this angle, the city that dominated the broad plain before them appeared endless, a monstrous labyrinth of concrete and rock, from which thick plumes of smoke rose and spread. Kell took a steadying breath. The largest gathering she'd ever seen was The Wheel, but this . . . She couldn't see the end of it. She glanced to her brother and saw Jor's eyes were shining.

As they drew closer, the scent of the air changed, became thick with the odor of a river and of damp stones under heat, with the spice and funk of many, many bodies. Kell wrinkled her nose. While desert smells were sere and sparse and clean, the reek of this place was filthy and made her feel dirty in turn. She pulled her scarf across her face, breathing through the familiar scent of the fabric.

All the myriad travelers whose roads had met theirs were funneled into one path leading to the city's main gates. Kell's sense of time raced, even though their pace grew slower with the congestion. The jumble of traffic somehow became a line that stamped and snorted and shifted its weight. Customs officials at the city's gate asked travelers questions and gave bored looks of authority at the answers. Before she knew it, she and Jor were only a few cart lengths from the entrance, and they rushed to gather their packs from Silaya's horse.

Kell's mind buzzed as she unbuckled straps and double-checked her essentials, including the two pouches of chips the council had given her. The People were more inclined to trade among one another—barter was much more practical than money—but they reserved a treasury for use with outsiders. Ama had told her to put one pouch in her pack and hide one under her shirt, in case she was robbed. Kell now feared this was inevitable, and every face around her took on the leering menace of a thief. She leaned into the horse and tucked one pouch into the bindings around her chest—she wasn't particularly well endowed, but long travel was still uncomfortable without support. The press of the hidden pouch against her restored a small amount of Kell's confidence.

The line shuffled forward, and the officers were near enough that Kell could see the mole on the cheek of one and hear the slight stutter of another.

"What do I say?" she asked Silaya in a panic.

"Just tell them why you're here," she said, her voice soothing but her eyes like knives. "Tell them you want an audience."

"What if they say no?" Kell's heart was racing, and it was difficult to swallow.

She thought of her prayer smoke drifting back toward the desert and felt impossibly far from Home. Silaya's eyed darkened and Kell felt a glimmer of something—was that contempt or just her own nerves? As Silaya's warm hands closed around her own, Kell realized with a flash of embarrassment that her own fingers must be icy. Silaya kissed her then, a rough, hard kiss that made her mouth burn, and then she took Kell's face firmly in her hands.

"You will do this. You and your brother. We need you." Kell nodded. "Do you hear me?" Silaya stared into her as if forcing the words in through her eyes. "You will *not* fail."

"I will not fail," she repeated.

And then Silaya was leading the horse away, and Kiche was saying something to her brother, and Jor was slipping the beacon amulet back into his shirt and adjusting his collar. Silaya gave Jor a wave that could have been a salute and clicked her tongue. The horse turned and began moving deftly against the flow of travelers. Kiche hugged Kell briefly, and then he, too, was gone, and it was just Kell and Jor, their packs on the ground beside them, the press of the crowd pushing them toward the gates of the city.

An officer barked them forward, and Kell watched in amazement as Jor smiled and gently took control of the conversation. Dancing nimbly around potentially dangerous questions about their purpose, Jor even managed to draw out hazy directions to the temple in the process. By the time they were done, the customs officer actually chuckled and gave Jor a playful clap on the back, wishing them both a good stay in the great City of Soogway.

"How did you do that?" she asked as they hoisted their satchels over their shoulders and stepped through the massive stone arch that marked the entrance to the city proper.

Jor shrugged. "People want to feel noticed," he said.

"Sure, but that man gets plenty of attention. People are groveling at him all day long. He was practically ready to buy you a meal."

"People grovel at his station and what he can do for them," he corrected. "That's not the same. He's a function to them, not a person. He enjoyed being seen." He lifted his eyebrows as if to suggest that, in another situation, Jor, too, might have poured him a drink.

Kell shoved him playfully. "He was *not* good-looking."

Jor shrugged, and both siblings wore smiles as they stepped into the thronging streets. Kell craned her neck and noticed the gates had doors made of wood thicker than her own body, held together with massive metal studs. In the desert, structures were temporary and portable, shifting like the dunes, and she had never seen anything so tall. Her mouth opened against her will, and she closed it again, determined not to look like the simple desert folk she suddenly felt herself and her brother to be. Jor shone with delight, clearly not as gobsmacked as she was, which Kell found a comfort.

"That's why *you're* the ambassador," she said.

Jor stopped and turned to her, forcing the foot traffic to flow around them. "And you're the teller," he said. "If we have to fight, you fight." She swallowed the small moan that tried to escape her chest. "Kell," he said, placing his hands on her shoulders. "You're one of the best tellers I've ever seen."

The confused warmth in her chest was followed by sudden tears, and Kell blinked them away. A man bumped into her, and she glared at him, wiping her face, but he was already gone, lost to the sea of people and animals and carts streaming into the main plaza beyond the gates.

"So, we know how to get to the temple?" she asked with a sniff.

"Let's find a place to stay first," he said. "I don't know about you, but I'm starving."

He turned and began carving a path through the crowd as easily as if he were a guide. People parted to make way, and Kell followed in the wake of his confidence.

"Sometimes all it takes is a quick wash and a fresh braid, and everything feels new again."
—Shade's mother

23. HITTING THE MARK

Shade watched the strange branch draw a lazy circle in the water as it drifted downstream. The water seemed even greener than usual, sluggish and thick, as it disappeared beneath the bridge and entered the canals downtown, carrying the stench of its accidental cargo throughout the city. Branches came from trees, and trees were more valuable than cubes or the finest tech. How one this size had made it all the way from wherever trees still existed without being dragged from the water and sold for a small fortune was beyond Shade. They considered diving in after it. After all, they were here to bathe, their soap and a small cloth for drying off clutched in a plastic shopping bag.

Shade looked around for a chain or length of twine, but the ground here was mostly gravel, broken glass, and the remains of bamboo crates long since smashed. They slipped off their shoes and waded into the edge of the water, enjoying the squish of the river mud between their toes. As they leaned toward the branch, a cloud of flies burst forth. Shade could see, then, the rounded belly below the surface. The wet fur they'd taken for bark was the putrefying leg of an ox drifting placidly downstream. Shade gagged and stumbled back out of the river. Today they'd spend the five chips on the public steam baths, instead.

Going to the baths was a rare treat that always made Shade feel like a proper grown-up, a sensation they both enjoyed and feared. They had lived alone for years—that wasn't the part of adulthood that bothered them. It was the sense that, sooner or later, they might have to find regular work rather than eking out their means picking pockets and hustling the odd fight. Being in the same place every day, doing the same thing? A job sounded like hell.

All the same, a steady income would be nice, Shade mused as they lathered and rinsed. To feel like they could eat when they wanted, pay for baths when they wanted. They could get used to that. Besides, now that Go's sponsorship and tutelage had proven valuable in ways they couldn't have imagined, Shade felt generally indestructible. They had the best of both worlds: immunity from safes, and none of the creepy hassle of learning Go's tricks. They walked with a little more swagger as they exited the baths and paused to look at themself in the mirror.

They had combed out their hair and redone their dark braids just as their mother used to do. The part was so tight their scalp itched, but it made them feel strapped in, ready for the day. They could see their mother's hazel eyes in their own reflection and their father's olive skin, though Shade's own frame was still slight, a quality neither of their parents had passed on. They put on their hat and turned, cocking one hip, admiring themself from a new angle. The swagger looked good, and they kept it on as they strode out the door to make some money.

They had been steering clear of the Shipping District for the past few days, and the Box still felt off-limits, as well. Their usual haunts like the gator hole and Commercial Street had been overrun with gangs of kids lately, and working there was like picking in the path of locusts—nothing left in their wake. Shade decided it was time to check out the other side of the city, closer to the gates, where traveling merchants and wealthy tourists streamed into Soogway with full pockets and stars in their eyes. Safety enforcers were usually thick over there, but those were no longer the worry they once had been now that Shade was under Go's protection. This felt like a perfect moment to take advantage of it.

It was a long walk, and by the time they'd found their way to the Traveler's Quarter, Shade was hungry and in need of a restroom. A side street off the main plaza revealed a row of cheap inns, overnight spots for business folk and traders, and Shade figured they could duck into one for a few minutes and relieve themself, grab a snack, and scope out possible marks. The first they came to was too noisy, the patrons already well into the hooch despite the early afternoon hour, and Shade pulled down their hat as they passed, hoping to remain invisible. The second was too quiet—if there were patrons, they weren't enjoying much. Shade continued until they found an inn that appeared to do a pleasant amount of business without too much fanciness or funny stuff.

They went in, used the bathroom, and paid for a bowl of soup at the bar, which was unexpectedly delicious, more so than a few chips warranted. It came with spongy bread, half of which Shade devoured; the remainder they forced themself to squirrel away in their pocket for later.

Shade had taken a seat at the bar, which faced the door. It was never a good idea to scope a mark indoors and then hit them in the same place unless there were lots of exits. Still Shade was able to get a good sense of the pickings from here. The inn had a solid clientele—travelers and merchants, mostly, some from the Nong Plateau, by the sound of their accents, who'd taken the dry route rather than the river, and others from the south, which Shade knew less about. Southerners often traded in minerals, they knew, and were therefore asset rich but cash poor. They made bad marks unless you had a fence for gems, which Shade did not.

They wondered idly if any were from the Broken Forest and had a moment of fierce, irrational jealousy. Did they see trees every day? Did they appreciate what they had? Probably not. Shade figured they'd have to tax them for their lack of gratitude and then wondered where that thought had come from.

They thanked the barkeep for the soup and received a smile and a nod in return. Hopping off their stool, Shade followed behind a merchant who had had a few drinks with their lunch and grown noticeably loud and boastful with the other patrons as time had worn on. Shade figured they could walk right up to him and dip into his pocket for all he'd feel it. Outside, though, the man smoothed his jacket and straightened up, slipping from the slouch and stagger he'd adopted inside to a brisk, professional pace.

I'll be damned, Shade thought to themself. *A fellow player.*

They winked in salute at the man's back as he disappeared into the plaza crowd, likely in search of another target. Among the hustle of workers there, Shade spotted a wealthy-looking woman walking a small fox on a leash. The animal looked as if its fur had been washed and then blown dry in a hot wind, and it minced down the street, fluffy and proud. Shade now fell into step behind the woman, eyeing her for her pockets until the fox paused, sniffing the air, and then turned to bare its tiny teeth in a fierce little snarl. Shade put up their palms in apology and leaned against the stone wall of the lane, pulling their hat down low.

Two travelers wandered down the street, their eyes up and the city shock still upon their faces. They walked too slowly, and the flow of traffic had to part around them. Desert folk, Shade guessed, noting the tattoos on the one and the head wrap on the other. They each carried a single bulging satchel slung over their shoulders without precaution. Shade paused. Rule number two was never to steal from poor folks. But these two looked well fed and clean; they had enough money to travel, that part was for certain.

Shade could see pouch cords around their necks—chips that would not be easily lifted. They figured they probably had more, though—most did.

And I'm guessing they're right . . . there. Shade eyed a protuberance on the side of the smaller one's bag where it hung down her back. It might break the Don't Be Greedy rule, but it was hard to snag single chips from travelers. At least it wasn't *all* she had.

Shade allowed them to pass and then followed at a reasonable distance, waiting for a cluster of people to pass in the opposite direction, providing cover for the bump. Shade timed it perfectly, coming up close just as the two had to step out of the way of a passing cart and its driver. They bumped and slipped their hand in the outside pocket, lifting the small, full pouch, which Shade quickly transferred to their jacket.

The woman turned and glared.

"Watch out!" she hissed. *That accent. Desert folk, for sure.*

"Sorry," Shade mumbled.

She looked them up and down, her eyes flashing and suspicious. She was very nervous. Probably her first time in the city. Shade moved to pass them, but a hand snaked out and grabbed their sleeve, hard. They spun and shrugged off the grip.

"Hey!" the desert woman shouted. She had stopped walking, her eyes locked on them, her shoulders hunched and feet in a fighting stance. Her casting palm was already up, though Shade could see it was trembling.

Oh, great. A teller.

Shade had no interest in fighting this tumbleweed. The crowd parted around them, leaving a clearing to avoid their confrontation. Shade checked for safes out of habit and rearranged their face into what they hoped looked like surprise.

"That's mine," she said. Her voice was shaking too. She pointed at the tassels of the pouch poking out of Shade's jacket pocket.

They cursed to themself. *Sloppy.* They'd have to play this one straight.

"I've never seen you before," they said, raising one hand in a gesture of gross innocence. "I don't know what you're talking about."

"Give. It. Back," she spat. She looked much more focused now; it was her companion's turn to look nervous.

The impulse to fight came on so quickly, Shade forgot they could just keep walking. It was as if the story were already waiting at the gates of their chest, and they prepared their body accordingly. Their casting hand began to glow. Light bubbled in their palm like the vats of melting glue at the killing yard, slow and thick. Shade took a deep breath and rooted their feet into the street. In the back of their mind, they sifted through Go's tricks and picked one to test out here in the wild.

"This pouch is mine," they began, their mouth working to catch up with the pace of their heartbeat. "My aunt gave it to me before she p—"

A wall of light rushed toward Shade, eclipsing their view. They ducked, almost losing the thread of their words. An enormous glowing desert cat had cleared the gap between them in a single leap and pounced on the gathering light above Shade's hand, knocking it to the ground. Spikes erupted from its leonine shoulders as it trapped their nascent innocence story beneath its razored paws, which were expanding now, each roughly the size of a large serving platter.

The cat's jaws yawned, ready to devour the wriggling glow it had crushed to the cobblestones. Shade looked at the woman, eyes wide. She wasn't even watching, so absorbed was she in her telling. The crowd sounds drowned out her voice, so Shade found it difficult to hear her, which unsettled them further. Something about a spirit in a tree and some poisonous seeds.

Time to get serious, they decided, rolling up their sleeves.

Shade muttered a few lines about their poor dear aunt from whom they'd inherited the pouch and then rapidly shifted tactics. A series of penetrating questions spun their story from a narrative into a rhetorical puzzle, quickly dismantling the assumptions her story was based on. The glow trapped against the cobblestones leaked like oil from underneath the cat's paws and then solidified into a sheet, folding into a series of rotating blades, which began to spin faster and faster. The cat leaped back at once, but the blades followed. In an instant, it looked as if the desert cat had been minced into confetti of light, a rough, luminous dust suspended in the air above a set of whirring swords.

Shade smirked. That had worked even better than they'd expected it to. They looked to the woman's face to appreciate the defeat they'd find there, but instead they found a smile painted across her lips as she continued to tell. It was a grimace that said triumph tasted sour, but deliciously so.

"When the winds came, as come they do, each shivering pod trembled at the end of its branch, ripe with purpose, dry as the soul of the sand," she said, her voice clear now, a singsong above the noise of the crowd. "The storm spirit realized its mistake, but already it had unleashed its force, and the tree gave itself up to that power, releasing each seed into the gale . . . "

Shade had only an instant to register their story before it was too late.

Each speck of minced cat had begun to swell and sprout wings of its own. Where they hung in the air, they coalesced and turned, slowly and in patient defiance of the blades, counter to their frantic rotation. The bits grew larger, first the size of chips, then the length of Shade's fingers. The flurry began to duck and whir as they turned, accelerating. Their light dimmed, and they took on an almost realistic look: a storm of locusts.

The cyclone of enormous bugs spun and then erupted into the air, soaring above the tops of the buildings around them. Passersby were no longer just avoiding the two fighting in the street but running now, shouts of fear and amazement as traffic scattered below the gathering cloud. It made no sound—like all storylight—but it *felt* as if it were humming, clicking, emitting some horrible insectile threat that Shade could feel in their skin. They panicked. They tried to twist the blades into paddles, great bug swatters, and send them upward, but they found their rhetorical strategy was weakening, too far outside their natural style. They diverted quickly into a story they'd won in a fight some months ago, one that manifested as an enormous spider, hoping to draw the insects into a web.

The locusts gathered in a shape like a massive spear tip and shot toward Shade. Every cell in their body screamed for them to leap out of the way, but Shade held firm.

It's just a story, just a goddamn story, it can't hurt y—

The swarm of giant bugs split inches from their face, spilling around either side of them like a parting sea, more shadow than light. Shade could swear they felt the breeze of them, the wall of air pressure that followed, the sinister click and hiss of their myriad wings a scream en masse. Shade squeezed their eyes shut and gritted their teeth, their own story forgotten.

There was shouting. A man's voice and then the woman's, angry and defiant. The sensation of pressure abated. Shade opened their eyes.

The desert teller was panting, her shoulders rising and falling with her breath, though from the murderous look in her eyes, Shade guessed it was from emotion rather than exertion. Her companion had one hand on her back and was murmuring in the kind of voice a mother might use to calm a small child. The locusts and blades were gone, both seeping into the stones as puddles that refused to mix. Shade swallowed and gathered their story back into their palm, and the woman did the same, her eyes still shooting barbs. They eyed her sidelong.

"It's taboo to attack the teller," they said.

"I didn't touch you," she growled.

"My sister—" the companion began, as if that were an apology on its own.

"I have a name," she snapped. "I'm Kell. Red sandbeast. And you stole my pouch."

The brother dug into a pocket Shade had missed and produced a small handful of chips. "Here," he said. "Take this if you're hungry. But give her back the resin."

Shade scowled. "I'm not hungry," they snarled, resisting the absurd urge to show them the bread in their pocket. *Wait—resin?*

"Then why'd you try to take it?" Kell demanded.

Shade kicked a lump of horse dung on the street. "Doesn't matter," they said. "You wouldn't get it."

They dug the pouch out of their other pocket and looked inside. Instead of chips, the bag contained what looked like small nuggets of amber, which they sniffed.

All this for a bag of incense.

Rule number two had never come up in this way before, but Shade realized that keeping the girl's resin out of spite would probably count as being greedy. Dammit. It felt strange handing the pouch back, but they did, and Kell quickly placed it deep inside her shoulder bag and secured it with an unnecessary number of buckles.

"Thank you," said the brother, extending his hand.

Shade looked at it a moment before taking it. The man was tall and good-looking, and something about him made Shade like him despite themself. They felt a sudden stab of protectiveness.

"You two need to learn to walk better," they said. "And faster. You're going to get hit by more than just me. The little ones will eat you alive."

"We'll try," said the brother. "Thanks for the tip—?" He paused, waiting for a name.

"Shade."

"I'm Jor. And this is—"

"Kell," Shade interrupted. "Got that."

Jor grinned and cuffed Shade's shoulder as if they were old friends. "I think she had you."

Kell had wrapped her scarf around her head and glared over the top of it. It made her eyes even more intense, and Shade ducked under the brim of their hat.

"Good story," they offered. "The thing with the bugs, I . . . hadn't seen that before."

"What are you, twelve?"

Shade pulled their braids flat against their chest and puffed up. "More like twenty," they retorted. *More or less.* "I've fought plenty."

Jor was looking at them thoughtfully. Shade couldn't tell if they felt exposed or strangely grateful. "I'll bet you have," he said.

Shade turned to leave, exaggerating their cocky swagger. The city was going to eat those two alive.

"Some of us can't afford to lose."
—Shade's father

24. SECRETS

Shade managed to keep their swagger until they turned the corner and began to run.

Something about that whole interaction was off—their sloppy grab-and-stash, the way they'd slipped into a fight, their softening to the brother's kindness. They barely recognized themself. *I got scared by a couple of bugs*, they chided themself as they dodged carts and pedestrians. *I got greedy and tried to lift a bag of incense.* Ever since they'd met Mr. Go, things had gotten farther and farther off track.

But no more. What they needed was a good meal and a quick count of their winnings to get their head straight. They could take the night off and sleep. *Tomorrow will be back to normal*, they decided. *No more lessons. No more tricks.*

The neighborhoods melted past them as they ran, a blur of sameness, both familiar and strange, alleyways and trash bins, small storefronts with bored shopkeepers leaning against doorways beneath cheerfully blinking signs. Bamboo carts rattled past, and plastic bags littered the cobblestones. Shade reached out to touch a statue as they ran by, their foot landing square in a filthy puddle and making a satisfying splash.

Eventually they tired and slowed. It was a long way home, and the late afternoon sun had heated the stone and concrete until the alleys felt like little ovens. They pulled the leftover spongy bread from their pocket and ate it as they walked. It was still delicious, but now they had a pocket full of crumbs. Shade licked their fingers.

When I get to the Broken Forest, there will be fruit growing from trees, they thought. *No more scrounging and scrimping. No more roasted beans. Fresh fruit from trees and berries from bushes. It'll be shady and cool, and I'll climb branches and sit in the leaves and look at the ferns . . .*

The fantasy carried them all the way to the outskirts of the Arbor. Shade decided to go through the front door of their building for a change, so they took Commercial Street straight past the dumpling shops. They slipped into the shelter of a doorway as a safety enforcer and their unit strolled past, more out of habit than real fear. Once the street was clear, they nodded hello to the mute old woman who was a fixture on the bench outside their apartments. Shade realized with a start that it had been too long since they'd checked on the D Street kids, and they cursed under their breath as they went inside. Another thing that needed to get back to normal.

The stairwell was dim and clammy, but a welcome respite from the street. Shade's footsteps made a familiar pinging as they mounted the stairs, one hand on the railing, the other touching their thumb to a fingertip to count the steps. It was always the same number, but Shade counted every time, anyway. On the fourth floor, they reached the landing and made their way down the hall past identical doorways opening onto dingy little homes packed tightly together like a beehive made of stone. Shade could smell the boiled roots of suppers past and thought briefly of the weeds on the roof, wondering which were kitchen herbs.

Shade's room wasn't a proper room. It was a repurposed janitor's closet, so their door looked more like a panel in the wall, streaked where rain had leaked in and carried with it mineral deposits from the roof. Shade liked to pretend it was art. They drew their key from where it hung on a string around their waist and unlocked the metal door.

Inside was a scent Shade couldn't quite place, but it lingered over the top of the vegetal funk of dinner from the hallway and the dank mildew that bloomed beneath their mattress. It was a delicate aroma, floral. The hair on the back of their neck stood up.

Broken daylight fell through the barred window, and Shade blinked as their eyes adjusted. They didn't have much—a street sign they'd found in a trash heap rested on a stack of cinderblocks to serve as a table, and plastic crates held their few possessions: some clothes and dried food, a large ball of string they'd been adding scraps to for years, a small collection of rocks and pieces of glass. Their bed lay in the corner, the blankets in need of a wash but folded neatly at the foot of the mattress.

Shade never folded their blankets.

A sound came out of them then, the strangled squeak of an animal. Someone had been here. For a suspended moment, they became curiously weightless, then they leaped across the room, scrambling across the mattress to the far side, where they dug underneath, desperately reaching for their hidden stash. Nothing.

They stood and grabbed the edge of the bed, heaving it upward. Shouted. Stumbled. They fell against the table, knocking it from its blocks, landing hard against the concrete floor. They struggled to their feet and climbed over the unwieldy bulk of the bed, running their hands across it like a blind man who'd dropped his only chip. The tear was there, where they hid their entire savings, their ticket out of the city and back to the Broken Forest, but the familiar lump, the pouch full of scrimped chips and scant cubes, their treasure, their only hope—it was gone.

Shade slowly withdrew their hand and grazed against something within the soft mattress stuffing. Their fingers closed around it, and they pulled out a small white card made, no doubt, of real paper. There were words on it, Shade could tell—indecipherable scribbles that swam and danced as their eyes filled with tears.

They crumpled the card with a shaking hand and stood, though they had the uncanny sensation that they had floated up through the top of their own head and were no longer in their body. This wasn't like traveling through the floor. It was like being picked up by a wave and stranded on a high cliff above themself. Nothing was under their control, not even their own limbs.

As if in a dream, they watched themself flip their mattress back over. Odd details gleamed. They noticed specks of dark mold they'd never seen before. The mattress landed with a whump, and Shade left it as it was, jutting into the room at an uneven angle. They gathered the blankets and placed them on the mattress and righted the makeshift table. Dust coated their shelves. Shade couldn't feel their hands as they worked, or their own heartbeat. The light through the window bars made a geometric pattern on the floor.

Cheap.

Shade watched themself close the door behind them and retrace their steps down the stairwell, their arms held slightly away from their body as if dripping wet. The crumpled card in their pocket rustled as they walked, and the blur of the scribbles glowed in their mind's eye.

I need Cheap.

Despite the sunshine, they could not feel the heat. They walked, and blocks passed, though whether it took hours or moments Shade could not have said. The thought bubbled up that the street was unusually silent, then they realized it wasn't silent but rather all the sounds were drowned out by another noise. Shade noted dully that the other noise was screaming, then understood that the sound was only in their head; they were screaming, but not with their mouth. Their mouth was too far to reach. Trapped in a silent scream, they floated down the street to find Cheap. Shade needed him to read the words that would tell them where their dreams had gone.

The sight of Cheap's stand broke the dam in their chest, and tears soaked into the collar of their shirt. Their braids clung to the sides of their face uncomfortably, and Shade wanted to run but all the rush had left them. They couldn't do more than walk, their hands hanging awkwardly away from their sides.

Cheap sat hunched on a scuffed metal stool, as always, though the happy box in his hands looked different, newer. Fancy. He didn't look up when Shade pushed aside the plastic tarp and took the stool next to him. Shade wiped their face with hands covered in dust and grime from the floor. They could feel it all turning to mud on their cheeks, but they didn't care.

"Cheap."

The old man's eyes flicked to them and then back to the fancy new happy box. He grunted. Shade noticed Cheap was wearing new clothes. When they reached down for a scoop, they noticed he was wearing new shoes, as well. Confused, Shade replaced the scoop. They didn't want roasted beans. They took off their hat and twisted it in their hands.

"Something's happened, Cheap."

Cheap flicked a switch on the side of the happy box that made the patterns on the screen go dark. Shade shivered, looking at it. It was something alive in their friend's hands, a dangerous animal briefly asleep. Cheap turned it so the blank screen, like a single, staring eye, faced the ground and glanced at Shade over his shoulder.

"It's yer own damn fault," he growled.

Shade frowned. Their breath came faster, and their eyes felt hot. "I—"

"I *told you* not to let him in." For a moment, Cheap's voice sounded almost regretful, as if he wrestled with an inner conflict. But then he snarled, "Now you've gone and made him angry."

Shade slid off the stool. They did not recognize this old man. Their heart pounded, the card in their pocket forgotten.

"You coulda had it all, kiddo, but you had to go and—"

"Wh-what are you talking about?" Shade stammered. "Cheap." Their voice was a plea.

"He was gonna give you everything, and you thought you could just walk off? Not hold up your side of the bargain? Just who do you think you are, you worthless rat?"

Shade backed away from this monster that looked like Cheap. The box. The clothes. It all started to make a horrible kind of sense. They pushed aside the plastic of the tent and held it, staring at the old man as he switched the device back on. Their hands were shaking, and tears burned their cheeks.

"Go on, get out of here." Cheap's voice cracked, and for the briefest moment, Shade thought it was from sorrow, a hope that was immediately doused. "And Shade?" Cheap turned, at last looking them in the eyes. Shade's own searched the old man's face but found only shadow beneath the folds of his brows. Shade wanted to reach toward him, to nudge him or to slap him and bring him back to himself, but they saw nothing of their friend there.

"He's gonna find you. Doesn't matter where you go. You belong to *him* now." Cheap wheezed this last and was racked with a dry cough.

Shade let the plastic fall and backed away, their feet carrying them they didn't know where.

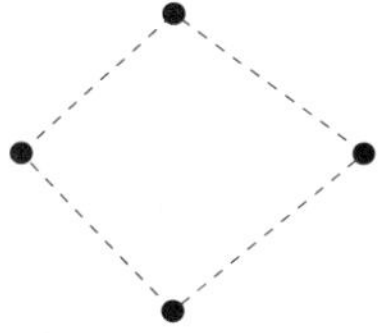

The Lantern: South

25. ONLY A DREAM

Soogway stank. Kell hoped she would get used to it, but many hours later, the reek of the place still distracted her, a foul mix of fish in mud and laundry moldering. Everything was damp and sullied, as if the city itself were in the early stages of rot. Kell imagined the stench clung to her the way dust did after a sandstorm, and time and again she resisted the urge to wipe herself clean. Jor didn't seem bothered by it, but he was too busy marveling at the details of their room to notice.

"How do they do it?" he asked for the fifth time. He was standing at the door, pulling on a small cord that somehow activated a light that hung overhead, flooding the tiny quarters with an artificial glare. Click. Darkness. Click. Garish light. Click. Darkness. Click. More light.

"Ancestors help us, Jor. *Enough*."

He climbed onto the bed to look closer at the lamp, but it appeared to be little more than a box suspended by a thick string, revealing no clues to its mechanism. Jor touched it with a finger and then turned it with his whole hand.

"It's warm!"

Kell rolled her eyes. The room was very small. Kell was accustomed to the broad reach of the family tent or sleeping under the vault of the sky. The closeness of the walls here made it difficult to breathe, and she felt like she couldn't turn around without bumping elbows with her brother, whose enjoyment of everything she found increasingly difficult to bear.

The room did have a window and a tiny balcony. They were on the third floor, and except for cliffs and canyon ledges, Kell had never been so high up in her life. Looking down to the street below gave her a weird sense of vertigo, but she could also see over the top of the building across the way, and the perspective onto the streets before them gave her a small feeling of comfort in this crowded city. Seeing through this tiny corner of the maze, she thought she might make sense of her surroundings after all.

The sun had set sometime in the last hour, she could tell by the color of the sky, but the buildings made it difficult to see exactly where it had gone down, and she disliked the feeling of disorientation. She looked up to find the early stars, but the gloom of the clouds only reflected the lights from below. It was like sitting too close to the fire—the light made one blind to constellations.

Thinking of the fire made her think of smoke, which reminded her of incense, which brought back the events of the afternoon. Her own ferocity had surprised her. She had already been on edge, and then that thief had tried to steal her resin, of all things. *Ancestors, forgive them.* She felt strangely sorry for them.

What was their name? Something strange. Shadow? Clearly for all its wonders, the city had no interest in taking care of its own. The People would never let someone go hungry or become so desperate as to resort to stealing.

But Kell had to admit, the thief was a decent combat teller. Excellent, really. That unusual stance and the clear, musical voice. She had never seen anything like those spinning blades. The idea made her nervous—if a street urchin knew tricks like that, what must the combat general's arsenal look like? She shook off the thought, warming herself with the memory of Silaya's hands on her face. *I will not fail.*

"Look at that," Jor breathed, marveling at the rooftops. He had joined her on the cramped balcony, and she found herself both irritated at his closeness and grateful to have him near. Being in the city had already brought something out in him—like a small child with a new desert kitten to play with. She hadn't seen the edges of his smile fade since they had arrived.

"It smells," she said.

He shrugged. "It's damp here. It's different."

"I wanted to look at the stars, but it's too bright."

The sky was darkening rapidly. All around was the blink and flash of signs and lanterns marking territory and making offers on the streets below—food, entertainment, places to stay or to drink or to buy any manner of things. Voices and laughter drifted up, revelers from inns staggering back into the night, their spirits improved. The roll and clatter of carts and clop of hooves. There was an undeniable energy to it.

"I was going to sleep on the floor, but there's no room," she said.

"Trying a city bed won't kill you."

She turned and eyed the raised platform and its lumpy, excessive mattress.

"It might." She wrinkled her nose.

As night fell, more lights flickered on in the distance, and Kell had the strange impression that the sky had come down to rest, that the stars were nestled in the buildings, shining in strange new patterns. She was deeply tired but unable to relax. The mattress she shared with her brother was softer than the roll she slept on at home but surprisingly comfortable, which annoyed her. As the city's lights and sounds continued, she was afraid she might never rest, but sleep overtook her as quickly as if she had fallen backward into a bottomless cave.

Kell tried to run, but the grove around her was too dense. It wasn't made of trees but of bamboo, thick stands of green reaching higher than she could see, creaking and whispering in a breeze she could not feel. She was frantic. It was almost too late, and it was her fault. Leaves and small branches whipped against her face as she struggled, her feet churning but carrying her nowhere. She put out her hands and felt the pulse of the stones, but it came from every direction at once, and she wept in confusion. Her hands throbbed. The bamboo, smooth and rigid, made her feel like she had been caged—and then it *was* a cage, a tall cage of ironwood. When she looked up, the bars reached into the clouds and there was no roof, and she could scarcely see through the cage wall, the bars were so closely spaced. When she slipped her fingertips through, her knuckles got stuck. She leaned close to peer between them with one eye and saw a ring of stones. Hurry, *hurry*. Each stone was pulsing so loudly now it thrummed in her chest, disrupting her breathing and her own heartbeat. She couldn't breathe—her breath was being stolen from her. The stones were too strong, too near. Her hands were on fire, and she banged them on the bars, trying to cool them or break herself free. The stones began to crumble then, the pitch of the sound shifting higher and higher until it was a high whine, a shrill shriek—

A whistle blew.

Kell opened her eyes. The sound faded, followed by a shuffle of activity from the street below. She pulled herself upright and went to the balcony, her joints stiff and awkward after a night on the soft mattress. People were squeezing along the sides of the alley as a crew of sweepers pushed their way through with brooms, reminding her of a caterpillar chewing its way through a leaf. A cloud of grime and refuse traveled down the street before them. Jor was still sleeping, a soft snore coming from his side of the bed.

A sense of urgency remained with her, but she couldn't remember whether she had dreamed or not. She thought she had—something about her hands. She yawned hugely and leaned out.

In the morning light, Kell saw that the windows across the street were nearly all flanked with small garden boxes, from which unruly plants and vines strained upward and lent small bits of color to the miserable stone gray. The scent of something deliciously fried and meat-filled drifted up, and her stomach growled despite herself. A woman appeared at a balcony across the way and shook out a rug. Her eyes met Kell's briefly, and she nodded in greeting. Kell nodded back, suddenly shy, having felt invisible until that moment.

She turned from the window and rummaged through her pack. She regarded the small pouch of incense in her hand and thought how precious it seemed now that she had nearly lost it. It was so stupid—just a small amount of resin, not valuable by any measure, but she had been willing to unleash a nightmare to regain it. The contents of the pouch felt like a tangible link to everything she knew and loved well, and she needed that if she was going to survive in this place with her spirit intact.

Longing for a flint, she fished out Jor's lighter and her small dish and lit the resin, exhaling gratitude that the small piece of tech hadn't broken in her hands or somehow set the room ablaze. The sweet smoke instantly calmed her nerves, and she allowed herself to be transported. As she settled into prayer, she heard Jor stirring behind her. He rinsed his face with water from the basin but did not join her on the floor. It had been ages since he'd prayed with her, but all he had to do was sit. *What goes on in that heart of yours, Brother?*

As if hearing her thoughts, he said, "All I can think about is getting some breakfast."

She finished her devotions and stood. "Then let's find some and get to the temple."

"In such a hurry," he laughed. "We could take the day and look around." He strolled to the balcony and looked out. "Get a sense of the city, see what there is to see. What's the rush?"

"What's the *rush?*" Kell didn't want to start the morning with a fight, but tension was already boiling up inside her, ready to burst in a cloud of anger. "Are you *serious*? Every minute we're not stopping the extractions is a minute they're stealing the stones. This isn't an adventure, Jor—we're not tourists."

"I know why we're here, Kell." His voice was calm but cold. "I just think it would be a good idea for us to have a better sense of the city before we jump into something we don't understand well. That's all."

She turned away from him and began stuffing her few belongings into her pack. A piece of the resin was still hot, and she winced. "We're going to the temple today," she said.

He sighed heavily. "Fine, but we should leave our packs here."

She whirled on him. "What?! And let some innkeeper steal everything we have, our chips, our clothes?"

"You almost lost your precious resin yesterday on the street! If we leave our things here, we have a better chance of not being robbed by pickpockets."

"What's to keep our things safe here?"

"Nobody needs your clothes, Kell. It's an *inn*. It's what people *do*."

"How would you know what people do? You've never been in an inn in your life, and you know it."

"You look like a tourist with that bag on your back!"

"I *am* a tourist!" she shouted.

Jor smirked at her. Her face burned.

"You know what I mean."

Jor came and put his arms around her, which startled her, but she didn't resist. She leaned into his broad chest, and he held her until she felt the anger ebbing away. She felt small, and he smelled like Home, and she had to blink quickly.

"It'll be OK," he said softly. She nodded into his shirt. Through the fabric, the beacon pressed into her cheek.

His stomach growled then, and they both laughed. Kell wiped her eyes.

"Something smells good down there," she admitted. They put their packs under the bed, distributed some chips among their pockets, locked the door behind them with the key they'd been given, and went down to the street to eat.

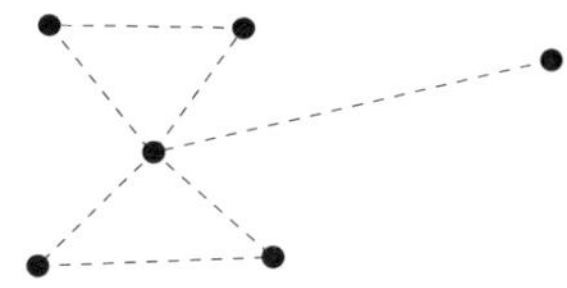

The Councilor: Western horizon, bird migration

26. TREE RINGS

Kell reluctantly conceded that the dumplings were some of the best things she had ever tasted. Spicy, rich, somehow both crisp and chewy, with just the right amount of grease. She licked her fingers and was dismayed to find she had already finished the two she had purchased. She wondered idly how many Silaya could eat and dug out another chip to buy a third.

"Aye, the best in Greenwood," said the round woman who plopped the raw dumpling into the vat of hot oil, poking it with her bamboo tongs. Kell eyed the dumpling as it floated in grease, sizzling and turning perfectly golden brown. Her mouth watered.

"Why do they call it that?" asked Jor, sucking air around a hot mouthful—rudely, Kell thought, but the dumpling woman didn't seem to mind.

"Call it what?" She propped a fist on an ample hip. Kell could not tell if she was smiling or if her eyes were always squeezed half shut. Jor swallowed his bite and made a sound of delicious appreciation before clearing his throat.

"Greenwood. It seems . . . " He gestured around at the concrete canyon that surrounded them. The woman was definitely smiling.

"Soogway's got a queer sense of humor, don't it?" she laughed. "Aye, it were green once, to be sure, but that was before my Oma's time. *Her* Oma might have remembered when they cut 'em all down." Her face grew thoughtful. "They say it were beautiful, the main boulevards lined with giant trees, old ones. The canopy about blocked out the sky. And there were birds in 'em, and they say you could hear 'em singing, day and night."

Jor flashed her a grin. "That does sound beautiful."

"T'were cooler then, too," the woman went on. "Not like the big stone oven we got now." She wiped the spattered edge of her ancient apron across her forehead.

"What happened?" Kell asked, hoping the answer wouldn't delay her dumpling.

The woman snorted, stirring the oil. She shook her head. "What d'ye think? The city government chopped 'em all down for wood an' paper. First the outer forest, then the inner. Lumber prices got so high, fools didn't think to save some for later. Now we just got the farms."

"Tree farms?" Jor had finished his dumplings and was looking around for a place to wipe his hands. The woman offered a corner of her apron, and he took it like a true diplomat. Eyeing the stains, Kell wished for some nice clean sand instead.

"Bamboo farms," the dumpling woman explained. "Where you think we get all this?" She gestured at the crates stacked behind her and wagged the tongs in her hand. "Grows quick," she said, and plucked Kell's third dumpling from the oil, waving it in the air to cool it and remove excess grease.

"We passed through one of those on our way here," Kell offered. "We don't have many trees where we live, either."

The woman extended the tongs toward Kell and dropped the dumpling into her hands. It was clear she had mastered the timing required to cool a dumpling down to the precise degree it was no longer dangerous.

"I figured as much," the woman nodded, pleased. "What are ye, desert Roamers?"

Jor bowed with a flourish that embarrassed Kell, but the sound the woman made was almost a giggle. Kell directed her attention to her third dumpling so she wouldn't be caught rolling her eyes.

"What brings you so far from home?"

Jor spoke carefully. "We've come on behalf of our People's . . . resources. We are seeking an audience with the city government."

The woman busied her hands, chopping something fragrant and tossing it in a large bowl for more filling.

"Ye'll be heading for the temple, then."

Jor nodded. "We received directions at the gate, but we're a little turned around. We'd be grateful to hear the way again from someone with your knowledge of the city," he said.

She shooed the compliment away with one hand, like a fly. "I can tell ye how to get there, for sure," she said, though her voice indicated that she didn't think it a worthwhile destination. The woman's knife was a blur as it turned a mound of undefined meat into mince. "I don't have much use for the temple, myself," she continued, speaking loudly over the sound of chopping. She looked up at Kell, who worried the woman would lose her fingers if she didn't better attend to the blade. "You will see some trees there, though."

Kell wrinkled her brow and swallowed the remainder of the dumpling. "I thought you said they were all gone," she said.

"They're gone for folks like us, to be sure," said the woman. "Trees are for the rich and powerful now, aren't they?" Her voice was matter of fact.

Despite her directions, they still got lost en route to the temple. The city was a maze at the street level. It was laid out in rings, not unlike the People's camps, but the height of the buildings and the lack of any familiar landmarks made it difficult to know when to turn. Even Jor became frustrated.

"I wish we had a bug," he said as he scowled up at one of the strange statues that loomed in the neighborhoods. Kell was almost certain they'd seen that one before and had gotten turned around.

"Why can't we just use the Way at Ease?" Kell asked.

"You're the one who's afraid of getting robbed. What better target than two people who look like we do, singing down the street after a floating snake? Besides, I'm not even sure it would work here."

"Why wouldn't it?"

"Isn't the Way supposed to be one of the gifts of the gods to the First Pathfinder?"

"So?" She bristled at his *supposed to*.

"So, it requires the presence of the stones. We're nowhere near them now."

Kell chewed her lip. It hadn't occurred to her that they would ever be too far from the stones to feel them, though it was obvious now. They had always been a part of the world around her—the heartbeat of the land itself. The notion of their true absence now made her stomach and its dumplings uneasy. The city loomed around her, fussing and noisy yet also dead somehow, like one of the mud golems Ama had told stories of around the fires at night to frighten children. Mud golems were loud and shuffling but held no stories inside them, moving purely by ill will. Now that they were lost inside it, the city felt much the same.

She sighed. "You're right."

Jor looked as if he took no pleasure in winning the argument. "Which way do you want to try?"

She stepped out of the way of a small parade of people in long robes, none of whom noticed her. The buildings felt as if they tilted in toward them as Kell scanned the lattice strips of sky above. She missed the openness of the desert. How was anyone supposed to know where they were here?

"Tough without yer snakey, huh?" A voice interrupted her thoughts, and she turned. Someone was lounging against the statue they had just passed, watching them, a woman around Kell's age, twirling a slender knife.

"What would you know about it?" Kell snapped. Jor placed a hand on her shoulder, which made her doubly furious. Without thinking, she put her palms over the pockets where she'd stuffed her chips, shielding them from imminent theft.

"I know you don't wanna show 'em where yer keeping the good stuff, that's for certain." The woman laughed then, but without malice, a high and braying laugh that threw her head back, revealing a wide set of alarmingly brown teeth. She slipped the knife into a small sheath at her waist, spat noisily into the street, and stepped forward, leaning into Kell and Jor conspiratorially. Kell caught the scent of whetstones and chewing leaf. The woman looked over one shoulder and then the next, and whispered loudly, "So, do you wanna know how to get to the temple? Without the snakey? No singin' required?"

"As a matter of fact—" Jor began. Kell glared at him, and he stopped.

The strange young woman laughed again, throwing an arm around each of their shoulders. "It's OK," she crooned. "I know where you're headed. As it happens, I'm headed there, too." She took a few steps like that before Kell shrugged out from under her arm.

"Hands off!" Kell hissed.

The woman shrugged and began walking backward, smiling at her. Kell wanted to scream. She didn't care how this person knew where they were going—with two people obviously not from the city, that was no great feat of mindreading—but the last thing they needed was some pushy stranger to lead them astray and then empty their pockets.

"Alls I'm sayin' is, I'm going to the temple, and probably you are, too. We all gotta chat with the clerks from time to time, now, don't we? 'Specially when they got their eyes on what's not theirs."

Kell evaluated the stranger, trying to decide whether she was more afraid of losing time or of losing chips. This woman didn't look like anyone they'd seen so far in the city. In fact, her golden-brown clothing seemed made of a fabric not unlike what scouts wore back Home, but without the loose cut the desert heat required. Her shirt was stained, and her pants were a motley of pockets and clasps, her body crisscrossed with straps and small packs of every description. Her tangled mess of golden-brown curls had long been a stranger to combs. Every part of her was golden brown, Kell realized, as if she'd been carved from oiled wood. The woman crooked the pointer finger of each hand at Kell and her brother and beckoned them.

"Come *on* then," she said, and the two couldn't help but follow.

In the torrent of words that accompanied her quick stride through the city's rings, their odd new companion informed them that she was a visitor, too, though she turned out to be an accurate guide. They had learned her name (Winty), her age (between 22 and 25—she'd lost track), her profession (trader), and her favorite bird (gyrfalcon) before either Kell or Jor had got a word in edgewise. This woman seemed to be composed of two speeds: rapid or languorous. She chattered and strode through the circuitous route as if she'd lived in this neighborhood since she was a babe, but then would pause and lounge against a wall as she digressed further from a point, or swagger up to a statue and trace its curves as if they had no destination whatsoever. Kell found it maddening, though Jor was predictably enchanted. Kell swallowed hard every time he laughed at one of the stranger's jokes. His flirting would get them both robbed, or worse.

Kell gritted her teeth and willed them forward. She found it difficult to anticipate what would catch this stranger's eye and what would not. They passed several statues that looked to Kell every bit as unusual as the last, but Winty paid them no more mind than she did the glowering street sweepers or the beasts pulling heavy laden carts. She did pause at one shop display, scowling in at the rainbow of colorful headwear and feathers, and her monologue halted long enough that Kell thought perhaps she'd at last run out of words. Kell wasn't sure whether the prattle or the delay irritated her more.

At one point Winty spun on her heel mid-story and walked backward, facing them. Kell spotted a glimmer in her hands even in the pale glare of daylight. With a surprising flash of jealousy, Kell realized that the woman was a teller like herself, though she did not see the creature manifesting the tale. Then a small face, furred and flat, with long, silky whiskers, popped up from under her golden-brown collar. Kell gasped.

Winty's eyes traveled downward to her shoulder, but she made no sign of having noticed anything out of the ordinary. Instead, she turned and sauntered off down another unexpected turn, leaving Jor and Kell jogging to catch up. The buildings here were denser and the streets narrower, and Kell knew, deep down, they were following this odd person straight into a trap.

A'LAN SPEAKS: HEART STORIES

There are many kinds of telling, girl. I know you know it. I know you feel *it. You feel when the ancestors come with their lessons and their lore. You know the rhythm of them, the ways they build and recede, how different they are from fireside games or songs. You feel it in the sharp turns and tricks of combat. You know what it is to lose a fight, to feel the story drain out of you, never to return unless you win it back—and even then, you know how it shifts and changes, touched by the thoughts of another. You know how it's never the same story twice.*

But do you know how to tell the truth? Do you know what it means to lay your own heart bare?

No, I don't believe you.

That is also a power, you know. Sharing that hurt. Opening yourself to others so they can see you are one of them, can see they are not alone. It's not just about the past, child. Not everything is tradition. It's the now. It's how you know you are alive.

You will know it when it comes because it will shake you. Your breath will quake, your hands will vibrate as with fever or with cold. You will be one bare nerve then, vulnerable, electric. You will want to tell and keep on telling, to be seen and held, whole and entire. You will feel your soul exposed. Then you will know you are telling the truth. Then you will tell a heart story.

"It's not just knowing your story or your opponent. You have to be aware of your situation. Your surroundings, your timing—it's all part of the tale."
—Shade's father

27. THE GROVE

Evening welled up around Shade like water from a flooding sewer, and they waded through it, their legs foul with darkness. Bright lights punctured the blurred shadows around them. Sometimes their feet carried them quickly, sometimes they shuffled along like one of the old broom ladies who swept the path before wealthy tourists, hoping for a chip. They followed one city ring and then another, winding between the neighborhoods until nothing looked familiar but everything looked the same. Trash cats hissed as they passed, their eyes round reflections like tiny golden moons.

Always running, Rat. Where do you think you're going? Go's voice whispered and nipped at them. They could no longer tell if they were imagining it or if he were somehow really in their head. There was no difference. They could hear him either way. They had let Go in. Cheap told them not to, but they'd done it anyway.

Cheap.

Shade felt a flash of something, an awful pain in their chest, followed by an unpleasant numbness that extended into their thoughts. It was hard to pay attention. They tried to think about Cheap, about how Go had somehow bought their friend—but they felt dull and blank. *You shouldn't have trusted him either.*

Shade gagged briefly and stumbled. They just had to get as far away as possible. They had to keep going.

Until what, Rat?

Shade didn't know.

The Arbor was rough around the edges, but it was nothing like the neighborhood where Shade found themself now. Hooch heads lay sprawled across curbs and curled into doorways, their clothes stained and their faces slack or crumpled with drink. Vendors barked aggressively under the glare of streetlamps, demanding passersby stop and check their wares, often little more than bits of broken tech strewn on sheets of plastic spread on the sidewalk. Shade ducked to avoid one such trash dealer, and the man made a lewd sound, grabbing Shade's shoulder and pulling them backward. They yanked easily from the man's grip, but they could feel the impression of his fingers on their skin for blocks after.

Shade hugged their jacket tight. Their stomach echoed like an angry well, and their feet were beginning to drag. They were being sloppy, they knew it, but they just didn't care. What difference did it make if they got marked? They had nothing anyone could steal. They thought about their few possessions back in their room and wondered if they would ever go back there. Maybe they should have gone to see the D Street kids—they would have given Shade a place to sleep, at least. But if Shade had been followed . . . They didn't want Go anywhere near the little ones.

There was no place they could go.

A red light stained the sidewalk ahead, and a row of prostitutes in outlandish outfits purred and posed beneath it. Shade crossed the street to avoid interaction, but something made them pause. They slunk into a doorway and crouched in the shadow to make themself as small as they could. Their tired feet ached beneath them. Shade peered out at the swaying, murmuring lineup—they were tellers, all of them. Beneath the red light, the glow of stories curled and twisted like bright smoke.

A man approached, his hands in his pockets. The storytellers became animated then, not moving faster but with exaggerated gestures, their stories louder. Shade could just make out their voices—one in particular rose above the city sounds, belonging to a tall, thin person with short, spiked hair. Their hips jutted through the sheer dress they wore—at least Shade thought it was a dress. It was little more than an afterthought of fabric, something shiny that rippled and moved against their body like a sheet of water. Shade strained to hear them describe a warm, safe nest filled with comforts—Shade could almost smell the flowers and sweet smokes, feel the softness of the cushions. They wanted to close their eyes, to rest, but as the man reached the tall, shiny teller, something about the story changed and drew Shade's attention.

A long, luxurious tail sprouted from behind the teller, fluffy and prehensile, like that of a massive fox. Shade held their breath. What sort of story was this? They had never seen anyone change their own body this way—stories were creatures of their own, animals or chimera. They weren't appendages or illusions to augment the teller.

The memory of the glowing manacles burned at their wrists, and they realized maybe this was just one more thing they believed that had turned out to be wrong. Still, something about this use of the telling made Shade shiver.

Shiny was purring now, their tail draping over the man's shoulder as he tried to pass. He stumbled and muttered something, holding up his hands apologetically. Shiny didn't seem to mind. Instead, their story grew bolder, and they narrated the kinds of things that could happen in their cozy nest.

Shade blushed. This was not their kind of story. They'd never so much as kissed another person, nor did they plan to.

The other tellers on the street corner had grown new bits of their own, too—glowing tentacles that grabbed, curling and twining about the man's legs, wings like a dragonfly's fluttering in a blur. One sprouted what looked like a whip from their forehead, from which dangled a globe of bright storylight, and Shade thought they saw the shapes of needle-like teeth between their telling lips. All these stories tickled and reached for the man's shoulders and hair as he passed, teasing but ineffectual. Even though story was weightless, substanceless, the taboo of story interacting with, of *touching* one's opponent in any way did not seem to apply here. Shade stood, trying to shake off the feeling in their belly.

They stole another glance at the needle-like teeth and decided that they didn't want any part of it. Shade stifled the itch in their mind that longed to try it for themself. What would they add to their body if they could? Their stomach gurgled loudly. *A dumpling.*

They stepped quietly back into the street, patting their pockets for stray chips and finding none. They still had a few in the pouch around their neck, but they would need to make those last. They followed the ring road and turned toward the center.

Within blocks the smell of spices and roasted meats overpowered the stench of damp concrete and trash. Colorful lights blinked and spun from snack stands, and the street was thick with pedestrians, despite the late hour. Shade paused to observe the patrons. Many wore robes rather than the common pants of the poor. These people had money.

First things first, though. They needed food more than chips, and some water. Most of the stands kept their wares behind plastic screens, but they caught a glimpse down the way of an artful stack of something—a pyramid of loaves. Shade recognized the braiding that indicated delicious filling inside: nuts and dried fruit, maybe, or stewed meats. Their mother had made those for special occasions when the family could afford it. Shade's mouth watered at the memory.

They slipped behind a trio of revelers with their arms around one another's waists. One swung a bottle wildly as all three laughed, their robes just skimming the ground. Shade was their quiet shadow, scanning the moving wall of bodies for possible exit points and finding several. *Good.* Another scan side to side beneath the brim of their hat—*no safes.*

The three marks staggered through the crowd, loud enough to part the way, and as they came even with the bread stand, Shade snaked out a hand and gripped the end of a loaf, tugging quickly to pull it from the stack. At the same moment, one of the revelers stumbled and stopped short, and Shade bumped into them from behind, jostling the pyramid.

"Watch it!" the robed man's laugh turned to a snarl as his eyes tried to focus on Shade. Shade clutched the loaf to their chest, heart hammering. But the one holding the bottle had been pulled off balance and fell against the counter then, sending the pyramid of ornate breads tumbling to the ground. The baker roared and reached through the window to clutch at the drunk's robe as the other two began shouting in defense, protesting the inconvenient location of the stand in their path. Shade stuffed the loaf inside the front of their jacket and melded into the crowd that had paused to enjoy the commotion.

Shade considered tearing into the bread right there—they might have been invisible for all anyone cared—but something told them to wait. Beneath the frantic hunger in their gut was a need to feel hidden, safe, even if for a moment. They bargained with their stomach for just a little longer, searching for a darkened doorway in which to eat in peace.

There. Behind a hooch trailer strewn with blinking lights was a large dumpster, and beyond that, Shade could make out . . . nothing. A perfectly dark spot to rest. They sighed with relief and passed between a pair of robed figures, angling for the trailer's nearest corner. The crowd was denser closer to the booze. As Shade pushed through the people milling and drinking, they thought they felt hands on them, shoving them, groping them, marking them.

Not hands. A hand. Just one, tapping their shoulder.

Shade turned.

"Nice loaf," the towering safety enforcer said. His unit—a dog—curled its lips to reveal teeth dripping with storylight saliva. "You're the one Go's looking for."

Terror flooded Shade's chest. They wheeled and pushed through the crush of bodies, throwing themself down the market street, a ripple of angry murmurs in their wake. The dog loped after them, the safe's footsteps in time with their own.

"Don't be stupid," the safe growled. "You're already bought, you little shit."

Shade lunged and stumbled past carts and stacks of crates. Colored lights melted into a blur in their peripheral vision, and they looked for exit points off the ring into other streets. They zigged left and then right, then left again.

As they ran, the snack stands dissolved into other late-night commerce and then into darkened windows and concrete archways, bricks, looming statues exaggerated by the few streetlights. The shapes were different here, somehow all wrong. They could hear their own breath coming in gasps, the panicked burst of energy waning and their legs turning to lead. The dog was right behind them. Shade remembered the sting of the manacles on their wrists and pushed harder into the ground as they ran.

The safe barked after Shade, his voice too close. They couldn't keep this pace up much longer, and the smell of the bread crushed to their chest made them dizzy with hunger. They turned onto a smaller alley and saw that the end was fenced off. Glancing upward, they saw a trellis at the end of the block and aimed for it.

A large metal garbage can was near enough the base—with their last burst of panic, they launched themself up onto the can, scrabbling onto the trellis and pulling themself up. They felt the loaf fall from their jacket and cursed. There was a barked command behind them, and something icy clamped around their ankle and yanked. Shade gripped the trellis with everything they had, but the unit's jaws surrounded their leg now. Shade had the uncanny impression that their entire foot had been locked in a block of ice. They tried to kick but felt nothing below the left knee. They gripped the trellis tightly but found that they were moving downward now—it had come unstuck from the building, and they were falling.

The trellis groaned as it leaned away from the building. The safe was shouting, and Shade thrashed, trying to free themself from the unit. Metal trash cans clattered and spilled. The falling trellis pulled away from the unit, landing with a jolt against the fence. A sharp pain shot through Shade's side as they crashed into it too. Their leg was now frozen up to the hip, and they had the bizarre sensation that they might wet their pants. They grabbed the edge of the fence behind them and flailed their legs, striking something. They heard an angry shout, and then the feeling in their leg diminished.

With the last of their energy, Shade launched themself and toppled headfirst over the fence into a tangle of crates. They bounced hard and skidded downward, tumbling even farther. Bright agony flared around their skull. There was a loud bang, a falling sensation, and Shade found themself sliding down a long surface in the dark. Pain came from all sides, and Shade noted vaguely the bread-shaped hole in their stomach, but they had no strength left to feel it or to care.

Dark weight settled across Shade's mind, and they succumbed to a lightless and hopeless sleep.

Hours later, Shade opened their eyes to trees.

"A forest is like no other place.
You'll understand when you see it."
—Shade's mother

28. BREATHING THE GREEN

"But what do we *do* with them?"

"We do what we do. What *they* do will be entirely up to them, I suspect."

"And if they were followed?"

"If they were followed, we would already be found. Perhaps the upper supply trap needs tightening, if one can so easily fall through. You are quite good at that sort of thing, are you not?"

Shade lay as still as they could, listening to the two voices—one young and anxious, the other rasping yet calm. A set of footsteps retreated, and Shade blinked rapidly, trying to adjust their eyes to the dim light. Their head hurt. They weren't seeing or thinking correctly—they could swear they saw branches arching overhead, great spindly limbs that split into countless tiny twigs with leaves rustling at their ends. A soft glow formed an ambient bowl behind the canopy above.

They *were* trees. Shade was sure of it now. As awareness rushed back into their body, they noticed much more—small sounds, unfamiliar ones: shushes and drips, tiny croaks and whirrs, a soft trickle of water into a pool. Underneath that, they heard quiet voices repeating something rhythmic, like chanters but without the grandeur or aggression, only gentle repetition in unison. The sound tugged at something in their chest, and Shade was bewildered to find tears leaking down their face.

"It's quite beautiful, isn't it?" The rasping voice echoed faintly in the cavernous space. Shade tilted their head to see a figure approaching. They sat up and immediately regretted it, discomfort entering every joint and soft surface of their body. They felt like a child's doll, stitched together out of rags and stuffed with pain. They couldn't run if they wanted to—and, oddly, Shade didn't. They examined themself and saw that they had bandages on one wrist and a stiff splint stabilizing an ankle. Wherever they were now, they had been cared for.

They sat on a raised mat, one cot among many, they realized, as if this place were both sanctuary and dormitory. The figure paused as it neared, evaluating Shade, before choosing the cot directly beside them on which to sit. Though the light was weak and dappled, Shade could clearly discern the man's features as he regarded them with a curious smile. His face was deeply lined—not as old as Cheap, but old. His hair was cropped so short Shade could only make out the glint of gray. He raised his eyebrows as if waiting for something, and Shade realized he had asked a question.

"I guess," Shade croaked. Even their throat was sore.

They were in an enormous hall with a floor of packed earth and round openings to passageways leading off in many directions. A small stream snaked a path through the center of the hall, ending in a stone-ringed pool. Dozens of trees clustered around the water, reaching for the weak light that filled the dome overhead. Some had silvering bark that peeled like old skin; others were thick and gnarled, like candle wax that had dripped and cooled. Still others shivered, spindly and naked, their branches whisker fine. Shade's mouth hung open, and they closed it, swallowing painfully.

Something about the trees looked strange, though Shade did not actually know how trees were meant to look. They had seen them only in their bedtime stories and in dreams, as well as the scant few that remained on the temple promenade, where they'd once dared to lift a few chips. These here seemed sickly, starved for something, yet they sprouted stubbornly with a will to live, leaves outstretched like beggar children demanding sunlight.

Something leaped from a branch and wheeled overhead, cutting a circle through the air before flitting and disappearing again among the leaves. Shade flinched, which made their shoulders jerk painfully.

"Was that a *bird?*"

The man laughed softly. "It was."

To Shade's great embarrassment, tears continued to trace their cheeks unabated. They were just so tired, they realized, and everything was so strange, and they were tired of strangeness and tired of being tired. They were tired of running, and being lonely, and being broke. Gazing up into the branches with the uncanny glow behind them, something in their chest snapped. Shade took a deep breath, feeling every ache in their ribs, and let it out. What escaped was something between a cough and a sob. They reached to pull their hat down over their ears and discovered it was gone, lost in their tumble through the crates.

"We found this next to you," said the man. His voice was comforting, soft with an accent Shade couldn't quite place. They turned to look, wiping their face gingerly, and saw the man extending a rumple of soft brown cloth. Shade took their hat, twisting it familiarly between their hands.

The sound of locks turning echoed from one of the tunnels, followed by footsteps. A figure in a simple tunic and loose pants entered the great hall, guiding a bent old woman leaning heavily on a cane. The figure took her gently by the elbow and slowed their pace to assist her as she shuffled toward the pool. The elderly woman murmured something indistinct and settled herself onto a bench near the water's edge, a detail Shade had missed before. The guide bowed and retreated, and the old woman set her cane aside and relaxed into stillness as Shade watched. The soft chanting continued, punctuated only with the hum of insects. An unseen bird sang a brief melody, as if testing its song, and then repeated it with more certainty.

Shade looked back at their companion. He was wearing the same simple gray clothes as the guide, and Shade realized it was a uniform. The man regarded them, as if waiting patiently for them to ask the next question.

"What is this place?" Shade asked.

"This, young tumbler, which you so cleverly found," he said, lowering his voice, "is the Grove."

They heard the locks turn again, and this time a small group entered, bowing reverentially and speaking to one another in whispers that traveled unimpeded across the great space. They, too, made their way to the pool but settled instead on their knees in the packed earth. One dipped their fingers in the stream, muttering, and touched their forehead with the wet. Another bent with their face nearly touching the ground. Shade saw their eyes were closed as they inhaled, smelling the dirt.

"What are they doing?"

"Praying," said the man, "Meditating, thinking. Not-thinking." He sat calmly, his hands folded in his lap as he regarded Shade. "Breathing the Green."

"Breathing the what?"

"Humans need the Green. Trees, plants. The Green is good for us, for our bodies and our minds. It helps us feel safe and relaxed. It helps us focus. It allows our bodies to fight disease." The old man looked into their eyes. "Or to heal. Do you feel it?"

Shade looked away. Mostly they felt broken and exhausted, and—now that they thought of it—unbelievably hungry. But they also didn't feel like they were in danger, which was a pleasant change. Something about the place made Shade melancholic, as if they had misplaced something important but could no longer remember where or what it was. They took a deep breath in, feeling every stab and hitch in their ribcage. The air was richer, somehow. Like the air had more . . . *air* in it.

"Mm," they answered noncommittally. Their stomach growled loudly, remembering the abandoned loaf, and the man smiled and put his hand on Shade's shoulder. Shade shrugged it off.

"Forgive me, young tumbler," he said. "Now that you are awake, we must find you some food. Stay here. I'll be back soon." Shade watched the man disappear into one of the tunnels.

They were very happy not to move, and their stomach cramped painfully at the thought of a meal. They put on their hat and arranged their braids flat against their chest. They knew they needed to pay more attention—look for exits, figure out what time of day it was, make a plan—but they couldn't seem to muster the urgency. The man was right—they *did* feel calmer.

If just a room full of trees does this, what would it be like in the Broken Forest? Out of habit, they reached for the familiar fantasy, the one that had sustained them through countless trials and fights: hefting the pouch stuffed with cubes and chips, purchasing papers for transit and a seat on the right carriage, watching the city gates close behind them, the road to the Broken Forest unfurling like a welcoming carpet. The dream always grew hazy at this point—time sped forward to find Shade surrounded by lush green, pawing an indent into rich, moist loam and dropping the acorn they wore around their neck . . . *You will plant it, and it will grow.*

The edges of the fantasy blurred and disintegrated. They were tired and broke and sore. They were lost and in the company of strangers. Still, something about this place felt right.

Shade peered around them. The more they looked, they more they saw. What they had initially taken for uniform green at the base of the trees, they now saw was a varied tapestry of flowers and plants, more shapes than they could count. The cots around them were angled to allow occupants to sit and look without staring into the back of another's head. Lying down, one could run one's fingers through the bits of green bobbing at the base of the cot. It wasn't comfortable exactly, but it was *comforting.*

Shade curled onto their side and let their hand dangle, brushing the small plants below with their fingertips. The stems were springy, and the leaves gave off a scent that Shade didn't have a name for—something spicy but also fresh and cold-smelling. They pinched some between their fingers and held it to their nose. It made them feel like they had swallowed a breeze.

Shade heard a noise beneath them and leaned to peek under their cot. This proved too painful, and they lay back down again. The sound returned, and then they felt something wet against their hand, a ticklish lump that moved. They jerked their hand back and bolted upright, to the dismay of every joint. Shade stared.

Beneath them sat a small frog. They had never seen a live frog before—the river waters were too foul by the time they reached the city—but they had seen them sold as meat at the market, dangling from bamboo poles by their back legs. They were more compact than Shade had expected, wadded up. The frog leaped away from their cot, and Shade gasped. When it jumped, the entire creature unfolded and became so long, then regathered itself again. Shade was taken with a wild urge to chase after it, which their body overruled. They watched the frog make its way toward the pond and disappear into the water with a satisfying plop.

The man returned to their bedside and presented Shade with a small round of bread filled with a fragrant vegetable soup. Shade thought they might faint. They tore the edge from the bowl, nearly spilling it, dunked it, and crammed it in their mouth. They closed their eyes as they chewed and opened them to a look of amusement on the man's face.

"I would have brought it sooner, had I known," he said mildly.

Shade ignored this but grabbed the spoon that was offered with a nod and began shoveling the soup in. The man seemed content to sit quietly as Shade destroyed the bread bowl, and he looked politely elsewhere as both contents and vessel disappeared into Shade's mouth. When Shade finished, the man gently took their spoon away and offered a handkerchief he produced from a pocket. Shade realized there was a ceramic mug of water beside the cot, which they quickly emptied.

With a full belly, Shade felt like they might survive. Wiping their face with the rough cloth of the handkerchief, they narrowed their eyes at the man.

"What do you want from me?" Shade asked. The man tilted his head at the question.

"This is a place to heal," he said, choosing his words carefully. "Some people return often, as if drinking from a spring. Some only come when they are very tired or very sad." The man paused, holding Shade's gaze. They felt bare and vulnerable, altogether too visible beneath his look. "Some come to stay and never leave," he continued. "They are drawn to the Grove and see the power of it, understand its importance. They make the Grove their own work."

Shade had the distinct impression they were being asked a question. Was this a test?

The man waited in silence. Shade avoided his gaze and returned their attention to the hall around them. There was something about the shape of the ceiling that reminded them of . . . something—they just couldn't put their finger on what. Another figure in gray descended a staircase that Shade had taken for the back wall. Everything here was hidden by foliage, and it was easy to mistake stone for shadow. The person was met halfway by another in the same uniform; they greeted each other with a double handclasp and then passed by on the stairs, the second heading up in the direction the first had come.

The man cleared his throat. "Why don't you tell me how you came to tumble into our Grove, young one?"

"Shade."

"I beg your pardon?"

"My name is Shade."

The man's face split in an unexpectedly bright smile. "You honor me with your name, Shade," he said. "I am Xylem."

"I don't have any idea how I got here, Xylem," Shade said, and they meant it.

"The Grove called you, to be sure," he said. The man radiated deep patience, as if he had no other purpose in life but to listen to them. "Why don't you start from the beginning?"

Shade sighed and looked at their hands. Perhaps their full belly gave them an unusual sense of security. Maybe they were too worn out to care what happened next. Whatever it was, Shade told this gentle stranger everything.

They told of losing their parents, of living alone for so long scrambling for chips and food they'd lost track of their own age. They told of their few friends—of the D Street kids, how they looked out for the little ones, but how the children were their rivals in the streets when it came to picking pockets, their camaraderie conditional and specific. They told of Ma Bud's surly care, of Cheap's poor jokes. They felt a deep warmth in their chest as they spoke, something fierce and strong. Their hands fell open in their lap, and a glow formed in their casting palm without volition, a bright mouse wriggling to life, leaping and dashing, scurrying through the air stealing luminous crumbs that materialized before them. Shade told of the Broken Forest, describing scenes of lush greenery their parents had painted for them. Their chest ached with longing, and Xylem's eyes glittered in the storylight. Whether they were wet with tears or with age, Shade was uncertain, but they knew they had him spellbound. Yet this was not a telling for an audience—Shade was overcome with the swell of their own story, their teeth chattering as they shook with a feeling of exposure and release.

Shade recounted their combat rounds, winning at places like the Box to make money for food, saving the odd chip for their escape fund. The mouse grew wings and sprouted fangs as it badgered shadowed enemies in the air before them. Shade told of Mr. Go, of the lessons and the surveillance, the terrifying mix of power and servitude that relationship had brought. The mouse shifted, grew large and uncanny, strange appendages bristling from its parts. Shade described the loss of their savings, of Cheap's betrayal, of their flight from the Arbor, and all they had seen since, the stolen loaf and subsequent chase. The mouse elongated into a blur, whipping through a maze as a ball of light, growing limbs again and climbing, then falling . . .

Shade's sides heaved. They gathered the storylight back into their palm and discovered that they were weeping, their breath coming in deep shudders. They shook with the raw, singular chill of telling a heart story.

They again felt Xylem's hand on their shoulder, and again they leaned away from it, even as something inside them screamed to be held. Shade felt empty and wrung out, free from the weight they'd been carrying but free of everything else as well—their sense of purpose, their hope. The Broken Forest was out of reach now, no more a possibility than competing in the Cycle. Or having their family back.

They wept until they were dry, and then they rubbed their face with the handkerchief. They felt sticky and hot and wanted to go to the baths, and they realized they had no idea where the baths were, had no idea where *they* were. They felt entirely dependent upon this gentle man, a feeling they disliked very much.

"You are welcome here," Xylem offered in his comforting lilt. "You can stay as long as you like. We could use someone of your—talents."

Shade peered at him from under their hat brim.

"How do you mean?"

Xylem raised his eyes to the canopy of leaves. "The trees," he said. "How do you think we keep them alive down here in the sewers?"

The sewers! That was the shape that looked so familiar—they were in an abandoned waterway under the City. Shade had slogged through more than one of those tunnels dodging safes in the past. Some of the kids had a whole network of them they used to get from place to place unseen, though they were wet and dark and full of creatures that did not like having children wading through. This place was dry and comfortable, and—

"How is it so bright?"

Xylem's face softened into a wrinkled smile. "How do you think?" He asked. He pointed along the back wall and the ceiling. Shade looked and listened. That glow, that sound of soft chanting . . . They blinked.

Xylem nodded. "That's right," he said. "We tell them stories."

"Storylight?" Shade gaped. "Trees can live on storylight? But I thought—" Shade paused. They weren't sure *what* they thought anymore. Shade had always been sure that stories couldn't touch you, couldn't make a sound, had always assumed they had no impact in the physical world at all. But there had been the manacles, the odd appendages of the sex workers in the street. In their head, Shade replayed their conversation with Go about remaking reality: his trick with the business card, the spider that had moved an object, the object that had changed before their eyes. Shade was no longer sure what was possible. All things considered, storylight helping a plant grow seemed the least surprising thing they'd learned lately.

"It takes a lot of work," Xylem agreed. "We have tenders chanting together from false dawn to false dusk. They tell in shifts." The old man indicated the stairwell leading up the back wall. "Together, we have created story patterns that generate just the right balance of light for photosynthesis."

"Imagine what the city would do if they knew this was here," Shade said with not a little bitterness. Xylem's face darkened.

"Which is why we keep this place well-hidden. I do not believe it was by chance that you tumbled into our supply chute, young teller, but it is important that nobody followed you—nobody that you do not trust," he added. "The Grove is a sanctuary for many. A safe place, but I believe it is also holy. And sacred things must be protected."

Shade nodded. They were spent and had no energy left for talking.

"Shade," Xylem said softly. "I wonder if you would consider this as a place you might—remain. You are in need of rest, and my hope is that the Grove may enrich you with the spirit of its origins." The old man paused, his look asking if his meaning was clear. When Shade said nothing, he continued. "Many of the trees we care for here were rescued as small saplings from the Broken Forest, in an attempt to save some corner of the diversity it once held." The old man folded his hands in his lap in both resignation and apology. "What you see is what remains."

Shade received the news with blankness, as if some part of them had already known this to be true. They clutched at their amulet beneath their shirt and felt nothing but a hollow space where their hopes of escape once lay.

There was nothing left to save. In some ways, it was easier. Shade was so tired.

You will plant it, and it will grow. You'll do this, won't you?

They lay back on their cot without a word and closed their eyes. They felt Xylem's hand on their head but did not move away. They heard his footsteps retreating on the carpet of green, heard the trickle of water in the pool, heard the soft chant keeping the trees alive. And then they escaped into sleep.

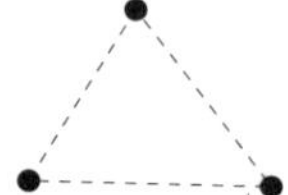

The Empty Cup: Southeastern upper quarter, flood season

29. GROWTH

To Kell's begrudging surprise, Winty led them not to a den of thieves but to the city's core. The central ring was encircled by a metal fence, though to call it that missed its effect entirely. Worked in the form of twisting vines and flowers, the dark iron bloomed lifelike and beautiful. From a distance, Kell thought it was a wall, but once they approached, she was able to see the space between its metallic curves, and the gardens and temple it obscured. Guards were posted every few paces, armed with units of different shapes and sizes—though mostly the sizes were large. Kell clenched and unclenched her jaw to match the pulse of her nervous heart.

One guard asked them their business, which Jor explained with his utmost charm, an effort that was lost on his audience. The guard only nodded, and an unseen mechanism opened the gate, the vines clicking apart to swing inward. Winty trailed along inside as if she were attendant to their mission, which irritated Kell. But the only thing that mattered was that she was going to get the stones back and get out of this godsforsaken city and back Home, where they—where *she* belonged.

Kell's determination not to be impressed by the temple was quickly lost to awe. The excess and filigree that appeared on the city things that made their way to the desert—like the sled with the antelope, she recalled with a frown—were wrought here a hundredfold. Ornate lampposts sprouted from the earth like enormous flowers on towering stems, and every structure bloomed with decorative curls. Trees rustled and swayed along a broad avenue made entirely of mosaic, patterns swirling and dancing at their feet. It was like stepping on a story, she thought. Here the restless heat of the city vanished and was replaced with cool shade. Kell felt almost peaceful as they neared the temple, though her heart hammered with purpose.

The temple itself rose before them, majestic and wholly unlike the brutal concrete reaches of the city. The structure was made entirely of wood, its vast surfaces carved in loops and whorls, beasts and tableaux writhing across its exterior. It accordioned skyward, every story slightly narrower than the last, terminating in a point so far above they had to crane their necks just to take it all in. As Kell stared, it occurred to her the temple wasn't any taller than many of the other buildings in the city, but being set apart from the dense construction of the city's outer rings made it look more imposing. She told herself that it was a trick of perspective, designed to intimidate—but it worked.

As at the city gates, they were again greeted by a row of guards, only these were brisk and efficient rather than stern and seated in an orderly row at a broad desk. Clerks in lieu of safety officers, she decided.

"State your business," the man before them droned, not bothering to look up as he shuffled through a handful of papers and wooden tokens. Kell had never seen so much paper in one place.

Jor bowed. "Ma'ani," he began. "May you find home wherever you are. We thank you for welcoming us into the heart of great Soogway—reports of its glory are truly understated outside its formidable walls. We are representatives of the northern deserts, sent as a delegation to discuss the reappropriation of geologic resour—"

"This man doesn't give a hare's ass who we are," Kell muttered, louder than she'd intended. She thought of Silaya's hands on her face, her demand that they succeed, and stifled a jolt of impatience. Hearing that kind of groveling city speak coming from Jor's mouth made her want to put a torch to the temple and be done with it. Winty giggled behind her. Jor's face maintained a stiff mask of charm.

"This is my part," he hissed under his breath. "If I do this right, you don't have to do yours." Kell lifted her chin but said nothing, fighting the urge to fidget. He was right, of course, but now that they were here, she found she didn't care about doing things the proper way. She just wanted what rightfully belonged to her People. And then to get the hell out of here.

The clerk, however, barely registered that she had spoken. He turned and muttered something to the guard at his left, who opened a small box (also wooden, she noticed) and flicked through a stack of tiles that clicked neatly as he made his selection, handing one back to the clerk.

"Second floor, fourth audience chamber. Complaints and entreaties," the clerk instructed, passing the token to Jor.

"But where—"

"She knows," the clerk said, indicating Winty with his chin.

Kell wheeled around. "What?"

"You didn't ask," Winty shrugged, offering a little wave of farewell to the guards as she passed. One of them returned the wave, tossing her a wooden token of her own, which she caught easily and secreted into a pocket.

Kell and Jor stared as Winty sauntered through the entry ahead and out of sight. They both spoke at once.

"This is perfect," Jor said.

"This is a nightmare," said Kell. Her brother grinned, and Kell felt a curious dread awaken in her, like a golem stirring to life.

"Who *is* she?" she whispered between gritted teeth. "Why is she with us? Why are we *following her*?" Jor shrugged.

"She's our guide," he said, and headed in the direction Winty had gone. "Be grateful."

Kell scowled. *Ancestors grant me patience.*

Inside the temple, Kell's footsteps struck the polished wood floors and her pulse thrummed in her ears, her vision both sharp and dreamlike. Through the tunnel of her anxiety, all she could do was train her focus on their strange golden-brown guide who was leading them gods knew where. Winty, meanwhile, strolled over mosaics and past magnificent columns like she'd lived there all her life.

A loud clatter made Kell nearly jump from her skin. Jor had dropped the wooden tile, and as he stooped to retrieve it, the beacon slipped from his shirt and hung around his neck. It pointed at the token on the floor, the long dark line of the chain like a serpent from the Way at Ease. Kell shivered. It was a sign, she knew: the only way home was through this process. Jor slipped the tile into his pocket, returning the beacon to its place beneath his clothes.

Winty led them through a series of twisting hallways and up a flight of stairs that looked to be hewn from a single tree, the steps worn smooth and rounded by countless footfalls. Doors flanked them on either side, some round like portals and others narrow or sliding. All were ornately carved, surrounded by filigree and, in some places, even living plants set into the walls themselves. A few of the doors hung open, and Kell heard music come from one as they passed, soft murmurs of conversation from another. From a third came the sound of running water, and Jor slowed to peek in, but Winty tugged at his sleeve and shook her head.

"This way," she said.

They passed other people, some gliding along in the long robes of dignitaries, others dressed as common folk, perhaps supplicants like themselves. Kell twisted the edge of her scarf as they walked. No one took note of them, and she had the odd sensation that she had become invisible.

Down one hallway of windows was a giant cage made of thin bamboo and wires. Plants bristled all around it, and it nearly filled the corridor, reaching all the way to the ceiling. Here, Winty stopped and leaned into the bars, pressing her hands flat against them. A small bird hopped from one metal perch to another, offering a series of melancholy trills. Winty's face contracted, and Kell feared for a moment the other woman might cry, but she only whispered to the bird, then turned again, leading them at last to a door flanked by more guards.

Kell wondered again who Winty was and why on dry earth they trusted her. The forest guide smiled at her then, amber eyes glinting as if she had read her thoughts. Kell could almost feel Jor being drawn to her, a wayfinder pulling toward camp. She swallowed, hoping his judgment wasn't so easily bought.

"Show them," Winty said, utterly at ease.

Jor produced the token from his pocket. The guard made a display of examining it, then escorted the three of them into a large audience chamber. Kell noticed he'd given Winty's token only a cursory glance.

For all its finery, the chamber was a very big waiting room. It was round and recessed, which, when she tried to figure out how it fit into the rest of the building, made Kell's head hurt. At the back, more functionaries sat behind a dais amid piles of paper and stacked tiles. The room reminded Kell of the old stone amphitheater her camp had visited once in the red zone, except the walls here were covered in carvings—not the whorls or constellations sometimes found on ancient cliff faces in the desert, but stiff, exaggerated images of machines. Looking at them made her lip curl against her will.

They descended a series of steps that turned into risers. Yet another guard stopped them to inspect their tokens and then gestured for them to take a seat. Kell saw dozens of other supplicants seated around the rings, some with anxious, pinched expressions, others having given in to the intense gravity of boredom, their faces and shoulders sagging.

Winty sprawled on a riser with a loud sigh, her attitude aggressively casual. She produced a knife from one of her many pockets and began playing a game with her own hand, the rules of which appeared to involve coming as close to losing a finger as possible without actually getting cut.

"You might want to get comfortable," she said as the knife blurred between her fingers. "It's gonna be a while." Kell expected her to launch into another of her long, prattling discourses, but Winty stayed quiet.

Jor sat beside Kell, his eyes scanning the ceiling and walls. Kell knew he was admiring the tech that allowed the room to be so brightly lit without any apparent source, and she hated him a little for it. She perched uneasily on the edge of the riser, trying to hear what was being said at the front of the room. The acoustics here seemed the opposite of an amphitheater, somehow, as if the clerks on the dais were only mouthing their words—no sound reached her at all. A stifling stillness filled the chamber, as if they were each trapped in their own thoughts as they waited. Kell heard a man to her right yawn loudly and was relieved.

"How many times have you been here?" Jor asked.

Winty shrugged.

"Too many," she said. "Folks where I'm from don't like coming to Soogway much. They get the jumps, like me. But I can handle it better than most, so I usually get sent whenever they have new deals that need making."

"And where is that, exactly?" Kell asked, more sharply than she'd intended.

"Where is what?"

"Where you're from."

Winty smiled. "I'm from the woods," she said with pride. "The real ones, where things don't grow in rows, and everything gets to just be."

"I thought the woods were all gone."

"Sure, the city axed all they had, but there be plenty of forests left elsewhere. We just make sure the Soogers can't find them." Winty winked.

"Soogers?" Kell asked.

"City folk!" The golden-brown woman's teeth showed as she grinned. "That's what we call 'em where I'm from. They have stuff we want, and we have stuff they need. So long as they don't find us, we're happy to trade."

"That's why you come here all the time?" Jor asked. "To trade?"

Winty raised her eyebrows. "Only when I have to," she said. "And I try to leave before I get the jumps."

Kell didn't know what the jumps were but was pretty sure she had them, too. She had no idea how long it would be before Jor got to speak to the whoever-it-was there in the front, and the tense, unnatural quiet of the room made her stomach hurt. She stared at the bland functionaries on their dais surrounded by their carved tech worship, and a liquid fury began to move through her veins. *These* were the people who would decide the fate of her kin? These severed bureaucrats had the power to withhold the ancient and rightful pulse of her Home? She briefly wondered what a god story might look like unleashed indoors.

Kell took a deep breath in and envisioned the sweet smoke of her makeshift altar back at the inn, imagined it wafting onto the balcony and drifting through the filthy maze of streets toward the gate. She pictured it traveling, snakelike, over the stump-studded grassland and the rocky terrain at the edge of the desert, before gliding with fierce speed into the rolling sands of Home. She held tight to the tendril of smoke in her mind and sent her prayers where they belonged. *We must not fail*, she repeated as her blood burned.

Movement at the front of the room interrupted her thoughts. The petitioners standing before the dais turned and trudged back up the stairs. As they passed, Kell could see the defeat on their faces. There was a shimmer above the dais, and something small and glowing wriggled up from among the clerks and unfurled in the air like a giant insect drying its wings. It formed itself into a symbol, and Kell saw many waiting look down at their tokens. One person stood and made their way to the front, and the symbol vanished.

Kell scowled. "They're using a teller to call people's turns?" *What a disgusting use of sacred power.*

"Clever," said Jor.

Winty launched into a list of all the ridiculous things she'd seen city bureaucrats do, her words a restless, uninterrupted stream. Kell leaned back against the riser, grateful at least that the strange acoustics of the room muted Winty's voice. They waited.

After what felt like hours, the shimmering symbol matched the one on the tile Jor clutched. He rose stiffly, adjusted his clothing, and straightened his shoulders. Kell watched him gather his courage and his charm. She stood too, then, and took his hand, turning him to look at her.

"Ancestors guide your words," she said. "I know you can do this."

He nodded, his tattoos dancing across his skin. She squeezed his hand, and then he was gone, stepping silently toward the panel of clerks. She studied his body language as he greeted them, his gestures smoothly conveying both respect and authority. If there was one thing Jor was good at, it was talking to people. She wondered, though, whether these officials registered such subtle cues.

"They never let you settle on your first time," Winty said, nudging Kell like she was sharing a joke.

"What do you mean?" Kell didn't take her eyes off her brother.

"They test you out, get a sense of your moves, your branches, how you respond. How much you'd be willing to lose."

Kell turned at this. The golden-brown woman was looking at her placidly, but her eyes held a sadness that unsettled her.

"We aren't willing to lose anything," she said. "That's why we're here."

"I think it's great what you're doing," Winty whispered, leaning in. Kell noted that the strange smell of this woman was quite pleasing. "I hope you win."

Kell angled away from her. "Of course we will," she said gruffly. Her brother was listening as one of the clerks spoke at length. A teller, from the looks of it, as small sparks sloughed from their casting hand. Kell tried to read the angle of Jor's shoulders, but he held himself carefully, betraying no reaction to the clerk's words. Kell wanted to smash all the tech in the room.

Winty sighed heavily, as if she were watching a fight, and her teller had just lost. The woman's words reformed in her head.

"And what do you even know about it?" Kell snapped, several seconds too late.

"You said you want your rocks back," the forest dweller answered simply. "I hope you get them."

Kell felt a twinge of regret—Winty had done nothing but help them so far, but there was something about her that made Kell uncomfortable. She had just appeared when they needed a guide, and she knew about wayfinding and the missing stones, not to mention her easy rapport with the temple guards. It was too much, almost like—

Help from the gods. Just as I asked for.

Kell looked at Winty and found her looking back, again giving Kell the strange sense that she had overheard her thoughts.

"The Soogers'll take anything they can," Winty said softly. "It's up to the rest of us to protect what's left." Her face was serious now, the mocking nonchalance replaced with a grief that mirrored Kell's own.

Kell nodded. "It's up to us."

Jor appeared beside them, his approach silenced by the strange acoustics of the chamber. Kell searched his face for a sign of the news he brought.

"Poor timing," he said, taking a seat between them. His voice was too casual—Kell knew he was trying to put her at ease, which only doubled her anxiety. "Apparently there is some big event in a week or so," he went on.

"The Cycle," Winty agreed. "When all the fancy folk show off their dragons and whatnot."

"What does that have to do with us?" Kell asked.

Jor took her hand, a pacifying gesture that made her snatch it back. Her chest tightened. She could hear her own exhales, and she noted that she was breathing too fast. It was the same sensation she had when she had to tell for a crowd, before the story swept her away.

"They have stayed all decisions of treaty renegotiations until after the Cycle. I think they're trying to encourage petitioners to engage in the event. There will be a host of challenges prior to the competition. In front of the public."

Kell shook her head. "I don't understand."

"They're giving us all a choice," he said. "We can wait—sit here, explore the city, bide our time until they are ready to hear pleas again after this Cycle, whatever it is, though they said there is no guarantee when that would be. Or—"

"Or what?!" Kell barely contained her shriek. Waiting weeks was unthinkable. The extraction machines were out there *right now*.

"Or you challenge the general to combat. In the Cycle."

Kell dropped his hand and stared. From behind Jor, Winty caught her eyes. In place of the waiting and uncertainty, Kell felt suddenly cold and still, as if the silence of the room had crept into her blood. This choice was no choice at all.

You will not fail.

Kell stood. "Fine," she said. "I will fight."

The Four Points: Western upper quarter

30. POWER

The walk back to the inn was a blur of heat and concrete. After the clerks had given Kell instructions for the challenge and Winty had had her audience as well, the forest dweller offered to guide them back to the Traveler's Quarter near the gate. She and Jor were now locked in discussion several paces ahead, the two talking animatedly with their hands. Winty's story creature, or whatever it was, crept out from under her golden-brown jacket and scampered around her shoulders, only to disappear again into a pocket.

Kell's thoughts swam—part of her wanted nothing more than a chance to wreak devastation on the city's smug narrative, to summon all the awesome power of the ancestors and the gods in defense of the stones. How sweet it would be to watch her desert creation sting their hollow displays to death, tear their tropes to pieces, and scatter them to the winds. She thought of her false god, with all its storms and vengeance, and smiled bitterly. The satisfaction faded quickly, however, when she pictured the massive Soogway audience, and her misgivings about combat flared. The idea of a very public battle—a *spectacle*, from the sound of it—with her entire People's way of life at stake, made her want to vomit. She fought to remind herself what Ama had always told her when she grew anxious before a fight.

It is an honor to be met in combat.

In stories, honor sounded like a shining thing, something light and vibrant that lent strength to its bearer and armored the teller against doubt. Kell saw now that it was instead a weight, a burden to be born. Ama had known this, certainly, and believed Kell capable of carrying it. Hadn't she?

At the thought of her grandmother, a sweet ache pierced her chest. Imperious, brilliant Ma'Shifra who could silence a crowd with a glance and topple even the fiercest warrior with her clever, vicious storytelling. Yet she had taken Kell and Jor in with such warmth when their mother had left their camp to follow a man she'd only just met. When their mother had broken Kell's heart.

Ama, who smelled like almonds and resin and ozone, like a ritual cast in lightning. Ama with the sweet singing voice, who had made the constellations leap to life through story so Kell and Jor would remember them when they were far from camp. She wouldn't have sent Kell here if she didn't think her up to this task. Or had she simply assumed Jor would succeed? Had she sent Kell only out of necessity, as her own health prevented her from making the trip? Kell had to believe that Ama had faith in her—that the entire council believed she could win. She considered the false god story they had prepared. Could Kell summon it on her own? And if she did, could she control it?

So immersed was she in these thoughts that she nearly walked straight into Jor's back, not realizing their arrival at the Traveler's Quarter. Jor and Winty were still talking—something about city tech Kell didn't care to follow. It was clear Jor did not want the strange forest guide to leave, nor was she in any hurry to do so on her own.

"Let's get something to eat," he suggested, and Winty quickly agreed. Relieved to be back in familiar surroundings, Kell followed them into the inn, hoping her belongings were still where she'd left them in their room.

Over bowls of thin, grayish soup, Winty explained the limits of her trade with Soogway. The forests of her home were rich in nuts and oils that were highly prized among the wealthy artisans and the ruling class of city officials. This gave her people some leverage. But in turn, they had to take great pains to keep their territory hidden from city scouts. Kell remembered the sea of stumps surrounding the city walls, and her appetite fled.

Pushing her bowl away, she looked at Winty, who seemed equally disinclined to finish her meal. "Why not just stay hidden and avoid the city altogether?"

The forest guide raised her eyes mid-slurp. "They gots things we want, don't they?" She sucked the broth off the spoon loudly and made a face. "City tech, it's more than just them fancy lights and stupid-boxes . . . "

Kell snorted at this, despite herself.

"They don't even know what they got," Winty continued. "My people do things with it these Soogers haven't dreamed of. They keep cutting things down, but we're making up ways to help things grow. Did you know, you can use them power cells to run pumps and make smokeless cookfires just by adapting them to act more like plants?" Kell felt her eyes glaze over, but Jor leaned in, his soup forgotten. "You can make them soak up the sun, just like leaves do," Winty went on. "And then you got your juice right there. No need to burn trees or dig up them flashy stones."

Kell choked, but Jor spoke first. "What do you mean, 'flashy stones'?"

Winty laughed her wide-mouthed laugh and slapped the table. "You mean you don't even know what they're digging them up for? They suck the juice out of 'em! Run their little boxes and their blinkies and all the beep-beep." Winty made a bizarre series of hand gestures in an effective parody of navigating a busy city street.

Kell's soup threatened to come back up. "You mean, they're harvesting the most ancient part of our land so they can turn lights on at night?" Her voice came out too high, almost a squeak.

"Incredible," Jor shook his head thoughtfully. "It never occurred to me they could be harnessed in that way—"

"Are you out of your severed mind? Jor!" Kell gripped the edge of the table to keep from flipping it over. "You think it's an interesting use of the stones? You think it's *clever*?" He looked at her as if returning from somewhere far away.

"No, no," he repeated, which somehow made it worse. "I just feel like there's so much we don't understand about what they are and what they do."

"They are gifts. From the *gods*." Kell was shaking. "They don't need to *do* anything."

Jor nodded, distracted. Kell felt at once furious with him, and also very, very lonely. Winty was absorbed with something at the bottom of her bowl.

"She just said there are other ways these people could produce power," Kell said, fighting to keep her voice down. The noise of the inn had settled to a low murmur, and the tingle at her neck said their conversation was now being attended to by the ears of strangers. "All we need to do is get our stones back," she said in a hoarse whisper. "And make sure they don't take any more."

There was a long, uncomfortable pause in which Winty played with her spoon. Finally, Jor said, "So, you have a week to prepare. What's your plan?"

"Ma'Shifra had an idea for how to beat the general back at camp, but I don't know if it's the right move for this."

"You tell the truth, right? An honest appeal will create its own power. 'Trust the ancestors.'"

"Don't. You know it's not that simple."

"You're the teller—I'm not trying to tell you how to do your work," he said, though the arrogant tilt of his head said otherwise. Then he softened. "There's a lot at stake."

"I know that," she snapped. "It's just . . . a heart story might not work."

Kell relayed Silaya's warning, how Upepo had lost to the combat general who took the first stone, the strangeness of his tactics. Ama's plan to use a false god instead, she explained, would intimidate the city's teller with a display of fake power, dressed in the symbols of Home.

Winty whistled in appreciation. "Not a bad idea, that," she said. "They gonna do the same thing to you—intimidate, I mean."

Kell frowned. "That means the general will be ready for a big display. I feel like I need something more, something they haven't seen before."

"It seems a little late to prepare new tricks, doesn't it?" Jor sounded irritated. Kell hated that she agreed.

"I didn't ask to do this," she reminded him. "I'm just trying to figure out the best way. I don't want to risk something sacred, but I also don't want to do what the general will expect. Whether it's lore or heart stories or this false god, they all feel to me like they're missing a piece." She shifted uncomfortably in her chair. How did people sit in these all the time? She wished she were back in Ama's tent, listening to the sand shifting and the crackle of watchfires, the gentle snort of sandbeasts signaling that all was well.

"Who could teach you?" Winty asked.

"What difference does it make?" Jor said. "We don't know anyone here, and if we did, the chances of them being a gifted teller . . . " He trailed off thoughtfully.

"What?" Kell nudged him under the table with her foot.

"What about that one we met?"

"What one?" Winty asked.

"The *thief*?" Kell scoffed. That pickpocket who'd taken her resin, thinking it was ironwood chips. She'd nearly made them pee their trousers with the poison tree story, she remembered. Then she recalled the blades, and the other unusual moves the small teller had made. She chewed her lip. She hadn't seen any of that before. Maybe it wasn't a terrible idea.

"OK," she nodded. "I'm listening. How would we find them?"

Jor shrugged. "We ran into them right outside of here. Maybe they'll come by again?"

"Doubt it," Winty broke in. "If they're a thief, they'll hit different places all the time. Those street folk do make great tellers, though," she said. "There was one time when I was down by the gator hole, and this whole little crew of 'em made some folks think they were falling into the pit, and then they got rescued by a giant spider—except one of them had a rope around their waist, and while all the Soogers leaned in to see what was what, another kiddo was stripping their pockets clean!" Winty threw her head back in that laugh of hers, the sound like a wild dog shouting at the sky. "It was brilliant." She wiped her eyes, chuckling.

"So then how do we find them?" Kell was impatient, drawn toward this new idea as if pushed by a strong wind.

"Could—could we use the Way at Ease to locate a person?" Jor asked.

Kell grimaced. The Way at Ease was a song that used the presence of the stones to triangulate paths through featureless deserts, not a surveillance tool for individuals. *Ancestors forgive him.*

"Think about it," Jor said. "When we find our way to camp, it's often not the place itself we're locating, right?" Kell frowned. "The camp *moves*," he went on. "It isn't in the same place as when we left. So, what is it that we're finding? Is it the place, or is it the People?"

"It's the place," Kell insisted. "We can use it to find springs and—and we used it to find the way to the city." But now she felt uncertain. What if it was also the People? The stones were a part of them—*gods, could the stones feel the People, too?*

Jor looked at her and raised his eyebrows. His tattoos looked faded in the false lights of the inn. He could almost be mistaken for a city person, she thought unhappily. *A Sooger*.

She shook her head. "Even if we could do it—and I'm not saying we could," she warned as his eyes lit up, "It requires the presence of the stones. So, it's the same thing as before when we were trying to find the temple. The stones are too far."

Winty was smiling around her spoon. She pulled it out with a pop and grinned. "No, they ain't."

"Yes, they are."

"No," Winty sat up straight and flourished the spoon. "They ain't. Not the ones already been taken. They got them crated up in them warehouses near the power plant. I seen 'em pulling one in once—those flashy rocks are *noisy*, ain't they? Hurt my ears." She shook her head as if clearing it.

Jor's mouth hung open. "You can *hear* them?" The People only felt the stone's power in their palms; they assumed outsiders were unable to sense them at all.

Winty hung her spoon on her nose. "Of course."

Kell ignored the flash of confused jealousy this revelation brought. If the stones had been taken, obviously they would now be here, in the city. A little wisp of hopefulness wound up her chest. The presence of the pulsar stones—even ones that had been defiled and extracted—made her more confident, and she barely felt irritated with herself for not having thought of it before. Maybe they could find the young thief again and convince them to help her prepare a story that the combat general would never suspect.

Thank you, ancestors.

Maybe it would work.

They decided to wait until nightfall to avoid the unwanted attention they were bound to get, singing after a floating serpent. Kell insisted they bring their things with them—leaving their bags unattended at night felt too risky, and there was no way they would be mistaken for locals anyway, so Jor conceded. Now in a quiet alley, Kell clenched and unclenched her jaw. Everything about this felt both wrong and necessary, and she struggled to reconcile the two feelings in her chest. In place of whispering dunes, they were surrounded by clammy concrete walls that sent their voices back to them at odd angles. Instead of singing their way home, they were reaching into their memories—unpleasant ones, at least for Kell—for a scrap of familiarity with someone they had barely met. The connection would be weak, at best. That Jor had shaken the young thief's hand would help, she hoped.

Trust the Way. Kell closed her eyes and opened her palms to the stones. One struck her hand immediately, bright and fierce, and she gasped. It was close—almost too close—and the sensation was like grasping a live ember. It pulsed quickly, as if it, too, were frightened.

"Got one," she whispered. She waited for long moments, seeking another. When it came, it was almost undetectable, eclipsed by the flare and sensation of the first. This second pulse was very faint, and its angle of approach so near the first that it was difficult to separate them save for their different frequencies. Kell had never had to tease apart the signals in such a way before, and she had the bizarre sense that she was balancing on the end of a stick, trying to steer her weight between two close-set points. She opened her eyes and began to hum.

The snake slid along her neck, coiling briefly at her breastbone before slithering the rest of the way down her body and onto the stone street. It didn't seem to mind the unusual setting, which steadied her nerves. Beside her, Jor had found his own two points—each hand cupping the pulses as they came. Kell realized that meant *at least* four stones had been taken and stored here in the city. She wondered how many were already gone, and how Soogway had managed to do such damage before the People had realized what was happening.

Kell's and Jor's snakes twined together, then formed an egg. Winty managed to stay silent, gods be thanked—Kell needed to concentrate if this had any chance of working. Jor sang his part softly at first but gained power as the egg burst and the guiding serpent emerged. Kell loved the warm tones of his voice, the rich, velvet edges of it, and the way it balanced her own golden timbre. The harmony was like the surface of the dunes, rolling up and down and meeting at oblique angles, but always smooth and shifting. Their voices slid over one another and past, creating an undulation that the serpent rode in its sidewinding drift. It writhed through the air, bunching and stretching, its tongue a tiny ribbon of flame, tasting the fetid city smells, seeking its strange destination. Kell breathed in through her nose and hummed, keeping her breath circular despite the impulse to hold it, nervous at what might come next.

The guiding serpent corkscrewed the air, then straightened into an easy walking pace, leading them down the alley. With a glance at one another, they shouldered their bags and followed, Winty trailing behind.

To Kell's surprise, the snake seemed to know to keep them off main streets—it had never occurred to her that the Way at Ease might include an awareness of social and not just physical barriers to travel. She and Jor had often been led carefully around chasms to river fords, away from dangerous quicksand or waterless routes—it had always been *the way*. But as the snake led them through unlit corridors and behind crumbling, abandoned structures, pausing at intersections and waiting for empty streets before proceeding, she realized that it was much more of a sentient guide than she knew, with a good understanding of their purpose. The ancestors were wise and generous, even if their gifts were sometimes inscrutable.

The city was far larger even than Kell had imagined, and hours passed as they made their furtive way through the shadows and back alleys. The smell of garbage and rot was strong, as if it had cooked all day in the sun and now was steaming into the cooler night air. She was glad she hadn't finished her soup.

They encountered animals, which surprised her. Small packs of strange, furred creatures roamed and rooted through the trash. They looked like the badgers that lived in the stony parts of the ash zone, but with fluffy tails and dark patches across their faces. They picked through the refuse with humanlike hands, and their eyes gleamed like storylight when they passed. One hissed and bared tiny sharp teeth. Winty spoke to it in a low voice, and it eyed her carefully, reconsidering. When she caught back up with Kell and Jor, she bubbled over with small animal stories, narrating in a whisper much louder than her speaking voice. Kell ground her teeth as they walked.

They passed darkened windows shuttered with metal bars, hollowed-out buildings that reminded Kell of the bleached sandbeast skulls one finds in the desert, far from springs. They skirted the tired remains of night markets closing, where the smells of grease and alcohol lingered as vendors locked up their stands and swept the day's trash into piles. Here and there, twisting statues loomed from the sidewalk, and Kell ignored the compulsion to touch them. The endless vigilance of wayfinding in the city was exhausting. They no longer had to sing, the serpent having fully actualized hours ago, but they hummed from time to time, encouraging it.

Seeds of doubt began to take root in Kell's mind. What if this thief lived in a hole with a bunch of other thieves? She felt stupid now for having brought all her belongings. What if they didn't want to be found?

The snake made a few rapid turns. They were walking very quickly now, and Kell jogged to stay apace of her brother's longer stride. They turned through a succession of small alleys, and once even through a narrow gate that stood open. The first weak light of morning was beginning to tinge the sky and give muddy edges to the shadows. Kell's feet dragged.

"Almost there," Jor murmured. The snake stretched straight and true.

The three of them rounded a final corner as the snake gleamed, limning a puddle on the stones. It sank to the concrete, dissipating into a ribbon of light that seeped into the ground, indicating their arrival.

Kell's heart sank as she stared into a blank, featureless wall. They were at a dead end.

"Sometimes a story has its own momentum. You can't always control what happens next, even when you're the teller."
—Shade's father

31. FOUND

Shade awoke at the first murmurs of the dawn story. Xylem had explained that, just like people, the trees needed to rest in the dark, so the acolytes allowed for six hours of silence in the Grove at night. When the first shift of tellers took their places, they began the arduously repetitive task of creating false morning deep in the sewers, murmuring in what sounded to Shade's ears at first like a soft cacophony, but which revealed patterns and harmony when they listened closely. Over time, it was easy not to hear it at all.

A bird chirped. The trickle of the small stream reminded Shade that they had to pee. They had made their way to the latrine and relieved themself, washed, and returned to their cot to straighten their bedclothes and look for small tasks with which to busy themself. Xylem wanted them to begin training as a Grove tender, but they weren't yet sure. They loved the trees, that was certain. But after dreaming of the

Broken Forest for so long, the small spot of green hidden in the sewers of Soogway, right under the feet of Mr. Go and everything else they wanted to leave behind, felt like a poor compromise. *The Broken Forest.*

The notion of escape had once driven all their actions, justified their every choice and sacrifice. Now that the resolve steering them had evaporated, their chest was full of an aching directionlessness. If they didn't think hard about placing their feet on the ground, one after the other, they might just drift away. Perhaps tending the Grove was a way to stay rooted and find new purpose.

The sensation of drifting came upon them, then, but tangibly, physically. It was different from the aimless, dissociated float they experienced telling their heart story with Xylem. It was as if the floor had tilted subtly one way, and gravity was pulling them down its slope. Shade took an unbalanced step in that direction to steady themself, but the sensation grew stronger, and with it, the faintest tickle of warmth. Shade followed.

They didn't need to think about where to go—they were drawn to the end of the great hall, away from the Grove, and toward one of the many tunnels that led out. They passed several Grove tenders in their plain uniforms, each of whom smiled politely but did not ask where they were going, nor could Shade have told them. They felt no alarm or unease—more like they had fallen asleep and were pacing through a dream.

They were let out of the locking gates by the acolyte serving as a guard that morning. She nodded but also said nothing. The blue gleam of a small electric lamp at the mouth of the tunnel made Shade's shadow compress then stretch into a snake leading the way. The warm feeling spread through their hands and feet as they turned left then right then left again. Quickly, the sewers became a featureless maze, the blue lamps few and far between, but Shade walked on. Their gait quickened as if the invisible slope had grown steeper, and they were tempted to run to keep their balance. At last, the heat in their limbs grew uncomfortable, and they paused to catch their breath at an intersection of tunnels.

Up, the pull urged. On the wall before them an old metal ladder extended upward beyond the reach of the light. They gripped the rungs and began to climb.

It took the better part of a minute to reach the top—Shade had sensed the Grove was deep, but now they realized exactly how far it lay beneath the city. By the time they ran out of rungs, they were in complete darkness. With one hand, they groped in the shadows above them and felt a handle. It turned with some effort, protesting its long disuse in a rusty voice. Shade shoved their shoulder against the hatch, and mercifully, the ceiling above them gave way, letting in the weak early morning light of the outer world.

The air was fresh but reeked of the street, a smell both familiar as home and repellent after their days spent in the green. The morning was quiet around them but for distant shouts and the rattle of carts. There, in the dead end of an alley, stood three people regarding the stone wall before them, their backs to Shade. The pulling sensation had ceased, and the excess heat leaked from their limbs. They hauled themself out of the hatch and onto the cobblestones.

The three figures turned at the sound. Shade blinked. Normally, they would have run—strangers never meant anything good unless their attention was elsewhere and their pockets full—but Shade still felt in the grip of a dream, and it was a good one. All three of the strangers' faces changed upon seeing them, frustration melting into clear wonder. Shade wiped their hands on the loose pants they'd been given in the Grove, though they had kept Ma Bud's jacket on for the pockets, and stood awkwardly, not knowing what to do next.

"It's you!" The young woman in the middle exclaimed, relief apparent in her voice. Shade took in her scarf and the pack slung around her shoulder and recognition flickered. The one with the resin. Confusion clouded their thoughts. Her brother was there, and seemed excited to see them, as well. The third person Shade didn't recognize at first. They looked like another traveler, dressed in soft brown clothes with straps and buckles. Then the realization hit like they'd walked into a wall: the woman from the private fight club. The terrible singer. The one to whom Go had forced Shade to lose. What was going on?

The one with the resin stepped forward. "I don't know if you remember me," she began. They did—and the storm of insects she had flung at their head. Then she pressed a hand to her chest in a gesture of peace. "But I think I need your help."

An hour later, Shade had led the three down through the maze of the sewers and back to the Grove. They couldn't say exactly why they agreed to do it. The young woman's chances of winning against the combat general were nil—about the same as their own competing in the Cycle without Go's support. Maybe they felt sorry for their first encounter, though to be fair, they had given the resin back. Maybe it was the strangeness of finding them, which had left Shade with an inexplicable feeling of connection to the two desert Roamers. It unnerved Shade, but it also felt nice—like being close without being touched. Mostly, though, Shade was grateful to have something to do. Helping this person learn a few tricks—and Shade had tricks—would fill the space the loss of the Broken Forest had left, at least for the moment, and they were happy for the distraction. Maybe something was still able to be saved. Luckily, Xylem approved once he heard about their purpose. He even offered them all space to stay for as long as they needed to rest and train.

The desert folk were impressed by the Grove, both trailing their fingers in the stream and listening to the day-story illuminating the ceiling above the trees. But the woman in brown, Winty, was restless and uncomfortable. Shade thought she was a pain in the ass, which had nothing to do with having lost to her in the fight.

"They don't like it, you know," she said, standing next to Shade. A small, rodent-like creature had crawled out from one of her sleeves and was perched on her wrist. Winty spoke as if to the animal, never turning her head to look at them.

"Who doesn't like what?" Shade demanded.

"The trees," she said and petted the creature, leaning her nose close to its fur. If she recognized them from the club, she gave no sign. Shade didn't think their performance had been *that* forgettable.

"Those two seem to like the trees just fine," Shade said, nodding at Kell and Jor, who squatted near the water, gazing up into the branches.

"I mean the *trees* don't like it," she said brusquely. "They think it's weird, and they don't feel good. They're all bunchy-woozy, right?" Winty at last deigned to look at Shade, though she did so down her nose, one fist propped on a hip. Shade itched to summon a conqueror's tale and pound her flat with a squid.

"The Grove is a sacred place," they snapped. "It gives people hope."

The girl gave out a braying laugh and turned away. "I'll show you sacred," she said and strolled off, missing the rude gesture Shade made at her back.

Xylem appeared at their side, smiling. "Your new friends are settling in well, I see?"

Shade made a sound of disgust. "They are," they said, indicating the two by the pool.

"Be patient with that one," the old man nodded toward Winty's golden-brown shape disappearing into one of the tunnels. "Folks from the wild have no tolerance for captivity of any sort," he said. "It's hard for her to imagine any being needing a place like this."

"You think these trees are *captive*?" Shade asked. The idea was somehow troubling.

"They did not choose to plant their roots here, to be sure," he said. "But the nuts and seeds that were secreted here to create this place were done so with love and care. And now they live." He raised his palms in a gesture of celebration. "Besides," he caught Shade's eye. "Isn't it better to strive in a sewer than never to live at all?"

The corners of his mouth tugged up as if he'd made a joke, but Shade supposed they, too, were one of these trees—a seed taken from the wild and planted in the bowels of the city. Were they thriving? Shade traced the edges of their acorn under the material of their Grove uniform.

No. But they were alive, and they would find a new place to put down roots and grow. In the meantime, they had a safe place to stay, and now they had a job to do: to show this desert teller some new moves so they could get their giant rocks back. Shade didn't quite understand what they were, but somehow they had helped Kell and Jor find Shade. The reality of that experience was all the proof Shade needed.

Besides, these people had sought them out for their expertise, and Shade liked feeling like the expert for a change. They'd have to see what she could do first, of course, and then they'd think about what to share. As they ran through a mental inventory of tactics, they realized they were shying away from Go's lessons, despite their obvious power. Those stories and tricks felt tainted to Shade, as if using them could poison the outcome.

Be careful, Rat. Shade shivered. They made their way to where Kell and Jor were resting and announced it was time for some practice.

That night, after the dusk story had ended and the only sounds were the creaks of small frogs and the burble of the stream, Shade lay in the dark and let their mind wander. When they couldn't sleep, they imagined themself lying on a giant leaf, drifting down a lazy, warm river—a trick their mother had taught them. The water would turn them this way and that as they floated, branches and stars overhead. When they were very small, this worked every time, the leaf ferrying them off into gentle dreams.

The images did not come easily this time. Shade found themself drifting into dark waters, the leaf a scrap of plastic then a bamboo crate, and they floundered, splashing and cold. The warm river had become the foul waterways of the active sewers, and Shade was lost in a labyrinth of lightless tunnels, wet and shivering as something dark and hungry pursued them. They reached out for a passing branch, only for it to become the stiffened, rotting hoof of a cow. A cloud of flies burst from its swollen belly when Shade disturbed it, and the flies became a storm of locusts, swirling and clicking, diving for Shade's head. Shade tried to shout, but their mouth filled with black water, and they were kicking, flailing, to keep their head above the surface.

I thought rats could swim, came a familiar voice that made Shade's skin crawl. It was soft, sleepy, almost musical. A scent of flowers.

Shade thrashed, the water impossibly deep. If they could make it to the edge, maybe they could outrun the voice. Their fingertips grasped concrete, but everything was slippery with muck, and they struggled to grip it.

Such a small rat, the voice purred.

Shade threw an arm out onto the walkway, banging their elbow hard, and hauled themself out of the water. Immediately they were dry, but their clothing began to fall apart into rags. Their pants, their shirt tore like cobwebs at the slightest touch. They looked for their jacket, but it was missing. They knew there used to be something around their neck, but they couldn't remember what it was. Instead, they had to run.

They turned to race away from the voice, but it was coming upon them too quickly. It would find them anywhere. There was no place in these sewers where the voice wasn't. Shade took a step, but it took ages for their foot to land, and when it did, it drifted uselessly, as if they were stepping on air. They dragged their other leg forward. They were trapped in a floating, leaden run that would take them nowhere.

They could never escape it. *You're mine, Rat.*

Shade awoke in the dark, their heart hammering and the blanket on their cot damp with sweat. They lay still, willing their breathing to slow. They could hear the sleeping sounds of their companions nearby, where all three chose to sleep on the ground rather than on the cots, and Shade found the soft rhythms of their exhales comforting.

They reached down and plucked a small bit of the herb that grew under their bed, crushing it between their fingers. The fresh, cold scent blew away the sick feeling the dream had left behind. Shade felt a new resolve take root in them.

I am not captive, they thought. *I am free*.

They turned over beneath the clammy blanket and listened to the patter of the running water. They thought of the trees at rest, the birds roosted in their branches, the small creatures that made their homes in the Grove. And then they closed their eyes and willed themself into a clear and dreamless sleep.

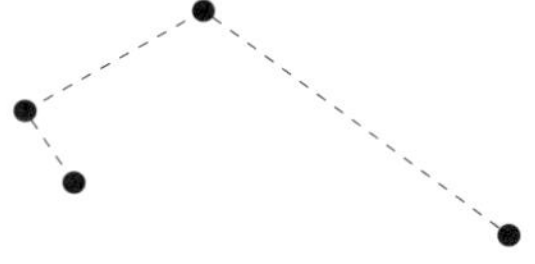

The Bear: East, flood season

32. ROLES

Shade was not a bad teacher. Though at least three or four years younger than herself, Kell figured, there was a self-sufficiency to them that made them seem older, and they were surprisingly patient, despite their cockiness. And they saw things in her work that surprised her, habits that had crept in, tells, like her tendency to drop her chin before an attack. Even though she'd sought them out to expand her tools, they knew more than just tricks. At some point in their life, someone had taken the time to invest them with a philosophy of storytelling and combat, someone subtle and disciplined and hopeful. Shade understood the intimacy of listening and paid attention to body language; there was more to their drills and ideas than just scraps picked up in street fights, she was sure. She was impressed with the breadth of their repertoire and told them so.

"Every time I win, I get to keep the story," Shade shrugged. Kell knew this, of course, but was suddenly acutely aware of how little combat she'd engaged in comparatively, particularly with people outside her own camp. She and the other young tellers had always jousted and played at mock-battles, and she'd come into her own fighting bandits and rangers on scouting missions. But she'd always preferred lore work or histories, the familiar myths that shaped tradition, the comfort of the ancient tales charting landmarks and constellations. Seeing how many unusual stories Shade had at their command made her envy their time in fighting pits. She tried to picture them squaring off with the gritty, older tellers she imagined must frequent such places and felt a pang of protectiveness.

"It must surprise them when they lose to you," she said, then she flinched. She hadn't meant it as an insult. Shade didn't seem bothered, however.

"That's my advantage," they said with a smirk. "Everyone expects me to lose—that's why I'm glad I'm small. I use surprise *in* the stories, too, when I can. It makes it harder for them to prepare and defend against it, especially if they're really committed to a classic."

"We don't use surprise so much," she said thoughtfully. "We rely on the beauty of the story, or the importance of it to do the work. Many of the stories are very, very old, and they have the power of hundreds of tellers behind them. It makes them strange, sometimes." She admitted.

"All old stories have extra parts, or pieces that don't make sense anymore," Shade agreed. "Sometimes that's the surprise. Or inspiration makes the story weird."

Kell nodded, but she knew there was something fundamentally different in their approaches to storytelling. She loved the old stories because she could feel her ancestors telling them through her, feel the continuity of time and practice as if she were simply a conduit, opening her mouth and letting the desert wind pass through as her voice. It didn't feel like her words at all. Sometimes she scarcely knew what she was saying until she said it. More than inspiration, it was submission, opening to the flow of the past. She hoped that the combination of her style and Shade's would create something stronger than the sum of its parts, not just another strange chimera with inexplicable horns or flightless wings.

They were in a large, dim space similar to the Grove's great hall, but empty, a dry reservoir in the sewers that had been abandoned ages ago. The lack of light made story glow luminous and clear, so it was easy to focus on effects.

"What was that thing you did with the blades? The ones that chopped up my desert cat," she asked.

Shade explained—it sounded terrible—but Kell asked if she could try it out on them, perhaps with something they both knew that could be shared again easily, a simple folktale.

Shade thought for a moment. "Like Rabbit and the Rain?"

She smiled. "I know that one. Though we tell it as a sand hare—are you OK with that?" If she successfully destroyed their story, she would have to retell them the tale, and her version would become their own. It was a common enough trade among tellers—at bazaars and gatherings at Home, at least—but it was polite to seek consent.

"It makes no difference to me," Shade said, and lifted their casting palm, settling into an easy, noncommittal combat stance as if they were going to arm wrestle a small child. Kell marveled at their lack of sentimentality. Kell thought she would be quite sad to lose her own version of the tale—why would a desert Person tell anything but a desert story?—but she admired Shade's lack of attachment. She adopted her own stance and noticed how much more strained it was than theirs, almost a crouch. It was only a practice joust. Trying new techniques made her tense.

"Long ago, Rabbit walked upright, with her people," Shade began. "She was tall and calm, strolling among the bushes and eating berries and leaves in the sunshine, and all was good."

Kell watched the storylight pool in Shade's hand and coalesce, taking the form of Rabbit. It was leggy and had strange, elongated ears and legs, as if the animal had been made of honey sweets and then pulled in two directions. She suspected that Shade had never actually seen a rabbit before in real life, but the story was old and familiar and had the strength of countless tellers giving it shape.

As Shade continued, a tiny glowing butterfly burst from an invisible branch, and Kell chuckled. She knew she had to take the story apart, but it was hard when it was so well told. She wanted to let it work its magic on her. Instead, she shook her head to clear it and readied her response.

"One day, the clouds covered the sun, and Rabbit got angry with them," Shade went on, their voice darkening. "'Who are you to rob me of light and warmth?' she demanded. The clouds did not answer. Rabbit stretched taller, standing high on the tips of her paws and pointed her ears at the sky. 'Bring it back!' she shouted. 'Bring it back, or my people and I, we . . . ' she cast about for a worthy threat. 'We will EAT you!'"

A bolt of light shot from the ceiling of the domed room and fanned out around the glowing rabbit in concentric circles, an impressive display of the clouds' offense. Kell startled, but began murmuring her rhetorical counterattack: "Why does Rabbit think she is capable of reaching the sky? Is this an empty threat? You ask me to believe the impossible, and while I am distracted by the fantasy, logic dictates that I seek a mechanism . . . "

The words felt strange in Kell's mouth, thick and tasteless, as if she had slept with her lips wide and awoken thirsty. There was nothing pleasant about treating a story this way, but she watched as a handful of throwing knives hovered above her palm and began to rotate slowly through the air toward Rabbit and her dignified outrage.

Shade had gotten to the part where the rains poured upon Rabbit and her people, making them cower and flinch. They were particularly good at storms, she noted, and thought to ask them later if they had ever worked with sand. Glowing puddles of rainwater appeared on the stone floor of the room, and Rabbit was forced to leap over them, hopping rather than walking, to keep her paws dry.

"Rabbits move the way they do due to their role in the ecosystems of which they are a part and their unique bodies, shaped by nature for that purpose," Kell continued her dissection of the myth. It was joyless telling, and it missed the point of the folktale entirely, but she kept on, elaborating point by point, as the knives began to slice through Shade's story. At first, the glowing Rabbit only wavered as the blade interrupted its path, but eventually the entire tableau collapsed into distasteful pieces, becoming amorphous blobs of light that clung to the edges of the knives and gathered on the stone floor at Kell's feet. She collected it all back into her palm and frowned.

"I hated that," she declared. She felt faintly sick to her stomach.

Shade shrugged. "Yeah, it's gross, but it'll get the goods in a pinch. Just add it to your bag, you know? That was good."

Kell hadn't thought of her story work as a metaphorical satchel before, but the idea helped her get a little distance on what was bothering her.

"How do you, you know . . . " she cast about for the right words. "How do you know when to use an old story, and how do you know when to make something new?"

Shade looked at her, evaluating. Their almond eyes were bright beneath the brim of the hat they always wore. Their smooth, black braids hung down nearly to their waist, and Kell wondered vaguely if they'd ever cut their hair. She felt silly posing such an important tactical question to someone so young, but she didn't know who else she might ask.

"It depends," they began cautiously. "You gotta read the situation, right? You gotta know what you're up against, who you're fighting. That makes all the difference." They paused and wrinkled their nose, their hands jammed into their pockets. "But also, like—it's always new?" Shade's voice went up as if they were asking Kell, instead.

"What do you mean? We were just talking about how the old stories have all these weird parts and things people have forgotten what to do with or why they're there. How can that be new?" She was irritated. She wanted a rule to follow, not a riddle.

"Every time you tell it, you make it your own." Their voice was frustrated, like the question bothered them. "I dunno. It feels like both." They kicked at something small on the ground. "Like we have all these stories in us, they come from other people or the past or they're classics or whatever, so yeah, they're old. But when you tell it, doesn't it feel like you're making something new? Like you can make it be anything you want?"

Kell felt like she was digging in the sand for something she couldn't quite see. How could she name the fear she felt? "What I like about lore," she began, "is that I don't have to make anything new. It feels so comforting to me to just . . . give myself up to the old traditions and let the ancestors tell through me. I feel like I'm a part of something bigger, like there is a long river running through my People, and I am only the channel to let it flow through. It's like I just—disappear. There's no me to make mistakes or ruin it. All I have to do is carry it."

Shade looked at her for a long moment as if they were weighing something.

"Do you want to play a game?"

Kell rolled her eyes. "We're supposed to be training," she said.

Shade shook their head. "I mean a story game. It's something we used to do as kids. I think it might help." Kell scowled. A'Lan never used games as teaching devices, she realized. Story was too sober or reverential for such things. She felt suddenly awkward—was she *too serious*?

"Trust me," they said, raising their eyebrows and cracking their knuckles as if to say she was in for it. She couldn't help but laugh and agreed.

"OK, so you are standing on the street in the middle of the city. No, wait," Shade interrupted, "You are on a vast plain, standing beside a river. There are wildflowers underfoot, and a mountain range juts up in the distance to your right. If you threw a stone as far as you could ten times, you'd hit a small copse of trees to your left. The river winds away from you and drops into a valley."

As Shade spoke, storylight began to glimmer in their palm again, only this time, it had a watery quality, full of shimmer and particulate. The storylight coiled and wended its way up from Shade's palm, forming something vaguely animal shaped. Unfinished. Full of potential.

"Who are you?" they asked.

Kell blinked at them. *What on dry earth?*

"Who are you?" They repeated. "What are you wearing? Where are you going? Why are you there?"

"Oh!" Kell said, understanding dawning. Frowning, she tilted her head and considered for a moment. "I am a traveling musician," Kell said, and thought briefly of the strange tumblers they had passed on the road to the city. "I have a bandolier across my chest—the kind hunters use for darts, but mine . . . " she paused, closing her eyes to see it more clearly. "Mine is filled with flutes of many sizes—little ones and big ones, reed pipes and metal pipes and bamboo, too. And some clay ones," she added.

The animal sprouted elegant joints and paws and began to pace delicately through the air.

"Where are you from?" Shade asked, smiling.

"I'm from . . . " *Home*, she wanted to say, and a pang of homesickness lanced through her sharply, as if she'd fried a wayfinder bug and stuck her finger in its circuits. "The mountains," she said instead. "I have long white hair that I tie up with strips of bark from the many trees in my homeland," she went on, picturing it clearly in her mind's eye. "I am old, and strong." *Like Ama.*

Light was streaming from her palm as well now, twining with Shade's to fill in the creature's details. It grew ears and a rounded snout. Luminous eyes blinked as it peered about, examining its imaginary surroundings.

"You are fishing in the river, and you catch a fish," Shade prompted. "You spear it with a long sharp stick you have in your hand. You consider building a fire, but you can see rainclouds coming on the horizon. What would you like to do?"

"I want to carry my fish toward the trees and then build a fire." She paused. "Can I do that?"

"You can do anything you want," Shade said. "Do you have a fire starter?"

"Do I?" she asked. They looked at her patiently. "Yes," she decided. "I have a fire starter kit. And a length of rope in my pack. And thread."

"OK, you start making your way toward the trees. As you get close, you hear a sound behind you, and you realize that something is bearing down on you quickly."

"Wait, what? What is it?" She felt suddenly frightened, as if she were in real peril.

"A bear!" They laughed wickedly, and she shoved Shade's shoulder.

"Ancestors help me," she groaned. "What do I do?"

Shade shrugged. "It's up to you. What do you want to do?"

"How close is the bear?"

"It's right there! It's almost on you!" Shade shouted, pointing over her shoulder. The creature scrambled in a panic. It sprouted a thick, bushy tail and tiny little horns. It wasn't an animal Kell had ever seen before.

"I . . . " Kell's heart raced as she grasped for a solution. "I . . . take the fish off my spear and throw it far away from me!"

"The bear lunges for the fish! It's skinny and hungry. It's springtime and it has just woken up."

"I take my spear and stab it in the side?"

Shade grimaced. "Remind me not to mess with you," they said, only half in jest. "OK, you take your spear and stab it in the side. The bear dies, but dies with a fish in its mouth, so it was kind of happy, I guess. The rainclouds move in closer."

"I get to the tree line and build a fire. And take my very sharp knife that I cleverly packed in my bags and skin the bear. And I have roast bear for dinner and a new cloak. And I make a very striking necklace from one of its teeth." Kell realized with a start that she felt light for the first time since she'd known about the stones being taken. "I sit beside my fire, warm, and fed, and I compose a song about the bear on one of my flutes," she concluded.

They both laughed at this, and the storybeast they had created bucked and leaped as if dancing about a fire. Kell marveled at it, the ease with which she had been so utterly transported into the character, how she'd really felt, for a moment, that she was a traveling musician from the mountains. It was such a different way of thinking, of telling.

"See?" Shade said. "You're good at making things up on the fly."

"Combat is so different, though. That's why I'm not great at it," she sighed. The lightness in her faded, and she again felt heavy and uncertain. "And why it scares me."

The storylight dissipated in the air between them and separated to their respective palms.

"What do you mean? You were terrifying," Shade protested. "You know, when I took your resin. You were so fierce, and everything you did was unexpected. Jor was right—you definitely had me." They smiled sheepishly. "And that doesn't happen very often."

Kell groaned. "I don't even know what I *did*. It just came out." Secretly, she felt pleased at their admiration.

"That's what I mean," Shade said. "You're a natural."

"But how can I trust that it will happen again if I don't know what I did?"

Shade shrugged. "You just do it," they said. "Or you practice, I guess. Until you know that you can."

Kell's mind whirled. When she challenged the general, should she choose something sincere and beautiful, a classic to show the value of the People's ways and traditions, how they deserved to remain the stewards of the stones? Would she risk a heart story? What about the false god?

"Ma'Shifra—my grandmother—she had a plan," she said.

Shade squatted on the floor to listen, and Kell sat as well. She felt desperate and vulnerable; she could barely believe she was going to reveal Ama's secret strategy to someone who only days ago had tried to pick her pocket on the street. But she had no choice. And Shade was easy to talk to. This street kid was surprisingly sensitive for one who made a living lifting chips from tourists and beating up other people's stories in underground fights.

"She didn't want to use a heart story," Kell started. "We've heard—well, we've heard that they don't work on city generals, somehow." Shade said nothing. "And she thought folktales and lore wouldn't be strong enough, so she had this idea."

She took a deep breath before continuing. *Ama, forgive me.*

"We have something called a god story. We are guided by our ancestors mostly—they watch over us and help us make the right decisions. They offer small protections. But our gods are more distant. Bigger. Much, much bigger. And they don't often get involved with human things. They're more likely to intercede with nature, change the route of a river . . . They don't often fight." She paused.

"But . . . ?"

"But Ama—I mean, Ma'Shifra—she thought we should use a god story to represent the power of our traditions and demonstrate our kinship with the land and with the stones. It would be colossal, the kind of thing that could wipe out countless everyday stories with the flick of its finger—or whatever a god has. The soul of a sandstorm turned into a weapon."

Kell watched Shade take this in. Their eyes were shining in the dim light. She thought of Silaya and the way her face had glowed when she had first heard the plan. The potential of wielding such power made people light up. Kell, on the other hand, could feel her palms starting to sweat.

"What would happen if you lost?" Shade asked. "What would happen to your god?"

"That's the trick," she confided. "There's no such thing as a sandstorm god. We invented a false one, one that could summon the feeling of the desert without risking any of its true lore or pieces of our culture. It would look and feel like a real one to an outsider who didn't know any better, but it would all be made up. We even created a false history for it, just in case."

Shade chuckled. "That's a good idea."

"Yeah."

"You don't like it?"

Kell didn't know *what* she liked anymore. "I don't know what else to do," she confessed.

"So, it's a good idea, but it's not *your* idea," they said.

"I guess so."

"And to feel confident, you need to know you control it."

"Maybe. Or at least it needs to feel like it comes from me, like I *know* it," she said.

"So, basically, you're saying you want to make things up, not just rely on something you've been given. See? You *are* a natural!" Shade looked pleased, as if they had caught her in a contradiction.

"Not exactly," she said. She realized what she felt as the words left her mouth. "I don't want to lie, to just make something up. I want what I tell to be true. I want the truth to be what brings the stones home."

Shade nodded, but the glimmer had left their eyes. They tugged their hat down over their ears and said in a too-cheery voice that echoed in the chamber, "Well. I hope it works."

XYLEM SPEAKS: THE DAWN STORY

Dark is the earth and
the earth is the turn and
the turn is the source of the darkness
The turn is the source and
the source is the glow and
the glow is the line of the turning
The glow is the first and
the first is the curve and
the curve opens into the glowing
The curve is the source and
the source is the sun and
the sun is the light's true curvature
The light is the growth and
the growth is awake and
awake is the birth of the light

The birth is the life and
the life is the cell and
the cell is the place of the birthing
The cell is the green and
the green is the growth and
the growth is the heart of the cell
The heart is the core and
the core is the song and
the song is the dawn where the heart lives
The dawn is the source and
the sun is awake and
the growth is the heart of the dawning

"There's always different ways to find yourself, should you get lost—like moss on the north side of trees. Or that queer feeling that tells you which way's home."
—Shade's father

33. BAD DREAMS

Shade had always been good with direction. Even in the repetitive rings of the neighborhoods, they rarely got lost, though every color was that of damp stone, and every building wore the same facade, studded with window boxes and edged with crumbling filigree that had once been leaves and vines but now, old and eroded, looked like worms boring into the concrete.

Some nights, Shade would lie in bed and find their way around in their mind. It was like being a ghost in a ghost of the real world, and they would float or fly through its contours far faster than their feet could ever carry them.

They had seen tech that reproduced the streets in miniature, little flashing arrows pointing left and right. People carried them in their hands, tourists often, but lazy locals, too, their eyes fixed to their screens as they bumped into passersby and struggled to find their way. But Shade preferred the feeling of folding all of space up in their head and then uncovering little corners of it as they needed. It wasn't hard, and they didn't have to hold the whole map at once. They just followed a street in their mind's eye, and the space to come, the shapes and landmarks, appeared as they went. Sometimes there were other cues, too—the smell of dumpling carts or particularly ripe trash, the fishmonger's stall or the place where the tanners dyed animal hides. Those were hard to miss, and they acted like magnets, pushing or pulling them along their way in real time.

They followed one of these now, enjoying the sensation of unfolding their map in their head as they connected the location of the Grove to the rest of the city they knew. Another corner to fold and keep. It was a long walk back to the Arbor, but they needed the time to clear their head after days of training with Kell and nights of—

Shade shivered and hugged their jacket tighter around them despite the heat of the day. Their nightmares had only gotten worse. Last night, they had seen the D Street kids get pushed off a pier into the river by a group of thugs who smelled of flowers. The water had boiled with aggressive, carnivorous fish that morphed into ropes as the kids were pulled below the surface, the ropes squirming into a net that had pinned them all to the bottom of the river. Shade had seen their faces under the water, their eyes and mouths like hollow ohs, their little hands reaching for Shade to help.

It would be a quick visit. A welfare check. Besides Ma Bud, the kids were the closest thing Shade had to family, especially now that Cheap was lost to—whatever had taken his attention. Shade needed to see with their own eyes that Go hadn't somehow gotten to the kids too.

As they walked, Shade saw Cheap's darkened face and heard his cold voice, called up against their will. *I told you not to let him in. You belong to him now.* They pushed the memory down and closed the lid on it, hoping they would never find it again.

Avoiding the old man's bean stand added a couple of blocks to their route, and the detour squeezed at their heart. They longed to march right up to the familiar rickety bamboo poles and plastic tarps, listen to one of Cheap's inscrutable jokes, tell him about everything that had happened. Hell, Shade would even let him rub their head and muss up their braids in that obnoxious way of his if it meant things could be normal again. Shade pushed this down, too. No sense wishing for things that couldn't be. While they were at it, they'd like a juicy roast and a pair of wings.

They had changed into their old shirt, more for anonymity than nostalgia—the Grove uniform would have been out of place and thus noteworthy to anyone with eyes out—and packed a small bag with extra food for the kids. As they drew nearer, Shade felt a peculiar anxiety rise in their chest. Their old neighborhood no longer felt like home. They had pieced together whatever they had needed from the few people they could trust, and if nothing else, the Arbor had been familiar. Yet as they rounded the corner near the Box and cut through an alley to Commercial Street, Shade had the weird sense that the place had changed, subtly, but certainly. Or maybe they had. Whatever it was, they no longer fit, and they winced as they turned the corner onto D Street, as if they were slipping into shoes long outgrown.

Shade stole into the empty doorway of the abandoned building and stood in the sudden dark of the interior. They listened carefully for long moments, knowing a guard would be posted if the kids were around. Their breathing made the faintest of echoes as the shapes of the broken entryway sent the sound back at odd angles.

Shade gave a low whistle that bounced off a dozen surfaces and died away, unreturned. Shade's eyes strained into the darkness but found no movement, no suggestion of life, no guard or otherwise. Shade whistled again, the high-low pair of tones this time that Shade's mother had said was the call of a bird she loved. Shade had never known it in real life, but they liked the lonely sound of it. There was no response.

They turned to leave when they heard the faintest of rustles above. Shade froze, then relaxed. Probably just a trash cat. What they needed was a light, just to be sure.

They didn't like to use story for this purpose—it felt cheap and unnecessary, like using real paper to wipe your ass—but it would do in a pinch. They settled their feet and lifted their palm. The first thing that came to mind was the Sand Hare and the Rain, the folktale Kell had shared a couple of days ago to replace the one she'd dissected.

"Long ago, Sand Hare walked upright, with her People," they began, relishing the new version's flavor on their tongue. "She was tall and calm, a beauty," they continued. The glimmer in their palms stretched and leaped into the air as they recited the tale, storylight strolling upward as if ascending a hill. The light was shallow and soft, revealing the edges and shadows of the collapsed staircase more than illuminating the room.

"One day, the clouds covered the sun. The sands grew cold and the flatlands dark. Sand Hare grew angry with them."

The glowing story creature paused at the first landing, and Shade's voice faltered. The light traced the edges of something shiny, a small rhyming shape, one then another. Shoes.

"Still gathering other people's tricks, I see," came a soft voice from above.

Shade's blood turned to ice. Mr. Go's face was carved in soft pale light, but his eyes reflected none of it as he looked down at Shade. They took a step backward but were stopped by something large on the floor behind them, and they sagged, paralyzed. All their nightmares were true. The Sand Hare melted away into falling sparks, and Go was again hidden in complete darkness. Shade gathered the folktale into their shaking palm and readied another.

There was no escaping this man or what he could do. Shade had the same slow panic as in their dreams; they wanted to run or fight or scream, but their motions were sluggish and dumb, their thoughts like two pans clanging together in their head.

"The Cycle is in just a couple of days, street rat." The voice drifted from the balcony like poison, soft and terrible. "Time for your end of the deal."

"I'm not fighting for you." Shade sounded small, and they hated it.

"But you will," said Go. "In some ways, you already are. You and your friends."

Shade's stomach wobbled and they wondered how much Go really knew. Did he mean the desert folk or the D Street kids? Where *were* the kids? Did he know about the Grove and its tenders? Could this man's army of spies and thugs find it? Guilt shot through Shade—fear they had led Go right to everyone and everything they cared about. Maybe Shade was the poison, after all. They had let him in.

Their breathing echoed loudly in the room, and they tried to stifle it. The darkness was their only advantage right now. If they could just slip out, they could be blocks away before Go could get down from the second floor. How had he gotten up the drainpipe?

Where would you go, Rat? Shade couldn't tell if they thought it or Go put it there, and their heart raced. It was true—they were trapped.

"It hasn't been easy for you, has it, kiddo?" Go's soft voice was everywhere, above and below, around their head and in it. "You didn't ask for much—you didn't ask for *anything*, did you? Just a shot. You wanted a shot at proving you could take care of yourself."

Shade saw the faintest glimmer of storylight creeping down the wall from the second floor, then trail across the entryway in the shapes of vines.

"And you have. When your father died, spending all his secrets, selling himself to save his skin, turning himself into a husk, you kept going. You learned and kept your heart stories to yourself. And when your mom left you, too, well. What were you supposed to do? What would anyone do?"

"It wasn't like that," Shade mumbled, trying to muster a counter-story, but their mouth was numb. "She died, you asshole."

"Of course it wasn't." Go ignored the epithet, his voice was little more than a whisper, yet it cut through the dark with eerie precision. "Yet what else is death than leaving, leaving where none can follow?"

Shade felt hot. Their eye sockets burned, and they blinked quickly, trying to cool the strange fire burning in their face and in their veins. Their heart had become a ragged wound, bruised and bleeding, unhealed after all this time, unfit to do its work. As it pounded in their chest, Shade feared their blood would burst its bonds, spill out of their body and onto the floor.

"You can never bring them back, you know." Go's voice chilled, its edges sharper as it grew louder. "Not through good works or through bad. You think you can justify anything through the need to survive—you can take whatever you like, as long as it gets you to the place you imagine, your precious forest, where you flatter yourself you could finally make things grow."

Shade's mind rebelled against Go's words, even as part of them was crumbling. Their casting palm twitched, and they raised their free hand to the acorn beneath their shirt.

"They said it was beautiful," Shade said in a strained voice. They cleared their throat, but a lump remained there. "I wanted to see it. Trees live so much longer than people." There was no use lying or evading now.

"But the forest *didn't* live longer, did it? You knew you'd never make it there. That was an excuse to justify yourself, to get away with anything you wanted. That forest is gone for good, and you always knew it. You need another distraction now."

Shade shook their head in the dark, but Go's vines were slithering closer. One had already twined about their ankle and was twisting up their shin. At first, they felt nothing—it was just storylight, after all—but then the vine began to sprout leaves, and a strange buzzing vibrated through their pant leg.

"You're a thief, Shade. A fake." They felt a squeeze. "All you do is take the things of others. You have nothing that is your own—not your stories, not your personality. Not even those pants you're wearing." At this, the vines bristled with small thorns, and Shade cried out. It felt like being crushed in the jaws of a sharp-toothed animal, the thorns sinking into the muscle of their calf. They watched in horror as another vine snaked its way up their other leg. Shade tried to turn and run, but the vines held them rooted to the floor. They gasped and searched their body for signs that Go was inside them, stealing their breath, but it was only panic robbing them of air.

"You're wrong!" They managed to shout between gulping breaths, but a voice in their head said, *You're right, you're right, you're right.*

"There's only one thing you have that is yours, Shade. Do you know what that is?" Go was hidden in shadow, only his casting palm visible above the balcony, held casually in the air as if he were skipping invisible stones in a river.

Shade shook their head. Their mind cast about for a story—any story—to take their focus off Go's voice. If they could begin telling, maybe they could block out his words for a little while longer . . .

"H-have you heard the one about the merchant and the fishmonger's daughter?" The light in their hand sputtered but held, a tiny candle cupped against the wind.

"That's right," Go went on. "Your talent. It is *unique*."

"One—once there was a poor merchant who loved to eat." Shade struggled to remember how it went. A small, duck-billed lizard waddled from their palm and fell to the floor. A tendril shot out from the vines and wrapped it up like a spider swaddling a freshly caught fly. The lizard spasmed then dissolved, and Shade let their casting hand drop.

"But the problem with being that good, Shade, is that it's hard to find people who can teach you things, isn't it? And this is why you need me. You're still learning, still raw. There are still countless moves you've never even dreamed of."

The vines tightened around their legs, and Shade faltered. It was difficult to stand. *Stories can't hurt you*, their mind screamed. Yet real pain coursed through their ankles and feet. Only the strange vibration kept them upright. Shade feared they would collapse without it, even as their nerves begged for an end to the stabbing thorns that lashed them to the floor.

"Speaking of dreams, how have you been sleeping?"

Shade blinked. A torrent of images flashed before their eyes: rising water in the sewers, the kids below the surface with open mouths, the rats and the rats and the rats . . .

"You're nothing without me." Go's voice closed like iron bands around Shade's chest. Restraints that were cold and solid—certain. They could just sink into them, they thought, stop trying so hard to fight for something—anything—else. Shade realized how tired they were of fighting. So. Incredibly. Tired. The buzzing in their legs had crept into their torso, and they thought they might nod off. It was lulling, that sensation, that pain could carry them off to rest—

"You should be ashamed of yourself, using it like that." A familiar voice broke through their haze, but it came from far away. Shade couldn't place it.

A small creature scampered across the floor toward Shade's feet. The rodent-like shape glowed very faintly, but Shade noticed blearily that it also looked, well, *real*. As if a living animal had been dusted with storylight or caught in the crossfire of a messy battle. The creature began gnawing furiously at the vines that rooted Shade in place.

"The forest exists, Shade. It's just not where you think it is. Not where *he* thinks it is." The pain in Shade's legs receded. The buzzing sensation softened to a gentle hum.

"Winty?"

"You're just lucky you're so easy to track. I lost you at that last street, though, your little cut-short. Do you know how many of these ugly buildings I've had to poke my head in, looking for you? Too many. That's how."

The creature had managed to free one of Shade's ankles and moved on to the next. Shade shook out their unbound leg. It stung as if it had fallen asleep from being too long in one position. Above them, Go gave a soft chuckle.

"Here or there, Shade. Now or later."

"Now you listen up, Mister," Winty said in a voice like she was ordering a herd of children into a line. "There's places that's stronger than folks, wild places, that'll barely notice you're even there. All your sneaking and money and people who's scared of you don't amount to nothin' in places like that. You'd be lost and wandering, you sad old coot. You'd scarce be able to find the clouds, even, with the overstory and canopy in all its puzzle-completeness. The birds and the snakes and the bugs, they know every single thing that goes on, but you, you'd be deaf and blind, lost and thirsty like a baby, crying and full of tantrum with no one to carry you home."

As Winty spoke, soft tendrils of storylight bloomed around Shade, dozens at first, and then hundreds of tendrils. They unfurled in myriad shapes—blades and fronds, saplings and stalks. Upward they grew with uncanny speed, popping and bursting into flower and trunk. The light filled the old shell of a building, and for a moment, Shade saw Winty crack into a grin, and then she was hidden by the growing trees. It was like being in the Grove only denser, stranger, *wilder*, they thought. The floor was lost to thick underbrush and a tangled carpet of storylight plants. Go's mask of fury gave Shade the sudden thought he had been turned to stone, but then Go flinched as a tree shot up beside him and extended its branches. Another grew past the balcony, and another, until the thicket hemmed him in entirely, a prison of glowing forest.

Shade looked down and saw the storylight vines had been absorbed by Winty's trees. She stepped out, pushing aside an enormous, luminous leaf that swayed on its stem amid a clump of others like it.

"Told you I'd show you sacred," she muttered to Shade as she grabbed their arm and dragged them, stunned, outside into the light.

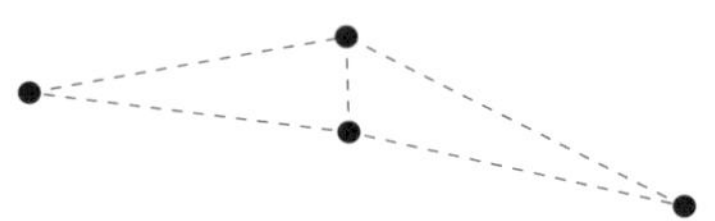

The Bind: Southwestern horizon, bird migration

34. THE STONES

Nothing and nobody was where they were supposed to be, and Kell was done with it. Shade had up and left the morning before, and then Winty had as well. Jor paced the sewers outside the Grove like he'd lost something precious, and Kell was jealous of his attention. He was always enamored with one person or another, but right now she needed his support, and he was busy moping after a strange girl they barely knew. When the forest dweller and the street urchin both returned in the middle of the night together—which was strange, considering Winty made it clear she wanted little to do with Shade, or the Grove, for that matter—Kell felt out of balance, as if she had pitched camp on shifting sand.

And on top of everything, tomorrow was the beginning of the Cycle. How could she focus when everyone else was pulled in different directions? Wasn't this contest the entire purpose of their being here? Her heart felt like a wild animal that had been stuffed inside a basket and taken to market; sometimes it slept, but mostly it thrashed and howled and clawed to be free.

Xylem brought Kell a bowl of tea, which she accepted gratefully. The taste reminded her of A'Lan's ease-herb decoction, and for a moment she was afraid she might cry. The old man smiled and invited her to spend a few minutes by the stream. "To wash away the nerves," he said, and she agreed, his perceptive hospitality increasing her melancholy and resolve in equal measure.

Kneeling in the damp earth, she dangled her fingertips in the water, watching how quickly the patterns they made were reabsorbed into the greater flow. Her eyes followed the stream to the small pool that formed at the base of a cluster of trees, and she saw a flash of color beneath its surface. *Fish!* She had no idea they were here, too. The glint of purple disappeared into shadow, and she wondered if she'd imagined it. Then a flare of orange kissed the skin of the water, and she could see the outline of fins clearly for a moment before it darted back down beneath a thicket of roots.

"Those kinds of fishies wouldn't live together in the wild," came a voice at her shoulder. Kell found Winty crouching beside her, squinting at the pool with distaste. Kell didn't know what to say and dried her hand on her scarf.

"I like the sound of the water," she said. "It's very peaceful." Kell thought of the story of the spirit trapped in the rocks whose tears formed a stream in an oasis, but Winty only shrugged.

The little creature that accompanied Winty everywhere crawled out from beneath her collar and fixed Kell with wide, round eyes. It blinked. A tiny tongue flicked out, as if it had finished something delicious. Kell couldn't help but smile.

"May I ask, what *is* that?"

"Her name is After-the-Rain-But-Before-Things-Are-Dry. She's a smell."

Kell stared. "I beg your pardon?"

"A smell. You know that smell?"

Kell was baffled. She guessed she did. She reached a hand toward the creature, but it shied from her touch, burrowing back into the folds of Winty's clothing.

"You mean its fur smells like that? That's why you gave it that name?"

Winty crossed her arms over her chest in long-suffering patience, as if ridding Kell of her stupidity was clearly going to take some time.

"*She*. She is a smell. I didn't name her—it's what she is. I don't create her nature any more'n she creates mine." After-the-Rain-But-Before-Things-Are-Dry poked her head out from the opening of Winty's jacket and placed two little paws on a buckle. Kell noticed the creature had a faint glow to it—*her*, she corrected herself. Understanding began to creep in, but it was too strange for Kell to accept.

"Wait. She's a *story*?" She couldn't keep the incredulity from her voice.

"She's a smell, like I said," Winty explained patiently. "Kind of like a story, if you want to think about it like that. But a smell's got no beginning or end, does it? It's just there when it's there. So, there she is."

"But—" Kell had so many questions she didn't know where to start. "How does it work? Why don't you have to tell it? Why is she here, even though it hasn't rained? Why do you keep her?"

Winty laughed that braying laugh of hers and shook her head. "You got it wrong, desert lady. She's not mine. She's a wild thing. Wild things do as they please. They don't need tellers, or folk to summon them or to give them names or make them real. She's realer than I am, that's for certain. And she'll still be here long after you and I and this whole pile of rocks here is done for." She gestured vaguely at the dome of the Grove. The chanting of the tenders went on in the silence between them, and Kell shivered. The world felt stranger and much bigger than ever, and homesickness squeezed her ribs.

"Then, why is she with you?" Kell asked more cautiously. What she didn't say was, *Why don't* we *have anything like that?*

Winty squinted at her and smiled. "She likes adventure," she said, as if that would explain everything. "She loves to come to the city when I make my trips. But once we're back to the forest, she'll be gone." After-the-Rain-But-Before-Things-Are-Dry seemed to know she was the subject of discussion and made a show of scampering to the top of Winty's head. She bunched up and took a leap into the foliage at the base of the trees then disappeared up a trunk. Winty kept her eyes on Kell.

Who are *you?* Kell wanted to ask, but she bit her tongue. "I thought you said you didn't come to the city often."

"Not often, but oftener than most folks where I'm from. We're working on so many tinkers, you see—busy a lot, except for when we're not. Too many projects takes up the mind, makes you noisy, and then you stop hearing and seeing. But still, we need some of the tech to make things better. Soogers're doing it wrong. We gotta show them better ways before they figure out where we're at, and then we'd gotta deal with them, too."

"So, you're trying to teach the city folk something about tech?" Kell rolled her eyes. "Good luck with that."

Winty snorted. "Nah, folks don't listen none unless you're tellin' them what they already think. We gotta *show* them."

"What is it you want to show them?"

Winty's face stilled, and she leaned in so close that Kell tilted away and lost her balance where she sat. The stone-and-leaf smell of the forest guide was strong, as if her body had heated up and was radiating scent like herbs tossed on a fire. Her golden-brown eyes locked onto her own, and Kell had the discomfiting certainty that she was being evaluated by a wild animal, one that might flee or strike with equal swiftness.

"That they don't gotta burn it all down." The girl's drawl came out a fierce whisper. Kell prayed to the ancestors that Winty would blink, but she did not. Kell felt her own eyes twitching under the other's fevered gaze. "There's plenty for all, but you gotta know how to do it right."

This was a new side of her that Kell had not seen before. Gone was the brash, raw teller always grinning or lounging. In her place was someone serious, driven by a single purpose—like Kell herself. Despite her many off-putting qualities, Kell had to admit that Winty had a strange magnetism to her, as if she were somehow just a little more alive than everyone else. Not alive, Kell amended, *vivid*. She was the first to break the gaze. Kell looked back into the pool, pretending to search for fish, but she could feel those eyes still pinning her in place.

"They don't get it," Winty continued. "And there'll be no talking sense to them. They want to dig them all up, just like they did with the trees." Kell's heart stuttered, thinking of the desolate sea of stumps they'd passed while walking beside Silaya's horse. That felt like ages ago.

"How do you know?" She frowned at Winty, tired of being talked to like she didn't see the big picture. "And how do you know what *we* want, for that matter? Why are you even here?" Kell's words sounded harsher than she'd intended, but once they were out, she felt relief.

Winty's lip twitched. She settled back on her heels and spat a wad of brown juice into the foliage. "Folks what be on the same side need to know so," she said. "You're fighting for the stones; we're fighting for the wild. There's others, too, you know. River protectors, other forests . . . It's all the same fight."

"It's hardly the same." The stones were gifts from the gods, granted to the ancestors. They weren't ore or trees, no matter how precious those resources may be. They were sacred guardians, with . . . *personalities*, almost. They were the only means of finding one's way through the desert—*besides tech*, she thought bitterly. Anyway, Kell didn't care about distant rivers and forests. She just wanted to protect her People.

"Pigeons."

Kell blinked, thinking she had missed part of what Winty had said. "What?"

"Pigeons," Winty repeated. "That's how I know—pigeons talk. They told me how to find you, what you're after, and all that. They heard it from some hawks, who heard it from some of them desert birdies you got."

Kell felt certain the forest guide was making fun of her, but if she was, her delivery was uncharacteristically deadpan. Her creature scrambled out from behind an enormous leaf and scurried back up Winty's pant leg and into her jacket.

"Even if you win, you know, they ain't gonna give them stones back." Her expression was solemn, yet Kell wanted to blast the look off her face with a well-aimed whirlwind of sand. "If our tinkers go like we plan, we can show them a better way to can their juice, and then everybody'll be happy, see? It's not about getting rid of the tech—it's about using it right."

Kell barked a short laugh of disgust. "You sound like my brother." Winty raised her eyebrows in what could have been agreement.

Just then, Jor appeared as if summoned and sauntered over to join them by the pool. He and Winty exchanged conspiratorial smiles, and Kell swallowed the jealousy that sprang unexpectedly up in her chest.

"Come here," he said to Winty, radiating the attentive energy that people responded to so readily in him. "I want to show you something." He jerked his chin toward one of the tunnels, and the forest guide popped to her feet. Jor gave Kell a small wave of weak farewell or apology, and the pair were gone, shoulder to shoulder, talking in animated whispers.

Kell refused to watch them go. She glared at the surface of the pool and forced herself to take calm, deep breaths. She had much more important things to worry about than her brother's endless romances.

The general. How would they open? Would they come on strong, trying to dominate from the beginning, or would they try to make a good show of it for the audience, toying with her and letting her keep some hope alive before they crushed her?

She tried to focus on what *she* had to do, which was win, but something had stuck and wouldn't let go. *Even if you win, you know, they ain't gonna give the stones back*. Was that true? What was the point of fighting, then—just for the spectacle of it? To make it look like Kell had a chance, like petitions held power and weren't the sham they actually were?

Kell refused to believe it. The council had sent her as their combat teller in the event a battle for the stones was required, and so combat is what the general would get. The council believed in her. Ama believed in her. Even if the council had no idea what they really faced, Kell couldn't let doubt shake her now. *Ancestors, guide me.*

Something in her heart turned hard and clear then, like a gem. She felt more focused and surer than she had in weeks. It was decided. She ran it through in her mind—the swirling sand, the rage, the darkness in the middle of day. She would use the false god story and bring havoc to whatever the city planned.

Kell's sense of calm persisted through her afternoon training session with Shade. They were so impressed they started calling her The Desert Menace, which made her laugh. She was embarrassed at how good it felt, but Shade was a gifted teller after all—that praise *was* the assessment of an expert—and it wasn't like anyone else was paying attention to her preparations. Shade had seen enough of past Cycles to know she was likely to fight early in the program, and Kell found even this small insight was a comfort.

Kell had asked Shade to be her second, and while the streetfighter had never heard of such a thing—backup was hard to come by in pit fights, apparently—they quickly agreed. She assured them that they wouldn't have to engage in actual combat. The role of the second was to serve as a coach and as emotional support, not to take over for the combat teller except in very rare circumstances. Shade seemed unconcerned about the possibility of fighting.

The two reviewed the scant instructions Jor had received at the temple, decided on a departure time, and drilled scenarios until Kell's voice went hoarse. They ran through every possible outcome they could think of until Kell was numb. Shade, too, had stopped focusing, fiddling with their hat as they stared into space.

"Let's take a break," Kell suggested when they heard the bell for the evening meal. "I think we've done all we can." Shade perked up like a drooping plant given a taste of rain. They were about to dash out of the chamber toward dinner when they stopped and turned.

"You're more creative than you think," they said. "You're going to do great. You're a menace, remember? Just, you know, let yourself go. Listen, release, disrupt. Just like we practiced."

Listen. Disrupt. Just like Ma'Shifra says, too. Kell smiled at them, partly in gratitude, and partly to reassure them that she was clear and confident, too. Inside, the sandstorm had already begun. *Let's hope great is enough.*

Shade pulled their hat down over their ears and wheeled away toward the smell of food.

Winty was absent for the meal, and Kell was relieved to get her brother alone for a few moments, or as alone as they could be, surrounded by the motley community that made up the Grove. Some aged seekers sat near the pool, enjoying a tranquil dinner together, and Shade was in a corner, talking with Xylem between bites. The tenders who weren't currently chanting the twilight into evening above them sat scattered around the cots and benches with bowls on their laps. There was no prohibition against speaking in the Grove, though something about the place encouraged silence, and beneath the rhythmic murmur of the ongoing story overhead were the scrapes of spoons against bowls and the chirp and croak of small frogs.

Kell swallowed a mouthful of soup made from legumes and water and wrinkled her nose. She missed the spices of Home. Though one of those dumplings they had on the street near the inn would be welcome right now, too, she thought. Jor tucked hungrily into his meal as if flavor were of no concern.

"I think I'm ready," she offered, hoping for conversation. Jor felt so far away to her, she wanted to throw a rope around him and haul him back. She wished they needed the Way at Ease so they could sing together—anything to bridge the distance that had grown between them over the course of the trip. Jor glanced at her, swallowing, and nodded.

"Hope so," he said, taking another a bland spoonful. Kell bristled but said nothing. After a long span of more scrapes and croaks, she tried again.

"Jor," she began. "It's time to press the beacon. The challenge is tomorrow, and if I win—I mean, *when* I win," she amended, "we'll be able to go home right away. They said it would take almost a week to get here. Jor, I don't think I can stand more than another week in this place."

Jor continued eating but looked at her sidelong, as if turning his head would be too much trouble. Pausing for a long drink of water, he said, "There are a lot of things to take care of."

"Like what?"

"Diplomatic things, Kell. Agreements, treaties, things to sign. It's a complicated process, getting policies changed. We'll go home when it's time to go."

As if you have any clue what diplomacy entails.

"It's time, Jor!" she hissed. A few faces turned toward them, and she struggled to keep her voice low. "We don't belong here. I know you're happy making new friends and playing with city tech, but this place is killing me. I want to win the stones back and go *home*." She felt desperate, as if the door she had been about to step through turned out to be a wall, after all. "Please, Jor. Press the beacon."

Jor set his bowl down beside him and turned to face her at last. In an uncommon gesture, he picked up one of her hands in his own, holding it gently and looking into her palm before meeting her eyes.

"Kell, I need you to trust me," he said intently. "You do your part, and I'll do mine. OK?" She coughed and realized she was on the verge of tears. "And listen," he went on, "if anything happens, you need to get to the gate and get out of the city, no matter what. Do you understand?"

She did not understand. She shook her head and jerked her hand free, a dark confusion yawning open beneath her feet. "We'll be together," she said. "You'll be with me, and we'll leave together, Jor." She searched his face for clues to what he wasn't saying.

"Just promise," he said. His dark eyes betrayed nothing of the thoughts behind them, and Kell felt as if she were falling into a bottomless hole.

"No!" she shouted, drawing stares. She clenched her fists and forced her voice into a harsh whisper. "I won't do it," she spat. "I won't promise. If you're so sure that I'm going to lose, why are we even trying? Why put me through it at all? Especially when your new *girlfriend* there says it doesn't matter whether we win the challenge anyway." She tossed a dismissive hand toward an invisible Winty. "They're just going to take the stones no matter what, right? To power all the precious junk you love so much. Well, good for you! I hope you two enjoy it. But I'm going to fight for our People, because *that's why we're here, Jor.*"

Jor's face had hardened into an impassive mask that, for Kell, was worse than his anger. He shook his head, negating her and everything she cared about. His eyes told her he thought she was not a combat teller, not defending the People in any real way, just a distraction in a political game she had no clue how to play. Just as she feared.

"You have no idea what I love," Jor said. "And you understand nothing of why we're here." He got up silently and walked out, leaving Kell alone to ignore the stares in the Grove as frustration and shame consumed her.

"The three strands come together like this. Always put the outer one into the center."
—Shade's mother

35. THE SECOND

Shade rebraided their hair in a ritual of concentration. They loved the tight feeling of the plaits pulling against their scalp, the itch of it. First one side was done, and the imbalance felt as if it tugged their entire face to the left; then they did the other side, their fingers nimble and sure even without the aid of a mirror, and the tension in their head was balanced. Their vision came into clearer focus when their braids were fresh, the discomfort keeping them alert. They felt ready. They pulled the soft protection of their hat over top as if sheathing a sharp blade.

The Cycle.

They had to admit, this wasn't how they'd pictured it happening. They had been in the audience a few times, of course, sneaking in with the other street kids when they were younger, ducking around knees in the crowd and elbowing for glimpses of the spectacle below as the best tellers battled for untold wealth and status in the arena. It was a kind of storytelling far beyond what happened in the pits and alleys of Soogway—those stories were common, clever, poetic, even, but they lacked the grandeur and scale of the Cycle.

Shade knew that Kell's challenge against the general was just part of the warm-up act. Along with the other petitioners, these were bits of political theater to get the crowds roaring and hungry for the main events, but Shade felt a thrill to be part of it, nonetheless. Their father had always dreamed of competing, but their family had lacked the entry funds. Shade wished he could see them today, stepping into the arena, walking proudly into the center to face the general.

They realized with some irritation that they were a little bit nervous. Their last run-in with Go had frightened them deeply. In fact, they had decided to get as far away from the city as they could, immediately. Their plans to save up and travel to the Broken Forest had been ruined in any number of ways—they were now completely broke with nowhere to run. Yet staying in Soogway no longer felt like an option, with no corner of the city where Go or his agents didn't have some sway.

Shade didn't know what to expect from the challenge but acting as Kell's second was a sure way through the arena gates, if nothing else. There had to be some way to leverage that into a job or an invitation to . . . somewhere. At this point, they would consider slipping into the back of a wagon hidden among the luggage. Anywhere, anyway would be fine. And the sooner, the better.

Shade came to the first Grove guard and then the second, and each nodded them through, the gates locking shut behind them with a clank that echoed and briefly obscured the sound of chanting like a stone rippling through a pool. The Grove never failed to calm them. Shade took a deep breath of the green—they knew what Xylem meant now—and let it out, feeling some of their tension go with it. The trees that once had seemed sickly to them now appeared determined and serene. Shade tried to absorb as much of that feeling as they could.

They looked for Kell and found her by scent before they spotted her. A thin tendril of smoke wended its way from the back corner where she knelt in prayer, her scarf over her head. The air in the Grove was still, and Shade could see the shapes the incense made as it curled above her and dissipated. Shade knew she felt conflicted about the strategy her grandmother had set, but they'd seen Kell come to embrace it over the last few days. This brought a marked shift in her confidence, even if she hadn't shown Shade her god story yet.

Xylem approached, and Shade smiled at the old man, who returned it and patted Shade's shoulder in friendly greeting. Shade tensed, but there was something reassuring in the touch as well.

"She's been there all morning, Master Tumbler. She hasn't eaten yet, either. Perhaps she's waiting for you?" Xylem raised an eyebrow. Had they eaten yet? They couldn't remember. Then their stomach gurgled. "There are fresh rolls in the corner, and a pitcher of sweet tea." Xylem's tendency to mother them was an unfamiliar but welcome experience.

"Thanks. I'll be sure to grab something before we go." Xylem stood quietly for a moment, his hands crossed before him in that patient way of his. They both regarded the desert teller where she kneeled across the great hall. Small birds chirped and flitted in the false morning light, and a few tenders quietly prepared for their shift.

"You will always be welcome here," Xylem said, apropos of nothing. "No matter what happens today."

Shade studied him. The old man's eyes were soft and kind. He wore an expression that was at once tired and full of love.

"Thank you, Xylem." An unspoken conversation passed between them. Shade felt a flicker of something—was it regret? It was almost like they *missed* him, even though Xylem was standing right there. Like Cheap—only if Cheap had abandoned Shade, now Shade was the one doing the leaving. They felt the strangest sensation of their life splitting in half—there were two paths now, and on one, Shade remained here and became a tender of the Grove. They would be well fed and cared for and have access to trees and the green. They would feel peaceful and safe—maybe. They would have something like a family.

But could whatever hid the Grove from the city officials and the bustle of the streets also keep it hidden from Go? Shade couldn't take that chance. Go's reach seemed endless, and they wouldn't be the one to draw him here, to ruin this one beautiful thing in an otherwise ugly city. They were already on the other path, they realized. What they felt now was the loss of that life, the one they might have had here, had circumstances been otherwise.

The old man gave Shade's hand an unexpected squeeze, looking into their eyes, as if he could read their thoughts. "You are just at the beginning of your road, Shade. It is too early for you to stop walking. But when you come to the end of your journey or need somewhere to rest, remember this place." Without further ceremony, Xylem turned and made his way to the pool to sit with a pair of Grove visitors in quiet contemplation.

Shade stuffed a pair of warm rolls into their jacket pockets. They crossed the great hall and approached Kell, fidgeting with the hem of their shirt as they stood behind her, unsure whether it was okay to interrupt.

"It's time," Shade said gently.

Kell sighed deeply and stood. She lowered her scarf from her head, her eyes flashing. Her expression, when Shade caught it, looked . . . *dangerous.*

"Let's go," she said.

Resurfacing felt strange. The sun was intense, and the air was rank with city smells. How odd it was that the outdoors would feel stale while the Grove sewer was fresh, but it was true. Air without the green was incomplete, Shade thought.

After so much time in the calm of the Grove, Shade found the world aboveground impossibly hectic. Vendors shouted from stalls and sidewalk blankets. Passersby of every shape, size, and color jostled and chattered in a tangle of accents. The crowds clotted and stalled, bunched and sped as they were pumped through the arteries of the streets. Old habits quickly returned, however, and Shade knew the way and led Kell through the clamor, their eyes sharp for threats. They were accustomed to looking out for safes, but Go and his agents were much harder to spot.

"What are you doing?" Kell hissed once when they held her back and pressed her into the side of a building, both of them flat against the stones.

"Shhh," they hushed her. A safety enforcer strolled into view, a giant glowing insect unit marching at its heels. The insect paused once, angling its shiny head toward them before pulling two spindly forelegs from the cobblestones and preening its antennae, twisting its head this way and that. If it saw them, it made no sign and trotted after its safe. Shade let out a long breath.

"Look," they said, turning to Kell. "There are a lot of people around here who'd rather hassle you than give you a 'good day,' so just do as I say if you want to get to your fight."

"Gods," Kell muttered, her face saying plainly what she thought of city life.

"Just trust me," Shade said, peering both ways at the corner before giving her a small push in the back to hurry her along. Kell tripped and let out a small yelp but didn't argue further.

“Where's your brother?” Shade asked after they had passed several more ring streets in silence. “I figured he would come with you.”

“So did I,” she said.

“What happened? Did you two have a fight?”

Kell shrugged helplessly. “I don't really know,” she said. “We were sent to do this together. He would do his part, and if that failed, I—I would do mine. But I thought he would be a part of this, too.” Shade wasn't sure if she meant they were a poor substitute for a brother.

“I'm sorry he isn't here,” is all they said.

“Me too,” she whispered. There was a long pause before the sharp edges returned to her voice. “I think he doesn't really want to go back home. I think he wants to stay here with that—that forest girl and play with city gadgets for the rest of his life. I think that would make him really happy.”

“But what about the stones?” Shade asked.

“Exactly.” Kell set her jaw and pulled her green scarf over her closely cropped hair. “What about the stones.”

Shade tried to think of something useful to say, then remembered the rolls they'd brought and offered her one. She took it silently, and it disappeared in a few bites.

“I know he's proud of you,” they ventured. “He knows what a good teller you are.”

Kell snorted. “I wish *I* knew that,” she scoffed. “And anyway, I don't know if that's true. He thinks I ruin everything.”

“Well, you don't.” Shade was way out of their depth. They had no idea how to make her feel better. They just knew she needed to be sharp to win, and this moping wasn't it.

The arena lay near the temple, at the center of the city's rings. If Soogway was a tree, the temple was its heartwood, and the streets grew denser and drier as they neared, accordingly. The clamor of trade and the decrepit sameness of the concrete buildings gave way to statelier residences, as cinderblock gradually turned to carved stone and even brick. Garish electric signs became filigreed moldings over doorways. Archways loomed over sidewalks, layered with clambering vines that offered moments of cool shade. They passed one neighborhood where each home sought to outdo the next with ever more elaborate awnings, billows, and sails of fabric and tassels.

The wealthier part of town was much less crowded, so there were fewer potential threats. Safes were bound to run thick, though—there was no doubt whom they served in Soogway—and Shade could feel their heart beating in their neck as they drew nearer the temple and the arena that lay on its far side.

The crowds swelled again as the rings grew closer together at the city's center, residences giving way to bureaucratic offices in the prime real estate surrounding the temple and its gated gardens. Thousands of spectators waited at a standstill to enter the arena, and Shade and Kell at last had to push their way through. Shade hunkered low out of habit, slipping between people's hips or knees, and they hoped Kell was able to keep up. Here and there Shade snagged a chip easily, their light fingers moving almost without thinking, as they forced a line through the crowd toward the rear of the arena.

Over a sea of heads and shoulders, Shade saw the flags that marked the entrance where the clerks had told Kell to register. A crush of people trying to bluff their way in made the participants' gateway thick with jostling fans, some of whom already reeked with the stench of hooch though the sun was still high in the sky.

Shade turned to Kell but saw only a wall of tunics behind them, an eager mass of browns and grays that threatened to flatten them. They searched for a flash of her green scarf, but she was gone. They called out her name, but it was lost in the noise of the crowd. For all her ferocity, Kell was still a fish out of water in the city. Shade went cold, despite the heat of the day, as an irrational fear gripped them.

Had Go taken her? Shade spun, shoving their way blindly between spectators, their arms wheeling to make way between the bodies that blocked their view. There were people of every description—tall and short, thick and thin, skins and hair a rainbow, but all wore the drab, sun-faded colors that formed the unofficial uniform of Soogway's working class. Shade's eyes searched for the shock of green, that sign of life, a defiant sprig in a pile of rubble. But Kell was nowhere.

Shade cursed themself for not thinking, not holding on to her. They pictured Go smiling his confident, rich-man smile at her and then sucking Kell's breath out through her feet. They wanted to scream.

Raised voices broke through Shade's spiraling thoughts, a scuffle too far through the mass for them to see the source. There were shouts, and then Shade was stumbling, falling, pushed onto the concrete by a wave of pressure from the crowd. They scrambled to their feet to avoid being trampled, but the press of bodies unexpectedly loosened around them, a wall of empty space burgeoning as people shoved in reverse, backing away from something.

Shade gripped their hat with one hand and broke through the ring that surrounded whatever it was, yet nearly dropped it when they saw the source of the commotion. There was Kell, her voice deep with threat, telling a story in which her every word was spat out like a curse. Her entire body crawled with scorpions, their countless tails wagging with menace, under which Shade could barely make out the green of her scarf. Kell's eyes gleamed, and for an instant they met Shade's own with pure fury before recognition softened them. Shade realized then they were genuinely afraid of her and of what she could do.

The tension in her shoulders visibly relaxed, and she stopped her telling. It appeared Kell had only been creating space for herself; there was no one on the receiving end of her rage. Relief propelled Shade toward her, but the uneasy crowd gave them both a wide berth. She dropped her arms, and the scorpions melted into storylight, running in rivulets down her body, draining into her palm.

"Found you," Shade said. They smiled though their knees were shaking.

"I hate this place," Kell replied, and took Shade's hand in her own, as if she were their big sister and had done so a thousand times before.

If Shade had hoped for the two of them to be greeted like heroes at the participants' entrance—and they had been, they had to admit—they were disappointed. A battery of clerks and safes checked and double-checked Kell's name then shuffled through more paper and tokens than Shade had ever seen. Kell had to press her thumb into a variety of substances: soft wax, ink, sheets of guidelines, as they verified her identity, her willingness to abide by the rules, and her complete and total submission to the outcome of the challenge. In other words, if she lost, her thumbprint promised that she wouldn't make a fuss. The whole ordeal took far longer than Shade had anticipated, and they had grown hungry and restless by the time they both were let through the rear gates. The clerks had been unable to find any rule prohibiting the use of a second and so had reluctantly permitted Shade to accompany Kell, provided they didn't fight unless called.

Shade and Kell were led through several winding halls, all of which were plainer and less grand than the temple arena might have intimated, and then past three guarded checkpoints. At one, a safe stood at attention with a small glowing worm on his shoulder, and Shade nearly laughed out loud—though they knew better than to question the power of small things. They definitely did not want to find out what that worm could do.

When they finally entered the waiting area, Shade couldn't help but let out a sound of wonder at its view of the arena. The stands were already nearly full despite the hordes of hopefuls waiting outside. The noise was tremendous. With a trick of geometry that made Shade's head spin, the oval arena was much larger inside than seemed possible from the exterior. The space was so vast, they could barely make out the faces of people on the far end. From this vantage point, Shade could see the entire arena, grounds, and spectators—a very different experience from the stolen glimpses they'd managed to snatch in the past.

The lower levels of the arena's seating were filled with people in administrative robes and the bright colors of the rich, who had undoubtedly arrived via their own entrance away from the hordes. These people laughed and chatted and unfurled tiny silk parasols against the glare of the early afternoon sun. In the tiers above them, the less comfortable still angled for space—the stone benches crammed tight. From their clothing, Shade guessed these were common business owners who'd gotten lucky enough to buy a spot. On even higher tiers, poor folk jostled and shifted on their feet, without seating to allow the greatest number to press into the stands. Shade's eyes picked out a few littles pushing under the elbows of the grown-ups and secretly applauded their success at sneaking in.

They turned to find Kell had retreated to a nearby corner of the waiting room, seated as if in prayer. The other challengers sat on the chairs and cushions provided, chewing their nails and glancing nervously at one another in silence, careful to avoid each other's eyes. Metal trays laden with snacks and cloth napkins stretched along one length of the room. Shade sidled over and helped themself to a piece of fruit and a small meat pie before returning to watch the arena.

The Welcome Ceremony had already taken place, but the jester acts were still on, which were some of Shade's favorites. These were professional comics, goofy tellers who pretended to do battle in ridiculous ways. There were five of them on the field now, each dressed in a different color. A signature of the act was that each jester would make their storylight match the color of their outfit so the crowd could more easily track which story belonged to whom. High above the arena's dirt floor, a purple cow was walking on its hind legs, bullying an enormous green moth by shoving it with its belly, its purple udders wagging with the effort. An unlucky yellow *something*—part-trashcat, part-fish, thought Shade—was being throttled by both the red creature and the blue. The crowd was still so uproarious, it was difficult to hear anything these jesters were saying, and no one much cared to listen anyway—though Shade knew the later acts would be different.

The acoustics of the arena were such that the crowd could hear even the softest whisper, a fact that good tellers used to strange and powerful advantage. Shade turned to mention it to Kell, but by the look on her face, she had gone somewhere far away in preparation, and Shade let it go.

The colored creatures destroyed one another in increasingly violent and absurd ways—red turned yellow into an ax with which to chop up green; blue stomped an opponent into small purple bits, which rebounded into tiny copies of the original and swarmed blue in turn, devouring it like termites. Shade cheered and laughed, and their meat pie and fruit were eventually joined by two slices of sweet paste and some pickled roots that squeaked between their teeth when they chewed. The sun began to push the shadows of the comic combatants longer down the field, and soon it was time for the challenges.

The first few challenges were simple enough—some formal disputes between citizens who fought one another, with the spectators as witnesses. There were several that followed in which the tellers faced minor clerks or ministers, as if the internal workings of municipal government could be reasonably solved through the clashing of monsters. The crowd roared in appreciation, however, and Shade mused that it was at least one way to create civic engagement with the mundane issues of water distribution or the power grid. Something itched at Shade, though. *Where was the general?*

One by one, the nervous combatants in the waiting room were called to the arena until only a few remained. Shade had expected something less . . . bureaucratic. None of these matches had the kind of grandeur that the rest of the Cycle was sure to offer. They allowed themself a cautious moment of hope—maybe even more than hope. They caught themself feeling certain.

She might really do it, they thought. *If this is all it is, she just might win.*

Then a hush fell over the crowd. It was as if someone had used a damp blanket to douse a fire; tension billowed and smoked through the stands, but the voices of the throng all ceased in eerie unison. A figure had stepped into the arena and was walking slowly into the center of the field. There was an odd stiffness to their movements that unnerved Shade. Were they wearing armor? Contact with the teller was forbidden, so there was no need to protect the body, and a costume callback to the ancient days of blood combat was gauche, at best. Shade twisted their hat in their hands as they tried to glean everything they could from the figure's gestures and stance, but it was difficult to see much. They were draped neck to toe in a pale robe that hung loosely about them. Only their arms were free of its folds, and these were sheathed in dark leather gloves that reached the shoulder. A broad, round hat crowned the figure's head like a small halo of sunshine, and a veil hung from the brim to further obscure their face.

The figure stopped and gave a short, jerky bow in Shade and Kell's direction, then the robed figure turned their back, raising their arms above their head toward the crowd. The entire audience leaped up at once, the sound a pounding of feet and a crushing wave of applause that shook the very air of the arena.

The general had arrived.

The Warrior: Overhead

36. THE GENERAL

Despite all the hooting and cheering, the pressure, her feelings of terror and grief, Kell had allowed herself to become very still. It was as if she were dreaming, her body safely curled on her rug somewhere far from this place, the rustle of sand hissing against the sides of her tent. The familiar smells of smoke and skin surrounded her while the spectacle raging in the arena danced beneath her eyelids, as if none of it were real.

Home is real.

Her feet carried her forward, past Shade, past the open wall that faced the arena. Shade said something to her as she passed, but she didn't hear the words. She could barely feel the earth beneath her, scarcely notice the thousands of expectant expressions waiting hungrily for what came next.

The ancestors are real.

She opened her heart, and one by one, she felt them pour into her, all of those who had come before: the tellers and the rest—the ancestors who made up who and what she was and all she stood for, the wisdom and continuity of the ages, of her People. A liquid warmth flowed through her, rushing to her toes and fingertips, flooding her chest with a sense of calm and rightness. Behind her eyes were the eyes of countless others like her, witnessing her and all that was to come. She stood before the general but barely saw them—the figure before her was inconsequential, a single person, a functionary. A barrier to be removed. To be obliterated.

The gods are real.

She closed her eyes and thought of the desert, of the way light moved over the surface of the sand, of the winds that scoured its skin, of the creatures that raced and lurked and skittered through its heat and shade. Severe, rich, endless in its variety. Kell thought of Home. Of the stars. Of the constellations on her brother's skin.

She opened her eyes. Someone was reading the terms of her challenge, voicing the complaint of the People, as it had been recorded in Jor's audience with the clerks a lifetime ago. A clerk approached her now and gestured for her to state her intent, and she found herself speaking aloud.

"My name is A'Kell," she said clearly. Her voice rang out across the arena. She could sense the amplifying trick of the acoustics, and it brought her power. She looked directly at the veiled general before her. "I represent the Roamer People of Home. I have come to reclaim the pulsar stones and see them returned to their rightful places."

The general nodded at her slowly, in formal acceptance, and then the two assumed their fighting stances. Kell cast her arm wide and invited the entire stadium into her circle, drawing in the crowd as surely as if she held them with a tether.

"The Hunter was a great one," she began. "She was afraid of neither man nor beast. Fast of foot was she, and long of limb. Some even said she could disguise her shape, to become a stone by a watering hole or even a sister beast, running alongside the herd in their skin."

A glowing desert hare leaped from Kell's palm and began an elegant tour of the arena, bounding in slow motion, as if the crowd themselves were dreaming. Its ears were too long, and its paws flashed with sharp claws beneath its luminous fur. The hare grew and grew as it made its loop, until it returned to Kell the size of an elephant. It crouched, wrinkling its nose. An ear twitched at a comic angle, and a rumble of appreciative laughter rolled through the stands.

Then the general began. "Once there was a child. Just a common child, nothing special, nothing great." His voice was strange. It sounded to Kell as if more than one person spoke at once, an eerie chord of voices that strained away from one another until they found a common pitch and then resolved. "This child lived in a common world where everything was simple. Or so they thought." The strange effect faded, and Kell wondered briefly if she had imagined it, before turning her attention instead to the large kitten that had begun prowling the arena, playfully stalking the enormous hare. The kitten lunged toward her and fell short, tumbling head over heels. The crowd loved it.

"There was not a single shadow in that land the Hunter did not know, not a grain of sand nor crook of branch she didn't greet as part of herself and herself as part of it. When she moved through the deserts of Home, every step was an embrace, every breath a kiss—the air, a dancer; the stone, a lover." The hare sprouted small wings and leaped playfully, its strength evident in the tension of its great hind legs, its joy visible in the stretch and reach of its massive body. The winged hare climbed the air over the arena, largely ignoring the kitten on the ground, describing with its movements the wonder and freedom that Kell hoped would kindle a sweet ache in the hearts of the audience.

The plan was to use some of the basic lore to set the stage. Kell wanted the spectators to love the desert, to see it and feel it. She knew her opponent's kitten was a cheap ploy, that it would likely grow into a jaguar or tiger and try to eat the hare. It was a standard move—shockingly simple, in fact. She had expected more and was starting to wonder if maybe she had over-prepared. She searched for Shade's eyes and shook off the arrogance that threatened to distract her.

The general was setting up a classic hero tale, thin on worldbuilding but heavy on emotion—the child's mother had left him, leaving him lonely and insecure. Kell flinched, feeling the sharp edge of her own mother's abandonment, her own uncertain upbringing. It was fertile and obvious ground for the making of a triumphant conclusion.

Ama, be with me. Kell launched into the next phase of her story, a strange and frightening mix of truth and fantasy where enormous machines prowled the desert on massive iron wheels, crushing the dunes and the nests of ground birds, flattening small lizards too slow to move aside. The machines had monstrous jaws that creaked open and shut, devouring sunlight and stone, threatening to leave the desert in smooth darkness. The hare fled in circles, muscles bunching.

"One by one, the pieces of the sky were swallowed up by the bottomless hunger of the machines. The very blue above cracked apart like glass, and piece by piece, the machines gulped it down, their tremendous jaws crunching and groaning as they left permanent night in their wake. A spiderweb of darkness followed the machines as they roved the sands. What would they do with the sky? What could the Hunter do to stop them?"

The hare raced and strained at the edges of the arena, its movements increasingly human and dance-like. Its eyes were wide and terrified, and the audience shifted uncomfortably, tracking the hare's path with open mouths as Kell narrated the destruction of Home.

The kitten only blinked at these theatrics. It licked a paw.

"The child picked a fight he could not win. He entered a realm he did not understand." From behind the veil, the general's voice was blank, almost bored. Kell's attention was absorbed describing the devastation of Home.

Then, instinctively, she looked out sharply, sensing a trick: the kitten began to melt. First its ears folded, then its paws began to spread, pooling beneath its little belly and merging with the storylight of its tail. The kitten's head oozed disturbingly downward like hot wax, and the entire body spread into a puddle of light that widened. And widened.

The hare bolted, running ahead of unseen machines, and tore across the field, skimming the ground. Terror flattened its ears and elongated its limbs as it sailed over top of the glimmering pool that oozed now where the kitten had been. The merest tip of its hindclaw grazed the pool as it vaulted over, and the hare's foot froze to the surface. The hare's body hurtled intractably forward, and its powerful leg jerked out behind it at an unnatural angle. The animal flailed and thrashed, but it was as if the hare had stepped into a pit of tar, and the more it moved, the more it sank into the stillness of the puddle.

Kell's heart pounded, matching the frantic speed of the hare's. Fear accelerated her words, but she drove the story forward.

"The Hunter knew these machines were beyond her strength to stop. She could not speak to them the way she could whisper to the beasts, for they had no ears. She could not hide from them, for they gulped down the stones that offered her shade and cover. Her arrows failed to pierce their armored hides and clanged uselessly to the sand, to be crushed like twigs beneath their great iron wheels."

The hare floundered, and its ears melted and disappeared, then a forepaw, then its round spine softened. The crowd roared at the general's trick, thousands screaming for the death of the hare. Kell felt strangely removed as she watched it happen. Part of her had hoped that her love of the desert would be enough. She wanted to believe the story itself would save her People—that if only the audience could see what was happening, could feel what she felt, the challenge would be hers.

She realized now that all they wanted was a spectacle. They didn't want the truth. They wanted to be entertained.

Kell shuddered briefly, coming into her body as if her spirit had left and then returned. She was awake. Her mind was clear. She knew what must come next, but she wasn't sure she had the courage to do it. She looked across the arena, where Shade was standing, perpetually wringing that hat of theirs in their hands. They were shouting, but she could not hear them over the din of the crowd.

Kell took a deep breath and allowed the hare to sink beneath the surface and disappear.

A'LAN SPEAKS: FUNERAL PRAYER

Ancestors, hear us.

Our teller will soon be among you. Come now and guide them so they may learn to walk as you do. See them, know their face. Hold their hands and lift them so they may again be light, free from the weight of the earth from which we're made.

Ancestors, be with us.

Share your wisdom so we may celebrate, so we cease to weep. Help us laugh and dance at the sound of our teller's name. Ease our hearts that we may release our grief and know the truth of all endings and beginnings.

Ancestors, open us.

Raise the voice of our teller that they may share all they know, all they have carried for you. Open our ears and minds that we may become better vessels for the stories that move through us, belonging to all and to none. Let not a word be lost. Let no silence escape into void.

Ancestors, trust us.

As you learned from yours and we learn from you, we are, all of us, a river and not a rain, a torrent and not a lake. On and on, we carry. On and on, light passes through. We are all the past, as we were once the future. Let it always be so.

Ancestors, hear us.

Let it always be so.

"Like a weed."
—Mr. Go

37. THE GOLEM

The hare thrashed once in the glowing tar pit and disappeared. Shade wrung their hat. The trap was inescapable, that was for sure. Being a second was agonizing—how were they supposed to just watch as Kell's story struggled and dissolved before their eyes? She needed to stop trying to get free and switch strategies, *quickly*, or the challenge would be over before it had barely begun. They wanted desperately to help, but Kell didn't even seem to see them. Shade shouted reminders to stick to the plan, to ignore the general's tricks, but their voice was a drop in a river amid the roar of the crowd.

They paced back and forth at the edge of the arena. The clerks had said Shade wasn't allowed past the first few dusty feet of the field, having determined a second could only support. They were barred from entering the central grounds of the contest. Shade felt like a pit dog on a chain, straining against it and longing to get their teeth in the battle. They wracked their brain for a trick to make the hare slither or spread, to be less a hare and more a snake, something that could climb and pull free.

Like a vine.

Shade stopped pacing. It was an outrageous thought. Almost unthinkable. And yet, there they were: thinking it.

Across the arena, Kell's voice wavered, and Shade thought they could hear the threat of tears in her story. The general was calmly narrating the pride and sorrow that drives people to terrible mistakes. The crowd bayed like dogs after a trashcat. Shade had to do something.

They pulled their hat down over their ears and smoothed their braids against their chest. They gave the acorn beneath their shirt a little squeeze. The hare had lost all definition now, boiling, roiling in lumps, a jumble of weird shapes like an animal trapped in a sack. They took a long, deep breath, planting their feet wide for balance, and set their gaze on the general before they could lose their nerve. *Down.*

It happened much more quickly with practice; Go was right. Almost immediately, the clamor of the crowd grew muffled and distant, reminding Shade of bathing in the river and dunking their ears below the surface, muting the city noises into rumbles and snippets of sound. They felt the sense of pressure as they slipped into the ground. *Forward.*

The packed earth of the arena was different from the dense concrete of the warehouse where Shade and Go had their lessons, both sharper and more porous, and Shade found traveling through it easier yet much less comfortable. It felt like worming their way through broken glass, though they moved with surprising speed and quickly found their bearing.

Above them, the general's rhythmic cant continued, dragging Kell's story inexorably into its own. The words were distorted and unclear—something about a hero overreaching—but the tempo was strong and strident as a drumbeat. Through the earth, Shade had the impression that there were several voices speaking at once, each at a slightly different pitch, creating a dissonant tangle of vibrations in the dirt around them. They pushed farther forward, seeking the general's feet.

Shade's eyes grew heavy, and they blinked out at the spectacle of the arena through weighted lids. They wavered and reached out a hand to steady themself on a post at the entryway. Their stomach had begun to turn. *Now, up.*

Shade felt the general's feet directly above them, the solid weight pressing into the ground that indicated the presence of something other.

They paused, their heart racing like a frightened bird, flapping at the cage of their ribs. Nausea gripped them, and they felt their body convulse at the waist, clutching at the post. Shade remembered what had happened the last time they'd tried this, but they promised themself they wouldn't take it that far. They could control it—they were sure of it. Just long enough to snatch a breath, to disrupt the story. That's all it would be. Kell needed them.

Shade waited out a deep pulse of nausea as it washed over them and then pushed upward. Immense pain bloomed like a spike into the top of their head. *Don't push!* they reminded themself. *Grow.*

And they did. From a tiny seed in the crumbling earth, Shade stretched easily upward like the merest plumule, a tender shoot wending its patient way not toward sunlight but toward the darkness inside the general. Shade felt first the hard casing of his boots, then the horrible tension of skin, the fatty, popping sensation of entering the body, and then they were in.

Shade was struck with a wall of sound. A dense shrieking filled their head, coupled with a symphony of clicks and buzzes and deep thrums that pounded into them, driving them back downward. It was as if an entire warehouse of machinery were beating Shade into the floor, pile drivers and millstones and an incessant, high-pitched whine composed of many voices at once. They were deafened and disoriented; they had the clear sensation of being torn in two. Terror froze the tiny sprout that was Shade, but it was too late. They were sucked up into the machinery and ground between cogs and plates, shot through arteries and shredded into small bits, their consciousness scattered and thin.

Screaming. Was that Shade, or something else? Dark, jumbled noise and motion, hard, sharp edges, and always the relentless pounding. Sparking, something burning and icy at once, a jolt and then another. They should not be here. A grip seized around them. They had the sensation of being deeply, utterly observed, then rejected. A push-pull flow like that of blood but not blood—no, not blood at all. Cold. Oil. Shade was battered and whipped from one darkness to another, their root lost completely. How could they ever return? There was no sprout, only grit and fuel, bits being shot and flushed, churned and flattened.

Shade's mind could find no direction, but one question floated up before being destroyed under the slamming and grinding of the general's interior: *Where is the breath?*

The shriek repeated in arrhythmic bursts, a staccato tattoo followed by a long, piercing screech. The sound burrowed into Shade's mind and slipped between its folds like a fistful of naked wires, plunging sharp points into every soft surface of their thoughts. It continued until Shade could no longer hear it—or felt that there was nothing else to hear, never had been—the only sound in the world, driven forward with the thrum and pulse of machinery.

Shade was fading. They had the muddy impression that Kell's story had come to life, that the creations she said had ravaged the desert were here, had devoured the sky and trapped Shade under their wheels. They were dust.

Shade felt heat and wondered distantly whether it was hotter in the desert than the city. And then they succumbed to the noise and the pressure and the nausea boiling over into their head and were gone.

Of the two other challengers remaining in the waiting area, one was crouching over Shade when they awoke. He had Shade's head cradled on a cushion on the floor and was dabbing their face with a napkin. He looked uncomfortable and frightened, though of them or the general in the arena, Shade didn't know. They blinked, confused, and saw that the cloth was stained dark red.

"My son gets 'em, too," he offered weakly.

"What?" Shade managed. Their throat felt raspy and dry.

"Nosebleeds. You were pouring out for a minute there. Looks like it dropped you. I dragged you back in here—couldn't lift ye on account of my back. Hope that's OK," he added apologetically. "I pinched it off. Looks like it's stopped. Just gettin' you cleaned up."

Shade looked down and saw their jacket and shirt were spattered in blood. They thought of the hare and panic seized them. They struggled to sit up.

"How long was I . . . ?"

"Just a few minutes. Your friend is up to something out there. She's quite a fighter, isn't she? I never seen nothin' like it." The man's expression softened with admiration.

Shade turned to look at the arena, and another wave of nausea washed over them, breaking over their head in a liquid wash as pain stabbed through both ears. They retched and had to swallow to keep their meat pie down, hot gorge climbing into their throat. They spat into the dust of the floor.

"Sorry," they mumbled and wiped their mouth with their sleeve, but the man didn't seem to care. Now that Shade had revived, the man's attention was drawn back to the arena. He gave Shade a pat on the shoulder and returned to watch the bizarre combat unfolding between Kell and the general. The crowd had hushed, the tension like that before a terrible storm. Shade could feel them all leaning into the drama of it, hanging on Kell's every word as she began the next phase of the battle.

Shade closed their eyes and leaned back against the pillow. They knew they should be out there, encouraging her, but they felt so weak, they didn't think they could stand. Something had happened to them while they were seeking the general's breath, something bad. They felt . . . *poisoned.*

They discovered, to their great relief, a cup of water that the man had left beside them, and they drank it greedily. Their stomach revolted at first and then settled, begging for more, but they lacked the strength to get it. They worked on turning their head and body so they could watch as Kell tried to execute their plan. A sick feeling spread through Shade's belly, not the nausea from before but the awful creep of doubt.

The false god story, the possible heart moves, all of it—all of that was based on the idea of human experience, of being alive and privy to the wonder and terror of it. And now Shade knew better. Shade knew why Kell said a heart story hadn't worked. Somehow, they had to tell Kell, to warn her, but then what could she do instead? Her only hope was that the god story she conjured would somehow be powerful enough. And Shade knew nothing about the gods. Right now, they only knew one thing.

The general isn't human.

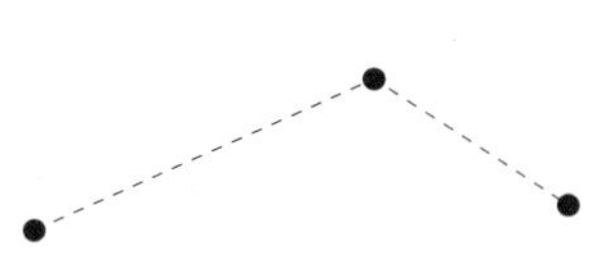

The Hare: Western quarter, early springs

38. DESTRUCTION

Kell stifled the sob that stuck in her throat as the last of the hare melted into the general's pool. It hadn't been absorbed—not yet—but that story was finished. It was time for her to tell the next. She paused, chilled. Her hands trembled, and she clenched her fists, twitching through a quick sequence of patterns to settle her nerves. Her grief at the loss felt cold and still, made of stone, but what she needed now was heat. A lot of it.

"The Hunter knelt in the desert and wept at its destruction," Kell told. "'Please,' she called to the gods. 'Please help.'"

Kell thought of the helplessness on her brother's face when he looked for the pulsar stone and found it missing. She thought of the beauty of A'Lan's stories and those among her clan who ignored them, preferring to spend their nights in their tents, glued to the tech of the city. She thought of Upepo and the heart story she sacrificed, and of the rudeness of the ambassador, and of Ama's faith in her. Warmth began to spread through Kell, a sharp, acid warmth. She thought of the desert—the vast, wild expanse that was at once Home and hostile—an environment that required familiarity and knowledge and community to survive in. That required love.

The general's story was wrapping up. Kell read disappointment in the slope of his shoulders at the ease with which his ploy had worked—clearly the Cycle planning committee hoped for a little more vigor in his warm-up acts. Their veiled face was directed toward hers, and with a start she recalled how he tried to bait her with her own abandonment.

How had this severed general known? Despite herself, Kell recalled the day she had been taken from her milk tent and given to Ama to be raised and trained as a teller, the wrenching and screaming that had shaken her little body as she tried to cling to her mother, her heart broken. She would not lose another home. She looked at the boiling pool of tar that was her story and the general's—a mass of telling, bubbling and seeping across the ground. There, she found the heat she needed.

Anger came quickly when summoned. It pushed aside the cold stillness of her sadness and split open the parts of her that had long ago turned hard. Her anger filled her, white-hot and radiant, lifting her chest and expanding her, as if she herself had grown luminous wings. She felt this anger blaze from her eyes and her casting palm, which she raised above her head as if she would call down the heavens themselves to assist her. *Gods be with me now.*

Kell began to narrate a new story, one not of tar but of ashes. She spoke of desolation and burning, of a world so parched by sun and heat that the very earth itself seized and shuddered and cracked into myriad specks of glass—sand. She spoke of an ebony sun that torched the sky, leaving the world in darkness but for its black radiance, a piercing, malevolent light that cooked all life and revealed shapes only through their shadows.

"The only movement in this bleak world was the wavering of the air, rendered snakelike in the heat that slithered upward, rays seeking their dark master, the black sun. In this ruined world, a new force was born, one with the power to bring shadow in daylight and to harness the powers of heat and devastation." Her voice came low from the depths of her chest. She tossed her head back in the way of the old summoners, giving herself over to the story as if it were the words telling her and not the other way around. She slammed an imaginary story staff into the earth beside her and heard the ghost of it rattle.

Around her, Kell realized dimly that evening had come, and that true darkness was beginning to fall on the arena. Small lights in the stands flickered on for the spectators, but the field itself was left dim to enhance the glow of the spectacle. The crowd was still.

Something huge rose in her chest, and Kell felt a glint of panic—her false god story had summoned something real, something horrible and true and utterly beyond her control. She struggled, trying to direct it, but she quickly gave up and let go. Whatever was coming, all she could do was set it free. *Release.*

"In the ashes of this earth, the power gathered, drawing to itself the heat and broken pieces of the land, the bits of sky, shattered stone, and shards of glass that remained. The wavering lines of heat became curves, and then loops, until the entire desert floor moved as one vast, grinding spiral into the air."

Storylight was lifting off the puddle as mist, a slow-churning miasma that struggled at first without form. It dragged itself skyward but took no animal shape, as if waiting to hear what it would become. Kell's head was still tilted toward the sky, the words belting from her throat like the bellow of a mother in labor. She scarcely recognized the voice that issued forth. It was not hers alone, she knew—it was the voices of endless lorists before her, come to lend their strength as she now birthed this strange and awful story.

"The gods had heard the Hunter and sent the wildest and most terrible among them—though as aid or punishment, no one could say. The churning darkness spun more quickly now, and its true shape emerged, howling and billowing upward into the sky."

The fog of storylight twisted and jerked as a spiral coalesced at its center, leaving whips and clouds of light-dust trailing around it. This was a newborn story, something raw and channeled, lacking the definition of old classics, the well-worn edges and chimeric additions. Anyone who witnessed it could see that it was coming into being for the first time with the unchecked energy of creation. The crowd shifted in their seats, unsure how to respond to this dangerous new entry upon the field. Kell could feel their attention like heat from a fire; from the corner of her vision, she was aware of slack jaws in the faces nearest her. They were listening.

"The broken sky was masked with bits of shattered glass and grit.

That which was clear became opaque. That which was earth became sky. That which was settled, shifting, became airborne and gained the speed of wrath."

Kell and the chorus of ancestors inside her unleashed the sandstorm upon the arena. From the central spiral a form drew together, a monstrous vision at once luminous and dark. Something in its shape recalled the rhinoceroses that roamed the fringes of the green zone of Home, the spiked wedged of its head and the thick folds of armored skin at its shoulders. The rest of it was something else, however, something unnatural to beasts, well outside the animal domain. Whisps of storylight curled and smoked from its hindquarters, recalling both erosion and gathering storms, a glowing cloud of menace writhing behind it like a tail. Though like all storylight it made no sound, veins of lightning flickered in its depths, and watching the sandstorm left the uncanny impression that it rumbled and howled.

Kell gazed at what she had created and felt a strange peace. This was all, oddly, out of her hands now. Her story would tell itself.

"Behold the true heart of power," she called to the still arena. "The god of the sandstorm." Kell paused to let the audience examine the monster. When she spoke next, she was lightheaded with release. "In the desert, destruction brings forth only more destruction. See now what you have summoned."

A wall of fury and light roared through the air above the arena, the false god at once a massive beast and a thunderous swirl of particles, glowing bits of sand hissing through the air like a million, million tiny knives. The crowd gasped, some cringing away from it, as it gathered itself high, boiling into the air in fierce cumulous towers before plummeting down again. The false god rushed the stands and poured itself out in a raging flood only inches from the spectators, who screamed and clutched at one another, pinned to their seats or against the standing crowd behind them by the enormous flank of the monster.

Kell told of the negating force of the sandstorm, the way it moved through the landscape like a barrier made of night, a scouring, burning thing of darkness that robbed the day of light and the air of breath. She called forth the storm's cleansing power, the countless tiny grains and how, individually, they are nothing, but together they can wipe filth from any surface, scrub life from any crook or hollow. Above the arena, the false god silently twisted and roared and plowed through space, magnificent and terrible.

Kell looked on her creation with a mix of love and sadness. It was exactly as Ama had planned: ruinous, excessive, perfect. Even if it wasn't the way Kell had hoped to win. Her heart ached with the knowledge now that sympathy had not moved the crowd. She felt a flush of embarrassment at how naive she had been; she had stubbornly believed—*insisted*—that if people could see the truth, the injustice would be clear and immediately corrected. Thank the ancestors Ma'Shifra had known otherwise. *Ama, you were right. It was a good plan.*

Kell felt the charged power of her teller lineage began to dwindle. Now that the false god had been brought forth, the rest was just technique and formula, letting the tale play out on its own—on Kell's own. She savored the sweet collective strength of her ancestors a moment more and offered a prayer of gratitude to them. Then she took a few shuddering breaths before continuing the story that would end the challenge and return the stones to her People.

The sandstorm coursed a final lap of the arena and then swirled into the center, like a dancer in a competition taking a last bow. Kell's knees were shaking as she surveyed the faces of the crowd, lit eerily from below by electrical lights in the stands. She looked to the waiting area for Shade but didn't see them in the doorway. In her reverie, she had almost forgotten the general altogether.

She barely had time to register that the puddle on the ground was gone before the dragon plunged headlong into the side of her rhinobeast.

"Our hero sneaks up on the monster when it least expects him," boomed the general's strange, chorded voice. "He is not afraid of darkness. For he knows—light shall ever prevail!"

The dragon punched a hole in the storm and came out the other side, streaming storylight behind it like gore. The crowd went wild, leaping to their feet. Cheers rained down on the arena from all sides. Kell looked wildly around her, trying to get her bearings, but the arena tilted suddenly, and she struggled to keep her balance.

The dragon now made its own tour of the playing field, this latecomer clearly a crowd favorite. Kell squinted at it, desperately trying to gather her thoughts—it was not a living dragon, though its shape was right and convincing. As it swooped past, Kell saw that it had been pieced together out of trash: bits of plastic and metal, broken tech, ragged sticks of bamboo, crumpled rags, and even discarded, moldering food moved together to craft the illusion of the dragon's form. Her stomach turned.

The audience took no notice of the dragon's construction, however, and screamed with cheery bloodlust as it corkscrewed upward into the night air.

What on dry earth is this? This deus ex machina of the general's was hardly even storytelling—nothing more than a cheap and boring move to save himself—and yet the dragon had done visible damage to her false god. She reflexively began narrating a countermove, but she had divined no continuity for this creature she had created, had not anticipated needing a further complication or climax after the denouement, and the earlier rapturous support of her ancestors had since drained away. She was alone in the arena, now. She told the first story she could think of.

"You all remember how we came to know our Home," she began. The rhinobeast thundered after the dragon overhead, and as she churned through the well-worn origin story of her People, her creature sprouted new lizard bits—its eyes grew reptilian, its feet long and spindled.

The general barked a chaotic mishmash of battle tropes—narrow misses, brave escapes. The dragon twirled and nipped at her false god, then raced in a circle, leaving glowing orbs in its wake. Kell could not say whether these were meant to be eggs or droppings, but it didn't matter because then the dragon made a second circle and belched a jet of fire at the orbs. These each exploded in turn, sending up enormous gouts of glitter and flame, at which the crowd shrieked with pleasure, clapping wildly at the spectacle. The edges of the false god grew blurred, and it stumbled once over its strange feet in its pursuit of the dragon.

Kell gritted her teeth and tried again, this time adding her own memories to the mix—the song for first bread, a memory of bathing in the Riverlands, the legend of the desert cat that purred babies to sleep. The rhinobeast reared up, sending a wall of sand toward the dragon. The dragon was momentarily flattened, tumbling over its side, and rolled. It was only feigning defeat, she realized, when it popped back up. New parts—machine parts, Kell noticed—whirred and cranked along its sides.

The dragon lunged again at the sandstorm god, swallowing bits of its angry cloud, as if paring it down to a manageable size. Gleaming sand dripped from its jaws, and the rhino ferociously pawed and jabbed at the dragon with its horn. But the dragon twisted out of its reach. Kell would almost swear the creature was grinning beneath its long whiskers, metallic teeth glinting along its garbage-laced snout.

She could not lose to this . . . thing. Whatever she could think of, Kell poured into the god. She called forth songs that she and Jor sung on long scouting missions, then a memory of burning herself while entranced by a lorist as she scooted too close to the fire; she told the story of why it rains. Dozens of stories flowed forth from her, twisting and transforming the false god in glorious, seemingly endless ways. The beast fluttered and changed, growing wings and lashes, sprouting spikes and fins at her words. It swam, danced, gnawed, and gnashed. It was angry but also beautiful, a rich and profound tapestry of meaning and symbol. Tears streamed down Kell's cheeks, but she was unable to stop—she gave herself to the god, praying that it would, in turn, save her People. The god of the sandstorm altered with each addition and became ever more fantastic and wonderful, and she sobbed, feeling it draw her heart out of her and into itself. *Take it*, she thought. *Use it. Take it all.*

Meanwhile, the dragon continued to feast. It consumed the god's tail like a bird gulping a worm. It batted at the god's flank and sent it onto its side, then retreated, pacing like a cat stalking an injured mouse. The tone of the audience was different now, the jubilant sounds had darkened to calls for death and conclusion. Some higher in the stands began to chant, and the chant caught around the arena, gathering power in unison. The dragon swelled in the night air, ragged sheet metal dangling from its chest like scales. Kell could see other debris sticking to it, elements she recognized from her stories alongside castoffs from countless others it had devoured, put to senseless use in its great hodgepodge body and rendered into meaningless junk.

The dragon grew so massive that it soon dwarfed what remained of the false god, filling the sky above the arena as a mountain of refuse and stolen parts. The chant of the crowd shook the stands, and Kell wept as the dragon opened its clockwork jaws and devoured her story whole.

Whether the crowd erupted or the cheers were deafening, Kell couldn't tell. She had gone utterly numb, clutching her stomach with both hands as the loss tore her stories from her, uprooting them from where they lived inside her and leaving instead a cool blankness, a horror of absence and theft. The false god was gone, and with it every memory and bit of lore she had fed it. She was ruined.

Kell blinked, but her tears were spent. She was simply hollow, filled only with the certainty that the challenge was one she could never have won. Silaya was right: the general's story had no honor.

She turned toward the general, wanting at least to see the face of the person who had taken everything from her and her People, but his face was still veiled as he gathered his story—and with it, her own—back into his palm. What would happen now? She had sworn to accept the results of the challenge. She felt strangely untethered, silent.

The general offered her a curt, mechanical bow, which she did not return. The people in the stands leaped and squirmed like so many worms, twisting in the night air. Kell blinked. Her own breath was loud in her ears. Everything else was a pantomime. Nothing was real.

Then the entire world moved sideways, and Kell was pushed aside by an unseen hand as a tremendous explosion rocked the earth beneath her. She felt it rather than heard it, a cracking of reality that splintered the air and sent waves of force through everything. The blast was immediately followed by two more, and she stumbled to her knees.

All the lights went out.

Sound returned to Kell now, screams of terror and confusion. The darkness in the arena was total, and Kell could hear the thousands in the stands above her shoving and stomping as they tried to get past one another. Safety enforcers barked commands that were lost in the frenzy.

Kell began to crawl on her hands and knees in the direction of where she thought the waiting area was, not knowing any other way out of the stadium. The grit of the field scraped into her hands and knees as she scrambled, the pitch black creating the illusion not of space but of pressure, as if the sky had fallen upon her. She heard a voice she recognized, and she pushed herself to her feet to shuffle toward it.

"Kell," it came again. A glimmer appeared, and she saw Shade then, murmuring a small story to give them light. It flickered weakly in their hand. Kell saw that they were lying on the ground, and she scrabbled toward them.

She knelt beside Shade and looked up, craning her neck to check that the sky was, in fact, where it should be. In the total darkness, pinpricks of light pierced the night overhead, and she noted distantly that she knew the pattern of the constellation.

Stars, she thought. *Finally.*

MA'SHIFRA SPEAKS: MAKING TEA

First, boil the water. The kettle is unimportant. Some are very fine, with ornate handles and specially shaped spouts, but does it taste any different? I doubt it. This old, dented pot of mine gets hot just the same.

Here—here is a bundle of stag's wood. Just take one. That's fine.

Now add this to the pot, along with some of this herb here. It's gentlenook. It will calm you. And here is some date syrup. It's just to make it a little sweet. No, it doesn't change it. No sense in making something foul to the taste, is there?

Now watch what happens in the kettle. See the way the color shifts? The plant breaks down entirely, but that is what releases the parts that we need. See it become soft and pliable? Let's wait and see how dark we can get it. I like it strong, don't you?

Without the hot water, it's just a stick and a fistful of weeds. It needs to boil and break before it can do what it must. Do you understand?

"Just do your best."
—Shade's father

39. TRIANGULATION

"What's happening?" Shade croaked. Their voice sounded strange in their ears, blurry and unclear. They were mumbling the simplest story they could think of to keep a light going, little more than a nursery rhyme, and the fox had almost reached the top of the mountain.

"I don't know, but we need to get out of here. Why are you on the ground?"

"I—I'm hurt," they managed. "Something happened." Shade had to tell her, had to warn her that it wasn't her fault. "Kell—"

"What did you do?" she snapped. "Did you do something?"

"The stones," they slurred, between snippets of story. "The general wasn't playing f—fair."

"I know that," she said. "Can you stand up?"

Shade struggled to their feet. The ground pitched toward them again, but Kell held them fast by one elbow—she was surprisingly strong for being so slight—and Shade reached one hand out toward the opening in the dark. Their fingers fumbled but found the post. They took a tentative step forward, testing their balance. Their guts swam, and their head screamed with pain as if someone had scooped their brains out with a metal cup then nailed their skull shut again.

"Can you keep that going?" Kell asked, meaning the light. Shade nodded and was immediately sorry they'd moved their head. They plucked another rhyme from their memory, their thick tongue laboring to enunciate the sweet treats Peat ate in the street, and kept the glimmer alive. The storylight danced in their palm in the shape of a jumping spider, and Shade held their hand outstretched before them like a lantern. Together, the two picked their way into the waiting area, arm in arm.

Inside, Shade heard the man who had nursed their nosebleed yelling for the other challenger to open the damn door. The arena was a cacophony of shouts, and relentless footsteps pounded above them, making it difficult to hear.

"It's locked!" the other shouted. "They locked us in here!" There was a frantic rattling as he tried the knob again.

"Then get out of my way," the first man snarled. The small glow from Shade's palm clarified little more than sharper edges to the shadows, and the second challenger began sputtering a small story of his own, panic leaving him out of breath. A dragonfly of light soon hovered helpfully above the locked door, and Shade watched as the first man's bulk gathered and heaved, and with a tremendous kick, the door swung open to the corridor outside. The dragonfly moved into the hall, revealing an empty passageway leading into darkness. The safes and their units had fled. The two men went first, their labored breathing echoing in the enclosure, and Kell and Shade followed.

Though they had come this way only hours before, nothing looked familiar in the dark. Shade's energy was flagging, and they gave up trying to keep the spider dancing on their palm with the rhyme. The first man kicked through another door and fell, as it was unlocked and gave way easily. He cursed and pulled himself back to his feet, one hand clutching his back, then limped along after the dragonfly. Shade guessed that many of these doors had been sealed with electricity, and now that the power was out, so was the security system. It was a detail that might have proved useful, in other circumstances.

Kell was gripping their upper arm hard as if she were trying to stanch a wound, and it hurt. Shade wanted to tell her to ease off, but their head reeled, and they feared that without her fierce attendance, they might spin away entirely. The corridors stretched on forever, though luckily there were no turns or choices to make. The building around them creaked and shuddered like a giant ship in a storm, with the weight of thousands of people, pressing and stampeding in the darkness. The thought made it difficult for Shade to breathe.

"We have to get to the gate," Kell hissed. Her voice was sharp and hot in their ear.

"The gate?" Shade was confused. Didn't they need to get back to the Grove? They wanted their cot and a bit of green. Some water might be nice, too. They were so thirsty . . .

"Yes." She sounded resolute. "Jor said that if anything happened, I had to get to the gate and get out of the city."

Shade felt dizzy and so, so tired. They didn't have the energy to argue. A chair came to view in the hallway, and Shade's knees buckled. Maybe they could just rest there for a moment? But Kell's grip on their arm dragged them forward, and they followed the small light of the dragonfly through the twisting dark.

Time passed in a blur of shadows, sounds, and pain. The two men bickered as they worked their way back to the beginning, questioning each other's judgments and getting in one another's way. They'd forgotten about the challenger and her second who followed them. Shade felt as if they'd been stumbling through the bowels of the arena for hours, maybe days, but then vaguely remembered it hadn't taken long at all going in. They stopped trying to think. At some point, the two men ceased arguing and together put their shoulders to a very heavy set of doors. Finally, the doors swung outward with a groan, and a flush of night air struck Shade's face. They were outside.

The men offered each other rough hand clasps and went their separate ways, disappearing into the jumbled chaos that was the plaza before them. Bodies pushed, and voices strained higher than usual with panic and disorientation. Here and there, flashes of orange lit faces grotesquely as some managed to procure torches and move into the darkened city with their meager flames held aloft. Shadows danced and flickered along the stone walls in echo. A stripe of pain cut through Shade's head, and they bent at the waist and retched onto the cobblestones.

"Can you walk?" Kell's voice was tight with concern.

"I think so." They *had* been walking, they thought. *How much farther?*

"We have to get to the gate," she repeated. "Can you find it from here?" Shade nodded and gestured with their free arm, and they set off across the plaza into the city's rings. Kell moved to Shade's other side to free her casting hand. She began singing a song under her breath, releasing a bright bird that arced and swooped before them. Her storylight was just enough to keep their steps clear—they could see the ground at their feet, but that was about all. Shade led them down one wrong turn and then another, and soon they found themselves backtracking over several blocks to correct their course. They plodded on, but Shade's feet were growing heavier and their thoughts increasingly muddled. The streets had grown strange in the darkness. Shade had the impression they were wandering inside the coil of a snake as it slowly cinched around them, ever tighter.

After several more wrong turns, Kell grew exasperated and made them stop.

"This isn't working," she said, shifting to deposit Shade's weight against a stone wall. "You need to rest." She kept up her repetitive little melody, humming more than singing now, Shade noticed. It had a nice pace to it, and they wondered if it was made for traveling. The bird alit on Kell's shoulder, and Shade slid onto the ground with their back against the clammy alley wall. Kell crouched beside them, her eyes glinting in the storylight. She turned her head as a trashcat waddled past. It paused, looking at them both, its eyes turned to pale lanterns by the light, then hissed and hurried off.

Kell cursed and muttered something about stones.

"What?" Shade's mouth felt gummed up, their jaw too heavy to move properly. She narrowed her eyes at them.

"I want to try something," she said. "Can you sing?" Shade shrugged. They had never really tried, they realized. Their mother had been a decent singer, but they had always just listened.

"We'll see." Their voice sounded like they were nose-deep in hooch, which frightened them.

Kell let the bird fade and gathered it back into her hand, leaving the two of them in darkness. Shade felt the delicious pull of sleep tugging them down, and they bit their tongue to stay awake. Kell's voice was urgent but calm.

"In the desert, we have two methods of finding our way—the Way at Ease and the Way in Haste. Both require singing, and both take two people to triangulate the course. Do you understand?"

"You—you want me to sing with you to find the gate?"

"Yes."

"Which one?"

Shade heard her sigh sharply before she spoke. "We need the Way in Haste, but you can't move quickly enough, so we'll pretend we're at ease, OK? But you'll need to go as fast as you can."

A large crash followed by shouting underscored her point. The city around them had become a weird and dangerous labyrinth without electricity, and the people of Soogway were responding with increasing panic. They heard glass breaking and then more footsteps. Some windows shone with the blue glow of battery-powered happy boxes as tenants waited out the blackout, but the streets were a tangled, frantic mess.

"You also must be able to feel the stones that my People use to navigate the desert. They give off pulses. We feel them here." She picked up one of their hands and pressed into their palm. "My People believe the pulses are—are . . . " she trailed off for a moment, as she tried hard to remember what. Pain clotted her voice as she continued. "You probably can't do it, but we have to try."

Shade sat up straighter. They wished they had some water.

"Close your eyes," she commanded. Shade was happy to comply. Their head drifted off to one side, and she jerked them upright again. "One of them is nearby and very strong," she went on. "If there's any chance you can sense the stones, that will be the one you find." She held Shade's limp arm up in a gesture not unlike their casting pose, roughly molding their hand into a cup. "Now, listen carefully. And *feel*. Feel for the pulse. Like a heartbeat."

Kell began to hum again, although this time the song was slow and meandering, not the brisk, happy march of the bird. Shade opened one eye to watch her. As she hummed, eyes closed in concentration, a luminous green line began to materialize at Shade's eye level, and they realized that the storylight was not coming from her casting palm but gathering around her neck. It slowly took the form of a snake and curled around the ball of her shoulder before slithering downward, under her clothes, and reemerging at her feet.

"Can you feel it?" Shade shook their head. Their hand felt soft and sweaty. Kell continued to sing, and Shade closed their eyes again, trying to follow the sound.

It reminded them of something, a dream they had, or an urge—it sounded like being pulled from oneself, like being homesick for a place they had never been. Shade realized it felt like the time Kell and her brother had found them in the Grove, when the serpent had pulled them from sleep and led them through the sewers to the street. As they focused, Shade felt the faintest tingle in their palm, not a pulse but an itch. They swallowed hard.

"I—I think I feel something." Their voice was hoarse.

"Your part goes like this," she said, her tone urgent. She began another wordless tune while the snake twined patiently on the stones between them. This countermelody was similar, a twisting, luxurious sound, but it took different turns and went lower in pitch. Shade tried to concentrate on the shape of it, but their head felt like a sieve. They reached for their part in the song and felt it run through the holes in their mind like water.

"Can you sing it again?" they asked. Kell did a second time, and then a third. Shade cleared their throat and tried, their voice at once both thick and reedy. They winced but continued.

Shade's fingers twitched at the itch in their palm, and they clutched at it, trying to hold on. The sensation grew hotter. Their singing faltered, and a cold band cinched their throat. Shade began to cough. Kell hummed her own part now, and Shade once more repeated theirs, trying to make them match. It was like trying to hold a live fish at the gator hole, gripping something slippery that didn't want to sit still. Shade's part lunged after Kell's and made a nice chord, but then it fell apart again, and the result made them both cringe. Patiently, Kell repeated hers again, and the snake circled in place, waiting.

Shade closed their eyes and listened to the course of the notes. There was a coolness there, and when they focused on it with all the tattered remnants of their attention, this coolness soothed them, eased their frayed mind and burning palm. It felt like a hand on their forehead, or a long sip of something fresh and clean. Shade let a hum pour from their throat, and this time the song came more easily. The notes were not perfect, but Shade felt a gentle slide across their neck nonetheless, and then something slipped from their collar and greeted the snake on the ground.

Shade opened their eyes. The two shapes glowed together: one a smooth, green serpent, magnificent and jewel-like; the other a squat, bunching shape covered in orange fur—a caterpillar?

The look of disgust on Kell's face was unmistakable even in the storylight, but she continued her part of the song. As they sang, their two shapes intertwined and formed what appeared to Shade to be an egg.

The egg shivered and burst, releasing a creature that Shade had no name for. It moved side to side like a snake but had shoulders and many tiny feet. Down its back were rows upon rows of what might have been wings but were far too small to give flight. It glowed brightly, however, and though Kell wrinkled her nose, she extended a hand to Shade, helping them up. Their ludicrous guide sniffed the air and began winding its way into the night, its many legs pumping furiously though it floated several feet off the ground.

"Gods," Kell breathed, clearly repelled. She frowned but raised her eyebrows at Shade like a shrug. "I guess we go that way," she said.

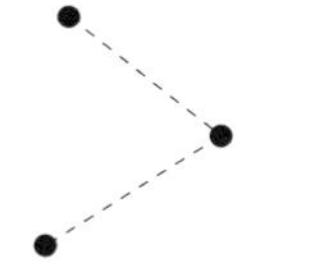

The Stranger: Northern horizon, market season

40. THE WAY IN HASTE

Beneath the tumult of shouts and intermittent crashes, there was a stillness to the streets that Kell couldn't put her finger on until she realized that all the machines had simply stopped running, all the lights had stopped buzzing. The city was dead inside. Rather than a return to nature, it felt like she and the street urchin were pushing their way through a corpse—the buildings vast bones jutting from skin, the alleys cramped, cold arteries. Kell shuddered at the thought but maintained her grip on Shade's arm, keeping them in motion. She didn't know what she would do with them once they reached the gate and found Jor, but she couldn't leave them in this state. Right now, all she could do was keep them walking.

How had Jor known something would go wrong? What had *gone wrong?* Whatever had blown took out the entire power grid and disrupted the Cycle. Would it restart again tomorrow in daylight? Would city officials come after her? Would they require her to somehow notarize her defeat, or had she simply failed to win the stones back?

Kell blinked these thoughts away like sandflies. Underneath her resolve, a tremendous hole yawned open inside her, its shape a horror of shame and absence. She thought of Silaya, the beautiful, fierce lines of her face as her eyes had burned into her own. *You will not fail.* And yet she had—she *had* failed, and she had lost not only the stones but huge swaths of herself in the process.

Hot tears flooded Kell's eyes as she strode after the small monstrosity marching before them. She walked as quickly as she dared, practically dragging the little thief by one arm, but neither wanted to get too close to the guide their Way at Ease had produced. It was an appalling thing, and Kell silently begged the ancestors' forgiveness for sharing one of their most sacred songs with an outsider. She hadn't known what else to do—and the poverty of her choice showed clearly in the result. Thankfully, everyone else on the streets was too preoccupied making their own way through the darkened city by torchlight or other means to pay much attention to their bizarre procession. Kell wiped her face with her sleeve, but the tears kept coming. She swallowed hard and tried to keep the acid down her throat. *Just get to Jor.*

Kell tripped and let go of Shade's arm to catch herself. She turned to see what had caught her foot, and she realized with alarm that it was someone's leg. A body lay sprawled across the sidewalk in the dark. She nudged the leg with her foot, fearing the worst, and a loud snore rattled from the body. A slack hand released its grip on a bottle, which clanked and rolled in a circle, the sound describing its emptiness.

"There's hooch heads everywhere," Shade slurred. They didn't seem concerned, but Kell was shocked.

"Shouldn't we move him somewhere safe?" she protested. It didn't seem right to leave a person lying in the street, especially if they couldn't look after themselves. "He might not even know there's a blackout."

"His whole life's a blackout," Shade mumbled and turned away from the man. The creature had rounded a corner, and they disappeared after it. Reluctantly, Kell followed, leaving the unconscious man to sleep off his demons.

The city without its electricity was so unlike the dark of the desert. Home was wide and open, a vaulting, star-studded night. This was like being locked in a box, as if the buildings were tipping toward her at every turn. It was stifling and claustrophobic, and she lost all sense of time. For comfort, Kell reached for a memory of A'Lan recounting the story of the First Pathfinder—one of her favorites since childhood—but found a shadow in its place, a terrible void where it had once lived. She swallowed a whimper and kept moving, her fingers flexing in and out of nervous fists.

Her eyes had adjusted to the thick, close black of the city, and she could draw details here and there from the creature's light. The cobblestones underfoot were smoother here, well-traveled. There were more doorways and bamboo crates. They turned onto what must have been a main thoroughfare, and suddenly light was everywhere, radiating from torches and firepots, braziers set into the street, and steel drums flickering with heat. People crowded around these, some laughing and passing bottles back and forth, though many still scrambled to get where they were going and pushed their way through the crowd.

"I know this place," Kell said, surprised. They had reached the row of inns in the Traveler's Quarter where she and Jor had first encountered Shade. She flushed in embarrassment at the memory, but it felt good to recognize something—*anything*—and they were very close to the gate.

Something bumped Kell, and she looked down to see that a small child had collided with her. They looked up at her with wide, sorrowful eyes. *Poor thing must be terrified.*

Shade reached around Kell and hissed at the child, shoving them roughly away. She whirled, ready to chide Shade, when she discovered another small urchin behind her back, their hands quickly searching her clothes for chips. She shooed them both off and spotted at least two more in the crowd nearby. She was a mark, that was for sure, and a snap of bitter laughter escaped her.

"Too bad for them," she said. "I have nothing at all on me—everything is back at the Grove." Shade grumbled something she didn't catch. She was about to ask when shouts nearby interrupted her.

A row of safety enforcers and their units had formed a line across the street leading to the main entry plaza and were attempting to block the flow of foot traffic toward the gates. Their glowing animals bristled with menace, those with teeth baring them in silent snarls. Shade froze beside her. Their guide creature ambled onward, straight toward the safe line, and Kell called out to it in her mind, begging the foolish creature to stop, to hide itself, though she knew it would do neither. A safety unit in the form of an enormous, leggy bird cocked its head at the wayfinder as it marched blithely forward, indicating the now-obvious path to the gates. That the Way had worked with an outsider at all was a minor miracle—expecting it to have the sentience of a true guide was beyond hope. Kell held her breath as the bird lunged at the strange creature, snapping at the thing's squat midsection. The wayfinder burst apart in a small cloud of glowing dust that dissipated quickly around the unit's beak. Kell exhaled when she saw that the unit's officer had missed the event entirely, their attention directed on the thronging crowd. She directed a small prayer of gratitude to the now-defunct monstrosity that had gotten them this far, even if its creation felt unclean. Shade's ability to sense the stone, however weakly, continued to make her uneasy. She had been taught that only the People could follow the pulsar stones, but Winty could hear them, and now Shade could feel them, too. What else had she learned, had she relied on as an essential truth, that was wrong?

One of the safes shouted orders into a cone that threw his voice against the surrounding buildings. *Everyone was to stay inside, there was a search in progress, the gates were closing, power would soon be restored.* He repeated it over and over with such monotonous authority Kell marveled that he himself wasn't made of the tech that trapped the ghosts of sound in a box. Shade looked a haggard wreck, but now they nudged her forcefully behind one of the steel drums of fire that cluttered the street, and she let herself be herded. Revelers and passersby alike grew tense and jostled to get farther from the safes, bodies driving away from the plaza nearest the gate.

Kell and Shade slipped to the edge of the street and skirted the bulk of the crowd, though Kell found she had to grip Shade even tighter now not to lose them in the flow of people. Shade stumbled on ahead of her, their small frame lowered into a crouch that made her stoop to hold on. Shade led her to a pile of crates along a wall right at the edge of the safe line and waited, panting. Kell wanted nothing more than to be somewhere else. The firelight danced on the faces of the safety enforcers, calling to mind sand demons in the frightening tales that had thrilled her as a child—she remembered flickers of imagery but struggled to summon the words. She groped for them in her mind but came back empty.

The mood of the crowd soured. Some who had been sharing a more festive attitude to the blackout were reluctant now to go home, and a few shouted profanities at the officers. Kell pressed herself against the stone wall beside her and tried to become invisible. The nearest unit was only feet away, an even larger version of a desert cat, which turned its head and fixed her with its glowing, unblinking eyes. Kell realized she had dropped Shade's arm and was now crushing their hand. They winced with pain, and she forced herself to relax her grip, though she kept her gaze on the enormous cat. It showed her its fangs.

Something sailed through the air and shattered at the safe's feet. The drunks had thrown a bottle, and then another. Shards of glass erupted and bounced, and the unit's head snapped its attention toward the revelers. On command, the line of safety enforcers split into an attack formation, some lunging forward and others dropping into a line behind. Kell felt her arm yanked from its socket as Shade somehow mustered the strength to propel them both past the safe line and into the crowd beyond.

They clung to each other as they fought the heaving chaos of the main entry plaza. Torches dotted the walls, but the center of the broad square was still completely dark, and people elbowed their way away from the gate in panic. *Where was Jor?*

Kell felt her footfalls sync with others' in a current moving toward the gate rather than away, and it carried her along with frightening strength. Within moments, she found herself at the massive wooden doors, one hand still in Shade's. She reached out for one of the metal studs to steady herself and realized the doors were in motion.

"They're closing!" she shouted. She looked around, desperately seeking any sign of her brother, but the torches offered only a flickering blur of faces as some people pushed into the city and others pushed out. Her eyes skimmed the crowd, seeking his height, his stride, but found nothing.

"Kell—," Shade began. Shade looked as if they could barely stand, their head nodded on their chest, then they jerked it back upright. Their skin was clammy and pale, even by firelight. She couldn't leave them here.

"What if he's outside?" Kell chewed her lip, her fingernails grinding anxious patterns into her free palm. Shade's hand was cold and sweaty and hung in hers like a rag, no longer holding hers back. She had to decide.

Clerks and guards were pushing people out of the gate, out of the city, as another set of safety enforcers and their units drove the rest into the side streets out of the plaza. A large guard holding a torch in front of her face approached them, her eyebrows cinched downward.

"Get moving," she growled.

"I'm waiting for someone," Kell pleaded, but the woman thrust her shoulder around, pushing her and Shade toward the giant doors.

"In or out," the woman commanded. "Now."

Kell took one last look into the plaza. It was draining of people, now that the safes had forced the crowd into the alleys. Jor was nowhere. She released Shade's hand long enough to wipe her palms on her clothes and then grasped it again, dragging Shade through the doors and out of the thick city walls.

Similar turmoil greeted her on the other side—darkness, torchlight, people milling and shouting, seeking one another, voices calling the same names in the same cadence over and over like the calls of terrified birds. Horses and other beasts of burden stamped and hawed, restless in the noise and agitation. Abandoned carts, parked at odd angles, created a puzzle of obstacles that jammed all flow of traffic leading away, out to the muddy plain and the sea of stumps beyond.

Kell's voice joined the others, calling her brother's name, first as a question but soon as a command as panic quickened her breath. Shade slumped beside her, crumpling to the ground as if all their joints had collapsed at once. Their hat slipped over one eye.

Kell climbed onto a bamboo crate that had fallen from a wagon and looked out over the darkened sea of people and things. Cold crept up her feet and into her legs. She called for Jor again, and again, but her voice was lost in the volley of other voices, shot over the crowd without hitting its mark. The cold moved into her stomach, and then her chest. She was being frozen, constricted with fear. She had lost the stones, and her stories, and her brother—he wasn't here.

Ancestors, please. Emptiness answered. The hollow inside her grew, eating away her insides until she felt only loss, until she thought she must be screaming, every cell in her body howling in grief, yet her voice was strangely silent. She stopped calling her brother's name. She was alone.

"Kell!"

Her name flew through the dark and struck true in her chest. She turned, seeking its source, and out of the mess of shadows and movement, two figures emerged. One threw back its scarf and revealed a face she knew in the torchlight.

"Kiche?"

He pushed through the crowd toward her, leading his horse by the bridle. Another rider followed, and Kell thought she might go wild with relief and joy. *Silaya.* The two maneuvered their way closer, and Kell jumped down from the box to greet them. Kiche wrapped her in a rough hug, and she was overwhelmed with the smells of woodsmoke and leather that clung to him, reminders of Home.

"I told you—you press that beacon, we come for you." His smile was wide and bright. Kell shook her head, fatigue and adrenaline muddling her thoughts. Her heart thudded in her chest.

"But we—"

The other rider removed their scarf, and Kell stopped. Kiche clapped a hand on Kell's shoulder and gestured to the unfamiliar rider.

"This my other cousin, Poley. He gonna ride with us."

"Where's Silaya?" Kiche's smile grew tight.

"She's busy. She got some things she's taking care of." His shoulders offered a soft apology. "Where's your brother?"

Kell opened her mouth to speak but a sob came out of her instead. Something about Kiche's easy manner made it so much harder to stay strong. She closed her lips on the howl in her chest, and it came out as tears, a hot flood burning her eyes and the back of her throat. Kiche wrapped his arms around her and patted her back like a child, and she wept into him, her shoulders jerking with every shaking breath.

"Okay, okay now," he repeated in a soft voice. "It's okay now. The city a hard place, I know."

"We didn't press the beacon," she said into his chest once she was able to speak. "I don't know where he is." Kiche held her out at arm's length and looked into her face.

"Your brother pressed it a week ago. He called us to come for you."

Kell blinked and wiped her face with both hands. "What?"

"You got to come home now, girl," he said. "Where's your stuff?"

"I don't—Kiche," she frowned, sniffling. She wiped her hands on her scarf. "I can't leave him here. We have to find him."

"Look. I was sent to get you, bring you back to your Ama. I don't know what Jor is doing or not doing, but we gotta go."

Guards had begun assembling in front of the gate, urging people along toward the road. There was a heavy clang and grinding sound, and Kell realized the massive doors were being barred from the inside.

Shade coughed on the ground behind her, and Kell noted with alarm that she had forgotten about them. She knelt and hauled them up like a sack of grain.

"This is Shade," she said to the riders. Without thinking, she announced, "They're coming with us." Shade hung limply from her arms, their head slumped forward on their narrow shoulders.

"Can they ride?" Poley sounded skeptical. Kiche shrugged and helped hoist the small, sagging thief into Poley's saddle, and Poley vaulted up behind them, gripping Shade before him and holding the reins with his other hand.

"We should move," Poley tilted his chin toward the road. "It's going to be . . . difficult tonight. There's a lot of people on the road." Kiche nodded and gestured for Kell to mount his horse. *A new horse,* Kell thought. She wondered vaguely if Kiche knew its name yet. As she placed her hands on the saddle to pull herself up, she noticed that the saddlebags looked thin and remembered her own things were still back at the Grove.

Kiche moved close, his face serious, holding her gaze.

"Ma'Shifra—" he said gently.

Kell stared at him. Whatever he was about to say, she was sure she didn't want to hear it. "Tell me," she demanded.

"She's real sick, like."

Ama. Kell didn't need to know anything else. She turned away from the burning torches and the noise and desperation of the city walled off inside itself. She turned from her brother, wherever he was, and the general, whatever it was. She didn't know which was more urgent, that she see Ama or that Ama see her. She had failed. Her stories were gone. Her heart was empty, a black space full of the night, a hole in the shape of Home.

"Take me to her," Kell said, looking into the darkness ahead.

DRAMATIS PERSONAE

Roamers, People of Home

Red Sandbeast Camp

Kell (A'Kell, formally): lorist and combat teller; pathfinder

Jor (Ma'Jor, formally): hunter and pathfinder; Kell's brother

Ama (Ma'Shifra, formally): combat teller and councilmember; Kell's grandmother

Clay Horse Camp

Silaya (Ma'Silaya, formally): weaver and pathfinder

Kiche (Si'Kiche, formally): weaver and pathfinder; Silaya's cousin

Upepo (A'Upepo, formally): Silaya's sister

Poley (A'Poley, formally): Kiche's cousin

People of Soogway

Shade: storyfighter and pickpocket

Cheap: roasted bean seller; Shade's friend

D Street Kids: crew of young pickpockets

Go: underworld crime boss; former storyfighter

Ma Bud: seamstress

Xylem: tender of the Grove

The general: imperial combat teller

People from elsewhere

Winty: Wild Forest scout; storyfighter

After-The-Rain-But-Before-Things-Are-Dry: Winty's travel companion

Map of Soogway Electrical Grid

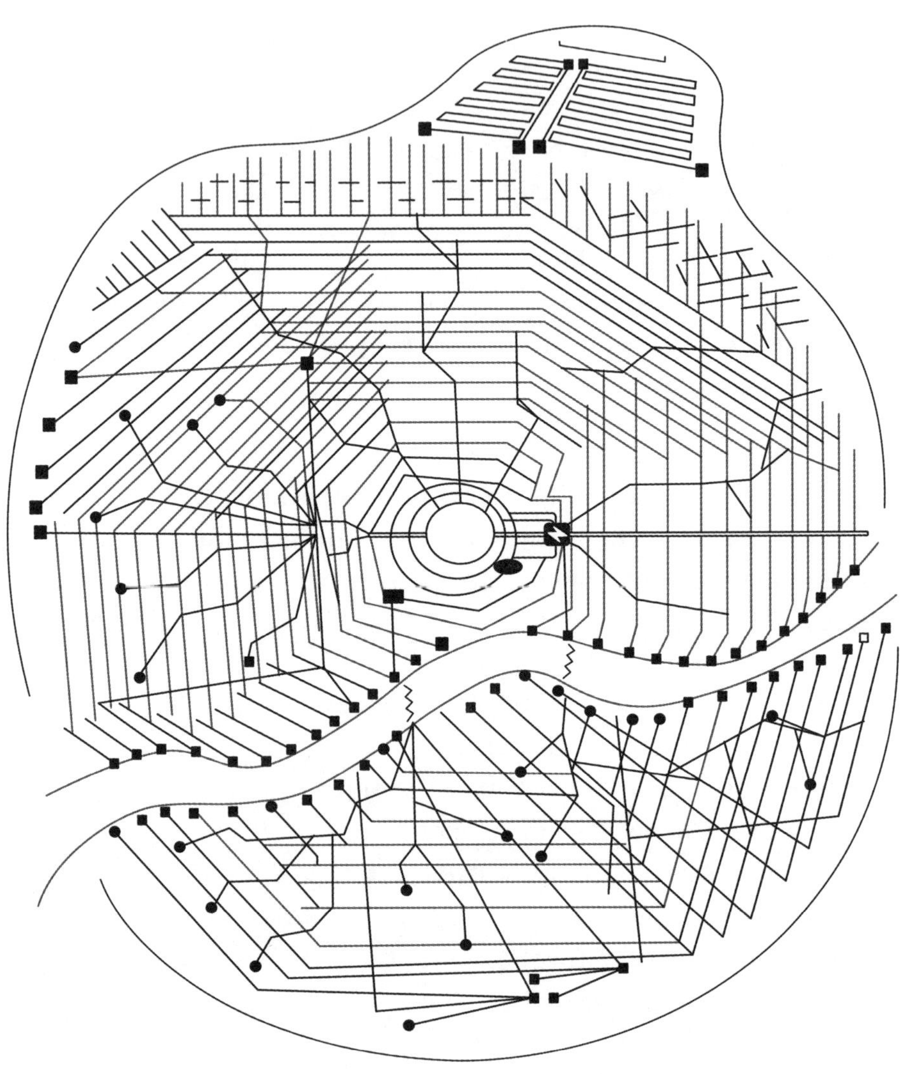

AUTHOR'S NOTE

While this is a work of fiction and no cultural groups or environments in the book are intended to represent specific people or places in the real world, I have allowed some global historical elements to shape aspects of Soogway's colonial violence against Indigenous groups like the People, as well as the city's attitudes toward extraction. The speech read by the ambassador in chapter 13, for instance, is based heavily on the language used in the 1789 Treaty with the Six Nations, which was intended to ensure a boundary line between US territory and that of the "Mohawks, Oneidas, Onondagas, Tuscaroras, Cayugas, and Senekas" (according to the original), an agreement the US government eventually violated. Also, the circular design of the People's camps was in part influenced by the work of anthropologists David Graeber and David Wengrow, who discuss horizontally organized cultures and rotational community structures in their book, *The Dawn of Everything.*

ACKNOWLEDGMENTS

Kell came to me in a dream and told me about her world, a place where combat took the form of storytelling instead of physical violence. Over time, she revealed to me a great many things about her Home, and I am grateful to her and the other characters for allowing me to visit and to share what they told me to the best of my abilities.

I want to thank my incredible writing community for helping me develop those skills and for being patient with my ongoing struggle to understand what kind of storyteller I want to be. Some noteworthy champions and heroes include Cody Luff, Megan Savage, Brenda Taulbee, Tracy Truels, Jamie Yourdon, Stephanie McCollough, Maren Williams, Alicia Jo Rabins, Liz Prato, Michael Keefe, Andrew McCollough, Frances Pai Ippolito, and Erik Grove. Thank you, too, to Blake Hausman for reading the manuscript with a careful eye. I am also deeply indebted to Zach and the rest of the collective at AK Press for taking a chance on this story, and especially to Angelica Sgouros, my editor, for her rigorous support.

I am grateful to N.K. Jemisin, Nnedi Okorafor, Ursula K. Le Guin, Octavia Butler, Tad Williams, Pat Rothfuss, and Jeff VanderMeer for writing the kinds of stories that have continued to fuel me at different points in my life and for modeling courageous speculative fiction. I am grateful to Paul and Silas for always being there, to Iommi for helping me type, and to Tana, without whose challenge this book never would have happened. This isn't the one where we win, but it's coming.